Memories

"Damon, I want no more pretense between us," she said. "Please hear me out."

He touched her hair and trailed his hand across her cheek. "Can we not talk later?" His lips touched her brow, then dipped down to her trembling mouth. "I have thought of little else but you for days."

A sob broke from deep inside her. "Damon, don't you know me?" She pulled away from him. "Search your mind."

He held her at arm's length. "No, damn it! I don't know you! Do you think I would ever forget you if we had met before?"

She shook her head sadly. "You once promised you would not forget me, but apparently you did."

With new awareness, he examined each lovely detail of her face. "My God, no!" he said, taking a quick step backward. "Royal Bradford!"

CONSTANCE O'BANYON

HarperPaperbacks
A Division of HarperCollins*Publishers*

This is a work of fiction. The characters, incidents, and dialogues are products of the author's imagination and are not to be construed as real. Any resemblance to actual events or persons, living or dead, is entirely coincidental.

HarperPaperbacks *A Division of* HarperCollins*Publishers*
10 East 53rd Street, New York, N.Y. 10022

Cover illustration by Pino Daeni

First printing: August 1991

Printed in the United States of America

HarperPaperbacks and colophon are trademarks of HarperCollins*Publishers*

10 9 8 7 6 5 4 3 2 1

My special gratitude
To my agent, Evan Marshal, for being there when I needed you. My lifeline on a sometimes stormy sea.

To my new editor, Karen Solem, thanks for believing in me.

And to Linda Henderson, who worked tirelessly with me on this one while I burned the midnight oil.

The grass has grown over the bare spot where you once played kick ball with your friends. Boxes of discarded action figures and comic books now line the walls of the garage. Somehow you caught me unaware when you abandoned childish mementoes for basketball and girls. I look at you in awe because the manners that were instilled in you have magically taken hold. Way to go, Jason, my son.

BATHE WITH ME IN THE FIERY FLOOD
AND MINGLE KISSES, TEARS AND SIGHS
LIFE OF THE LIFE WITHIN MY BLOOD,
LIGHT OF THE LIGHT WITHIN MINE EYES.

—Alfred, Lord Tennyson

PART ONE

A Promise Made

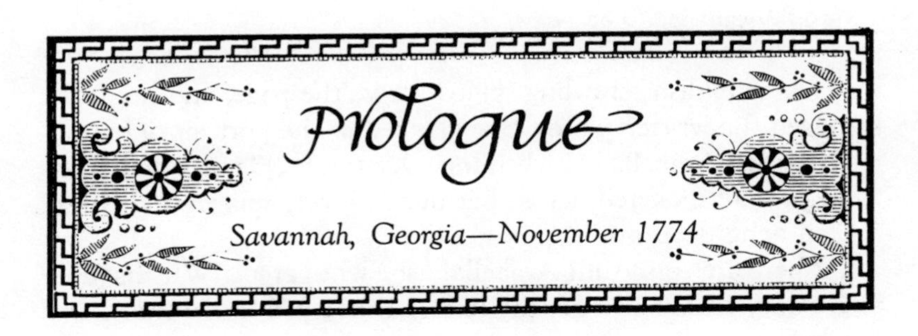

Prologue

Savannah, Georgia—November 1774

Royal Bradford sat at her father's massive oak desk, gazing across the street at Wright Square. She slowly became aware of the darkening sky, and she watched while a gust of wind twisted the branches of her father's prized mulberry tree, making it sway and bow from the fierce onslaught. Rain had begun to fall, and it pelted forcefully against the window.

Royal leaned back and reached for the black leather-bound journal her father had given her three months earlier on the occasion of her fourteenth birthday. Blinded by tears, she opened the journal to the first page, took up her pen, and began to write.

> Dearest Papa,
> When you first presented me with this journal and admonished me to keep a daily account of my life, I could not imagine anything to write about. How sad it is that I make my first entry on

the day you were buried. Sweet, kind adviser, beloved father, I find it difficult to comprehend that you are no longer with me. I am fearful that if I do not keep your memory alive, it will be as if you never existed; therefore, I have decided that each entry in this journal will be addressed to you. You were my father and my friend, and I will strive to grow into the kind of woman you would want me to be.

Royal's childish scrawling spilled across the page, and her tears smudged the written words. She glanced at the portrait of her father's sister, Arabella, which hung over the fireplace. The flames from the fire flickered across her aunt's lovely image, and Royal felt an ache deep inside.

"Where are you, Aunt Arabella?" she whispered. "Why haven't you come? Didn't you get my letter? Don't you know that Papa needed you—that I need you?"

Laying her head on the desk, Royal allowed her tears to flow freely. Deep sobs shook her body, and she lost herself in grief.

She was not aware of how long she had been sitting at her father's desk, but her tears had dried, and the candle flickered low, leaving the far corners of the library in shadows.

She glanced about the room where her father had conducted most of his business. The familiar aroma of leather mingled with the musty smell of the well-worn books that lined the mahogany bookshelves. Closing her eyes, Royal could almost feel her father's presence. The sound of a log falling against the fireplace grate brought her back to reality.

There were rumors of war between the Colonies and England, and the future appeared empty and frightening to Royal, who was all alone.

"Please hurry, Aunt Arabella," she cried. "You loved Papa, too, and we will need to comfort each other."

With a feeling of finality, she laid the journal aside.

Dearest Papa,

A week has passed since my last entry in this journal. I have not yet heard from Aunt Arabella. I know she will come, but when? I am so lonely, Papa, and I miss you dreadfully. I have been informed by Mr. Greenburg's office that the reading of your will takes place next Friday. Perhaps at that time I shall know your plans for my future.

Chapter 1

John Bartholomew's footsteps were noiseless as he moved off the fine Turkish carpet and onto the polished floor. In his meticulous manner, he pulled out his pocket watch and checked it against the hall clock to make certain they were synchronized—they were, as always.

Pausing before the heavy mahogany door of the library, the fastidious little man straightened his spectacles on the bridge of his nose. He did not relish the task that faced him.

On entering the library, he was astonished to find the room empty. Mr. Routhland was always punctual, so John wondered what could be keeping his employer from their appointed meeting. The spry little man had been employed by the Routhland family for twenty years, as secretary first for the father and now for the son. There had been a time when he'd considered becoming a schoolmaster, but he had never regretted his decision to work for Swanhouse Plantation.

With a perplexed expression, John glanced at the letter that had come in the morning post. It was from Oliver Greenburg, a prominent Savannah attorney, and the secretary dreaded calling the letter to Damon Routhland's attention. No, Mr. Routhland was not going to be pleased with the inconvenience this letter would cause. John had no time to speculate further on the dilemma because the door opened, and the master of Swanhouse Plantation entered.

Damon Routhland was of a towering height. His dark brown hair curled slightly at the nape of his neck and had streaks of sun gold that matched the unusual gold of his eyes. He was a handsome rogue, as many a young lady could attest. Since Damon had inherited the largest, most prosperous plantation in Chatham County, he was much sought after by the young marriageable ladies of quality and their ambitious mothers; thus far he had managed to evade all matrimonial traps.

"Good morning, John. I have some correspondence that needs to be answered. Let's get started straight away, because I am riding into Savannah this afternoon." He nodded at the official-looking document that John held in his hand. "Does that require my attention?"

John coughed to clear his throat. "I fear this will be rather a nuisance to you, Mr. Routhland. It seems that a Mr. Douglas Bradford has died and named you guardian of his fourteen-year-old daughter."

Damon arched a dark brow sardonically. "Surely you jest? No one would leave a young girl in my charge."

They both knew without saying that because of Damon's reputation with women, it was unthinkable that any father who cared about his daughter would consider him a suitable guardian.

"I believe if you read for yourself," the secretary offered, thrusting the letter forward, "you will better understand the predicament."

Damon took the letter and scanned the page, his brow furrowed in a frown.

> Dear Mr. Routhland,
> It is with profound sadness that I inform you of the passing of Douglas Bradford. . . .

Damon glanced up at his secretary. "I was aware Douglas Bradford had been ill for some time, but I don't understand how his death could possibly involve me. He was a friend of my father's, but I didn't know him at all well."

"If you would just read on, Mr. Routhland," John urged, "I believe it will be made clear to you."

Damon nodded and continued reading:

> You should know that Mr. Bradford's will appoints Damon Routhland as the guardian of his fourteen-year-old daughter, Royal. It was originally his intention that your father should take guardianship of Miss Bradford in the event of his death. Although I had advised Mr. Bradford on numerous occasions to change his will after the death of your father, he neglected to do so.
>
> Knowing this was his desire, and knowing you have the same name as your father, you should for legal reasons be present at the reading of Mr. Bradford's will. It will be a mere formality to clear up any misunderstanding. . . .

Damon's head snapped up, and he frowned at John. "My God, this is preposterous! Bradford's illness must have muddled his brain."

It was with astonishment that Damon returned to the letter.

> I am certain when you know that Royal Bradford is not without family to care for her, you need not feel duty bound to accept guardianship of her.
>
> She has an aunt, Arabella Bradford, who resides in France, and I have been contacted by Victor Bradford, a cousin on her father's side, who has evidenced a desire to raise Royal Bradford with his own children.
>
> If you find it convenient, I respectfully request that you attend

the reading of the will on Friday next at four o'clock in the afternoon at the Bradford home.

Until such time, I remain,

Respectfully yours,
Oliver Greenburg
Attorney-at-Law

Damon's jaw tightened and his eyes narrowed as he reread the part about Arabella Bradford. Old memories stirred to life within him—memories he had thought were dead—painful memories. So Arabella had been in France all these years, and she would now be returning to Savannah to assume the guardianship of her young niece.

Damon was unaware that he had crumpled the attorney's letter in his fist. After all this time, would he see Arabella again? Had she changed? he wondered. Surely her dissolute life as a stage actress would be reflected on her face. He pictured her once flawless skin with wrinkles, and her flaming red hair laced with gray. After all, eight years was a long time, especially to a woman of her age. She must be in her midthirties by now, he speculated.

As a headstrong youth, it had not mattered to him that Arabella had been ten years his senior. How young and foolish he had been at seventeen, he thought scornfully. How easily he had lost his heart to the beautiful but ruthless actress, and how mercilessly she had teased and tormented him when he had professed that love.

Damon glanced up at John, who had been watching him expectantly. "Yes, I shall definitely attend the reading of the will. Make a notation of the date and time and see that I don't forget."

Not that he would forget—how could he? Arabella had once filled his every thought. He still remembered vividly the night he had proposed marriage to her, only to have her laugh at him. Soon he would face her again, but this time he was not young or inexperienced—now he would face her as a man!

All concern for Royal Bradford had been pushed to the back of Damon's mind, for his thoughts were only of Arabella.

While tucking a strand of white hair beneath her stiff white cap, Alba Beemish turned to her husband with a disapproving expression.

"What's going to happen to Miss Royal?" the housekeeper demanded. "It's for certain she doesn't belong with Miss Arabella." Horror came into the woman's eyes. "An actress, of all things! It isn't suitable that she should have the raising of the young mistress."

Tobias avoided his wife's gaze. "Miss Arabella's not so bad, and she does love the girl," he answered in a soft voice that was characteristic of his easy manner. "Little Miss Royal's been through enough tragedy this past month, and she needs the comfort of her aunt."

"Humph." Alba snorted. "You are just like all men when it comes to a pretty face. Surely you don't think Arabella Bradford is a good example for Miss Royal? Goodness only knows what depravities the child would be exposed to in the company of that . . . that actress!"

Tobias knew it would not be wise to take Arabella Bradford's part against his wife. "There's the cousin on her father's side," he offered in a conciliatory manner. "He'll be the head of the family now. Most likely he'll take care of Miss Royal."

"Have you thought that we might be put out no matter what happens? If Miss Arabella takes custody of Miss Royal, she will take her away to France. And this Victor Bradford and his family, what do we know about them? In all the years we've worked in this house, there has hardly been a mention of them. Although he never said so, I always had the feeling that Mr. Bradford didn't like his cousin in the least, and I'm sure *I* won't like him, either."

With practiced tolerance, Tobias patted his wife's shoulder. "Not everyone can live up to your expectations, my dear."

But Alba would not be placated. "It seems strange to me that they didn't come while Mr. Bradford was so ill, but waited until he's dead and can't object. The lawyer said they would be arriving any day." Alba sniffed. "They didn't make it to the funeral, but you can be sure they'll be here in time for the reading of the will."

Tobias turned his wife to face him. "It isn't up to us to interfere, Alba," he reminded her. "Besides, it's not likely that Mr. Bradford left his daughter without providing for her. We shall know everything when the will is read."

Alba fixed her husband with a pensive gaze, but she spoke as if she had not heard him. "Miss Royal is an extraordinary young girl," she acknowledged. "Have we not seen an example of her courage this last year while she dealt with her father's illness? Her care and devotion to Mr. Bradford made it possible for him to pass on with dignity. We have both seen her accept responsibilities with determination and understanding that went far beyond her young age. Perhaps I am worrying needlessly."

Tobias nodded. "Be at peace, wife. The young miss has a strong spirit that has brought her though trial and tribulation up to now. It isn't likely that her courage will fail her when she needs it most. That one's a fighter and will never bow down in defeat. Have pity for anyone who mistakes her gentle nature for weakness."

"Even so"—Alba sighed—"I fear for her future. What if . . . what if—"

Tobias poked his hands in his pockets and took a deep draw on his newly lit pipe. "Now, Alba, I thought we had this resolved. Don't go borrowing trouble. Whatever happens, it's out of our hands, and we may as well be patient until the matter is settled. We will just have to wait and see."

The wind tore at Royal's cape, wrapping it about her body as she stooped to gather the bright yellow chrysanthemums that had been her father's favorite flowers. With her bouquet in hand, she rushed across Bull Street, staying to the path until she turned down Oglethorpe Avenue, which led her to the cemetery, where her father and mother were buried.

It was a dismal day. Smoky gray clouds blotted out the sun, and by now the wind had lulled to a crystalline breeze that tugged at the autumn leaves, sending them showering down on the freshly dug grave.

Royal stood shivering in the cold damp air, a silent prayer on her lips. Her lightweight cape did little to protect her against the steady stream of rain that plastered her hair to her face.

She raised her head and watched miserably as a lone leaf still clung to a sturdy branch of the ancient oak tree that would shade her father's grave in the hot summer months. She somehow felt like the solitary leaf that danced about from the force of the assaulting breeze. When a sudden gust of wind tore the leaf from its haven and sent it swirling to the ground, Royal felt as though a similar whirlwind had swept through her life, sending her world careening topsy-turvy and leaving her devastated with anguish and loss.

Bending down, she carefully placed the crumpled flowers on the fresh mound of dirt, while her tears mixed with rain. Although her father had been in ill health for over a year, she had not been prepared for his death.

Royal glanced down at the white marble stone that marked her mother's grave. Since her mother had died of consumption when Royal was but two years old, she had no recollection of her. Her father had been her whole world, and now he was gone. She tried to take comfort in the fact that he had been reunited with his beloved wife, and that he, at least, was not alone.

Standing up, Royal pulled her hood about her head while the heavy hand of depression settled on her shoulders. Unmindful of her actions, she made her way over the uneven bricks. She left the cemetery and fastened the iron gate behind her, thus closing a portal on a part of her life that could never be again.

Her footsteps lagged as she made her way back to her home, which stood like an old friend beckoning to her with a promise of warmth and solace. Slowly she climbed the wide steps to find Alba waiting for her with an expression of concern on her wrinkled face. Royal went readily into the housekeeper's outstretched arms.

There was a light rebuke in the older woman's voice when she spoke to her young mistress. "You are soaked to the skin and are likely to catch your death if you don't get out of your wet clothing at once!"

Royal obediently allowed Alba to lead her upstairs, strip off her wet gown and petticoats, and pull a clean white nightgown over her head. When the housekeeper yanked back the quilt, Royal climbed into bed and sank into the downy feather mattress.

Alba then shook the excess dampness from Royal's cape and hung it over a chair near the fireplace to dry. All the while she kept a watchful eye on her young charge, wishing she had the words to comfort the child.

"Now, now, Miss Royal, why don't you just rest a bit while I go fetch you some nice thick stew to warm you up. A steaming cup of apple cider with cinnamon ought to restore some of the color to your cheeks."

"I don't want anything to eat just now," Royal answered wearily. "All I want is to sleep."

Alba's eyes fastened on Royal's bent head, where riotous golden curls framed her small face. She thought how frail the girl appeared and how her slight body was dwarfed by the massive mahogany bed where she lay.

Alba lowered her gaze to the fingers that desperately clutched the quilted coverlet, noting the tiny blue veins that were visible in the well-shaped hands. Even though Royal was too thin, there was a promise of future beauty in her delicate features. It tugged at Alba's heart when Royal raised her blue eyes, and the housekeeper saw that tears clung to the girl's thick lashes.

"Be at peace, Miss Royal," she said gently. "Take comfort in the fact that God always seems to take care of the fools and the young of this world. He will surely take an interest in your plight. I believe that."

A slight smile tugged at Royal's lips. "Which do you consider me, Alba—the fool or the young?"

"Even if you are young in years, you're certainly no fool," Alba answered with assurance. "Most folks don't have half the gumption you've been blessed with."

Royal seemed totally unaware of the compliment. "I wish . . . I wish Aunt Arabella would arrive. What can be keeping her?"

Alba turned her back and moved toward the door. "I'm sure I don't know," she said stiffly. "It's time for you to get some sleep, Miss Royal. I'll be downstairs. Just ring if you need me for anything."

Wearily Royal's head sank into the soft pillow, and her eyes fluttered shut.

Tomorrow yawned before her with its dark uncertainties, and the present was just too painful to think about. She was too weary to protest and too heartsick to think. Perhaps rest was what she needed.

As the smoky blue sky of evening gave way to the ebony night, Royal snuggled beneath the warmth of the down quilt and fell into a fretful sleep.

Dearest Papa,

Aunt Arabella has not yet arrived. Each day I watch for her with great anticipation. Events have occurred so swiftly that I have had no time to record my thoughts. Nothing could have prepared me for Cousin Victor and his family, who arrived with trunks and valises in excess, thus leading me to believe it is their intention to remain in Savannah indefinitely. Since you would expect me to be a gracious hostess, I have extended every courtesy to make them feel welcome. Cousin Victor says he feels obligated to shape my future, and he is certain that is what you would have wanted. I hope you will not think me undutiful, but I despair at the notion that my future might be under his control. Already he deems himself your beneficiary. I do not know your feelings on this, Papa, but whatever your wish, I will abide by it.

Chapter 2

The mood in the dining room was solemn. Royal observed Alba as she bustled about, serving the meal with her lips pursed in a line of disapproval. It was clear the housekeeper did not like Cousin Victor. She removed the pewter serving dishes from a tray and placed them upon the snowy white linen tablecloth, then withdrew to the kitchen without a word.

Silently Royal watched the people seated about the table. Cousin Victor was a portly gentleman of medium height. With thinning hair and a long beaklike nose, he had the appearance of a man who was not at peace with himself, and he had the annoying habit of never looking at the person to whom he was speaking. Royal found it vexing that he had ensconced himself at the head of the table in her father's chair.

Cousin Victor's wife, Mary, was seated at the opposite end of the table. The woman was tall and thin, with black hair and equally black eyes. If she ever spoke, it was in a voice so low one had to lean close to hear her. There was a pinched look about her lips, and when she smiled it looked forced. There was a greedy light in her eyes as they darted about the room, assessing the worth of the furnishings.

Since Royal was seated beside their son Simon, she was forced to peep up at him from under her lashes. He was the oldest of Cousin Victor's children—she judged him to be in his early twenties. His hair was dark, and he had his mother's black eyes, while he was portly like his father. Royal found him watching her, and for some reason his close scrutiny repulsed her. He smiled smugly when she jerked away from the pressure of his leg when it brushed against hers.

Royal deliberately moved her chair away from Simon and turned her attention to her meal. She absently picked up her fork and pushed the meat around on her plate, wishing dinner was over so she could retreat to her room.

So completely had Victor Bradford taken over that Royal was beginning to feel like an outsider in her own home. Yesterday she had discovered him in the library going through her father's private papers. When she had objected, he had accused her of being a meddlesome child who needed discipline and had sent her to her room.

Now the tension deepened as Victor cleared his throat to speak. "What do you think of my son Simon?" he asked in a slow drawl, while watching Royal carefully. "I know he is older than you, but I believe, on observing your character, that you will need an older man to curb your headstrong ways."

Not understanding where the conversation was leading, Royal glanced at the three who were watching her intently, awaiting her answer. "I hardly know your son, sir." She glanced at Simon with repugnance. "But I do not believe we shall ever become good friends," she declared with an honesty that came from the fact that her father had always encouraged her to speak her mind. "And, yes, he is much older than myself."

Victor shrugged, feeling undaunted by her renunciation of his son. "Given time, you and Simon will come to know each other." He smiled slowly. "It is not unusual for cousins to marry. Especially since you and Simon are cousins three times removed."

Horror spread across Royal's features when she realized it was Victor's intention that she marry his odious son. She heard Alba drop a pewter serving dish, which clattered noisily across the floor.

Jumping to her feet, Royal declared hotly: "I am too young to consider marriage to anyone, sir! And I can assure you that if I were to marry, it would not be to your son!"

Victor had expected her objection and was unconcerned by her outburst. "Don't be too certain, my dear," he said calmly, wiping his mouth on a napkin, then folding it and placing it beside his plate.

Royal started to object, but he silenced her with the wave of his hand.

"You may as well know, young lady," he continued, oblivious of Royal's stricken expression, "that I will not tolerate your disrespect. It is obvious that your father has allowed you too many liberties, a situation which I shall soon rectify. I consider that I am already your guardian, and as such, *I* shall decide what is best for your future. And if I find it is in your best interests to marry my son—which I'm sure I shall—you *will* marry him. Make no mistake about that."

"The mistake is yours, Cousin Victor, if you think I would ever marry someone like your son." Her gaze brushed Simon's face, and she shuddered.

A leering smile twisted Simon's thick lips as he insultingly assessed her yet undeveloped young body. "You're not much of a prize yourself, Royal," he said, undaunted by her obvious dislike. "You're impudent, bad-tempered, and too skinny for my taste, but I'll take pleasure in taming you."

Royal gripped the back of her chair so tightly that her knuckles whitened. "That you will never do, Simon Bradford!" Sickened by the confrontation, her eyes locked with Victor's. "You are not yet my guardian," she said haughtily. "My father's wishes shall be made known this afternoon, when Mr. Greenburg reads the will. Until that time, I hope you will all remember you are guests in this house, and behave accordingly."

Angry red streaks ran up Victor's thick neck. "Don't take that tone with me, missy. Who else would be your guardian, if not the oldest living male Bradford?"

Suddenly the dining room door was thrown open, and like a whiff of fresh air, Arabella Bradford swept forward. Even dressed in black satin out of respect for her brother's death, she appeared beautiful and elegant.

"I came as quickly as I could, my dearest!" she cried, holding out her arms to her niece. When Royal flew across the room, Arabella gathered the young girl to her, while her cold glance went to Victor. "Do not worry, Royal, you will not have to marry anyone. It seems I arrived just in time. I have come to take you back to France with me."

Royal closed her eyes and rested her head against her aunt's shoulder. Now, everything would be all right—her aunt would see to that.

Victor came to his feet, his face red with rage. "I may have something to say about your taking Royal out of the country, Arabella."

There was an air of superiority about Arabella, as if she were dealing with an underling. "I do not believe for one moment that my brother meant for you to take possession of this dear child. I can imagine you were hoping I would not come at all, Victor," she said, nodding in Simon's direction. "I can assure you that neither my brother nor myself would approve of a match between your son and Royal."

"You always thought you were better than me," Victor stated, unable to hide his anger. "But you have looked down your nose at me and mine for the last time."

Arabella slipped her arm around Royal's waist and guided her toward the door. "Where else would one look to find a snake, Victor?" she threw over her shoulder.

Arabella did not stop until she had drawn Royal into the formal sitting room. Once there, she seated her niece on the sofa and sat down beside her. Raising Royal's head, she brushed away the girl's tears with a gloved finger. "There, there," she crooned. "You are trembling, dear. I am grievously sorry that odious man frightened you." A bright smile curved her mouth. "Don't pay any attention to Victor. I can assure you no one else does."

Royal felt all her hurt and anger melt away when she looked into her aunt's compassionate eyes. "I am so glad you have come at last."

"You knew I would, dear child."

"Yes, I knew, Aunt Arabella."

Arabella hugged her niece. "I am sorry I was not here for you when your father died, Royal. But we shall never be parted again. How would you like to go to France with me?"

Royal's eyes brightened. "Oh, yes, Aunt Arabella, I would like that above all else!"

The atmosphere in the library was strained. Everyone waited while Mr. Greenburg shuffled through several official-looking documents. Finally, glancing over the rim of his glasses, the attorney spoke. "I'm sorry for the delay, but we are waiting for one other party."

Royal was seated next to her aunt, while Victor and his family were huddled on the leather sofa. At the attorney's request, Alba and Tobias were present. The two servants stood near the door, feeling out of place among the family members.

"Who else could possibly be concerned with this afternoon's proceedings?" Victor demanded in an agitated voice. "We have no other family."

Mr. Greenburg merely turned his professional smile on the man. "I'm merely abiding by Douglas Bradford's wishes." The attorney suddenly glanced out the library window, which gave a broad view of the front of the house. "I believe the person I have been expecting has arrived."

Mr. Greenburg left the room to greet the newcomer. Those present focused their attention on the door as he and Damon Routhland entered the library.

Damon had not yet acknowledged anyone in the room, since he and the attorney were conversing in low tones. Victor, who was annoyed because of the delay, strained his ears, hoping he could hear their conversation.

Royal was mystified as to why this man should attend the reading of her father's will. She leaned toward her aunt and whispered, "Whatever can Damon Routhland be doing here?"

At first Arabella did not recognize the once starry-eyed young swain who had amused her for a whole summer when she had last been in Savannah. She realized with interest that he was no longer an untried youth, but a most attractive man. "Damon Routhland," she said reflectively. "It has been many years since I last saw him. Tell me, are you acquainted with him, dear?"

"No, not well at all," Royal answered. "Of course, I know who he is, but I doubt he knows me."

At last Mr. Greenburg turned to the others. "For those of you who do not know Damon Routhland, may I present him to you at this time?"

For just a moment Damon looked at Arabella, and in that instant she read many things on that arresting face: confidence, arrogance, insolence, haughtiness, but not one bit of warmth. There was about him an air of assurance, as if he knew he was attractive to women and accepted it with an air of indifference.

Lud, he was handsome, Arabella thought, staring at him in fascination. His blue jacket was cut of the finest velvet and fit smoothly across his broad shoulders. His blue trousers hugged his legs and disappeared into a pair of black riding boots. He was not the young man she had once known, she thought almost regretfully, wondering if he remembered her.

Damon's gaze swept Arabella's face. No, he thought grimly, she was neither old nor ugly. If anything, she was more stunning than she had been eight years earlier. The black gown she wore made her skin whiter and her red hair more pronounced than he remembered. When she smiled at him provocatively, he knew she was remembering the night they had last seen each other—the night she had refused his proposal of marriage.

Lazily and deliberately, Damon glanced at the young girl who was seated beside Arabella. There were dark circles under the child's eyes, and she looked so delicate he surmised she must be recovering from an illness, or perhaps her father's death had devastated her. He felt pity for her—an emotion he did not welcome under the circumstances.

Royal watched Damon lower himself onto the green leather chair directly across from the attorney. When he caught her eye, he nodded slightly, then appeared to dismiss her from his thoughts as his gaze unwillingly returned to Arabella.

"Now that we are all here," Mr. Greenburg stated, "I will proceed with the business at hand." He indicated that Alba and Tobias should come forward, then motioned for them to be seated. Picking up a thick document, he scanned it quickly. "It is not necessary to read the entire will, so with your permission, Mistress Bradford," he addressed Royal, "I will only read specific bequests."

When Royal nodded, Mr. Greenburg continued. "First of all, it was Douglas Bradford's wish that you, Alba and Tobias Beemish, should always have a home in this house, if you so desire. However, since you came over with the family from England, if it is your wish to return, Mr. Bradford has directed me to pay for your passage. In any event, he set aside for each of you the amount of five hundred pounds, for faithful service."

Alba dabbed at her eyes with her apron, while Tobias patted her shoulder. They had not expected such generosity and were momentarily overwhelmed.

"But that's a thousand pounds," Victor stated grudgingly.

Mr. Greenburg, who had taken an instant dislike to the belligerent cousin, nodded impatiently. "Thank you, Mr. Bradford. I believe your calculations are correct. Now, may I proceed?"

Victor cleared his throat and nodded indignantly but did not reply.

The attorney's voice rose as he began to read directly from the will:

> Since my wife and I were born and raised in England, it was always our intention that our daughter should be educated in the school her mother attended. Therefore, in accordance with my wife's wishes, I direct that Royal be sent to Fulham School for Young Ladies in London. There she is to complete her education.
>
> I further direct that my beloved daughter, Royal, should be under the guardianship of Damon Routhland, of Swanhouse Plantation, and he shall also be guardian of her estate, until the event of her twenty-first birthday, or until such time as she should be married with her guardian's consent.

A strangled gasp escaped Victor's throat. Then a heavy silence ensued while everyone in the room digested the attorney's shocking pronouncement.

At last Victor Bradford rose to his feet. "That's preposterous! What right has this man, who has no connection with the family, to be made responsible for Royal?"

Arabella leaned toward the attorney. "Surely there has been a mistake, Mr. Greenburg. I cannot believe that my brother would leave Royal in the hands of a man she hardly knows."

Damon observed the distress on Arabella's face. Could she really be interested in her niece, he wondered, or was her concern merely an act? He could clearly see the pain in her eyes. Perhaps she genuinely cared for the girl.

"I beg your indulgence for a moment longer, Mistress Bradford," Mr. Greenburg said. "I believe I can clear this up to everyone's satisfaction."

All eyes were on the attorney as he continued. "As I have already advised Mr. Routhland, when Douglas Bradford had this will drawn up, it was his intention that Mr. Routhland's father, also named Damon, be the guardian of Royal Bradford."

"Then the will is not valid," Victor said with relief.

"I can assure you, Mr. Bradford," the attorney stated emphatically, "the will is most certainly valid. I prepared it myself."

While Arabella and Victor continued their vehement protestations to the attorney, Damon turned his attention to Royal. Her life was the most affected by the day's proceedings, and yet for the moment everyone seemed to have forgotten about her. She was like a fragile piece of porcelain that had been handled too roughly. There was bewilderment in her eyes and hurt in her expression.

Royal sensed Damon's scrutiny, and when she looked up at him, he smiled at her sympathetically. "Do you understand the meaning of your father's will, Miss Bradford?"

Royal shook her head solemnly, blinking her eyes to keep the tears from falling. "No, I don't Mr. Routhland. I don't understand why he chose you as my guardian."

Arabella whirled around and faced Damon. "I must insist that you relinquish your claim on my niece to me," she demanded. "I can assure you I have the money to see that my sister-in-law's wishes are carried out. As a matter of fact, since I reside in Paris, it will be no hardship to visit my niece in London and to have her spend holidays with me."

"I protest," Victor chimed in. "As head of the family, I say Royal should be in my care."

The attorney, trying to bring order back to the proceedings, addressed Damon. "What do you say, Mr. Routhland? Are you willing to relinquish the guardianship of Royal Bradford to her relatives?"

Damon glanced at the girl, who was staring at him expectantly. It was evident that she wanted to be with her aunt. "Is it your belief, Mr. Greenburg, that Douglas Bradford intended his daughter to reside with Victor Bradford or"—he looked pointedly at Arabella—"with Arabella Bradford?"

The attorney struck a professional attitude. "In truth, Victor Bradford was not mentioned. However, your brother had this to say concerning you, Miss Bradford: 'While I love my sister, she knows I have not approved of her chosen way of life. I therefore direct that she will not, under any circumstances, have guardianship of my daughter, Royal.' "

Mr. Greenburg looked at Arabella apologetically. "You surely can follow your brother's thinking." His glance shifted to Damon. "Mr. Routhland, you are in no way obligated to accept the guardianship. As I told you in my letter, it is a mere formality for you to relinquish the responsibility. Since the will specifically excludes Arabella Bradford, the courts will most likely appoint Victor Bradford as the child's guardian."

Victor shot Arabella a triumphant look. "I knew I would be the likely choice to raise young Royal."

Arabella looked crestfallen but said nothing. Her eyes were seeking as she watched Damon. Everyone waited with anticipation while he pondered the girl's fate.

To Damon this was no longer a game. A young girl's future lay in his hands. He could well imagine that Douglas Bradford would not have wanted a man with Victor Bradford's temperament to raise his daughter.

Damon met the attorney's eyes in silent understanding and realized that he had been the intended guardian all along. "The will stands as written," he said at last. "I will accept the responsibility for, and the guardianship of, Royal Bradford."

"You cannot do this," Victor sputtered. "You're only interested in Royal's money."

Damon's eyes glinted dangerously, but he made no reply to the accusation.

Laying aside the will and removing his spectacles, Oliver Greenburg hastily intervened. "At this time, I should point out to all of you that Douglas Bradford's estate is not as large as it was when this will was drafted. As you may know, he invested heavily in silkworms, only to find they did not thrive well in this climate."

Royal was too shocked by the day's events to absorb the significance of all she was hearing. Was Mr. Greenburg implying that her father had lost his money? How was that possible?

With a new awareness, she looked at the faded spaces on the wall, where large and valuable paintings had once hung. When her father had sold them, Royal had not even questioned him. Now that she thought about it, several family heirlooms were missing. She also realized that the silver serving dishes that had been in the Bradford family for generations had been replaced with pewter.

Royal felt sad that her father must have been worried about money while he was so ill. Why had he not confided in her? And why had he never told her he was planning for her to go to England to be educated? What about Damon Routhland—did he consider her his responsibility? She felt her aunt's hand close comfortingly around hers.

"This is unthinkable!" Victor blustered angrily. "I shall not stand for such a miscarriage of . . . of . . . No, I will not have it!"

"Mr. Bradford, you have no say in the matter," Oliver Greenburg said sharply. "In accepting the guardianship, Mr. Routhland has complied with my client's wishes."

"Are you certain my cousin left nothing for me?" Victor pressed, reluctant to believe that his hopes for wealth had been dashed.

"I'm afraid not," the attorney confirmed, then raised an inquiring brow. "Unless, of course, you would be willing to accept any indebtedness Douglas Bradford might have left? Are you?"

Victor's face reddened, and for the first time he was speechless. Simon's face was drawn up in a frown, and his mother's expression was blank. The three of them realized that Douglas Bradford had excluded them from his will.

Impatiently Damon came to his feet. "If there is nothing further you require of me, I have other matters that require my attention."

"By all means, and thank you, Mr. Routhland," Mr. Greenburg said. "However, if you could come to my office at your earliest convenience, there will be papers that require your signature, and details we still need to discuss."

The two men shook hands, and Damon moved to stand before Royal. When the girl looked up at him with frightened eyes, on an impulse he knelt beside her. "Have no fear of me, Miss Bradford. I intend to follow your father's wishes for you, and nothing more. I will come to see you when everything is settled to my satisfaction. At that time, you and I shall discuss your future. I want only to help you."

Royal was too bewildered to answer, but Arabella turned on him furiously.

"You are doing this to spite me," she whispered through trembling lips. "You resent me for not accepting your marriage proposal."

When Damon looked at Arabella, he saw tears sparkling in her lovely eyes. "Oddly enough, this has nothing to do with you, Miss Bradford," he said stiffly. "You can believe that I have the girl's interests uppermost in my mind."

"I never knew you to be so self-sacrificing," Arabella taunted.

He stood to his full height. "You never knew me at all."

Her arms went around her niece protectively. "You haven't heard the last of this. I will fight you for guardianship of my niece."

Damon's golden eyes gleamed as if they were on fire. "I suspect you will—but you cannot win."

Royal was confused by the exchange between her aunt and Damon Routhland, but she had not fully understood many of the events of this day. She only half heard Damon Routhland when he spoke to Victor.

"I trust, Mr. Bradford, that you and your family will vacate my ward's house." His gaze was penetrating. "There is no need for haste—after breakfast tomorrow will be soon enough, I believe."

Angrily Victor stood up, jerked his wife to her feet, and motioned for his son to follow them out of the room. "We'll just see about this. We'll just see!"

Royal watched Damon Routhland depart. Then, in need of comfort, she laid her head on her aunt's shoulder. "What is to become of me?" she wanted to know.

Arabella hugged her. "I have not yet given up, my dear. That insufferable man has no right to dictate your future. Whatever was Douglas thinking about? I never knew he could be so cruel."

Royal wiped away tears on the back of her hand. "Promise you will not abandon me?"

"We will always have each other," Arabella assured her.

Mr. Greenburg gathered the scattered documents and placed

them in his leather valise. Nodding politely to Royal and her aunt, he moved out the door.

Once in the hallway, the attorney drew in a deep, cleansing breath. "So, Douglas, I know now why you never changed your will, no matter how hard I pressed. I believe your daughter will be in capable hands—but you knew how this would come out, didn't you, my clever friend?"

Dear Papa,

Soon after the reading of your will, Cousin Victor and his family took leave of Savannah without even saying good-bye. As of yet, I have heard nothing from Damon Routhland. I admit to being apprehensive about the future, but I am so grateful that Aunt Arabella is yet with me.

Royal put aside her journal and moved to the bow window that overlooked the square. There was an ache deep inside as she pondered her fate. Soon she would be ripped away from everything she held dear and sent to England where she knew no one. What was to become of her? she wondered frantically. Would she ever see her home again?

Each day she stood at this window and watched for Damon Routhland, but so far he had not arrived, and she was glad. He was a stranger to her and far above her socially. Everyone in Savannah was awed by the master of Swanhouse Plantation, but she was merely frightened of him.

His strange-colored golden eyes were too penetrating, as if they could see into her thoughts.

Royal sighed. When Mr. Routhland finally did appear, her life would be changed forever. She turned away from the window and moved out of the room in search of her aunt Arabella. Soon the day would come when they would be parted, and Royal would be alone again.

Arabella paid little heed to the view from the carriage window as the horses drew her closer to her destination. She was angry that her own brother would entrust the rearing of Royal to a virtual stranger. How could Douglas have turned against her? Surely he had known that she loved Royal and would take care of her.

She pressed her gloved fingers to her temples as her mind went spinning backward to the time when she had first come to the Colonies to visit her brother and niece. At that time she had been accustomed to the gaiety of London, so the parties and festivities offered by Savannah had bored her—that is, until the night of the Harvest Ball.

Of course she had heard of Damon Routhland since he had been the object of adoration of many of the young girls of Chatham County, and she had often seen him from a distance, but she had not expected to find him attractive.

Arabella closed her eyes and remembered vividly how Damon had looked the night he'd walked into the ballroom and surveyed the surroundings with boredom etched on his fine features.

She had felt challenged when he'd appeared uninterested in her—men seldom ignored Arabella Bradford. She supposed she had behaved badly to him, she reflected, but if so, he was entirely to blame—he had taken their little flirtation much too seriously.

The carriage came to a halt, bringing Arabella back to the present. She pressed a delicate foot forward and in a rustle of taffeta allowed Tobias to help her from the carriage. There was a determined sparkle in her brown eyes as she ascended the steps of Swanhouse.

She had come to persuade Damon Routhland that Royal belonged with her, and she was willing to use any means of persuasion to obtain that aim. Royal was miserable and frightened, and Arabella had no intention of leaving Savannah without her.

As she approached the wide double doors, they swung open, and a stiff-mannered butler greeted her with an inquisitive glance.

"Is Mr. Routhland at home?" Arabella inquired impatiently.

"Yes, ma'am, he is, but he isn't seeing callers this morning."

"He'll see me," she said, pushing past the man and into the entry hall. "Where is he?" she demanded. "Take me to him at once."

"That will be all, Davis," a commanding voice spoke up from the doorway of the library.

Arabella glanced up to see Damon observing her with a look one would bestow on a child who had just been caught misbehaving. "Miss Bradford, are you accustomed to bullying other people's servants?" Damon questioned lazily.

"I want to talk to you." She pushed past him and moved into the library, where she turned to face him.

He smiled slightly. "I take it this is not a social call." He deliberately left the door open and indicated that Arabella should take a chair, which she refused with a shake of her head.

"You know why I am here, Damon."

"To pretend otherwise would be to underestimate us both. I knew you would come. What took you so long? I've been expecting you these past few days."

Arabella was not about to admit that it had taken her several days to work up her courage to come to Swanhouse. "Since you know why I'm here, it will save time. It is my hope that you will agree to relinquish Royal to me." He was standing too near for her peace of mind—his golden eyes were too piercing. She clutched her hands nervously. "Please allow me to take Royal to Paris."

He shook his dark head. "I cannot permit that. Have you forgotten that it was your brother's wish that she be educated in London?"

"I have not forgotten. And I will honor my brother's wishes," Arabella promised, watching him expectantly. When Damon made no reply, she dropped down on the edge of the chair, her eyes pleading. "I will see that Royal is educated in London. I will do whatever you want, but do not take her from me. I have no family other than Royal."

"You have your cousin Victor and his family," Damon reminded her dryly.

She held out a beseeching hand. "Do not punish me, Damon. I know I hurt you in the past, but do not make an innocent girl suffer for my transgressions."

Damon glanced at her with a sardonic expression. "Surely you are not accusing me of an act of vengeance? Would you cast me as the villain?"

Arabella dabbed at her eyes with a lace handkerchief, an achievement that she had perfected for the stage. It had never failed to gain satisfactory results when practiced on unsuspecting gentlemen of her acquaintance. "The villain in this is death, because it has left Royal without parents. She has suffered so, poor dear." She peeked at him through her lashes. "Do not make her suffer more."

Damon clapped his hands and bowed to her. "Bravo, I applaud your performance, Arabella. It is little wonder you are such a sensation in Paris. However, I believe I should point out to you that I have read Escadaux, and recognized your speech from the third act of his play *Winds of Tomorrow.*"

Arabella gave a scornful toss of her head. "How was I supposed to know that you were a patron of the arts? One could not have expected you colonials to read Escadaux, since he has not been translated into English."

"Perhaps you would have been forewarned had you known that my mother was not only French, but also had a great love for the theater. She read all his works to me one summer when I was but a ten-year-old lad. There was a time when I could quote him word for word."

Arabella jumped to her feet and moved to Damon. "I would use trickery or anything I deemed necessary to sway you. Understand that my love for my niece is genuine, as is my desire to have her with me."

"Oh, I believe you, Arabella."

She placed her hand on his arm and looked up at him in earnest. "Please, Damon, forget what has passed between us. Let me have my niece. She is nothing to you. You don't even know her."

He glanced down at the dainty gloved hand that rested on his arm. "If you have it in your mind that I accepted guardianship of Royal Bradford out of some deep need to punish you, you are deceiving yourself, Arabella." He brushed her hand off and moved away. "I admit that curiosity contributed to my attendance at the reading of the will, and yes, I even admit I hoped to see you suffer, but that is no longer my motive. Whether you believe it or not, compassion for a very sad little girl persuaded me to become her guardian."

"Compassion? I can hardly credit that as an emotion a man would suffer from."

He smiled slightly. "It does seem a bit out of character, doesn't it?"

"There was a time when you were not so . . . cold. But now, I am not so sure."

His expression became serious. "How much do you know about your brother's affairs, Miss Bradford?"

"Very little," she admitted. "Douglas and I . . . since I became an actress by profession, my brother . . . chose to . . . he . . . you heard what he said about me in his will."

"It must have come as no surprise to you that your brother decided to look beyond you and Victor in choosing a guardian for his daughter."

Arabella appeared defeated for a moment. "It came as no surprise that he did not choose me. Nor would I have expected Douglas to leave the care of Royal to Victor." Her eyes sought his. "But why you, Damon?"

"Ah, I see. Can it be that you have been listening to gossip?"

"I have heard that you are a dashing rogue who sets women's

hearts atwitter." Her expression hardened. "Not a high recommendation for the care of a young, innocent girl such as my niece."

"Have no fear on your niece's behalf, Miss Bradford. Since she will be going almost immediately to England, I shall have very little personal contact with her. Do not be concerned that I shall try to seduce her. My taste runs more to older women—remember?"

She chose to ignore his barb. "If you will not let me have her, you surely don't intend to keep me from seeing her once she is in England, do you?"

"I have no objections to your seeing her." His golden eyes flamed. "However, I will not allow you to take her away from London."

Arabella drew in a resigned breath. "Tell me about your plans for Royal."

"I have no plans past abiding by your brother's wishes for her. I have written to the headmistress of Fulham School, asking that they admit Royal, and am now awaiting an answer. Until that time, you may remain with her."

Arabella leaned toward him. "I had a talk with Mr. Greenburg, and he informed me that my brother left his affairs in a muddle. The attorney also advised me that Royal would have lost the house had you not paid all my brother's creditors. Surely that was generous of you," she said. "I do not like the thought of Royal being indebted to you. I hope you will allow me to repay the debt."

"I don't want your money, Arabella. And don't credit me with sainthood. By paying your brother's creditors, I am merely insuring that after the girl has been educated and returns to Savannah, she will still have her own home, and therefore will not look to me for shelter."

There was a guarded look in Arabella's eyes. "Mr. Greenburg also informed me that you will be paying for Royal's education."

"I consider any monies I advance for your niece to be a negligible sum." His brows met in a frown. "I hope you will not tell your niece that her father left her penniless. She has had her share of heartaches. Let us not add to them. Allow her to believe it is her father's money that pays for her education."

"Royal is not a fool. She has already begun to suspect that my brother had no money."

"It is to be hoped that she will not learn of her father's indebtedness. She will not hear it from me—I trust you will not tell her, either."

"No, of course not." Arabella looked deeply into his golden eyes, wishing she could read his thoughts. "I know not if you are saint or devil, but you have put me in your debt, Damon Routhland. I am not without money myself. I will feel easier in my mind if you allow me to repay you for any monies you expend on my niece."

"As I said, the money is a mere trifle."

"To a wealthy man such as yourself, perhaps. I do not believe my niece would consider it a trifle. She is proud, Damon. If she ever discovers that she is living on your charity, it will devastate her. Not to mention what the gossips would make of that knowledge."

"No one need know—least of all Royal." He inclined his head, and suddenly his eyes grew cold. "Davis will escort you to the door. You might inform your niece that I shall be calling on her as soon as I hear from Fulham School."

Arabella moved across the room, knowing she was being dismissed. She had lost to Damon Routhland, and she felt as if she had just battled a whirlwind. Turning at the door, she stared into cold golden eyes. "Have you forgotten the summer we were . . . when you and I . . ."

His glance softened just a bit. "No, I haven't forgotten. What seventeen-year-old boy could have had a more beautiful and desirable woman to introduce him to . . . life, shall we say?"

"I hurt you."

"Perhaps just a little. But the knowledge I gained from the experience has often stood me in good stead."

"Perhaps I should have accepted your offer of marriage that summer."

"You did us both a favor by turning me down." He inclined his head with just the slightest smile tugging at his lips. "Good day to you, Miss Bradford."

Turning away, she found the butler waiting for her in the hallway. After her encounter with Damon Routhland, Arabella was no wiser than before. She had no insight into his motives as far as Royal was concerned. Perhaps it was as he said, and he felt sorry for the girl. Whatever the reason, she intended to watch the situation closely.

Dearest Papa,

It seems I spend my life waiting for something to happen. Weeks have passed, and still I have neither seen nor heard from Damon Routhland. Is it too much to hope he has forgotten about me? If that were only the case, I could go to France with Aunt Arabella.

Chapter 4

Royal was roused out of a deep sleep by someone shaking her.

"Wake up, Miss Royal," Alba urged. "Mr. Routhland is downstairs, asking to see you."

Royal tried to shake off the heavy drowsiness. "Surely Mr. Routhland would not be calling at this hour," she said, pulling the pillow over her head to shut out the intrusion. "Go away, Alba. It must be after midnight."

"Humph, it's after ten o'clock, but little does Damon Routhland care what time it is," Alba complained. "I don't like this business of that man being your guardian. Him with his high airs and demanding ways. Coming here after everyone's in bed and ordering me to bring you down to him because it suits his convenience."

Sleepily Royal rolled out of bed, allowing Alba to assist her into her pink velvet dressing gown. Still in the grip of drowsiness, Royal stood before the mirror and noticed that she did not look her best. Grabbing up her hairbrush, she quickly ran it through her tangled hair.

"Did you inform Aunt Arabella that Mr. Routhland is here? I feel certain she will want to know."

"I went to her room before I came here, even though I knew it would do no good. She complained earlier of being unable to sleep, so she took a sleeping draft, and I was unable to awaken her." Alba tied the bow at Royal's neck and stood back to inspect her. "Don't you worry none, Miss Royal, I won't leave you alone with that man for a moment."

Alba, accustomed to speaking her mind, did so now. "I don't know what your father could have been thinking about to make an unmarried man your guardian. I can only guess what the people of Savannah are making out of this. It just isn't decent for a young girl to be in the hands of a man like him."

Royal's eyes widened with apprehension. "Is there something wrong with Mr. Routhland?"

Alba placed her hands on her hips. "I am sure it's not my place to tell you about men like him."

"Why don't you like him, Alba?"

The housekeeper shook her head. "It's not for me to like or dislike him. As far as it goes, I have the highest respect for Mr. Routhland, but that does not make me approve of him as your guardian."

Royal squared her shoulders and braced herself for the meeting she had been dreading for so long. "Let's go below, Alba."

Moving through the hallway and descending the stairs, Royal had to quicken her pace to keep up with Alba. The housekeeper led her to the formal sitting room, where a welcome fire had been laid to ward off the night chill.

Damon Routhland was standing near the window, and Royal could feel his gaze on her as she crossed the room. He stood in the shadows, his silhouette little more than a dark outline.

"You wanted to see me, Mr. Routhland?" Royal asked, stopping ten paces from him. She stood like a frightened little bird ready to take flight, while the housekeeper hovered protectively next to her.

Damon moved out of the shadows to stand near the fireplace, and Royal noticed he was still wearing his greatcoat. It must be raining, she thought, because his dark hair, which was tied back in a queue, glistened in the firelight like silk. "Forgive me for the lateness of the hour," he said apologetically, "but I am forced to make an unexpected trip to Philadelphia, and I could not leave without seeing you since you will have sailed for England before I return."

With a heavy heart Royal asked, "When will I be leaving Savannah?"

"Within two weeks."

"How . . . long will I have to remain in England before I can come back home?"

"Until you have completed your education."

Damon watched Royal close her eyes as she drew in a shuddering breath. He wanted to assure her all would be well, that the time would pass quickly.

"Miss Bradford," he said gently, "may I call you Royal?"

"Yes, of course," she replied in surprise.

"Why don't you be seated so you'll be more comfortable." He moved a chair closer to the fireplace, and she obediently sat down, while Alba moved to stand just behind her.

"Now that's better." Damon sat down and gave her an encouraging smile. "I can guess how frightened you are about going to England where you have no friends or family, Royal. But I have been assured that Fulham is a good finishing school. Perhaps you will meet people there who remember your mother."

Royal only stared at him with large sad eyes, making Damon wonder if it was a mistake to send her so far away. "I am certain you will make friends right away, Royal. My only concern is that you may not want to return to Savannah after you complete your education."

Royal found much of her anxiety melting away under the softness of those golden eyes. "I have been concerned about finances,

Mr. Routhland. Mr. Greenburg made me suspect that my father left behind many debts. I am certain Fulham School is very costly."

Damon hesitated for a moment. He could not tell this young girl that her father had been unwise in his investments. He didn't want her to worry about finances. Looking into innocent blue eyes, he began spinning the half-lie that would divert her fears. "Fulham School is indeed costly, but you need have no concern. Your father made certain that your future is secure. I don't want you ever to worry about anything."

Royal's eyes brightened, for her first concern had been that she would lose her home. "My father was a wonderful man. I should have known he would provide for me."

"Indeed he was a fine man, Royal," Damon agreed, looking up at Alba and seeing a hint of respect reflected in her eyes. The severe line of the housekeeper's mouth turned up into an almost smile. It was apparent that Alba knew Douglas Bradford had made no monetary provision for his daughter, but Damon had the feeling she would keep his secret.

Royal stared in open curiosity at the man who now had control of her life. He was not as formidable as she had feared. There was something about him that inspired her trust, and she suddenly felt secure about the future. She saw the hint of amusement in his eyes as he realized she was assessing him, but she continued all the same.

"You do not know me very well, Royal, but I want you to believe that I am interested in your welfare."

"I thank you for that. But why should you trouble yourself about me?" she asked with her usual directness.

"It's very simple. Did you know that your father and mine were boys together in England?"

"Of course. I was well acquainted with your father, since he was often a guest here. I was very sad when he died two years ago."

Damon's voice deepened. "Both our fathers are dead now, Royal. Perhaps because of their friendship, you and I have a special bond between us."

Her eyes glistened. He was giving her something to hold on to—

a feeling of belonging. "I am so sorry for you," she managed to say past the lump in her throat. "I just realized how difficult it was for you to lose your father."

He moved forward, extracted his arms from his greatcoat, and flung it over the back of the chair before he answered her. "Grief has a way of lessening after a while. I know you don't believe that now, but time is a great healer."

"I . . . shall never forget my father."

"Of course not, nor should you."

For the first time Royal noticed the tiredness etched on Damon's face. His knee-high boots were splattered with mud, so he must have come on horseback. "I appreciate your coming out in the rain to talk to me, Mr. Routhland."

"Don't you think you could call me 'Damon'?"

"I don't think that would be proper, Mr. Routhland. My father would not have approved of my calling an older gentleman by his given name."

He laughed in amusement. This little girl was a real charmer. Golden ringlets framed her pretty face, and her eyes were large and luminous.

Royal covered a yawn with a childish smile of apology. Leaning her head back against the chair, she waited for him to tell her why he had roused her out of bed.

"I will not keep you from your sleep much longer. I only want to let you know my plans concerning your future. I thought you might feel less apprehensive that way."

She looked up at him coyly through her eyelashes. "I am glad that you are my guardian. I am indebted to you for your many kindnesses."

For a moment he turned his head and stared into the fire, as if he were remembering something. When he turned back to Royal, it appeared as if the firelight were reflected in the depths of his golden eyes. "Let us just say that by becoming your guardian, I am repaying an overdue debt to your father."

"What debt?" she asked curiously.

"My father came to the Colonies with your parents, but he had little money. It was your father who loaned him the money to buy land and build Swanhouse Plantation."

"I didn't know that. My father never told me."

"I can assure you 'tis true. Your father settled in Savannah, and my father chose country living, but they remained good friends. Shall I tell you a secret about your mother?"

Her eyes held a light of eagerness, for she knew so little about her mother. "Yes, please do."

"When I was a lad, I was in love with her. She was very lovely, and I suspect most of the gentlemen of Savannah admired her, but she loved only your father. In my mind she has always been the ideal woman. She once told me—I must have been about six years old—that if she had not married your father, she would have waited for me."

Royal eyed him admiringly. "Everyone in Chatham County is aware of how women flock around you."

Damon's laughter was deep. "You are an impudent little baggage. You should not repeat such rumors."

She curled her legs up under her, looking very like a little girl. "Surely you are aware that half the women in Savannah are in love with you?" she said seriously.

He arched an eyebrow at her. "Only half?"

"The other half are either married or too old. But I suspect some of them may be in love with you anyway."

Damon was aware of Alba's shocked gasp. He tilted up his head and pretended seriousness. "Keeping women attentive is a great responsibility for a man of my age."

"How old are you?" Royal inquired.

His smile was warm. "I am twenty-five, Royal."

He was not as old as she had thought, but old all the same to a fourteen-year-old girl's way of thinking. She was reflective for a moment. "At your age, you should be married."

"Well, little imp," he said, amused by her bold statement, "if you are to be believed, if I marry, I would break the hearts of half the women of Savannah. That would never do."

When she nodded in agreement, her face set in a serious expression, he resisted the urge to ruffle her golden curls. "Has anyone ever told you that you are precocious, Royal? You must have been a great source of amusement to your father."

She sighed wearily, and her tongue flicked out to lick her dry lips. "My father was my best friend." Her eyes clouded with unshed tears. "He will always be my best friend." Royal lowered her eyes, hoping to hide her tears. "It is sometimes painful to think about him."

Damon was suddenly stricken with tender feelings for this fragile little girl. His jaw tightened, but he softened his voice. "I can promise you that the time will come when you will smile when you remember your father."

Then he knelt beside her and took her small hand in his. "Will you allow me to be your friend, Royal?"

"Yes," she said. "We will be friends as our fathers were."

"Good." A half smile curved his lips. "Then feel comforted by the plans that have been made for your future. And don't forget that when you get to England, you will be closer to your aunt Arabella. She has assured me that she will visit you often."

Royal laid her free hand on his. "Must I leave? I am afraid of going to England."

"I thought you trusted me."

"I do, but—"

"I know you cannot imagine you will ever be happy again, but you will. What I do now is in accordance with your father's wishes, and I have no alternative."

"I don't suppose you would allow me to come and live with you at Swanhouse?" she asked hopefully, thinking that after all, living at the plantation would be better than leaving Georgia altogether.

Damon glanced up at Alba, and her eyes sparked with a warning. "No, little one. It would not be proper for you to live in a bachelor's household."

Suddenly Royal felt sad at the thought of being parted from her new friend, and with her usual honesty she said, "I shall miss you, Mr. Routhland."

He glanced down at her tiny hand. "The years will pass quickly,

Royal. Before you know it, you will be returning to Savannah. At that time I shall have decided about your future."

"May I write to you and tell you of my progress in school?"

His expression softened. "I will expect you to."

She threw back her tiny shoulders and brushed a tumbled lock of hair out of her face. "I am resigned to my fate, Mr. Routhland."

He stood up, laughing with delight. "Now that your immediate future is settled, I have a surprise for you."

Her eyes sparkled with interest. "What is it?"

"I have corresponded with Mrs. Fortescue, who is headmistress at Fulham School, and she has assured me that you will be allowed to have your own horse. As soon as you are settled in, I shall send you a suitable young mare from Swanhouse. Would you like that?"

Her eyes lit up, and she clapped her hands gleefully. "Oh, yes, Mr. Routhland, may I?"

"Have I not just said so? Also," he continued, "I have made arrangements with my London solicitor, a Mr. Webber, and he is to meet your ship when it docks at Plymouth. He will accompany you and your aunt to London, where he has been instructed to see to your needs. You are to have a complete new wardrobe"—he waved his hand—"and whatever else you will need to make you comfortable at the school."

"Thank you," she whispered through trembling lips. "Can Aunt Arabella stay with me until I am settled?"

"I see no reason why not."

Royal's eyes were shining with tears. "You are the kindest man, besides my father, that I have ever known."

Damon blinked his eyes in astonishment. No one before Royal had ever accused him of being kind. "I consider that high praise indeed."

He took her hand and pulled her to her feet. "Go to bed, now, little one, and dream of all the wonderful adventures that await you." He turned to the housekeeper. "See her tucked in, Alba. I shall find my own way out."

Reluctantly Royal moved to the door. Turning back, she blessed him with a smile. "I shall remember you in my prayers every night."

"Do that, Royal."

"Will you remember me?"

"Forever and a day," he pledged, "for you are etched in my mind."

"Is that a promise?"

"That's a promise."

A sad smile touched her lips, and Damon watched her disappear with Alba following behind. He saw months of loneliness ahead for Royal. Of course, Arabella had promised to visit the girl, but he felt sure that the actress would soon be caught up with her own friends in Paris and would forget about her niece.

He pulled on his greatcoat and left, closing the door behind him. As he mounted his horse, he noticed that the rain clouds had moved away and a blood red moon lit the sky.

Kicking his mount in the flanks, he headed for Swanhouse Plantation. He was concerned about the rumors of war with England, but hopefully war would not come, at least not until Royal returned. It would seem like a long time before he saw that charming little imp again.

He would instruct John Bartholomew to answer Royal's correspondence and see to her every need. "I am not the fatherly type," he muttered aloud. "What in the hell have I gotten myself into?"

It was the day before Royal and her aunt were to sail for England, and with an aching heart Royal had gone to place flowers on her father's and mother's graves. Standing in the shadow of the great oak tree, she whispered a prayer that the years away from home would pass quickly.

Later in the afternoon, as she went through the house with Alba and Tobias, closing most of the rooms and draping dust covers over the furniture, her uncertainty deepened—this act made her leaving seem so final.

That night after Alba and Tobias had gone to their own quarters and her aunt had retired for the night, Royal walked through each of the rooms, burning every familiar detail into her mind. When at last she climbed into her own bed, she was flooded with wonderful childhood memories. Finally, near dawn, she fell asleep.

Royal's saddest moments came the next morning in saying a tearful good-bye to Alba and Tobias. Both the servants stood on the front steps, waving to her until the carriage pulled out of sight.

Sunbeams danced on the surface of the water. Royal leaned against the railing of the British merchant ship *Excursion* and watched the shoreline of Georgia disappear in the distance. Then she turned questioning eyes to her aunt, who stood beside her.

Arabella pulled Royal into the circle of her arms. "I don't know when you will be coming back, my dear," she said, answering the unspoken question. "But be of good cheer. It won't be so bad. Think what fun you will have when you're fitted for a new wardrobe."

Royal sighed. "I don't look as good in black as you do, Aunt Arabella."

" 'Tis a pity you are in mourning and will have to wear black." Arabella shrugged. "Well, no matter, I merely consider this a challenge. I know all the fashionable shops, and with my guidance, you will be the best-dressed young lady at that school. Actually," she continued, "you are more fortunate than you know to be able to leave this backwater country."

Royal managed a brave smile. "Even though my mother and father were born in England, my roots are deeply embedded in Georgia's soil."

"I know, dear. But London is such an exciting city. At the height of the Season, there are so many parties and balls to attend. I know you are going to be enchanted with everything."

Staring into the foamy trail left by the ship, Royal frowned. "I am bothered by the conflict that has developed between the Colonies and England. Do you suppose there will be a war?"

"Of course not. There will always be a few hotheads who try

to incite dissension, but I am certain that cooler heads will prevail in this instance. Try not to think about anything but the adventure that awaits you."

"I'll try," Royal said doubtfully. She studied her aunt closely. "Why do you suppose Damon Routhland has been so kind to me?"

"I don't know, dearest. I've been wondering that myself. At first I thought it was because of me, but now I'm not sure."

"Were you once in love with him, Aunt Arabella?"

Arabella shook her head. "No, but I was enchanted with him. You will have to understand that at the time, he was too young for me—or so I thought."

"Did he love you?"

"He fancied he did, but I think what he felt for me was not really love."

Arabella's flaming hair was blowing in the breeze, and Royal thought no one could be more beautiful. "I am sure many men have been in love with you, Aunt Arabella."

"Yes, I suppose."

"Do you think I will be pretty when I grow up?"

Arabella's laughter was musical. "Dearest, when you become a young lady, there will not be a woman on either side of the Atlantic who will come close to you in beauty. Men will fight duels and die at your feet"—she smiled—"just as they have over me."

Royal did not want men to die for her. She thought of the darkly handsome Damon Routhland and wondered if he would ever think she was beautiful. Most probably he would be married by the time she returned to Savannah, she thought regretfully.

"It's very strange, Aunt Arabella. I have known Mr. Routhland for such a short time, and yet I find he dominates my thoughts. Why do you suppose that is?"

Arabella looked at her niece with new awareness. Royal's young body was beginning to develop, and her once pale skin had taken on a healthy glow. It troubled her how much Royal had to learn about men.

"You are no different from any other woman when it comes to Damon Routhland. Men like him draw women like bees to a honey pot. It is natural that you should be grateful to him, Royal, but do not ever lose your heart to him," she warned, "for I feel certain he is incapable of loving a woman. Most likely he has already dismissed you from his mind."

"He promised he would remember me, Aunt Arabella," Royal said with conviction, "and I believed him."

Dearest Papa,

Crossing the Atlantic was uneventful. The water was calm for most of the way. I suppose I was not in a mind to enjoy the voyage with the enthusiasm Aunt Arabella tried to arouse in me. I remained in my cabin most of the time, and poor Aunt Arabella thought I was seasick, when in truth I was homesick.

March 1775

Royal glanced out the window of the rumbling coach. The emerald-green glories of spring were complemented by a deep blue sky. The English countryside was so lovely it reminded her of a painting from some master artist's palette. The landscape was dotted with colorful wildflowers, while rolling hills gradually gave way to a small hamlet with thatch-roofed houses and cobblestone streets.

As Damon had promised, his London solicitor, Rupert Webber, had met Royal and her aunt when they docked at Plymouth. With him in command, the journey to London had thus far been trouble free. They now traveled aboard his well-sprung private coach, which was pulled by six matching grays.

"Are you not fatigued, dearest?" Arabella asked, noting the

heightened color in Royal's face. "The voyage has drained me, and the bustling crowds we encountered at the docks were unnerving to say the least."

"I am not at all tired, Aunt Arabella," Royal assured her. "I find the journey invigorating. Papa often told me about the beauty of the English countryside, and now I am seeing it for myself."

Mr. Webber nodded. "The exuberance of youth. Would that I could work up such enthusiasm over anything, Miss Bradford."

Royal turned her attention to the slightly built man whose powdered wig was a bit askew on his balding head. She glanced quickly out the window, fearing she would laugh if she looked at her aunt.

"Miss Bradford," the solicitor continued, "I trust you won't find it too difficult to adjust to our way of life. Everything in England is steeped in customs and traditions."

Her expression became serious. "My country is still so new. We are searching for direction."

He turned inquiring eyes on her. "Your country? My dear Miss Bradford, I was not aware that the colony of Georgia was a separate country from Britain."

"No, of course it isn't. It's just that England is so far away from Georgia that it's sometimes difficult to think of ourselves as your colony."

The solicitor burst into jovial laughter. "It's just such thinking that troubles many members of Parliament." Then, more seriously, he added, "Guard your tongue well, Miss Bradford, or you will be singled out to your disadvantage at Fulham School." The warning was issued in all sincerity, which gave Royal pause for thought.

Arabella had been listening to the exchange, and she now addressed Mr. Webber. "My niece has always been encouraged to speak her mind, and I hope she will continue to do so, no matter whom it offends."

The little man smiled, and his whole face creased into laugh lines. "Since Mr. Routhland has requested that I look after your niece's interests, I would be derelict in my duties if I did not point out the pitfalls awaiting her at Fulham School. I have to tell you that pressure was brought to bear to get her into the school as it was."

"Why is that?" Arabella asked. "My sister-in-law went there. I don't recall that she had any trouble getting in."

"This school is very prestigious. Some mothers enroll their daughters at birth to make certain that they will be accepted. Most of the pupils come from the nobility or upper classes."

"I won't tolerate any unkindness to Royal. And I take exception with anyone who thinks my niece is not good enough to be in that school," Arabella said haughtily.

"Rightly so, rightly so," Mr. Webber agreed. He held Royal's gaze. "When I called Mrs. Fortescue's attention to the fact that your mother had attended Fulham, she was more receptive to your enrollment."

Royal glanced out the window, wondering how she would ever feel at home in this country where people were separated into classes. Her footsteps had been set upon a path that was not of her making; however, she would try to behave in a manner that would make Mr. Routhland proud of her and reflect well on her mother.

"Look out the window, Royal," Arabella pointed out. "We are approaching London!"

The sight that met Royal's eyes was not at all what she had expected. The quaint, dirty, stall-lined streets were flanked by drab, crumbling warehouses. The smell of rotten vegetables and raw fish was so overpowering that Royal covered her nose with a handkerchief so she could breathe. The coach rattled over cobblestone streets, past garish inns that looked ready to collapse and public houses where dingy laundry had been hung out the windows to dry. The streets seemed to be filled with an endless swarm of disheveled men and women, trailed by shoeless, dirty children.

When the horses clopped across a wooden bridge, the scene began to change. It was as if they had entered another world. The sky was webbed with church steeples and towering buildings that gleamed in the afternoon sun.

"We are entering London's par excellence district, Miss Bradford," the solicitor informed Royal. "Here the highborn, titled, wealthy, and powerful dwell. The choicest section is said to be bound on the north by Piccadilly, on the south by Pall Mall, on the east by the Haymarket, and on the west by St. James's Street. Your new home, Fulham School, is, of course, within this domain."

If Mr. Webber was trying to make Royal feel at ease, he had failed. More and more she was convinced that she would not fit in, no matter how hard she tried.

They passed coaches with coats of arms boldly painted on their doors, symbolic of the nobility that rode inside. Royal gazed at the wide avenue with its age-old trees standing guard like sentinels, defying entrance to any outsider. Here, well-dressed men and women strolled in and out of fashionable shops. Royal was surprised when they passed stately homes with block gardens not unlike those in Savannah.

When the coach drew to a halt before the fashionable Devonshire House, the solicitor smiled. "This is where you will reside until such time as you are properly outfitted for Fulham School. On Mr. Routhland's instructions, I have made arrangements for you to patronize several of the shops. This is Monday. I should think by Monday next, you will be ready to be presented to the headmistress, Mrs. Fortescue."

Royal caught her aunt's eyes and received an encouraging smile. Drawing on her courage, she moved out of the coach. Whatever the future held for her she could not guess, but she was prepared to meet it bravely.

The office of the headmistress of Fulham was sparsely furnished, cold and impersonal. Two straight-backed chairs faced the cherrywood desk where a woman with cold, hard eyes looked Royal over from head to foot. Royal met the headmistress's assessing stare with interest.

It appeared that Mrs. Fortescue was in her late fifties or early sixties, but it was difficult to tell for certain. She was tall for a woman, big-boned, and wore her hair unpowdered and drawn tightly away from her face and covered with a stiff white cap. Thick glasses sat on the narrow bridge of her nose, and she tended to look over the rim rather than through the glasses.

Mr. Webber had warned Royal that the headmistress ruled with the same authority as a queen laying down laws for her lowly subjects. Royal felt certain that Mr. Webber had described the woman correctly.

Mrs. Fortescue glanced down at the log book on her desk, allowing Royal and her aunt to wait to be acknowledged. At last the woman raised her head.

Pale blue eyes seemed to bore right into Royal with an intensity that made her shiver with fear. The headmistress pointed to the chairs in front of her desk, indicating Royal and her aunt should be seated. Both quickly complied.

"I have been expecting you, Royal Bradford," Mrs. Fortescue said in a decidedly irritated voice, the words clipped and impeccably enunciated. "If you are to be a student at this school, you will be punctual at all times, and you will be dependable in all your habits."

"My niece only reached England nine days ago," Arabella stated in defense of Royal. "I was told that she was not expected until this week."

Mrs. Fortescue turned her cold stare on Arabella. "Yes, that is correct, and this week began two days ago. She was expected Monday morning."

"That would have been impossible, Mrs. Fortescue, because Royal had fittings for her new wardrobe. It was not easy finding black gowns that were flattering to my niece. You know she is in mourning for her father." Arabella drew in a breath. "And her shoes had not yet been—"

A tight smile pinched the headmistress's lips. "We have a rule here that is never broken, and that is: No excuses *ever*—only results."

"I'm sorry, Mrs. Fortescue," Royal apologized. "It will not happen again."

"See that it does not," came the reprimand. "You may as well know right now that we usually do not take girls from the . . . Colonies, here at Fulham." She pronounced the word *Colonies* as if it were some dread disease. "Fulham School is over two hundred and fifty years old and has the reputation of accepting only young ladies from our finest families."

Royal's eyes gleamed. "I make no apologies for my family."

The challenge went unanswered, and Mrs. Fortescue continued as if Royal had not spoken. "Fulham accommodates no more than twenty-five students. Of those twenty-five students, only you and the two granddaughters of the lord mayor of Edinburgh are not of noble birth. However," she continued frostily, "since your mother was a student here, and since your guardian, Mr. Routhland, is not without influence, we have decided to allow you in." Her eyes narrowed. "On a probationary basis, of course. You will find that if you tend to your own affairs and apply yourself to your studies, you will fare well enough."

Arabella came to her feet, her eyes blazing with anger. "It is inconceivable for me to leave my niece in a place that belittles and talks down to her! I am of a mind to take her away from here right now!"

Mrs. Fortescue seemed unruffled by Arabella's outburst. "You cannot take Royal away, Miss Bradford. The moment she walked through those doors this morning, she became my responsibility. As a matter of fact, I am going to ask you not to visit your niece for at least three months. We have a settling-in period, and we find the students adapt more easily to Fulham if their well-meaning relatives do not, shall we say, interfere."

"I am not bound by your outdated rules. It's barbaric to keep young girls away from their families. You cannot stop me from seeing my niece."

"But, you see, I can—and I shall."

The two women stared at each other until at last Arabella, realizing she could not win this confrontation, lowered her eyes. "Before I leave, at least assure me that Royal will be well treated here."

In a composed voice Mrs. Fortescue replied, "Better than that, your niece will learn to work with needle and shuttle and do fine embroidery. She will learn mathematics, history, and geography. She will learn to speak French and Latin, and if she does not know how to read and write, that will be taught her also. If she is adept in music, she will have voice lessons, and she can choose from several instruments in which to become proficient. She will be instructed in dance and, of course, the social graces. When your niece leaves Fulham, Miss Bradford, she will be presentable in any house in London, and at any table. No one could do more for her. Though the school year is under way, she will be expected to catch up with her classmates."

Arabella looked dejected. "Then I have no choice but to place her in your care. Will you give me time to take my leave of Royal in private?"

"No," Mrs. Fortescue said. "You may say your good-byes here and now. Already the two of you have disrupted my morning. Your niece is not the only student at our school, you know."

Royal stood up and rushed into her aunt's arms. "Must I stay, Aunt Arabella?"

Arabella's eyes clashed with the headmistress's, and she gave a resigned sigh—she could not win against this woman. "I'm afraid so, dearest." She tilted Royal's face up to her. "You are not to worry about anything. I will be in London for the rest of the week. After that I shall have to return to Paris, but I will keep in contact with you." She glanced at Mrs. Fortescue. "I would hope you have no objections if my niece and I correspond with each other?"

"I have no objections to letters. Just do not come yourself."

Tears gathered in Royal's eyes, and she wiped them on the back of her hand, bringing a disapproving frown from the headmistress. "Do not worry about me, Aunt Arabella," Royal said bravely. "I shall be fine."

"I think it's best that you leave now," Mrs. Fortescue instructed Arabella. "I will see your niece settled. Have no concern for her."

With a final embrace, Arabella moved hesitantly to the door, turned and smiled at Royal, and then left. She felt as if she were deserting the child, but what choice had she?

With the memory of Royal's forlorn little face in her mind, Arabella climbed into the waiting coach and instructed the driver to take her to Devonshire House.

Mrs. Fortescue looked Royal up and down with a critical eye. She took in her crisp, new black gown and her forlorn expression. "Have you brought your own maid to see to your needs, Miss Bradford?"

"Yes, madame. My aunt engaged a girl for me. She should arrive this afternoon."

"Very well. This interview is at a close. You may settle in now."

Then the headmistress said with a softness that surprised Royal: "You are going to have a difficult time here, Royal Bradford. You must remember on the days that are the darkest, the sun will be shining somewhere in the world. You remind me very much of myself at your age."

Without another word, Mrs. Fortescue moved to the door and called to someone who stood just outside. Royal was quickly introduced to Mrs. Hereford, the head housekeeper, a large, severe-looking woman who merely nodded and motioned for Royal to follow her.

As Royal moved into the hallway, her new shoes made a loud clicking noise against the polished floor. Dismayed, she tried tiptoeing to lessen the noise, but that only drew a reproachful glance from Mrs. Hereford.

They climbed the steep stairs and went down a long, dimly lit corridor before Mrs. Hereford stopped at a door. "I will direct the men to deliver your trunks. When your maid arrives, I'll send her up to you. Supper is at seven o'clock. If you arrive at the dining room late, you will not be allowed to eat." She looked down her beaked nose at Royal. "Of course, we dress for supper."

Royal nodded in understanding as the woman moved abruptly out the door, closing it with a snap behind her. Disheartened, she glanced about the room that was to be her home.

It was not a large room, but it was surprisingly cheerful and comfortable. A white lace coverlet adorned the bed, and matching lace curtains hung at the wide window, allowing a burst of sunlight into every corner of the room. There was a desk, a dressing table, and a chair, all of polished cherrywood. The marble fireplace meant that the room would be warm and cheery.

Royal walked to the window, which gave her a view of the long avenue at the front of the school. She watched as fashionable carriages came and went in a steady stream. Across the street was a park, and on the other side of the park she could just make out the roofs of several stately houses.

She was overcome with sadness, completely isolated in this unknown world.

What would her life be like for the next four years?

May 1775

It was after midnight, and the lights still glowed brightly at Swanhouse Plantation. Thirty gentlemen had gathered in the library to discuss the distressing news coming out of Massachusetts.

Damon Routhland held up his hand, calling for calm. "Gentlemen, gentlemen, this bickering among ourselves is not going to accomplish anything. All we know is that there was a skirmish at Lexington."

"War will come," Joseph Graham insisted. "It's just a matter of time until the British push us too far. What I want to know is who's going to stand with us—who demands freedom from our British enslavers?"

Some of the men raised their hands with a shout, others with more restraint.

"What about you, Damon?" Joseph demanded. "You haven't raised your hand."

Caleb Edwards came to his neighbor's rescue. "We all know that Damon is loyal to Georgia."

"For those of you who doubt my loyalties," Damon said, "let me assure you that if war comes, I will stand with you. I am not, nor have I ever been, a king's man."

"You have the most to lose if war comes," Joseph reminded him. "Since Swanhouse is the largest plantation in Georgia, you might be reluctant to join in a war."

"I repeat, gentlemen, if war comes, I'll stand with you—and war will come, make no mistake about that. But will we be ready?"

"Shouldn't we organize, form an army—do something?" Caleb asked, voicing everyone's concern.

"I suggest we do nothing for the moment," Damon injected. "Don't be in such a hurry to see destruction descend on us. It will arrive soon enough. We must be prepared."

Several men shook their heads. They all knew that Damon Routhland was right. When war came to the South they must be ready to fight.

"I ain't going to leave my home," Ezekiel Elman announced. "If I fight, it'll be right here."

"No army will take you, Ezekiel," Caleb told him. "You're long past your prime."

"That may be so," the old man admitted, "but I can still outshoot anyone in this room, 'cepting maybe Damon here, and I taught him."

Damon studied the old man with affection. From Ezekiel he had learned to hunt and how to survive in the swamps. The old man was indeed a good marksman, but he was in his seventies. Damon's gaze moved to each man in turn, assessing his value to an army. They were planters and shopkeepers—none of them had been trained as soldiers. Lord help them if war erupts!

"I suggest we do nothing for now, but wait and listen." Damon added under his breath, "And pray that when war comes, God will be on our side."

Dearest Papa,

Until now I have never known the meaning of loneliness. I have little hope of making friends here at Fulham School. So far I have only met the headmistress and the housekeeper, and neither has done much to recommend herself to me. I have been warned that I must not be late for supper, so I must close and make myself presentable.

Royal knew the black taffeta gown with its high, unadorned neck and long, loose-fitting sleeves was not flattering on her. She was certain to make an unfavorable impression on her first appearance in the dining room, she thought miserably. She was resigned to wearing black out of respect for her father, but, oh, it did make her look pale and insignificant.

Aided by Hannah, the maid her aunt Arabella had engaged, Royal arranged her hair in simple curls that were appropriate for a girl her age. Determined to add a touch of elegance to her toilette, she directed Hannah to weave a black ribbon through her unpowdered locks.

Downstairs, Royal paused at the dining room door and peered around the corner nervously. Several girls were already inside, laughing and talking among themselves. Shyly, Royal avoided their eyes and looked instead at the four long tables that were adorned with snowy white tablecloths and laid with crystal, china, and silver that sparkled in the dancing candlelight.

When she stepped into the room, Royal could feel everyone staring at her, but no one gave her a smile or indicated that she was welcome. She wished she could run back to the safety of her room, for she could feel hostility in the eyes that watched her.

Bravely she raised her head and moved forward until she attracted the attention of a serving girl, who bobbed a quick curtsy and led her to a table at the back of the room.

"I was told to remind you, Miss Bradford, that you will be eating at this same table for every meal, so you will always know your place," the servant instructed primly.

Besides herself, there were only two other girls at the long table. Both of them wore a red, wine, and green tartan sash, so Royal assumed that they were the Scottish sisters who, like her, were not of noble birth.

Royal smiled with uncertainty first at one girl and then at the other, fearful of being rebuffed. She did not feel up to facing another rejection today. Relief washed over her when both girls smiled back at her tentatively.

"We know who you are," one of the girls said, rolling her "R" with a heavy Scottish brogue. "You are the new girl from the Colonies."

"That's right. I am Royal Bradford, and yes, I do come from the Colonies."

"I am Meg MacGregor, and this is my sister, Fiona." The girl giggled. "Like us, it seems you have been banished to anonymity."

Royal glanced around the silent room and found that everyone was looking in her direction. Lifting her chin proudly, she replied: "I'm pleased to share this obscure corner with both of you." She nodded toward the center of the dining room. "I don't believe I should be comfortable there."

Meg MacGregor leaned closer to Royal and whispered, "You aren't likely to find out. It is doubtful that any of us will be invited to eat with the crème de la crème," she said pertly. "Not that I'd want to anyway."

Meg and Fiona were full of questions about the Colonies. By the time their food was served, the three girls were conversing like old friends. Occasionally Royal would glance up and find herself the object of whispered conversations from the other tables—this she tried to ignore, but she was aware of a coldness in the hostile eyes that intermittently met her gaze.

Fiona pointed to one girl who sat at the head of the first table. Royal had noticed her earlier because there was something queenly, yet fragile, about her. "That is the one who holds the power here at Fulham," she whispered.

Royal glanced at the girl who, though beautiful, appeared sullen and withdrawn. "Who is she?"

"That's none other than Lady Alissa Seaton. She is the sister of the duke of Chiswick, and the highest-ranking student at this school. If you are noticed by her, it will make you acceptable to the rest—if not"—Meg giggled—"you'll be left at this table with us."

"Lady Alissa is a monster," Fiona chimed in. "Of course, she's lame, and that could be the reason she's so often disagreeable."

"Lame?" Royal questioned, glancing once more at the girl at the head of the table. "What happened to her?"

"She was thrown by a horse," Meg informed her. "I overheard some of the other girls talking about it. They said the doctor thinks she might one day walk, but only if she tries. Of course, she never tries. I think she likes to be thought of as a cripple."

Fiona pursed her lips. "Why shouldn't she? Everyone falls all over themselves trying to do favors for her, and to please her. But not me—I never will belittle myself to gain her approval."

"I wish I were her friend," Meg said in a fanciful voice. "If for no other reason but to meet her brother, Lord Preston. He is quite handsome of face and manner. I would gladly fawn at Lady Alissa's feet if it would call me to his attention."

"Well, Meg," her sister declared in a disgusted voice, "You can get that notion right out of your head. Besides, even if you were acquainted with Lord Preston, his brother, the duke, would not allow anything to come of it. I am told that he and that wife of his have a sad view of anyone who is not of the nobility. You'll not be introduced to him, and neither will I." She glanced pointedly at Royal. "Nor will anyone at this table, for that matter. We are the social outcasts of Fulham."

" 'Tis a pity," Meg said in a resigned voice. "Oh, well. . . ." She shrugged. "Lord Preston is most probably as dull as dishwater, anyway. Still, I would like to find out for myself."

Intrigued, Royal looked across the invisible line that divided them from Lady Alissa's table. Royal judged her to be older than she was, perhaps fifteen or sixteen. Her hair was so light it was almost white, and she had the saddest eyes Royal had ever seen.

Royal glanced at the wheelchair, and she felt pity for the girl. It did not matter if Lady Alissa was acknowledged and spoiled by everyone—it could not be easy being lame.

At that moment Lady Alissa met Royal's compassionate glance, and she glared back at her. With a toss of her head, she obviously dismissed Royal as unimportant.

Royal lay in her darkened room, unable to sleep because the sounds outside her window were unfamiliar and disconcerting. She tried to think of something pleasant, and suddenly Damon Routhland's face came to her. It seemed that when she was troubled she always thought of him and was somehow comforted. She tried to imagine what he would be doing tonight. Probably entertaining some beautiful woman, she thought.

She slipped out of bed and lit a small candle. Sitting down at her dressing table and taking up pen and paper, she began to write:

> Dear Mr. Routhland,
> I plead with you to bring me home. I do not wish to be troublesome, but I must make you understand I do not belong here, and I am most disheartened. I know my father would not have wanted me to be unhappy. If you will allow me to return, I promise to

be no trouble to you. I beg you to consider my plight. I miss my friends and Savannah most dreadfully. Knowing you will consider my unhappiness, I will await your reply.

Your obedient,
Royal Bradford

Royal vented her loneliness in the letter to her guardian, then she folded it and put it away. She must not send a letter begging to come home—not yet, anyway.

Now at peace with herself, she crawled into bed and immediately fell asleep.

It had been a morning when everything had gone wrong. Royal had lost her slipper and finally found it beneath the folds of the bedcovers. Then she'd spilled water on her gown and had to change, which had made her late for class. Just last week, one of the teachers, Miss Mallory, had humiliated her before the class, making her apologize to everyone personally for what she'd termed "Royal's thoughtless behavior."

Royal moved up the stairs. When she reached the upper landing, she heard voices in the hallway below, one of which she identified as Lady Alissa's.

When a deep male voice spoke up, she moved to the railing and peered down to see who it was. "My dear sister," the man said, smiling at Alissa. "It's my hope that you will write to Mother and inform her I have been a dutiful brother in paying a visit to you."

"Lord Preston," gushed one of the girls, "would that my brother was half so attentive."

So, Royal thought, that was the brother Meg had spoken of so favorably. He was indeed handsome and most dashing. He wore buff trousers and a cream-colored coat. He wore his hair powdered and pulled back in a queue.

Royal glanced down at the faces of Lady Alissa's ever-present entourage. It appeared each girl hung on to every word Lord Preston spoke and worshiped him with adoring eyes. Their slavish adulation filled her with disgust; never had she seen girls behave so foolishly over a man. Her gaze moved to Lady Alissa's face, and she saw a softness reflected there. Apparently Lady Alissa was fond of her brother.

Lord Preston picked up his sister in his arms and carried her toward the stairs. "You have had enough excitement for one day. Perhaps you should rest this afternoon," he told her.

Alissa wound her arms around her brother's neck. "Must you go? I had hoped we would spend the whole day together."

He carried her up the stairs while the other girls followed. "Would that I could, Alissa, but, alas, I have another appointment that I dare not break."

"Redhead or brunette?" she asked petulantly.

His laughter was spontaneous. "You know me too well, little sister."

Royal had flattened herself against the wall, hoping to go unobserved, but she had not reckoned with the keen eye of Lord Preston Seaton. He paused before her and gave her a heart-wrenching smile. "Whom have we here?" he asked with interest.

"Pay no attention to her," said Kathleen Griffin. "She's of no importance."

Preston gazed into sad blue eyes. "You are wrong, Miss Griffin. I think she is someone very special—for who but one of great import could have eyes that rival a morning sky?"

Royal drew in a deep breath and blinked in astonishment. No gentleman had ever said anything half so marvelous to her.

"Preston," Alissa said in an icy voice that revealed her unwillingness to share her brother's attention with Royal, "meet Royal Bradford. She's from the Colonies, I believe."

Royal watched Lord Preston, waiting for his reaction, but he merely smiled. "Well, Miss Royal Bradford, the Colonies' loss is England's gain."

With a pounding heart, Royal turned away and rushed down the hallway. She could hear the giggling voices of the girls, and

Lady Alissa's voice was taunting. "She has no manners at all. Whatever possessed Mrs. Fortescue to accept such a student?"

Royal rushed into her room and closed the door behind her. Her eyes were soft as she remembered Lord Preston's words to her. Now she could not blame the other girls for acting such a fool—had not her own actions been far worse?

Lord Preston Seaton was wonderful—simply wonderful!

It was an hour before supper when Kathleen Griffin knocked on Royal's door. Then, without waiting to be invited in, she pushed open the door and looked about her with a curled lip. "How quaint," she said at last, her gaze boring into Royal.

Royal had been sitting by the window, but now she came to her feet, her eyes blazing with anger. "I didn't invite you into my room, so I don't have to endure your insults. Leave at once!"

Kathleen shrugged. "It was not my idea to come to see you. Lady Alissa asked me to tell you to come to her room immediately."

Royal moved to stand before the girl. "I'm not one of Lady Alissa's puppets. I will not go running to her any time she summons me." Her head went up a bit higher. "But I wager you do, don't you?"

For a moment the girl's dark eyes snapped with anger, then she smiled scornfully. "Is this what you want me to tell Lady Alissa?"

Royal turned away. "Tell her what you will. If she wants to see me, she can come here."

"She is lame," Kathleen reminded Royal, her eyes gleaming with satisfaction. "She won't like this, you know."

"Go and tell her I refused her summons," Royal said without turning around.

Malicious laughter filled the room as Kathleen crossed to the door. "Is this your last word?"

Royal turned to face her tormentor. "No. Don't come back—that's my last word."

"Very well, but I would not want to be the one to thwart Lady

Alissa. I can almost find it within me to feel pity for you—almost, but not quite."

After Kathleen had gone, Royal could not keep her hands from trembling. Should she have gone to Lady Alissa's room? She turned to the window. "No," she said aloud. "I will not allow anyone to treat me in such a shabby manner. I am Royal Bradford from Savannah, Georgia, and proud of it."

Royal rushed to the door and down the hallway toward Meg and Fiona MacGregor's room. Fiona answered the door and invited her inside. "You look pale, Royal," she observed. "Has something happened?"

Meg offered Royal a chair, and when she was seated she looked from one sister to the other. "I fear I have made a powerful enemy today."

She explained to the sisters about her encounter with Lady Alissa's brother and then about Kathleen Griffin's visit to her room. "I'm not sorry I didn't go with her. I just wish they would leave me alone."

Fiona's face whitened. "I fear they will not leave you alone now. They will take your refusal as a challenge."

Meg put her arms around Royal. "We have sad news to tell you that can only add to your troubles. Who will be your friends when we are gone?"

Royal looked up at Meg. "You are going home for a visit?"

"No," Fiona answered for her sister. "We are returning home to Scotland. Our grandfather is ill and our father wants us home."

"Oh, I am so sorry," Royal said, feeling sick inside. She glanced around the room and noticed that the girls were packing their trunks. "I do hope your grandfather will recover."

Fiona nodded sadly. "He will, I'm sure, but I do hate leaving you. What will you do?"

Royal came to her feet. "I have had worse things happen to me. I shall manage."

Her words were brave, but her eyes showed her distress. "When do you leave?" she asked at last.

Meg folded a lace shawl and placed it in the trunk, then

slammed the lid shut with finality. "In the morning." She glanced at the mantel clock. "Run along and make yourself ready so we can go down to supper together. At least you will not be singled out tonight with my sister and me beside you."

"Yes," Royal agreed. "At least the two of you will be with me tonight."

As she moved down the hallway, Royal saw Kathleen Griffin hurrying in the opposite direction. Had Kathleen just come from her room? she wondered. Surely not.

When she reached her room, she found the door was not closed tightly. Anger tugged at her mind. What had Kathleen been doing here? Perhaps she had only come with another summons from Lady Alissa.

With a firm set to her chin, she vowed never to kowtow to Lady Alissa!

Dearest Papa,

Supper last night was amazingly without incident. I kept waiting for something to happen, but I was gratefully ignored by Lady Alissa and her friends. This morning the MacGregor sisters left, and, oh, I do miss them so. It is lonely being without friends, but I have decided to devote myself to my studies and be the best student I can be.

Chapter 7

Royal closed her diary and set it aside. It was almost time for her singing lesson. She moved to the mirror and adjusted the black velvet bow in her hair. Mrs. Hargrove, the music teacher, had told Royal that she had a pleasing voice, and she did enjoy the lessons.

When she reached the music class, Kathleen Griffin stood before the door, barring Royal's way. "Mrs. Fortescue wants to see you," she said smoothly. "If I were you, I'd get there as quickly as possible."

Royal turned away, trying to ignore her irritation. That girl did test her sorely.

When she reached Mrs. Fortescue's office, she realized Kathleen was right behind her. "This is one summons you won't ignore,

Royal Bradford." The hateful girl leaned closer. "After today, we will have seen the last of you," she taunted.

Royal quickly entered the office, hoping to escape Kathleen, but the girl followed her inside. Not only was Mrs. Fortescue waiting for her, but Mrs. Hargrove was there as well. Royal sat down on the chair Mrs. Fortescue indicated and waited to hear what the headmistress had to say.

Mrs. Fortescue leaned back in her chair and glanced at Royal. "Mrs. Hargrove informed me that a valuable broach is missing from her room. Now it grieves me to think that you might be responsible, but Kathleen Griffin has accused you. If you took the broach, it would be wise for you to speak up at this time."

Royal whirled around to face her accuser, who stood near the door, a slight smile on her lips. Slowly Kathleen raised her hand and pointed an accusing finger at Royal. "She did it, Mrs. Fortescue! At the time, I thought it strange to see her coming out of Mrs. Hargrove's room, but now I know why."

"I was never in Mrs. Hargrove's room!" Royal turned beseeching eyes on the music teacher. "I have never stolen anything in my life. I could never steal! Besides, why would I want to hurt you by taking something that belonged to you?"

Mrs. Fortescue stared long and hard at Royal. "If that is so, then you won't mind if Mrs. Hargrove searches your room, will you?"

Pride battled with indignation. "I have nothing to hide." Her angry gaze settled on Kathleen. "I will expect an apology when nothing is found in the search."

Kathleen merely smiled, which gave Royal a moment of uncertainty. Mrs. Hargrove left the room, while Mrs. Fortescue busied herself with straightening the already orderly stack of papers on her desk.

Royal could hear the clock ticking away the minutes, and she began to suspect she had been caught in a trap. Kathleen was far too smug in her accusations. Something was afoot that made Royal apprehensive. She had the strongest urge to run from this place—to run and never look back!

After what seemed like long, painful hours, the door opened

and a dejected Mrs. Hargrove entered, a sad set to her mouth. "I have found it," she declared, looking regretfully at Royal. "It was hidden beneath your mattress."

Royal came to her feet, shaking her head as a feeling of helplessness wound through her mind. She tried to speak, but her voice seemed trapped in her dry throat. Could this really be happening to her?

"You will no longer be needed, Kathleen," Mrs. Fortescue announced stiffly. "Go to your room, and say nothing about this incident."

Kathleen brushed against Royal with a shove that sent her stumbling against the desk. "Out of my way, thief," she said acidly.

"That's quite enough, Kathleen," Mrs. Fortescue cut in. "I like an informer little better than I like a thief."

Royal was too stunned to heed the exchange between the headmistress and her accuser. She had never encountered anyone so brazenly vicious and wicked as Kathleen. Why had the girl deliberately set out to hurt her?

Mrs. Fortescue's voice brought Royal back to reality. She was surprised to find that Mrs. Hargrove had gone, too, and she was alone with the formidable headmistress.

"Be seated, Royal. I want to look into this matter further."

With resigned hopelessness, Royal sat down. "I didn't take the broach, Mrs. Fortescue. But I don't expect you to believe me."

The woman's face was stoic, giving away nothing of what she was feeling. "The broach was found in your room," she reminded Royal. "How could it have gotten there but by your hand?"

Royal shrugged her thin shoulders, her answer sounding unconvincing even to her own ears. "I don't know, Mrs. Fortescue."

"I know you haven't been happy here, Royal. I also know you are here against your will. Could you have committed this transgression in order to be sent home?"

A look of horror etched its way across Royal's face. "No matter if I am not happy here, I am not a thief, and I would never resolve my problems at the expense of Mrs. Hargrove. I like and admire her."

Royal could not have known how indignant she looked. When she raised her chin proudly, her eyes blazed. She repeated, "I am not a thief!"

Mrs. Fortescue sighed. "What am I to do with you? Should I send you back home in disgrace?"

Suddenly Royal considered how this would look to Damon Routhland. "Oh, please, do not do that. I want to go home, but do not send me like this." Tears stung her eyes and spilled down her cheeks. "I am innocent, please believe that!"

Mrs. Fortescue pushed a wisp of hair beneath her cap and looked thoughtful. "I am not going to do anything at this time. But I must insist that you confine yourself to your room and have no contact with the other students. You will even take your meals in your room, is that understood?"

"Yes, Mrs. Fortescue." Her eyes never wavered as she looked at the headmistress. "Must you inform my guardian about . . . about—"

Mrs. Fortescue shook her head slowly. "Not until I have all the particulars. This all seems a bit too contrived for me to—well, never mind." She stood up and bestowed a tight smile on Royal. "You may go to your room now. See that you talk to no one."

Mrs. Fortescue need not have worried about Royal talking to anyone; she wanted only to seek the safety of her room and avoid the other girls. She felt like a wounded animal, needing to hide and heal.

As she moved up the stairs and through the corridor, she thought she heard the sound of giggling, but she did not look back. There was no one she could turn to in this, her darkest hour—no one to believe in her innocence.

Royal stayed in her room all day, and when Hannah brought the evening meal to her, she pushed it away, too miserable to eat. Her sleep that night was dreamless; she tossed restlessly on the bed.

Two days passed with Royal confined to her room; her only contact with anyone else during this time was with Hannah. Royal lay upon her bed languishing, her tears now dry, her anger spent.

She closed her eyes, trying to shut out the voices that drifted up to her from the open window. Apparently the other girls were playing croquet, and the sounds of their joyous camaraderie only reminded her how alone she was.

Royal heard footsteps outside, and Hannah burst into the room. "Miss Royal, you will never believe what's happened!"

Royal had discovered that little went on at Fulham School that the servants did not know about. But she was in no mood to listen to gossip—she was too miserable to think past her own unhappy state. "I'm not interested, Hannah. I only want to be left alone."

"You'll want to know this, Miss Royal. The whole school's in a state over Miss Griffin's departure!"

Royal sprang off the bed and took Hannah by the shoulders. "What about Kathleen?"

"Well, the way I understood it, she left," Hannah said smugly. "Yessir, she just up and left."

"Do you mean for good?"

"That's what they say."

Royal saw that Hannah was determined to drag out the suspense. "I'm going to shake you if you don't tell me all you know—now!"

"She took trunks and every possession she owned. I was told she was in a rage and was saying horrid things about Mrs. Fortescue."

Royal dropped down on the bed. "I wonder what happened?"

"I don't know. But as I told the cook, it isn't my mistress that's going away with her head down," Hannah said loyally. "It's not you, but your accuser that was sent home."

"I wonder . . . ?" Royal's eyes brightened and then dulled. "I doubt that I have been cleared of Kathleen's accusations. If I had, Mrs. Fortescue would surely have sent for me."

Both Royal and Hannah jumped when a heavy rap fell on the door. Hannah rushed forward to admit Mrs. Hargrove. The teacher's smile was apologetic. "Mrs. Fortescue has asked to see you right away, Royal."

Royal gave Hannah a hopeful glance as she swept out the door after Mrs. Hargrove.

It had been a long, painful two days for Royal. She had been accused of being a thief and treated as a criminal. She was not so ready to accept anyone's apology—after all, she had been wronged.

By the time she was shown into Mrs. Fortescue's office, she had decided to be forgiving.

The headmistress merely nodded to Royal. "It has been proven that you are innocent. I hope you will allow this incident to pass. The guilty one has been punished. Just be grateful it was not you."

Royal blinked her eyes. She had just spent lengthy hours in solitude, pondering the unfairness of her situation. She had cringed inside, fearing the other students believed her to be a thief. But most of all, she had agonized over how the master of Swanhouse Plantation would react to the news that his ward had been accused of thievery. Now, Mrs. Fortescue merely dismissed the incident as if it had been of no import.

"Am I not allowed to face my accuser?" she asked with a proud tilt to her chin.

Mrs. Fortescue moved around the desk to stand over Royal. "Isn't it enough for you to know that you have been cleared of any wrongdoing?"

"It's not easy to forget when I have been branded a thief."

Mrs. Fortescue moved back to her desk and sat down. "I would advise you to forget about it. You were sent here to receive an education. So far I have been able to send your guardian fair reports about your progress. I would like to continue to do so."

Royal felt somehow unsatisfied. "You didn't inform Mr. Routhland that I was accused of being a thief, did you?"

"No."

Reluctantly she nodded. "Then it will suffice."

The headmistress fumbled through several letters, found one with Royal's name on it, and handed it to her. "This came for you yesterday. I believe, Miss Bradford, it will be ample reward for the indignation you have been forced to endure."

Royal glanced at the letter that had been posted from Savannah. "Go ahead," the headmistress urged. "Read your letter."

Royal needed no more urging. She broke the seal and began to read:

> Dear Miss Bradford,
> I have been instructed to inform you that my employer, Mr. Routhland, has had delivered to you at Fulham School a filly that was born and raised on Swanhouse Plantation. Her name is Enchantress. Knowing you are so far from home, Mr. Routhland hopes Enchantress will make you less lonely. I am instructed to tell you the filly is your birthday gift.

Royal stared in stunned silence at the signature of John Bartholomew. Damon had promised he would send her a horse, and he had not forgotten.

Mrs. Fortescue looked pleased. "I, too, received a letter from your guardian's secretary. You are a most fortunate girl to have a guardian who looks to your well-being."

"I wish . . . I had hoped the letter would be from Mr. Routhland."

"Go along, Royal," she said gently. "You will find your horse in the stable. It is hoped you will be dutiful in tending to the animal's needs."

Suddenly joy burst from Royal's heart. A horse of her very own! She moved quickly to the door and fumbled with the knob. "I'll take very good care of her," she said, smiling. "You have my word on that."

Mrs. Fortescue said so quietly that the girl who dashed out the door did not hear, "I have believed in you from the first day, Royal Bradford."

Enchantress was a glorious animal and certainly lived up to her name. At fifteen hands high, her coat was as glossy and shimmery as black satin. She was gentle and affectionate, but spirited nonetheless, and Royal loved her. At last she had a friend at Fulham School, but even so she wanted to go home.

She rode the animal around in a wide circle before leading her back to the stable and rubbing her down. After offering Enchantress a carrot, which the mare greedily accepted, Royal rushed to her room, her spirits high. A man who was kind enough to provide her with such a magnificent animal would surely understand her need to return to Savannah.

Dear Mr. Routhland,
Thank you, kind guardian, for the wonderful Enchantress. It was most generous of you to acknowledge my birthday, which is next Friday. Because you are so generous and understanding, I know you will realize it is impossible for me to remain here at Fulham. I am most unhappy and have no friends. Please! I beseech you, bring me and Enchantress home.

Dearest Papa,

Since the incident with Mrs. Hargrove's broach the other girls have turned colder and more distant. It's as if they think I am responsible for Kathleen being dismissed from Fulham. I am grateful that I have my studies and you to write to each evening, dear Papa. And, of course, Enchantress, who's always glad to see me.

Chapter 8

Two months had passed since Kathleen Griffin's departure, but her presence was still felt at Fulham. Every day Royal was met with frosty stares and accusing glances from the other students. Where she had been miserable and lonely before, she was now an outcast, despised and tormented by the others.

Although the leaves had not yet begun to turn, there was a touch of autumn in the air as Royal sat beside her window, glancing at the houses across the square. Today the school was having an outing, and she had searched her mind for an excuse not to go.

Her gaze moved to a white stone house where she had often seen children romping and playing in the yard. What would it feel like to belong, she wondered, to be part of a family?

Hannah knocked on the door and entered. "You got a letter, Miss Royal. It just arrived in the morning post."

Royal took the letter with trembling hands. Yes, it was from Savannah. Oh, please, she thought fervently, let this be permission to go home.

As she had suspected, the letter was not from Mr. Routhland, but from Mr. Bartholomew. Undaunted, she began to read:

> Dear Mistress Bradford,
> I am answering your last letter on behalf of Mr. Routhland. He has asked me to convey his hope that you will soon adjust to your environment. It is his wish that you exercise every effort to cultivate friendships. Study and make the most of your education.

Her hopes were dashed. Too stunned to cry, she could only stare at the letter. So it was Mr. Routhland's wish that she exercise every effort to cultivate friendships. How far away she was from home, and more than three years yawned before her like a bottomless pit. A lone tear trailed down Royal's cheek, and she turned away so Hannah would not see her cry.

Each day would be a trial for her. How much longer would she be forced to endure the spiteful innuendos that she was the cause of Kathleen Griffin's dismissal?

She should have written to her aunt rather than Damon Routhland. But, no, it would be cruel to upset Aunt Arabella, who would only suffer needlessly if she knew about Royal's misery, and she could do nothing about it anyway. Thus far Royal had managed to keep her letters to her aunt cheerful, stressing only the good in her life rather than dwelling on her unhappiness.

Hannah broke into Royal's thoughts. "Have you forgotten it's time to leave for the outing, Miss Royal? Mrs. Fortescue has asked that you come below where the others are already assembled."

With a heavy heart, Royal reached for her bonnet and tied it beneath her chin. She felt drab and ugly in her black riding habit, and she knew the others would be dressed in frosty pinks, bright yellows, and stunning reds.

She moved mechanically to the door. Today the students were

going to the country for a day of riding and picnicking. The other girls had talked of nothing else for weeks, while Royal had dreaded this day.

At the bottom of the stairs, she stood apart from the other girls while they filed out in an orderly manner. Mrs. Fortescue was directing them into the seven carriages lined along the front drive.

Royal's heart sank and she considered pretending illness when she realized Mrs. Fortescue was placing her in the second carriage with Lady Alissa. She felt her stomach churn, and just for a moment she did feel ill.

"Move along, Royal," Mrs. Fortescue urged. "That's right, in you go."

To Royal's dismay, when she climbed into the open carriage, she accidentally brushed against the shawl that lay across Lady Alissa's lap, causing it to fall to the floor.

"I am sorry . . . it was clumsy of—"

Lady Alissa's face was etched with fury. "I have often observed that gracefulness is not one of your strong points," she said in an irate voice. This drew giggles from the other two girls in the carriage.

Royal bent forward to retrieve the shawl, and Lady Alissa grabbed it from her. "Troublesome girl. One wonders if you will ever be taught manners. I have great sympathy for your teachers."

Royal felt her anger stir and with great effort brought it under control. There was nothing to be gained by quibbling with Lady Alissa. Her father had once told her that the best way to win an argument was to avoid it altogether. She would test that theory today and just ignore the other girls, Lady Alissa in particular.

Royal turned her attention to the eastern horizon, where the sun had just appeared from behind a cloud. The weather was balmy and the sky was blue, but for a few scattered clouds.

As the seven buggies pulled away from Fulham School in a procession, Royal leaned back and studied the tips of her fingers. It was going to be a long two hours, she thought, feeling a coldness in her heart.

The horses clopped along the wide avenue at a steady pace,

while Royal tried to ignore the remarks that were surely being made for her benefit. Deborah Stoughton, who always seemed to be Lady Alissa's shadow, was particularly hateful, and try as she might, Royal could not shut out the girl's high-pitched voice.

"If only Kathleen were here with us now." Her eyes sought Royal's. "Do you ever miss Kathleen, Royal?" she asked pointedly.

"I once had influenza. After it was gone, I did not miss it in the least," Royal replied before turning her face away. "Neither do I miss your friend."

Deborah reached toward Royal, but Lady Alissa caught and held her hands. "All will come in good time, Deborah. One has only to be patient."

Royal could not resist looking at Lady Alissa. Their eyes locked for a brief moment, then Royal glanced away. She supposed they were thinking up some new torment to use on her. So be it—she would not allow them to see her hurt.

"I am appalled by anything that comes from the Colonies," Deborah stated airily. "Their goods and materials are inferior, as is their workmanship. They are a backward people who incite riots, speak of war, and are ungrateful for all the help we British have given them. And if that weren't bad enough," she continued, glancing at Royal, "they have manners that would disgust an Englishman of the lowest birth."

Royal bit back an angry retort and kept reminding herself to follow her father's advice and ignore Deborah, although it was becoming more difficult all the time. She looked up to find Lady Alissa staring at her with what could only be interpreted as a quizzical expression. Without a word she moved farther into the corner and leaned back, closing her eyes. Let them try to torment her—she would just shut them out by thinking of something pleasant. Damon Routhland's face floated before her eyes, and she lost herself in the memory of a pair of golden eyes.

At last they reached the park area where the picnic was to be held. Royal waited until the other girls had disembarked before she scampered from the buggy. There were sounds of merriment as the girls paired off into their little groups, but Royal stood alone, ignored by everyone.

"Now girls," Mrs. Fortescue announced, making her way over the uneven ground with caution. "This is a private estate, belonging to Lady Alissa's brother, the duke of Chiswick. He has generously allowed us to have our outing here. This is to be a day of amusement. There will be games such as lawn bowling and races for those of you who wish to participate. Those of you who have horses and choose to ride must be back by two for luncheon."

Royal watched Mr. Moore, the groomsman, leading several horses into the makeshift paddock he had skillfully constructed with ropes. Enchantress restlessly ran the length of the enclosure, her coat glistening in the noonday sun. Royal rushed forward, taking her reins and patting the sleek ebony coat while the horse nudged her affectionately. Here, at least, she found a welcome.

"Where did you come by such an animal?" Deborah asked sharply, her voice laced with resentment as she came up behind Royal.

Royal tossed her saddle over the horse and tightened the cinch. "Her name is Enchantress," she replied, hoping Deborah would just move on and leave her in peace. She was in no mood to talk to anyone.

"I have seldom seen a finer animal," Deborah admitted grudgingly, with the eye of an experienced horsewoman. "Such sleek lines," she said, running her hand down Enchantress's neck. "I know a lot about horses. The finest in the world are raised on my father's estate. It's obvious this little filly is of superior bloodline."

Royal glanced at Lady Alissa, who was being placed in a horse cart since she was unable to ride sidesaddle like the other girls. "Enchantress is a gift from my guardian, and like myself, she is a product of the Colonies."

Leaving Deborah openmouthed with indignation, and the others to ponder her words, Royal allowed the groom to assist her into the saddle. She galloped toward the distant woods, glad she had escaped her chaperone.

No matter how much Royal pretended otherwise, she would

have liked to be accepted by the other girls. She would have enjoyed riding with them and talking about such things as gowns, the latest bonnets, and footwear.

Clearing her mind, she took a path that led her by a twisting little stream that cut its way through the heart of the valley. Once, she caught a glimpse of a huge gray brick structure in the distance with tall imposing turrets and gables. She realized it would be Chiswick Castle, Lady Alissa's home. She reined in Enchantress and stared at the castle, wondering what it would feel like to grow up in such a wondrous dwelling.

She nudged her mount forward. The air was filled with the scent of wildflowers and herbs that grew along the banks of the stream. A bracing wind cooled her face, and she soon lost herself in the joy of being mounted on excellent horseflesh. Enchantress responded to Royal's every command. They waded across narrow streams and explored well-worn pathways, and Enchantress seemed tireless.

After a while they reached a clearing where Royal had a magnificent view of the whole valley. She caught her breath as she stared at the lush green countryside.

Royal smiled, feeling it was good to be alive with the sun beaming down on her in the tranquillity of her surroundings. She shaded her eyes and gauged the sun. Mrs. Fortescue had said to be back by two, and she thought it was nearing that now. So, reluctantly, she turned Enchantress back in the direction they had come.

She soon reached the picnic area and found that with the exception of servants and teachers, there were few people about. She dismounted with a sense of dread when she saw that she and Lady Alissa appeared to be the only students present. Royal made a great pretense of rubbing down Enchantress, hoping Lady Alissa would ignore her, for she certainly intended to ignore Lady Alissa.

As she worked, Royal observed the servants setting up tables and covering them with white linen cloths. The aroma of food wafted through the air, reminding Royal she was hungry. She thought she would take her lunch and eat down by the creek.

She glanced over at Lady Alissa, who was still seated in the horse-drawn cart, her pink gown spread out about her. "It looks like rain," Royal observed, looking up at the overcast sky. "I hope it will hold off until we get back to London."

Lady Alissa pressed her lips together tightly, giving no sign that she had even heard Royal, but then Royal had not expected her to reply.

All of a sudden a jagged streak of lightning split the sky, and the ground rattled from the rumbling thunder that followed.

Several things happened at once, catching Royal off-guard. The horses hitched to Lady Alissa's cart reared and tore at the reins, rolling their eyes in fear. Wildly they lunged forward, jerking against the reins, while Lady Alissa used all her strength in an attempt to subdue them.

She might have succeeded in bringing them under control had not a second bolt of lightning jarred the ground. Thunder bellowed like a cannon shot across the valley, and the horses bolted out of control. Lady Alissa was thrown behind the seat and landed hard in the back of the cart, where she was helpless to check the frenzied animals.

Servants and teachers were scurrying about, trying to protect the food from the impending rain, apparently unaware of Lady Alissa's plight. When the girl cried for help, her voice was drowned out by yet another rumble of thunder, and only Royal heard her.

Royal did not hesitate. She grasped Enchantress's reins and hurried her to the mounting stump. Knowing time was important, she bounded into the saddle and turned her horse in the direction of the runaway cart. With a quick command and a jabbed heel into the filly's flanks, Royal prayed she would reach Lady Alissa before the cart entered the woods.

Enchantress shot forward with powerful strides. Time seemed suspended, yet Royal was aware of a bird's song in a nearby bush—she even felt the first drops of rain against her cheek.

Royal's heart lurched with fear when she saw the cart bounce over a fallen log and careen drunkenly, almost tipping over. By now Lady Alissa had managed to grab on to the sides of the cart, but the reins were dragging on the ground, making it impossible for her to reach them.

With added determination, Royal prodded her mount to a full stride. Enchantress gradually drew even with the back of the cart, and Royal could almost touch Lady Alissa's beseeching hand.

Glancing up, Royal saw the woods just ahead. The cart could not possibly get through the dense trees. Lady Alissa saw this, too, and cried out to Royal.

"Help me! Please help me!"

"Be brave," Royal called out above the din of thunder that rumbled angrily across the sky. "I'll have you in a moment."

Royal inched closer to the cart and reached out to Lady Alissa, but just as their fingers touched, the cart bumped over a jagged rock, and the terrified girl had to hold on to keep from being thrown out.

Royal knew that if she did not pull Lady Alissa free of the cart now, there would be disastrous results.

Jagged limbs tore at Royal's face, but she ignored the pain and thundered onward. Just ahead, the woods broke away to a deep crevice, and the fear-maddened team of horses was heading straight in that direction.

"Please, Royal," Lady Alissa pleaded. "I don't want to die! Help me!"

Enchantress, as though born to the task, kept her pace even with the cart as it bounced over fallen trees and huge rocks. Again Royal strained forward and, with a physical strength she did not know she possessed, clasped Lady Alissa's arm and held on. Slowly she managed to raise the girl out of the cart until she appeared to dangle in the air—her only lifeline was Royal's grip on her arm.

Lady Alissa tried to twist her body so she could hook her foot over Enchantress's back, but she could not make her useless legs obey.

"You must!" Royal insisted when she saw the effort Lady Alissa was making. "I haven't the strength to hold on for long. Help me save your life!"

Lady Alissa saw something in the young girl's eyes that gave her the strength to try again. Her fragile body trembled with the effort she was making. She could feel Royal struggling desperately to keep a grip on her arm. She gritted her teeth and willed her useless legs to move.

Lady Alissa's hair had come loose from its confines and blew across her face, blinding her. With an impatient gesture, she brushed her hair aside. She had never been so frightened in all her life. In a fraction of time she glanced back at Royal, and the look Royal gave her made her think she could do anything.

With a wild cry, Lady Alissa thrust her legs forward and made contact with the horse.

Royal dropped the reins and let Enchantress have her head so she could clasp Lady Alissa with both hands, thus pulling her free of the cart. A heartbeat later the frenzied horses tore loose from the flimsy rig and sent it careening toward the deep crevice. Both girls heard the splintering and shattering of wood as the cart slammed against a tree and broke apart before sliding over a bluff, to be lost from sight. A heavy silence ensued as both girls fought to keep Lady Alissa from falling.

Royal felt as if her arms were being pulled from their sockets, but she managed to keep a grip on Lady Alissa, and finally, with a surge of energy, she dragged the lame girl onto Enchantress's back.

Royal was unaware of the significance when Lady Alissa slipped her leg over Enchantress's back and gripped the horse with her knees. Lady Alissa herself was too exhausted to care that she had moved her legs; she only felt gratitude for being alive.

Royal reached out and grasped Enchantress's trailing reins and brought the filly to a halt. Both girls stared, horrified, at the spot where the cart had gone over the rocky bluff. They looked at each other, realizing that if Lady Alissa had been in the cart, she would also have been smashed on the rocks below!

"I . . . I am a bit shaky," Lady Alissa whispered. "Could we . . . dismount long enough for me to catch my breath? I have no wish to be near a horse at the moment."

Royal nodded. "Just allow me to dismount first, then I will help you down." She slid to the ground and held her arms up to Lady Alissa. "If you will trust me, I'll endeavor to bear your weight."

Lady Alissa smiled weakly. "You have just saved my life, at great risk to your own. There will never be a time when I do not trust you, Royal Bradford."

Royal braced herself against a tree and stood on tiptoes to grip Lady Alissa's tiny waist. "Perhaps you should not be too hasty with your trust. I may yet spill us both on the ground. Hold on."

As Royal supported her companion's entire weight, her knees almost buckled, but she managed to pull the frightened girl free of the horse. When she felt herself collapsing, Royal managed to deposit her burden safely on a pile of leaves. Emotionally and physically spent, Royal dropped to the ground, glad that the frightening ordeal was over.

"Are you all right?" Royal inquired, noticing how pale Lady Alissa was and how her eyes still held a hint of fear. "Is anything broken?"

Lady Alissa tested her arm. "Nothing's broken. That was a truly the most incredible, frightening moment of my life," she stated. "Considering all my misadventures with horses, I don't care to go near one of those animals ever again."

"My papa always told me if I was thrown from a horse, I should get right back on again." Royal paused. "I . . . am sorry. Of course, that would not apply in your case. I had heard that you lost your ability to walk because of a riding accident."

In a move that surprised Royal, Lady Alissa reached out and wrapped her fingers around hers. "From this day forward, Royal, you need never apologize to me for anything. You saved my life, and I am grateful. No one has ever done so much for me before."

She was thoughtful for a moment. "I don't understand why you would help me when I have been so unkind to you."

"I never stopped to consider the consequences. I only knew that if I didn't act quickly, you would either be killed or horribly injured. I'm sure you would have done the same for me under like circumstances."

Lady Alissa leaned her head back against the tree trunk and closed her eyes. "I would like to think so, but I'm not certain. . . ." She opened her eyes and stared at Royal. "I have been so wretched to you, and I don't know why, except that I am so unhappy, and you are everything I am not. I watched you proudly ignore us when we all made sport of you."

She squeezed Royal's hand. "Teach me to be as you are. Show me how to rise above disillusionment and torment. I want to be like you."

Royal blinked in astonishment. "I would be pleased to help you in any way I can. But I'm not special. I can assure you I have a temper, and at times it is hard to keep it under control."

"You will not regret this day, Royal Bradford. I intend to make up to you for all the hurt I have inflicted on you in the past."

Royal was uncomfortable. "You owe me nothing, Lady Alissa. What I did was instinctive—I would have done the same for anyone. I will not accept a friendship based on such a thin thread of gratitude."

Lady Alissa looked astonished. "Lud, you are a proud one! I would like to climb inside your head and know what makes you so independent in your thinking."

"It's not that. Just because you almost met with a fatal accident doesn't make me want to be your friend. I didn't like you before . . . why should I like you now?"

Lady Alissa had never been spoken to in such a manner. She stared at Royal with a growing respect. "That may be so, Royal Bradford, but I would like to have you as a friend. I am weary of those who only tell me what they think I want to hear. I have a feeling you would always be honest."

Royal stood up and dusted the dried grass from her black skirt.

"My papa often told me that to have a friend, you have to be a friend." Her eyes were sharp and penetrating as they connected with Lady Alissa's. "You get out of friendship what you put into it. I suspect you have bullied and prodded your friends until they are afraid to tell you the truth."

Lady Alissa jerked her head up. "Careful you do not go too far, Royal."

"Don't try to bully me, Lady Alissa. I am not one of your toads that grovel at your feet."

Suddenly amusement touched Lady Alissa's lips, and she smiled softly. "Is that how you think of my friends?"

Royal pushed a stray strand of hair beneath her black hat. "I don't mean to be unkind, but, yes, I often think of them as your sycophants."

Now Lady Alissa laughed aloud. "I have never met anyone as refreshing and original as you, Royal Bradford. I don't believe you would ever be a toad to anyone, would you."

Royal was surprised by the girl's sudden burst of humor. "No, not a toad, but I might be considered a mule since I am so stubborn."

"I would much rather you just be my friend and always tell me exactly what's on your mind. We can start with you calling me 'Alissa.' "

Royal was doubtful that the two of them would ever be friends, but she tested the name. "Alissa."

Lady Alissa did not hear Royal. She had reached down to her legs, daring to hope she could move them again. She concentrated all her strength on her right leg. Beads of perspiration popped out on her forehead, and she trembled from the intensity of her efforts.

Seeing Lady Alissa's pallor, Royal dropped down beside her. "Are you ill?"

"No," the girl said excitedly. "Watch this!" Had she moved her leg, or was it her imagination? "Did you see that?"

Royal stared in wonder. "I thought you were . . . lame?"

Lady Alissa closed her eyes as joy swept through her body. This time she moved both her legs, laughing and crying at the same time. "I did it—I did it!"

Royal sank back on the grass and watched with tears in her eyes as Lady Alissa took a deep breath, pulled her leg forward, and pushed it back. "It's a wondrous miracle," Royal declared. Then she looked at Lady Alissa, undecided. "Does this mean you can walk?"

Her new friend beamed at her. "I am hoping it does. I doubt I would ever have had the courage to try if the horses hadn't bolted . . . if I hadn't been forced to move my legs to keep from being crushed."

"I am truly happy for you. It is as if something wonderful came from a near tragedy."

"I owe it all to you, Royal," Lady Alissa said softly. "If it hadn't been for you, I would most probably be dead."

Disconcerted by Lady Alissa's praise, Royal glanced at the sky. The heavy thunderclouds had moved away, as had the threat of rain. "I believe we should return to the others. They will probably be concerned by now. Will you allow me to help you onto Enchantress's back?"

Lady Alissa shuddered. "I don't see that I have a choice."

Royal grasped her hands and helped her lean against the tree. "You will be safe. Don't forget, it was Enchantress who really saved you today."

Lady Alissa pushed down her fear. Leaning heavily on Royal, she reached for the saddle. Between them the two girls finally managed to get Lady Alissa firmly in the saddle.

"Climb up beside me," Lady Alissa offered.

"No, you are still shaky. It's but a short way back to camp, and I'm sure you will feel more secure if I lead Enchantress."

As Royal grasped the reins and pulled the horse forward, Lady Alissa spoke to her. "Tell no one that I can move my legs, Royal. I want to be able to walk before anyone finds out."

"It will be our secret, Lady—"

"Just Alissa," she reminded Royal.

It was a group of astonished teachers and students that watched Royal lead Enchantress out of the woods with Lady Alissa poised on the horse's back.

Deborah rushed forward, pushing Royal away. "What has happened? We were so worried about you, Alissa. Has there been an accident?"

Lady Alissa spoke softly. "I had a brush with death, but was saved by Royal." Lady Alissa's gaze traveled across the faces of the startled girls. "I will take it as a personal affront if any of you insult my friend," she said pointedly.

The groomsman came forward to help Lady Alissa from her lofty perch. She was soon surrounded by her personal servants and concerned teachers, who saw to her comfort. The girls gathered about as well, each wanting to do something to make her more comfortable and pressing her for details of her mishap.

Royal gave Lady Alissa an imperial glance. "Toads," she said airily.

Lady Alissa smiled. "If you want to know what happened, ask my friend Royal," she said, settling back on the padded seat where she had been placed.

Royal immediately found herself surrounded by chattering girls. She caught Lady Alissa's eye, and they both smiled. With only a few words from the duke of Chiswick's sister, Royal had gone from outcast to the center of attention. But she had a feeling that she had gained more than acceptance today; she had gained a friend.

As the girls were climbing into the carriages that would take them back to London, Lady Alissa insisted that only Royal ride with her. While the horses moved down the tree-lined roadway, Royal thought how circumstances could change one's life. If the horses had not bolted, and if she had not been there to rescue Lady Alissa, she would still be shunned by the other girls.

"How I envy you, Royal," Lady Alissa admitted. "I have observed with envy your pride and sweetness."

"I have too much pride."

Lady Alissa smiled and glanced at her torn and soiled pink gown. "You don't know what it is to envy someone, do you?"

"You are mistaken, Alissa. I envied the friendship you and the other girls had for one another."

"I saw a sweetness in you that I knew came from the heart, and for some reason unknown to me, I wanted to destroy that which I could not understand. I'm glad now I didn't succeed."

"I don't understand."

"No, you wouldn't." Lady Alissa pulled a dried piece of grass from the folds of her gown and flicked it out the carriage. "I hope you will believe me when I say I had nothing to do with the incident involving Mrs. Hargrove's broach."

"I thought you might have," Royal admitted with her usual honesty. "I've often wondered how Mrs. Fortescue found out the truth."

"Did you know it was Kathleen who placed the broach under your mattress?"

"I suspected as much."

"When I found out what she had done, I insisted she tell Mrs. Fortescue."

"So that was what happened. I never knew."

"I don't expect you to believe this, but Kathleen was never a friend of mine."

Royal shrugged. "It's in the past."

"Can we forget about what has passed and be friends, Royal?"

"I would like that."

Lady Alissa smiled and plucked a small twig from Royal's hair. "Tell me all about yourself. I want to know what your life was like before you came to England. I have been most curious about you, but would not allow myself to ask you before now."

The carriage ride home passed all too quickly, as Royal and Lady Alissa became better acquainted.

When they reached the edge of London, Lady Alissa reached forward and clasped Royal's hand. "I wonder if you are willing to help me?"

"Yes, but how?"

"I want to learn to walk again."

Royal's eyes were dazzling with delight. "Oh, do you think it's possible?"

"Yes, I do. As we have been talking, I have begun to feel a tingling sensation in my legs. There is feeling there—and if there is feeling, I will surely be able to walk."

"I will help you. But shouldn't we inform Mrs. Fortescue so she can have a physician examine you?"

"No, not just now. I have a plan, and I will need your help to carry it through."

"What is it?" Royal asked eagerly.

"The school gala is just two months away." Excitement stirred in Lady Alissa, and she giggled. "I want to be able to dance."

"Would that be possible?" Royal asked, hoping her new friend was not in for a disappointment.

"Will you come to my room every day at—" Lady Alissa was thoughtful for a moment. "Every day at three when we are supposed to be resting?"

"Yes. How will we keep the other girls from getting suspicious?"

The two conspirators put their heads together. "I know," Lady Alissa said at last. "Do you play chess?"

"Yes, of course."

"Perfect! We will tell everyone that you are teaching me how to play chess. So that it will not be a lie, you will teach me twenty minutes of chess each visit. The rest of the time we will devote to restoring the feeling in my legs."

"How can this be accomplished?"

"Our family doctor had encouraged leg massage and hot compresses. We shall try that."

Royal caught Lady Alissa's enthusiasm. "You will walk—I know you will!"

And so it happened that each day Royal would take her chess set and go to Lady Alissa's quarters. Soon, all thoughts of chess were abandoned as Lady Alissa's legs became stronger and stronger.

It was a long and painful ordeal for the lame girl, but whenever she grew weary and wanted to give up, Royal would encourage her to continue.

One day Lady Alissa took her first step, then another, and another.

Dearest Papa,

I can hardly wait for the social tonight. It will be such a wonderful surprise when Alissa's family learns she can walk. You would like Alissa, Papa. She is brave and determined in her character. As for me, life is quite wonderful. I awaken each morning knowing I have a friend. No more loneliness. Oh, Papa, you were so wise to insist I come to Fulham for my education.

Chapter 10

Tonight was the social all Fulham students looked forward to with great anticipation. It was the event where the young ladies could show off their newly acquired refinement to young gentlemen who had received the coveted invitations. They would be allowed to parade around in their finest frocks and bedazzle their family and friends.

Royal stared at her image in the mirror. Her year of mourning still not up, she wore a black velvet gown that fit snugly about her waist and flared out over a polonaise petticoat. Her hair was arranged in a soft, windblown style without a trace of formality or sophistication, making her feel colorless and insignificant.

She clipped a pearl broach at her high neck and turned to Hannah. "You should see Alissa's new gown. It's lemon-yellow taffeta.

The collar and cuffs are embroidered with gold thread and pearls. It's simply breathtaking."

"You look very nice, Miss Royal," Hannah assured her.

"I appreciate your loyalty, but my gown can hardly compare with a Paris creation. But no matter."

Royal could not have known how lovely she looked with her golden curls spilling down her back, the youthful blush on her cheeks, and the healthy glow in her blue eyes. Royal saw only the drabness of her costume and her yet undeveloped young body.

"You will stand out in a roomful of strutting peacocks with their fine feathers and bright colors."

"Oh, Hannah, you do say the funniest things. Imagine calling my friends peacocks." She stepped into her black kid slippers. "It doesn't matter how I look anyway, no one will notice me."

"If I was you, Miss Royal, I'd be right happy to be fluttering around, meeting all the grand gentlemen."

"In the first place, I am still in mourning for my father. And as for meeting gentlemen, I am not acquainted with any in London."

"You will be singing, and that'll get the gentlemen's attention. Your voice is pure like an angel's. With Lady Alissa playing the harp for you, the two of you will be the center of attention."

Royal picked up her black feathered fan, the only frivolity she had allowed herself, and moved to the door. "I'm so nervous about singing for all those people. I doubt I can manage the high notes." She turned back and looked at Hannah. "Did you place the two bouquets of flowers in the music room?"

"Yes, Miss Royal, just like you told me to."

Royal swept out the door and down the stairs to the music room, where her performance would take place. She paused, going over in her mind the surprise she and Lady Alissa had contrived for her friend's mother and brother. The plan was that after Royal finished singing, she would take a bouquet of flowers to the music teacher. Then Lady Alissa would rise, pick up a bouquet, and walk to her mother, the dowager duchess of Chiswick. Royal was so excited, she feared she would forget the words to her song, so she went over them in her mind. Tonight was so important for Alissa. Nothing must go wrong!

When Royal entered the music room, servants had already begun to seat the guests, and Lady Alissa was behind the harp. Royal's legs were shaking and her palms were damp as she moved to stand beside her friend.

"Are you ready?" Royal asked nervously.

"I suppose."

Royal's gaze moved around the room until she located Lady Alissa's brother, Lord Preston. He nodded at her and smiled slightly before turning back to his beautiful companion. Royal had no notion who she was but assumed the older woman seated at his right would be Lady Alissa's mother. She nervously worked her fingers in and out of her black lace gloves until a look of disapproval from Mrs. Fortescue caught her attention.

When everyone was seated, Mrs. Hargrove gave the signal that the performance was to begin. Lady Alissa pulled the harp to her, and her fingers nimbly rippled across the strings. Royal stepped forward and in a clear soprano voice began singing:

> Her lilies and roses were just in their prime,
> Yet lilies and roses are conquered by time:
> But in you, my love, age such a benefit flows,
> That we attend it more sweetly the bolder it grows.

No one in the audience stirred; all eyes were glued on the lovely young singer who held them spellbound. Lord Preston leaned forward, his gaze fastened on Royal. There was such a sweetness about her that it touched his heart.

"She is but a child," his companion reminded him in spitefulness when she saw where his attention was aimed.

"You are right, of course, my dear. But that does not keep me from admiring her lovely voice."

When Royal finished singing, and Lady Alissa's fingers had plucked the final vibrating refrain, the guests broke into vigorous applause. Royal was so astonished by the crowd's overwhelming reaction, she could only stare at them in wonder, until she caught the music teacher's stern glance that reminded her to curtsy to the guests.

Royal looked back at Lady Alissa and received a nod and an eager smile. Picking up a bouquet of flowers, she walked over to Mrs. Hargrove and presented it to her. The teacher smiled in appreciation and acknowledged Royal's thoughtful gesture.

Now the moment had come for Lady Alissa to reveal her surprise. At first no one but Royal noticed that Lady Alissa was standing on her own. She took a small step—her eyes on Royal for encouragement.

Hesitantly she moved toward her mother, who by now stood in shocked silence. The dowager gasped in disbelief while her eyes brimmed with tears. She would have rushed toward her daughter but for the restraining hand her son placed on her arm.

Preston, too, was moved by his sister's accomplishment. "It is important that you let her come to you, Mother."

By now everyone was watching Lady Alissa as she made her way slowly across the room, sometimes stopping to steady herself, sometimes almost stumbling, but always keeping her gaze on her mother.

Mrs. Fortescue's eyes opened wide in amazement. The students were silent, each girl willing Lady Alissa onward to her goal. Royal raised her hands and wiped the tears from her face. She could not remember any moment in her life where she had felt so proud. She would always remember how Lady Alissa looked in her triumph. Could anyone in this room understand how unceasingly her friend had worked to surprise her mother tonight?

Lady Alissa stopped before the dowager and handed her the bouquet. "For you, Mother."

The dowager embraced her daughter, and everyone pressed in around them, expressing their delight.

"I do declare," Mrs. Fortescue proclaimed. "I do declare!"

Royal was crying openly when a deep voice spoke up behind her. "Hello, Miss Bradford."

She turned to find Lord Preston at her elbow. "She is wonderful, is she not?" she asked, nodding at his sister.

"Yes," he agreed, his eyes resting on her small upturned face, noticing that tears clung to her silken lashes. "Truly wonderful."

Royal stood in the shadows of the ballroom, observing the dancers with a strange detachment. It did not matter to her that mourning kept her from joining in the festivities. She was too happy about Lady Alissa's accomplishment to think of anything else.

She did not realize that her foot was tapping to the music until Lord Preston appeared at her side. "My sister has told me all about your daring rescue. A fine feat of horsemanship, Miss Bradford. You are to be commended."

"You give me too much credit, Lord Preston. It was not nearly as daring as it sounds."

His eyes twinkled. "Perhaps we can ride together sometime, and I will judge for myself." He stared into the clearest, bluest eyes he had ever seen. "My sister has told my mother and me all about your devotion to her. Of course, we already knew you had saved her life. And now you've given her the courage to walk. How can we ever thank you?"

"Oh, no, you must not think that it is because of me that Lady Alissa can walk. Her brave spirit and perseverance have been an example to me."

Lord Preston had never met a girl who was so uncomfortable with a compliment. In his experience, more often than not women seemed to thrive on praise. Alissa was right—she seemed too good to be real. And he was fascinated by her.

"My sister also told me that you are in mourning for your father. Even so, you are very young to be denied a chance to dance, Miss Bradford."

"Even if I were not in mourning, Lord Preston, I have not yet come out. And I don't know any of the gentlemen here; so therefore I would not be dancing anyway," she answered, glancing up at him. Her smile was shy and hesitant.

"We have met before, Miss Bradford, so you are acquainted with me. Am I to take it you do not consider *me* a gentleman?" he said with mock seriousness.

"Oh," she said, hurrying to make amends. "I would never expect *you* to dance with me, Lord Preston."

His laughter was soft. Here was a girl who did not play coy games. Her face was so honest and open, he could read much of what she was thinking. Apparently she had not learned to mask the truth about her feelings—he hoped she never would. His laughter deepened when he realized that she was openly assessing him.

Lord Preston was tall, Royal thought, perhaps as tall as Damon Routhland. His shoulders were wide, and his tailored clothing fit him to perfection. He had a boyish look, and when he smiled at Royal, which he did often, she noticed that there were dimples in his cheeks. His hair was powdered and drawn back in a queue. She noted his blond eyebrows and lashes and guessed his hair would also be blond. He was so handsome, her heart was fluttering, and she thought she would faint.

As she gazed into dancing blue eyes, for just a moment Royal forgot about the golden eyes of Damon Routhland.

"If you were not in mourning, and if you had come out, Miss Bradford, I would surely ask you to dance with me. But by the time you are out of mourning, you will be surrounded by admirers, and I doubt I would be able to get near you."

She could not seem to find her voice, and she felt giddy. "I doubt I shall have any admirers. I am no beauty."

He stared at her in astonishment. "Has no one ever told you that you are lovely?"

She smiled. "Of course. My papa thought I was an 'incomparable.' But you see, he also thought I was brilliant. My mathematics teacher would tell you that's not the case."

Preston looked deeply into the little charmer's eyes. "I wonder if you will make me a promise, Miss Bradford?"

"Of course, if I can."

"The next time we meet at a social, and I can assure you there will be a next time, will you remember that you owe me at least one dance?"

"I will remember," she said in all sincerity.

"So shall I. Now, I wonder if you will do me another favor?"

This time her smile was not so hesitant. "Yes, I will."

"My mother has asked if you would attend her. She has been most anxious to thank you and pay her respects."

"But I told you I did—"

He extended his arm to her. "Shall we?"

Shyly she placed her gloved hand in the crook of his arm. She could feel her chest swell with pride to be escorted by such a handsome and important man.

"Let me warn you that my mother can appear reserved," he advised. "But don't be put off by her. She is really quite nice when you get to know her."

Royal took no comfort in his words. As they crossed the room, she felt the piercing scrutiny of the dowager's gaze. Lord Preston gave her a supportive smile.

"Courage," he said, as if he knew she was nervous.

When he presented Royal to his mother, the girl met the cool blue eyes that swept her from head to toe.

The dowager duchess of Chiswick leaned heavily on a pearl-handled walking stick. She was older than Royal had thought. Her gray hair needed no powder, and rather than styled in the latest fashion, it was reminiscent of the simpler, less extreme coiffure that had been popular twenty years earlier. Her rococo Watteau gown with silk cords and tassels was also a reminder of days gone by.

"My dear," the dowager said in a voice that was warm and soft. "I am so delighted to meet you. Come"—she motioned to the empty chair beside her—"sit with me so we can talk. I want to know all about my daughter's friend."

Royal slipped into the chair and folded her hands demurely in her lap. She was aware that Lord Preston had moved away to dance with the woman who had accompanied him to the social.

She spent the remainder of the evening sitting beside the dowager duchess, and in no time at all the older woman knew all about her life.

That night Royal's sleep was sweet as she dreamed of dancing with Lord Preston. She laughed and played coy as he whirled her around the dance floor, declaring she was a beauty. But when she looked into his handsome face, his image slowly began to fade and another took its place—a face with startling golden eyes . . . a face that always haunted her dreams.

Before, she had always welcomed the image of Damon Routhland, but tonight she had wanted to think only of Lord Preston.

With a heavy sigh, she turned onto her back, and for the rest of the night her sleep was dreamless.

John Bartholomew leafed through the bills that had arrived from London dressmakers, milliners, and cobblers. His expression was disapproving as he placed the neat stack before his employer for inspection. "For one in mourning, I believe Miss Bradford is spending an excessive amount of money on clothing, Mr. Routhland. Shall I make it clear to the London solicitor that her spending habits are not within her means, and that he should curb her extravagance without delay?"

Damon had been reading some correspondence, and he glanced up at John impatiently. "No, let the poor child have her diversions. God knows she has had little in her life to make her happy. If decking herself in finery will comfort her, then let her be."

John Bartholomew's chin jutted out at a reproachful angle, because in his methodical manner he could not accept frivolity. "I believe it would be remiss of me if I did not point out to you that Miss Bradford is already in your debt to a sum of more than five thousand pounds. Not to mention what you paid to settle her father's debts to save the Bradford home from the auction block.

The girl should be told that it is your money she is spending with such regularity."

Damon thumbed absently through the bills and then shoved them aside. "She is never to know that her father left her destitute. I want her to be young and carefree."

John looked with astonishment at the master of Swanhouse Plantation, seeing him with a new insight. Damon Routhland was a shrewd businessman, and it was not good business to put money into settling bad debts, but he would do as he was told.

"It will be as you wish, Mr. Routhland," he said at last. "I will instruct Mr. Webber to allow Miss Bradford a free hand." John cleared his throat. "I wonder, Mr. Routhland, if you have considered how Miss Bradford will subsist if war is declared?"

"I have thought about that. Has she mentioned being persecuted in any of her letters?"

"No, sir, she has not. Of late, she has even stopped asking to come home."

"If the time ever comes when she is harassed because of her loyalties, let me know, and I will strongly consider bringing her back."

"Yes, sir. Will there be anything else today?"

"No, that will be all, John."

As the secretary turned to leave, Damon's thoughts turned to the pretty redhead who had so charmed him at the ball the night before. "John," he called out, stopping his secretary at the door. "Instruct the gardener to gather three dozen perfect white roses and have them delivered with my card to Miss Darcy Maxwell's home."

Even as he tried to recall Darcy Maxwell's alluring smile, Damon had visions of a sad, angelic little face. Royal had again pushed her way into his consciousness to disturb his peace of mind.

Although the child was across an ocean from him, he felt her presence nonetheless. Perhaps because she had been such a melancholy little girl, she played upon his pity.

Absently picking up one of the bills for Royal's new gowns, he studied it. A small price to pay for a lost little girl's happiness, he thought.

The week seemed endless for Royal as conflicting reports reached England about a skirmish that had erupted in Boston at a place called Bunker Hill. The sketchy accounts said that the proud British soldiers had lost half their defending forces. There were those who were calling the colonists who died "rabble" and "dissenters," but reports recounted that Sir William Howe, the commander of the British forces, wept and sent word to the king that the rebels are not the despicable rabble many have supposed them to be.

A troubled Royal took up her journal and began to write:

> Dearest Papa,
> It seems there is no turning back the tide of war. I fear two prideful forces will soon face one another, and it won't be concluded until one or the other gives ground. Surprisingly, there are a few brave souls here in England whose voices are raised in anger against the King. John Selden, A member of Parliament caught the mood of the Colonies with his writing: "My penny is as much my own as the King's ten pence is his. If the King may defend his ten pence, why not Selden his penny?" Good night, Papa.

Dear Papa,

You would be happy to know I am quite in vogue. Where I once had no friends, now it seems everyone seeks my advice and counsel. Most of all, and by far the most glorious, is that I have a true friend in Alissa. I had hoped to spend the summer with Aunt Arabella, but it seems she is in Rome and cannot come to England this year. I have been invited to stay at Chiswick Castle, and I admit to being a bit nervous about the visit. I also admit I hope to see Lord Preston again. Will he remember me? I hope so. Good night, Dearest Papa.

Chapter 11

1776

Hannah laced Royal into her corset, then helped her into her new gray traveling gown and stood back to survey the result. "You won't have to be ashamed of your clothes, Miss Royal. Your new gowns are as nice as anyone's."

Royal glanced at the travel trunks that had been packed with all her new finery. Since she was no longer in mourning, she had found to her dismay that her old gowns no longer fit. She had been delighted, however, when Mr. Greenburg had informed her that Mr. Routhland was allowing her a free hand in replenishing her wardrobe. She had bought gowns for every occasion, with slippers and bonnets to match.

Hannah placed a bonnet on Royal's head. "You look beautiful, miss. It's all grown up, you are."

"Sixteen is not so grown up, Hannah. I wish I were seventeen, like Lady Alissa, so I could wear my hair arranged *à le bel oiseau,*" Royal said wistfully.

"The headmistress would never allow that, miss," Hannah replied gravely. "If you did such a thing, Mrs. Fortescue would have me out on the streets, and you wouldn't be far behind, I'll wager."

"I know," Royal admitted. "But, still, I wish I were older."

The maid held out the velvet cape that matched Royal's gown. "One thing's for certain, Miss Royal. If you live long enough, you'll get older."

"I intend to live a very long time," Royal informed Hannah. "There are many things I have not yet done." She walked to the door with Hannah trailing close behind. "I just want to be a woman so I will no longer have to attend school and can go home to Georgia."

Even as Royal spoke, she thought how far away Georgia seemed to her now and how remote the war was that raged between her country and England. She realized with a shock that she no longer felt homesick. She had become content with her life, and weeks would pass without her even thinking of Savannah, or Damon Routhland.

When the crested coach arrived at the front of the school, Royal's excitement mounted. She was ushered inside by a liveried footman, who stood stiffly at attention while Hannah climbed in the seat opposite her. Several students lined the steps and were waving farewell as the carriage pulled away.

Royal had only ventured away from school on picnics and occasional outings with the rest of the girls. Today would be the first time she had been invited as a guest in a private home. She nervously worked her fingers into her black kid gloves. Her invitation had come from Lady Alissa's mother, and she felt anxious at the thought of spending time with the dowager duchess.

While the well-sprung carriage clipped along at a steady pace,

Royal recalled seeing Chiswick Castle from a distance the day of Alissa's accident. That day she had certainly never imagined being invited to the castle as a guest.

Royal settled back into the black leather seat and stared out the window. She hoped Lord Preston would be there when she arrived. She glanced down at her new gown, knowing she looked her best. Would he think she was pretty?

She reached over to the basket of fruit that had been placed there for her comfort, took a red apple, and bit into it. This summer could possibly be the most exciting of her life.

It was just after the noon hour when the coach pulled to a stop before the wide steps leading to the castle. Royal swallowed her fear of the imposing structure, which looked twice as large as she remembered.

As her foot touched the ground, Lady Alissa came gliding down the steps with a wide smile of welcome. "I thought you would never get here! I have so many things planned for us, it will take the whole summer to accomplish them!"

Arm in arm, the two girls climbed the stairs. Royal took a steadying breath as, at last, she stood before the dowager duchess.

"Welcome to Chiswick, my dear. It is our desire that you will pass a pleasant summer with us."

Royal dipped into a curtsy. "Thank you, Your Grace. It is most kind of you to have me."

The dowager gripped the handle of her cane. "Alissa, take your friend inside and present her to your brother and his wife. Then the two of you are free to seek your own pleasures until afternoon tea."

Lady Alissa guided Royal into the cool hall. Royal stared at the high ceilings with their polished beams and the walls where ancient armor and weapons hung.

Lady Alissa giggled when she saw where Royal's gaze was directed. "It is a bit ostentatious, is it not? But pay it no attention—it is merely my brother's attempt to impress visitors."

"Lord Preston?"

"No, silly goose, my brother Nathan."

"Oh . . . the duke. I have seldom heard you speak of him."

"That's because he's been out of the country most of my life. His wife, Honora, considers England too dull. I can only hope they will soon tire of the country and leave again."

Royal stopped short. "But he's your brother!"

"Yes, but he doesn't seem like a brother. You see, he is in his forties. My mother had him early in her marriage to my father. She almost died giving birth to him, I believe, which is why she waited so long before Preston and I were born." Lady Alissa rolled her eyes. "And wait until I present you to Honora. If there is a more unpleasant creature on this earth, I have not yet met her."

"What do you mean?"

Lady Alissa tugged on Royal's arm. "You'll see when you meet her."

Royal was not looking forward to that prospect. She stood close to her friend as they entered the enormous drawing room. The duke and duchess were seated before the window drinking tea, and they looked up as if annoyed at the intrusion.

"Well, don't stand there dawdling, Alissa. Come forward and introduce me to your friend," the duke said in a voice that clearly showed he wasn't interested.

Lady Alissa cast her eyes to the ceiling in exasperation. "This is Royal Bradford, Nathan. Royal, my brother and sister-in-law, the duke and duchess of Chiswick."

Royal curtsied, while quickly assessing the couple. The duke looked nothing like Lady Alissa or Lord Preston. His forehead was wide, his nose narrow. He was a head shorter than Lord Preston, and the look of boredom in his eyes did nothing to enhance his appearance in Royal's eyes. The duchess was slender, almost too much so. Her face was thin, her cheeks sunken. It was apparent she wore a wig, for it was elaborate and dressed so high it looked as if it would topple over the moment she turned her head.

"I am pleased to meet you," Royal said in a trembling voice. "Thank you for having me this summer."

"I understand you are from the Colonies," the duke said dryly. "I always knew that barbaric country would cause us grief. I told the king so, too."

Royal made no reply. There seemed to be nothing she could say.

"It is not we you should thank, Miss Bradford." The duchess covered a yawn with her hand. "Alissa had to have someone to keep her occupied, since her mother insists that she remain in the country for the summer. I will expect you children to be as inconspicuous as possible. And see that you do not intrude upon us without an invitation."

Royal stepped back a pace to stand beside Lady Alissa. Her friend moved to the table, chose a plump grape from a bowl, and popped it into her mouth. "Have no fear, we shall try to avoid you both whenever possible," she said airily. "Come, Royal, let us seek more suitable entertainment."

"Tiresome girl," the duchess declared to her husband. "It makes me glad we don't have children of our own."

Lady Alissa smiled at Royal and whisked her out of the room. "I warned you they weren't pleasant. Now that I have done my duty by them, let me show you the rest of Chiswick."

Royal nodded, only too glad to be away from the duke and duchess.

The sun had painted the western sky with a rosy glow as Royal and Lady Alissa sat in the garden sipping cool lemonade.

"Tell me more about your guardian, Royal. Is he married?"

"No, Damon Routhland is not married as of yet. But he would be, if the women of Savannah had anything to say about it."

"I believe you said he was young and handsome."

"Not so young. He's twenty-six . . . no, he would be twenty-seven now. But he is indeed handsome, and very kind."

Lady Alissa laughed merrily. "Royal, twenty-seven is not old for a man. I am betrothed to a man who is twenty-nine, and he isn't old at all."

Royal's eyes rounded in wonder. "Of course I know you are betrothed, but I didn't know he was . . . so . . . was . . . twenty-nine. Do you love him?"

"Yes, he is truly wonderful! I can't wait until we are married. We have been betrothed since I was twelve." Her eyes took on a tender glow. "I cannot remember a time when I didn't love Holden." Lady Alissa glanced back at her friend. "But enough about me. Tell me more about your guardian."

"It's hard to describe Damon Routhland, but he is wonderful, too. I have often regretted I was born too late for him to think of me other than as a child." Royal looked into Lady Alissa's soft gray eyes. "Have you ever wanted something so badly that it hurts?"

"Yes, I have," Lady Alissa said sadly. "My fondest wish was to walk for Holden. And now I can."

"He must be so pleased."

"Tell me, if you could have your fondest wish, what would it be?" Lady Alissa asked.

Royal was reluctant to voice her frivolous yearning. "My want is not as noble as yours—in fact, it is quite selfish. I merely wish to grow up to be very beautiful so Damon Routhland will notice me." She pursed her lips. "Of course, he is accustomed to having beautiful females trying to catch his eye. I can't think why he would ever notice me."

Lady Alissa studied Royal's features, noting her delicate bone structure. "I believe you may get your wish, Royal. I have little doubt that you will one day be a great beauty. My brother Preston thinks you are pretty."

"He does? Has he told you so?"

"No, but I can tell all the same."

"Is he also betrothed?"

"Yes, he is, but Preston is not as fortunate as I. He doesn't like his betrothed, Lady Alice Stratton, and keeps putting off their wedding. Of course, since Nathan and Honora have no children, Preston is heir presumptive to the dukedom, so he must marry well. Lady Alice's family is a very old and influential one."

"Why do you suppose your brother and his wife have no children?"

"She was with child several times, but they were always born dead. I suppose it is sad, but I don't think Honora would make a good mother." The setting sun cast a warm glow on Lady Alissa's face. "Tell me about your aunt. She sounds exciting."

Royal's eyes sparkled. "Aunt Arabella is a glorious person. She is beautiful and witty." Royal leaned in closer to Lady Alissa and lowered her voice, as if she were afraid someone would overhear. "She is an actress!"

"Oh, I know that. But is she a good actress?" Lady Alissa asked eagerly.

"I am told she is. I know that many men have been in love with her."

"How marvelous to have someone so exciting in your family. Do you think I shall ever meet her?"

"I had thought she would come to visit before now." Royal's brow wrinkled into a frown. "She has promised to spend the Yule season with me. I hope she does."

Lady Alissa was thoughtful for a moment. "Preston was once enamored of an actress. Of course, Nathan ordered him to remain here at Chiswick while he sent the woman to Paris."

"Did he ever see her again?"

"Of course not." Lady Alissa was pensive. "At least I don't think so. But then, Preston doesn't confide in me about his love life." She looked at Royal speculatively. "I wonder if my brother could make you forget about Damon Routhland? Of course, Preston prefers older women, so we will probably never know."

Royal sighed. "That is always my problem. Young is not my favorite age to be."

The summer was spent in happy, golden days for Royal. She was introduced to a whole new way of life. She attended elegant teas, balls, and races. She was introduced to the nobility of England and, as Lady Alissa's friend, was accepted by all. She even met some interesting gentlemen who paid her marked attention. But Royal hardly noticed them. Her dreams were filled with thoughts of two men—one with blue eyes and the other with golden eyes.

To her disappointment, Lord Preston did not visit Chiswick, although his mother often read his letters to the girls. It seemed that the Season kept him in London. With a mischievous gleam in her eye, Lady Alissa confided to Royal that she had overheard the servants gossiping about a merchant's daughter who had caught Preston's eye.

All too soon the summer passed, and it was time to return to school. There Royal would again take up her studies, but with no thought of returning to Savannah. England, the birthplace of her beloved papa, had at last become her home.

Dearest Papa,

War is rampaging throughout the Colonies, but all that seems so far away from me here. Papa, what would you have thought of this war? I wish I knew. I don't like to think that men are dying over something as frivolous as taxes. Why don't the colonists just pay the taxes as everyone else does? Why must war divide two such fine and noble peoples?

Chapter 12

With a troubled mind, Royal laid the journal aside. She was just realizing she was not the same lost little girl who had first come to London. She had developed different beliefs, and her heart was turning away from old loyalties.

She began to see the war with the eyes of her British friends. As painful as it was, she could no longer defend her own countrymen, who had insisted on war in the first place. Why had they taken up arms against their mother country? she wondered again and again.

Even Aunt Arabella seemed a stranger to Royal now, for she no longer answered her letters, and she had not come to England in a very long time.

Royal's new friends now made up her world. She felt a strange detachment from her past until, at inopportune moments, the memory of golden eyes would intrude. When she thought of her life in Savannah, it was almost as if it had happened to someone else.

Why should she feel any ties with the Colonies? she reasoned. She had no one there anymore.

Royal picked up her journal and attempted to write, but no thoughts came to mind. She curled up on the bed and tried to sort out her true feelings about the conflict across the Atlantic. She had read every article she could find about the war, and it seemed to her that the colonists were entirely at fault.

Of course, she reasoned, everything she read had either been written for the English or by the English. She slid off the bed and walked to the window, where she stared out at the park across the street. She was not going to be sad or think about the war today. She was young, and she wanted to have fun.

Royal embraced her new life with enthusiasm. She had learned many things at Fulham School, and she was just finding out how important a proper education was. Of course, it was a definite advantage if a girl was also pretty. She was finding out that she was attractive to men and often drew their attention. It was a pleasant feeling.

Hannah entered the room, carrying a huge white box. With growing curiosity, she placed it on the bed. "This came for you, Miss Royal."

"It's not my birthday. Who could have sent it?"

"I don't know, Miss Royal. Why don't you open it? There may be a card inside."

With excitement stirring, Royal untied the yellow ribbon and gasped at what she saw. "It's the most beautiful creation I've ever seen!" she exclaimed, lifting out a shimmering white gown with silver embroidery across the hem and down the sleeves.

"Look, Miss Royal!" Hannah cried. "There're silver shoes to match."

Royal ran her hand down the soft gown, loving the feel of its silkiness. "See if there's a card," she instructed the maid, while she moved to the mirror and held the gown in front of her. "I have never had anything half so beautiful," Royal proclaimed. Then she looked somewhat doubtful. "But it is cut rather low in front. Dare I wear it?"

Hannah retrieved a letter from beneath the satin slippers and thrust it in Royal's hand, then waited expectantly for her to read it aloud.

"Could it be from your guardian?"

Royal gave Hannah the gown and quickly opened the envelope. "No . . . it's from Aunt Arabella!" she said excitedly. "And look, there's a ticket. I wonder what this can be?"

She quickly scanned the letter. "Hannah, my aunt's here in London, and she is performing tonight at Covent Garden. She is sending a carriage for me which will arrive at seven this evening."

"How long's it been since you've seen your aunt, miss?"

"Not since the day she left me at Fulham." Royal glanced down at the gown. "How wise of her to know I would no longer be a child." She touched the gown lightly, allowing her hand to drift to the silver trim. "This is a gown for a lady."

"It don't matter," Hannah stated with assurance. "Mrs. Fortescue won't let you go to Covent Garden unescorted. It isn't a fit place for a lady of your breeding."

Royal felt her happiness melt away. "You're right, of course. She would stop me from going . . . if . . . if she knew about it."

"Now, you aren't going to do anything foolish—are you, Miss Royal?"

"I have to go tonight, Hannah. I just have to!" She was thoughtful for a moment. "Go to Lady Alissa's room and tell her I need to see her at once."

Hannah seemed doubtful. "I know that look, Miss Royal. You're up to something."

Royal gave her maid a scathing glance and spoke sharply. "Hurry, Hannah. I am going to see my aunt perform tonight, and you and Lady Alissa are going to help me get past Mrs. Fortescue."

If Hannah had any notions about objecting, they disappeared beneath the determined light in her mistress's eyes. She quickly slipped out of the room, wondering what Miss Royal had in mind.

Royal pushed her foot into the silver slippers while Hannah marched around her, straightening the hem of her gown.

"If you don't hold still, Miss Royal, I'll never have you ready in time."

"I'm so apprehensive, Hannah. Suppose something goes wrong, and I am unable to see my aunt perform?"

"Well, it isn't going to do you any good to get yourself in a dither. Lady Alissa said she'd occupy Mrs. Fortescue while you slip away. Of course, you'll still have to get back in afterwards," the maid reminded her.

There was a knock on the door, and Lady Alissa poked her head inside. "Are you about ready?" She walked around Royal, her eyes wide with admiration. The low-cut bodice molded to Royal's young breasts with just a hint of daring, while the sleeves that tapered to her wrists were tied with silver bows.

"You're stunning," her friend declared. "No, you are incomparable." She looked at Royal's creamy complexion, made even creamier by the contrast of her powdered hair, which Hannah had arranged in an *à la Dauphine* coiffure. Silver ribbons were woven among the curls that spiraled down her back.

"If you weren't my friend, and if I didn't love you so dearly, I would hate you."

Royal stared at her own image in total astonishment. "I look . . . so . . . I *am* grown up."

Lady Alissa moved to the window and pulled the curtain aside. "The carriage should be here any moment. I'll go to Mrs. Fortescue's office and keep her occupied until I know you're gone. But you must be home by ten, so I can be at the front door to admit you."

Royal brushed her cheek against her friend's. "Thank you for helping me, Alissa."

Lady Alissa smiled. "That's what friends are for. Give me enough time to get to Mrs. Fortescue's office before you come downstairs. Have Hannah go before you to make certain no one sees you leave."

As Royal rushed through the hallway and down the steps, her pulse was thundering inside her. Never had she deceived the headmistress, and guilt lay heavily on her shoulders.

She hurried out the front door and down the steps, where she was helped into the carriage by a smiling coachman. She settled back against the cushioned seat and pressed her hand against her heart to quell its rapid beating. When the horses pulled away from the school, Royal let out her breath—she had made it safely away.

The coach moved down well-lit streets, through parks, and past elegant shops. After a time the broad avenues gave way to dark, narrow passages where ominous forms loomed out of the shadows. Royal observed women offered bawdy invitations to any gentleman who happened along. She felt a prickle of fear when hands reached through the window, and she shrank back against the seat on hearing the coachman's whip lash out and someone yelled in pain.

Royal was flooded with relief when, at last, the coach turned down King Street and the theater rose out of the darkness. Had she been foolish to come without an escort? she wondered. Surely her aunt would not have allowed her to travel alone unless it was safe to do so.

The coach came to a halt, and the coachman opened the door and offered her his arm. As she descended, she was certain she smelled strong spirits on the man's breath, but surely she was mistaken.

"I have been instructed to wait for you until the performance is over, Miss Bradford. And then I'll take you back to school."

"Yes, thank you. Please wait for me."

She moved up the wide steps and was soon engulfed by the crowd of people who had come to see the performance.

The inside of the opera house was decorated in bold reds and bright yellows. Shining mirrors lined the walls to reflect the many chandeliers that hung from the vaulted ceiling. Royal handed her ticket to an attendant, who looked startled, apparently because she was unescorted. When he saw her ticket, he smiled.

"Come with me, miss," he said. "I have been instructed to escort you to a private box."

As she moved gracefully beside the attendant, men looked at her in appreciation and women with envy. She was aware that she was receiving marked attention, but she didn't know why. She could not know how fresh and lovely she looked in her white satin gown.

Once she was seated in her box, Royal found a table laden with every conceivable delicacy and flowers so plentiful that the aroma was overpowering. After the attendant seated her, he withdrew, leaving her alone. There was a note on the table from her aunt.

> Dearest, I can hardly wait to see you. Come to my dressing room after the performance. I will expect you to sup with me afterward.

Royal glanced at the people being seated and waited impatiently for the performance to begin. Soon the lights were lowered, the mumbling voices ceased, and the curtain rose.

She had been so excited that she had not even noticed the name of the play. But now she recognized the words from *Othello.*

When Arabella appeared on stage as the gentle Desdemona, Royal could feel admiration ripple through the audience. Arabella was at the height of her beauty, and her clear, distinct voice captured the essence of the tragic heroine she played with passion and fire.

Unashamed tears rolled down Royal's cheeks as Desdemona was slain by her jealous husband and again, when the play reached its tragic end.

The curtain fell, and the audience reacted with resounding applause. When Arabella appeared on stage to take her bow, she received a deafening response. She looked in Royal's direction and blew a kiss.

Royal knew her aunt had attained great fame in Paris and Rome, and, at last, she was being acclaimed in her own country, as she deserved.

Royal brushed her tears away as the same attendant who had seated her reappeared. "If you will accompany me, Miss Bradford, your aunt will see you in her dressing room."

Royal followed the attendant through a narrow passageway that led backstage. When they reached her aunt's dressing room, the man bowed and left her abruptly.

Royal rapped softly on the door, which was immediately whisked open by her aunt. For a long moment the two of them could only stare at each other. Then Arabella embraced Royal, and the girl melted into her arms.

"My dearest, at last we are together."

"I have missed you," Royal said, realizing how much she had yearned for this dynamic influence in her life.

At last Arabella held Royal at arm's length and beamed at her approvingly. "It's like looking at myself as a girl, except you are much more beautiful than I ever was," she said generously.

Royal assessed each perfect feature of her aunt's face and doubted the truth of her statement. Arabella wore a yellow Chinese dressing gown that hugged her curvaceous body and enhanced her flaming red hair. "I could never hope to be as beautiful as you are."

"You will far surpass me, dearest."

"I love the gown, Aunt Arabella," Royal exclaimed, twirling around in a circle. "It's lovely."

"I knew it would be just right for you. You are a young lady now."

"Thank you," Royal said, her eyes moist with tears.

"Did you like the play, dearest?"

"Oh, Aunt Arabella, you were magnificent! I will remember your performance for the rest of my life. If Papa could only have seen you, he would have been so proud."

The two Bradford women looked into each other's eyes as renewed pain stirred to life—pain Arabella thought she had buried with her dead brother. "I always yearned for my brother's praise, Royal, but I only succeeded in arousing his disapproval."

"Who is this beauty?" a deep voice spoke from behind Arabella.

Royal had thought they were alone but for the maid who scurried about the room, gathering discarded clothing. She met the dark gaze of a man and turned inquiring eyes to her aunt.

"Royal, this is the Marquis de Moreau. Louis, my niece, Miss Royal Bradford."

The marquis was not a young man and was portly and short in stature. Yet while he could not be considered handsome, his eyes were lively and his smile genuine. "Charmed, mademoiselle. I have heard of little else but you since we arrived in London last week."

Royal turned hurt eyes to her aunt Arabella. "You arrived last week?"

Guilt was written on her aunt's lovely face, and her eyes were pleading. "Perhaps you are unaware of the torment an actress endures when she's preparing for a performance. You know how desperately I wanted to succeed here in London. I wanted everything to be perfect, and I devoted all my waking hours to rehearsing. You do understand, don't you, Royal?"

"Yes, of course," Royal said woodenly, still unable to disguise her hurt.

"I'll make it up to you, dearest. You will dine with Louis and me at the Goldsmiths tonight. Many of London's socially prominent will be there, and you will help me celebrate my conquest."

Royal realized she could not go with her aunt because Alissa would be waiting for her. The disappointment cut like a knife. "I can't, Aunt Arabella. I had to sneak away from Mrs. Fortescue, and I must be home by ten."

Arabella looked vexed. "That dreadful old woman, I remember her well. But are you sure you can't come with us?"

Deep inside, Royal hoped her aunt would insist that she go with her. "Yes, I am quite certain."

"If that's so, you must hurry on, dearest. I wouldn't want you to be locked out."

At that moment there was a commotion at the door and several people pressed into the room. They were all gushing and complimenting Arabella, so Royal was pushed to the background. With a last look at her aunt, she slipped out of the room. She never doubted her aunt's love for her—it was just that she was no longer a part of her world. With an aching heart, Royal realized she had no family.

As she moved through the deserted corridor and made her way to the front of the building, she resolved to remember only the good in her relationship with her aunt. Royal was proud of her aunt's accomplishments, and she wished happiness for her in the future.

When Royal reached the front steps of the opera house, she was startled to find only a few carriages remaining. She glanced about, hoping the driver who had delivered her would be watching for her. He had told her he would wait.

A carriage with a crest on the door pulled up in front of her, and a gentleman leaped out to stand before her, his gaze boldly raking her body. "Well, look at you, little beauty. Who could have left you waiting?"

She turned away, trying to ignore him, but he placed his hand on her shoulder. He staggered and almost lost his balance, and she realized he had been drinking. She tried to back away from him, but he only tightened his grip.

"Leave me alone!" she demanded, looking about for help—but there was no one to come to her aid.

"Come with me," the man insisted, steering her toward his carriage. "I'd never leave a pretty little toy like you waiting alone."

Feeling like a trapped animal, she looked for a way to escape this odious man. She twisted away, but he reached out and grabbed her in a viselike grip and brought her tightly against his body. His breath reeked of strong spirits.

Over her shoulder, Royal saw the man's coachman, who was ignoring what was happening to her. She knew she would get no help from him. "Please, sir, release me. I want to go home."

"Such a pretty little thing," he crooned, running his hand down her throat. She closed her eyes and gritted her teeth, hating his hands on her. "Skin's like silk."

She kicked and twisted when he grabbed the front of her gown and ripped it. He pulled her toward the steps, and she struggled with all her might.

"Release me!" she cried. The panic was so strong she could scarcely breathe.

"You heard the lady," a clipped voice spoke up. "Let her go."

With crushing relief, Royal looked into the angry blue eyes of Lord Preston. Her tormentor released her and stepped back a pace. "The devil take you, Preston! You always get the pretty ones."

"Perhaps you should just leave, Ralph," Lord Preston suggested with a bite to his tone.

"I'll do that, Preston," the man quickly agreed. "Don't want to intrude where I'm not wanted." He bowed to Royal. "I might have known you belonged to him." With a last glance at Lord Preston, he stumbled to his coach and disappeared inside.

Lord Preston turned anxious eyes on Royal. Seeing her ripped gown, he removed his coat and wrapped it around her. "Did he hurt you?"

She ducked her head, feeling ashamed. "No, I was but frightened. Thank you for saving me."

A frown hardened his features. "Miss Bradford, what are you doing here without an escort?"

She felt like an errant child. "I came to see my aunt perform. I . . . didn't . . . I . . ."

A muscle worked in his jaw. "How were you expecting to get back to school?"

"The coach that brought me was supposed to convey me home. The driver is not here."

Lord Preston thought of the pretty young actress who would be waiting for him and then dismissed her from his mind. Taking Royal by the arm, he steered her in the direction of his own carriage. "I will see you safely back to school."

Royal was too relieved to protest. Lord Preston helped her inside his coach and sat opposite her. He then instructed his driver to deliver them to Fulham. As the horses started off with a jerk, Royal sat tensely on the edge of the seat.

"It is hoped, Miss Bradford, that you do not often engage in this sort of foolishness."

"No, Lord Preston. This is the first time I have gone out on my own—I hope you believe that. I hadn't seen my aunt in such a long time." She ran her hand down her gown. "She sent me this gown . . . and a ticket for her . . . performance," she stammered, feeling as if she must appear to be no more than a foolish child.

"I knew Arabella Bradford was your aunt. Yes," he said, assessing Royal's features. "There is a strong resemblance. Why didn't your aunt see you safely home after the play?"

"She had made a previous engagement." Royal did not want Lord Preston to think badly of her aunt. "She had hired the driver to take me home. She would never have wanted me to—" She could not go on. Even to her own ears, her excuses merely made her aunt appear heartlessly neglectful.

Royal was not aware that she was crying until Lord Preston handed her his handkerchief. "Please don't cry, Miss Bradford. The ugly ordeal is behind you." He reached forward and drew her gently onto the seat beside him. "You are safe now."

She stiffened. "I would not want you to think I am—that I would—"

He smiled. "Have no fear of my intentions. I know you are an innocent, Miss Bradford. My sister keeps me informed of your progress. It might surprise you to learn that I know a great deal about your life."

"But why?"

He stared into her clear blue eyes. "Because you have always fascinated me," he admitted honestly, for Royal seemed to inspire truthfulness in him.

She glanced out the window shyly, her heart pounding because of his nearness. "I can't credit that you would give me more than a passing thought."

His laughter was amused. "I am watching your progress with great interest. I know when your birthday is. I know you have no family other than your aunt." His tone deepened. "And I am waiting until you are older."

She turned and stared at him with wide, innocent eyes. "But why?"

He lowered his gaze to her lips. "You are still a child. But, one day, I shall tell you why, Royal."

By now the carriage had pulled up before Fulham School. He leaned over and placed a chaste kiss on Royal's forehead. When she stared at him in wonder, he merely laughed.

"Can I suppose you have devised a plan to get back into the building?"

She hesitated for a moment but managed to nod. "Alissa is waiting to let me in," she confessed reluctantly.

"Ah," he said in amusement that was laced with affection. "Co-conspirators. My sister was always the crafty one."

He stepped out of the carriage and swung Royal to the ground. "I will see you again, Royal Bradford."

"Thank you, Lord Preston. I don't know what I would have done had you not come along."

"Apparently you need someone to look after you," he said in a more serious tone. "Promise me you will never repeat such an ill-conceived action."

She tried to cloak her shame by avoiding his eyes. "I promise I will never do such a thing again," she mumbled. "I hope you won't think badly of me because of my foolish actions tonight."

"I think that you went to see your only relative, and she, in her neglect, did not cherish you—I think you have no one to cherish you, sweet Royal."

Royal attempted to ignore the softness in his voice. She held out her hand to him. "I hope you do not think badly of Aunt Arabella. She means well. It's just that her life is . . . is . . ."

He reached out and took her hand. "Go in now, Royal. It's late, and little girls need to be in bed."

She had the strongest urge to lay her head against his shoulder and feel his arms close comfortingly around her. She moved up the steps before she gave in to that impulse. "Good night, Lord Preston."

"Good night, Miss Bradford."

He cursed under his breath as he climbed back in his carriage.

He had never seen anyone as sad and alone as Royal Bradford. And in spite of the fact that she was little more than a child, she intrigued him.

Royal held her journal on her lap, going over in her mind the events of the evening. In her short lifetime she had met two remarkable men, and each had played the part of her rescuer and had come to her in her need.

> Dear Papa,
> Life can be so confusing at times. If I were older and a great beauty, which man would I choose to love: the dark, brooding Damon Routhland or the light-hearted, often teasing Lord Preston? If I loved either of them, it would be to no avail—it would be like reaching for the unattainable.

She closed her journal and laid it on the dressing table. She then blew out the candle, and the strong tallow smell invaded her nostrils. Tonight she had come to the realization that Aunt Arabella was so immersed in her own life Royal had been all but forgotten.

Even though Royal had been hurt, she would always love her beautiful aunt. She believed her father would have wanted it that way, too.

Dear Papa,

War seems to be the topic of every conversation. I am often asked my opinion, since I lived in Georgia. I have come to believe that George Washington is an upstart and a rabble-rouser. If only cooler heads would prevail, so they could put an end to this war and both sides could get on with their lives.

December 1778

The war in the Colonies had escalated. It had turned south—and it had turned ugly.

On Christmas night, Lieutenant Colonel Archibald Campbell, commander of the British forces, sent soldiers ashore to scout out Savannah.

Like a sparkling jewel, Savannah sat vulnerable upon her lofty bluff. Behind her were marshes and pine-covered plains, making her isolated and hard to defend. The navigable Savannah River seemed to invite an invasion fleet because of the easy access from the Atlantic Ocean. The British scouts reported that Savannah would be easily taken, and two days later a battle ensued.

After a valiant effort from the Colonial army, Savannah fell to her enemy and was occupied by the British forces. Those who supported the Loyalists celebrated—those who wanted their freedom from the British cried bitter tears.

The defending army fled to join General Benjamin Lincoln in South Carolina.

Charles Town, South Carolina

The tattered banner of the Fifth Regiment, Continental Light Dragoons, whipped in the wind outside Colonel Damon Routhland's headquarters. Inside the tent, the lantern flickered as an icy gust of wind tore open the leather flap, sweeping across the camp desk and scattering papers in its wake. Damon's aide-de-camp, Corporal Thomas, scampered after them.

Damon was bent over the desk, his uniform disheveled, his boots muddy. Tired lines flared out from his eyes. He had been forced to watch his men die today. One boy, too young even to shave, had sustained a musket ball to his arm; the impact had thrown him from his mount, and he had been trampled beneath the horses of his enemy.

Damon's eyes burned, and he could hardly see the report he was writing. It was an urgent plea to Congress to dispatch more troops to the South where they were desperately needed.

"What's going to happen now, sir?" the aide asked, neatly restacking the papers on the folding desk.

Damon leaned back on his stool and studied the corporal, who could be no more than seventeen years old. Idealism showed in the eager young face, in contrast with the frustration that was etched in the hard line of Damon's jaw.

"Today is a sorrowful day for the South, Corporal, because the invasion has come to us. We must not look back, but must be prepared to defend our country at all costs."

"We will, sir! We'll drive the British dogs into the sea."

Damon stood up and moved to the opening of the tent, staring out at the camp. "That will take much forbearance and a miracle or two to accomplish, Corporal." He smiled. "But then, I have always believed in miracles."

"What do we do now, sir?"

"Tonight we lick our wounds, care for our injured, and bury our dead. The cost was high, and we are teetering on the edge of destruction. With today's defeat, the way is open for the British to sweep across the South. They realize that Savannah is a primary seaport. Now that they have captured Savannah, they will surely turn their eyes to Charles Town. But this time we must stop them!"

"We will stop them, sir," Thomas said with battered pride. "We'll stop them, by God! They can't hold Georgia, and we will never allow them to take Charles Town!"

Damon flexed his aching muscles, wishing he could muster as much faith as his young aide displayed. Having fought in many campaigns, Damon was now a seasoned veteran, and he was weary of watching men die. "I fear, now that the British have insinuated themselves in our midst, it will be difficult to be rid of them, Corporal."

"You just lead, and we'll follow, sir," Thomas vowed loyally. "The men who serve under your command would be willing to follow you into hell if you asked it of us."

Damon managed to smile. "Hell may look good after tomorrow. That's when we take to the swamps to avoid detection by enemy patrols."

He stood up and stretched his arms over his head, looking longingly at his cot. He had not been to bed in over twenty-four hours. "See that the sentinels are posted every twenty paces. It's getting dark, so pass the word to extinguish all fires and lanterns. We don't want to announce our presence to the enemy."

The young aide snapped to attention and gave a respectful salute. "Yes, sir." Turning on his heels, he rushed to do his colonel's bidding.

Wearily Damon sat down on his cot, where he unbuttoned his tunic and fell back, too weary to undress. Today had been agonizing for him. As a Southerner, the loss of Savannah had been a bitter defeat. He wondered if Swanhouse Plantation would escape the enemy's vengeful destruction.

His eyes drifted shut, his last thought of his ward's home in Savannah. Had it survived the torch? he wondered. Was the enemy occupying little Royal's house tonight?

His hand fell over the side of the bed, and he drifted into an exhausted sleep.

London

Snow drifted down in crystal flakes, settling like a blanket over St. James's Park. The few enterprising souls who had ventured forth on such a cold day were rewarded by the sight of a regiment of the king's guards sprightly marching up to their cannons and, with great ceremony, firing several volleys. A joyous cheer arose from the crowd.

Royal sat astride her prancing mount, watching the celebration with detachment. She turned to Lady Alissa, who had just ridden up beside her. "Whatever are they celebrating?" she inquired.

"I don't know," Lady Alissa replied, turning to a man who stood nearby. "You, sir, what is the reason for the revelry?"

"Haven't you heard?" he said in a boisterous voice. "Savannah, Georgia, fell into our hands like a ripe plum. And it only took two days!"

Lady Alissa turned quickly to her friend, but Royal had already spun Enchantress around and was riding across the park at breakneck speed. Lady Alissa considered riding after her but wisely concluded that Royal would need some time alone. . . .

Tears blinded Royal, and deep sobs tore from her throat. She rode until her mount was exhausted, and then she slid to the ground. Leaning her head against the trunk of a tree, she cried until all her tears had been spent.

Two months have passed since Royal discovered that Savannah had fallen. It was the night of the annual social, and she was not looking forward to the event with the same fervor as the other girls.

Royal wore a white gown with yellow rosebuds scattered across the front. Her hair was unpowdered and entwined with a yellow ribbon. She entered the music room that had been converted to a dance floor for the evening, dreading the hours that stretched before her. Since she had no beau, she would pass the time watching the other girls dance.

Already the music was playing, and couples were dancing a lively reel. Royal decided she would stay only a short time and then return to her room. But that was before she saw Lord Preston threading his way through the crowd toward her.

"Good evening, Miss Bradford," he said. "I began to despair that you were not coming tonight."

Royal tried to speak, but her throat went dry. She had not expected him to be here tonight. Could he hear her heart beating? Was her face flushed?

"Do you remember that you once promised to save a dance for me, Miss Bradford?"

"I recall a rash promise made to you by a very young girl."

His smile was spontaneous. "I have come to hold you to that promise."

He presented his arm to her, and she placed her hand on it reluctantly, allowing him to lead her to the dance floor. Royal panicked as she went over the steps in her mind. She hoped she would not make a complete fool of herself. What if she forgot a step? What if she was clumsy?

When they reached the parquet floor, Lord Preston took her hand and swung her around and around, leaving her breathless. Her eyes glowed, and she had the feeling she was floating on air. No, she had not forgotten the steps, and how wonderful it was to dance with a man who moved her so gracefully across the floor.

He gazed down at her sparkling eyes and drew in his breath at how lovely she was. "You are light on your feet, Miss Bradford."

She blushed at his compliment. "I've never danced with a man before," she confided, "except, of course, the dance master, and he's very old . . . thirty-seven, I believe."

Lord Preston laughed with delight. "You are a charmer, Miss Bradford. I am honored to be the first man to dance with you, except for the dance master, of course." Royal looked into his eyes.

"You look lovely tonight," he continued, feeling like a young boy with his first love. "Even more lovely than I remember."

"I believe you flatter me, Lord Preston."

"Not so. The time will come when you will know I speak only the truth."

She glowed beneath the warmth of his words. Around the floor he swung her, their hands lightly touching, their eyes speaking a language of admiration. Royal felt young and beautiful, and the grief over Savannah's tragic fate melted away beneath the glow of soft blue eyes.

The music ended all too soon for Royal. Lord Preston escorted her from the dance floor, but instead of excusing himself, he remained at her side.

His attentiveness did not go unobserved by others, nor did it escape Lady Alissa's notice. She frowned up at Lord Holden, her betrothed.

"Preston is showing too much attention to Royal," she stated in a worried voice. "I am aware of my brother's reputation with women, but I will not allow him to hurt her."

Lord Holden glanced over her head and observed that Preston and Royal were deep in conversation. "Do not concern yourself, Alissa. I will remind Preston that he must tread carefully where Miss Bradford is concerned. I'm sure he must realize she is too highborn to be a mistress, but too lowborn to be a wife. Preston should not put ideas into her head. He is already promised to another."

"Holden! How could you even suggest such a . . ." She glanced quickly at her friend and recognized adoration in her eyes. "I will never allow either of those situations to happen."

"I have rarely seen Preston so captivated by such a young miss," Lord Holden stated, now sharing some of Alissa's concern.

"When I think about it, Preston has always shown an interest in Royal." Her brow knitted. "Even if he is my brother, I will not allow him to turn Royal's head. Nothing could ever come of it."

"I'm sure you are distressing yourself unduly, Alissa. Preston knows where his duty lies." His eyes softened. "Forget about them. I want your whole attention tonight. Have I told you how lovely you look, and how I can hardly contain my impatience to make you mine?"

Lady Alissa's eyes took on the glow of a seductress, and already she had forgotten about Preston and Royal. . . .

Royal was unaware that she was the subject of much speculation. She was caught by Lord Preston's charm and fascinated by his quick wit.

"So, Royal Bradford, have you been applying yourself to your studies?" Lord Preston asked lightly.

"I am doing well enough," she replied, not wanting to tell him she was hailed as an extraordinary student by her teachers.

"Does that leave time for a beau?"

She shook her head. "Alissa could tell you I have no beau. My social life does not put me in such places where I would meet young gentlemen."

There was a satisfied gleam in his eyes. "I happen to know the only place you visit is Chiswick, and certainly the only unmarried gentleman you would encounter there is Holden, who has eyes only for my sister. I have arranged it so there will be no rivals for your affection."

She laughed at his banter, not seeing the seriousness in his expression. "You are wicked beyond belief! Besides, I happen to know you are betrothed, Lord Preston, and I doubt you ever give me a second thought."

His eyes lost their luster. "Yes, the betrothal—a barbarous tradition, don't you agree?"

When Royal did not answer, he bowed to her. "I expect I must be going. I only came to collect my dance."

She was sorry to see him leave. "I enjoyed the dance, Lord Preston."

He brushed her face with his eyes, then paused to stare at her parted lips. "Until another time, Royal Bradford. You have not seen the last of me."

She watched him walk away, wondering at his strange mood. Usually he bantered and joked—tonight he had been much too serious.

She glanced around the room and saw the others were all paired off, so she moved to the door and made her way upstairs. She wanted to be alone to think. Lord Preston had stirred something to life within her, but she did not want to examine it closely—she was too afraid!

While a sleepy Hannah helped her undress, Royal went over her conversation with Lord Preston. Why had he seemed so despondent? And had he really come only to dance with her?

She remembered that he was to be married and spent the rest of the evening trying to put him out of her mind.

PART TWO

A Promise Remembered

Dearest Papa,

It is the popular belief among my friends that the war will soon come to an end. Oh, Papa, I pray it is so. It's difficult to believe I have been in England for four years. I am not certain when I started thinking of London as my home, but the notion of returning to Savannah at the end of my studies is so disturbing that I can hardly bear to think about it. My life is here now. I only hope I can convince Damon Routhland to allow me to remain.

August 1779

Lady Alissa had completed her education, and a ball was being given to officially announce her engagement to Lord Holden. It appeared that everyone of significance was in attendance.

Royal stood just behind the dowager duchess of Chiswick while they watched the dancers whirl by on the polished ballroom floor. Many gentlemen had approached her seeking a dance, but she preferred to be an observer. There was only one gentleman here to interest her, and she had not yet seen him.

Royal had been a guest at the castle so often that she felt at ease there. She had a great fondness for Lady Alissa's family . . . well, most of them. She glanced over at the duke and duchess, who were presiding over the affair with bored indifference. Royal was honest enough to admit that she did not care for either of them. Of course, she had little reason to be in their company, and that suited her just fine.

Lady Alissa danced by, trailing a whisper of silk and looking lovingly at Lord Holden. She turned her head slightly and gave her mother a special smile, wrinkling her nose at Royal.

The dowager duchess looked at Royal with a sparkle of satisfaction in her eyes, and she spoke from behind her fan. "If the earth were to open and swallow up this room, England would be minus most of her nobility."

"I suspect you are right, Your Grace. It is apparent that Lady Alissa and Lord Holden are well received."

"They are suited to each other. After all, both of them come from distinguished lineage. Why, Holden's family came over with William the Conqueror. And of course the Seatons can be traced to Henry the First."

Royal had long ago realized that background and ancestry were important to the Seaton family. She felt fortunate that they had accepted her even though she was not of the nobility.

"There was a time when I was concerned about Alissa's happiness because her marriage was arranged by her father. I believe, however, they are fond of each other. Her expression became serious. "I want more than anything for Alissa to be happy. You are her best friend, Royal—is she happy?"

"Yes, Your Grace. She loves Lord Holden a great deal."

The dowager sighed with relief. "That is a blessing." She glanced up at Royal and tapped the chair beside her with her fan, indicating that Royal should be seated—a singular honor, one that was not missed by anyone in the room. "Had it not been for you, my dear, Alissa would never have had the determination to walk, and tonight would never have come about. This family will never forget that."

"Your Grace, it is I who am fortunate, since I have been rewarded by Lady Alissa's friendship and the kindness of her family."

"Look at my scandalous son," the dowager declared as she and Royal watched Lord Preston winding his way across the ballroom, dodging dancing couples while trying to balance two glasses of punch.

The dowager duchess leaned closer to Royal. "It is no secret to anyone that my younger son has rebelled against the marriage that was arranged for him, Royal. He tests my patience." She added as an afterthought: "But he is a good son, don't you agree?"

"Yes, Your Grace. I find him to be a man of great integrity."

The dowager glanced quickly at Royal, and her voice had a slight edge to it. "I have often thought that Preston pays marked attention to you, my dear."

Royal felt her face redden. "I hope you do not think that I have encouraged . . . that Lord Preston has ever indicated . . . that he—"

The dowager snapped open her fan and snapped it shut again. "Of course not. That would be unthinkable! It's just that I sometimes despair of my son ever settling down. I have noticed, Royal, that you seem to have a calming effect on him." Her brow furrowed. "Now that I think of it, it seems that the only time he comes for a visit is while you are here."

Royal was stunned by the dowager duchess's observation. "I can assure you that I . . . that you . . ."

The dowager changed the subject abruptly. "He's heading in our direction. Everyone in this room watches him, especially the ladies."

Royal saw that this was true. She smiled. "One would think he would be spoiled by all the attention, but he isn't, Your Grace."

The dowager let out an impatient breath. "I could wish he would pay more attention to Lady Alice, his intended bride. Too often he has neglected her." The dowager's expression became cold and piercing. "The alliance with the Stratton family is very important to the Seatons. If my son paid half the attention to Lady Alice that he does to you, they would already be married and have presented me with grandchildren."

Royal stared at the older woman with astonishment in her eyes. "Your Grace, I hope you do not think that I have in any way tried to encourage your son."

"But you like my son, do you not?"

"Yes. Of course, Your Grace, very much."

"Well then, it's up to you to see that his affections for you are discouraged." The shrewd old eyes sparkled. "I credit you with the good sense to do the right thing. Lady Alice isn't going to wait around forever for him to make up his mind. I am certain she has other prospects."

Not knowing how to answer, Royal remained silent. Surely the dowager was not implying that she was to blame for Lord Preston's neglect of his intended bride. She and Lord Preston had shared a special bond since the beginning of their acquaintance. For a brief time, when she was younger, she had been infatuated with him as any impressionable girl would have been. But she had never allowed herself to forget that he was of noble blood and she a commoner.

The dowager came to her feet. "I must talk to Smith about the seating arrangements." She lowered her voice and said softly so only Royal could hear, "I will expect you to talk to my son. He listens to you. Make him see the error of his ways."

When Royal glanced up Lord Preston towered above her, his eyes sparkling as they always did when he looked at her. She turned her head away quickly, hoping the dowager would not mistake her son's friendliness as anything else.

"How fortunate for me that I find you with my mother, Royal," Lord Preston said, handing her a glass of amber liquid, "and not surrounded by admirers."

She saw the teasing light in his eyes. "And what would you have done had I been surrounded by admirers?" His mother had been mistaken. He always treated her the same way he treated Alissa—like a sister.

He suddenly became serious. "If that had been the case, I would have called each one of them out and tested their fortitude with the point of my saber."

She tried to keep the conversation light. "Most likely that's why all the gentlemen in the room have been avoiding me all night."

She arched a silken eyebrow at him. "They see your presence as a threat to their safety."

He laughed down at her. "You are adorable, did you know that?"

She was glad his mother had not heard his statement, for she would never understand how harmless their banter was. "You should not make such flowery speeches to a poor, defenseless girl such as myself. Surely you will turn my head."

Suddenly Lord Preston's voice took on a solemn tone. "Have I the right to keep all others away from you, Royal? Will you grant me that right?"

For a moment she felt as if the air were trapped in her body. This was not the Preston she had come to know. Surely he was still teasing. She realized he was waiting for her response, and she did not know what to say to him. "I will always think of you as a dear friend, Lord Preston."

He drew in an impatient breath. "You should know by now that I want more than friendship from you, Royal!"

Against her will, she raised her head, her gaze locking with his. At last she read the heartbreaking truth in the clear depths of his eyes. She felt the sting of tears. "I know, Preston," she admitted with honesty, her words coming as no surprise to her. "I believe I have known for a long time, although I would not allow myself to admit it."

"Can I hope that you return my feelings?" he asked softly.

Her hand was trembling so badly she could not steady it. She took a sip of the punch, giving herself time to answer. "Preston, people are staring at us. I don't think this is the place to be having this discussion." Her expression was one of bewilderment as she stammered: "Your mother . . . I told her there was nothing . . . I . . . never . . ."

There was misery in Lord Preston's eyes when he took the punch glass from Royal and placed it on a tray. "Come and dance with me, so we can talk without arousing wagging tongues."

"No, Preston, we will not talk of anything so serious. This is your sister's night."

He sat down in the chair his mother had just vacated and crossed his long legs. "Tomorrow, then, we shall speak of our own future."

She was confused and wanted things to stay the way they were between her and Lord Preston. "I shall be returning to school tomorrow morning."

His smile made his eyes brighten. "We will have our talk before you leave. You cannot escape me, you know." His voice took on a deep warmth. "All that remains is for you to say 'yes,' and I shall have you forever."

Her eyes shifted from his as she tried to ignore the excitement that spread through her body. "Please don't say these things to me. It isn't proper. Your family wouldn't approve of our conversation."

"Ah, yes, my family," he said with an edge to his voice. "Nothing will change the way I feel about you."

"Neither your family nor my guardian will favor a match between you and me. You know that, Preston."

His eyes feasted on Royal. She had grown into an extraordinary beauty. Unpowdered, her hair shone like a golden halo of light. Her features were delicate and perfectly molded, her blue eyes soft and luminous. Her skin was creamy and smooth, and there was something almost ethereal about her. If it were not for the protected and secluded life she led, he knew she would be surrounded by admirers, and that thought tore at his heart.

Lord Preston now put forth a question that had been preying on his mind. "I have not asked you this before, because I feared the truth. Is it your plan to return to Savannah and resume your old life, Royal?"

She studied the tip of her satin slipper. "I feel that England is now my home. I don't know how my guardian will feel about that. I am, of course, obliged to answer to his wishes in the matter of where I live until I reach the age of twenty-one, or marry with his consent."

He glanced about the crowded room and wished they were alone so he could speak of his love. He wanted to explain to her that he must go away and ask her to wait for him. He feared that if he did not speak now, another man would win her heart while he was absent.

"I want to make a home for you, Royal." There was a sincere light in his eyes. "I want to take care of you."

She looked away from him, willing her tears not to fall. They were being watched, and she wanted to distract him before they became the object of gossip. "Perhaps we should have that dance after all."

Standing up, he took her arm and with light pressure about her waist guided her among the other dancers. As they had to change partners often, there was no time to talk. Royal concentrated on the intricate dance steps as she moved to another partner and then back to Lord Preston.

At last the music stopped, and Royal placed her hand to her temples. "I am very weary, Preston. Do you think anyone will mind if I slip away to my room?"

His eyes were filled with concern. "You do look pale. I hope I have not been the cause of your distress."

She did not hesitate. "Of course not. It's just that . . . I need time to think."

Unmindful of the gaping stares, Lord Preston raised her gloved hand to his lips. "I will wish you a good night. Will you ride with me in the morning before you leave?" He led her to the edge of the dance floor. "Will you, Royal?"

"Yes, I'll ride with you," she agreed. She was suddenly struck by how dear he was to her, and that realization was like a knife in her heart. Tomorrow she would be forced to discourage him.

She extracted her hand from Preston's grip and dipped into a quick curtsy. "I must say good night to your mother," she said, rushing away.

"Until tomorrow," he called after her.

Royal had been unable to find the dowager, so she made her way upstairs to the sanctuary of her room.

Hannah was not waiting for her when she reached the room, but then Royal knew she had not been expected back so early.

By the time she had removed her clothing and brushed her hair, she was trembling from the emotions Lord Preston had awakened in her.

She slipped beneath a delicate lace coverlet that some long-forgotten member of the Seaton family had painstakingly stitched. Looking at the portrait of an equally forgotten ancestor, she realized again how deep tradition ran in this family.

Some vague, troubling thought kept tugging at her mind, filling her with disquiet—but why? She thought about her conversation with the dowager earlier in the evening. Now everything was clear. Preston's mother had somehow known about her son's feelings for Royal and had been trying to explain that she would not be acceptable as his wife.

She leaned against the fluffy pillow and closed her eyes. Even with the bedroom door closed, she could still hear the faint sound of music from the ballroom below and tried to shut it out of her mind.

Since she always compared every gentleman with Damon Routhland, she did so now with Preston. Preston was like a safe, steady harbor, while Damon was like a turbulent sea. Preston would take care of a wife and cherish her—she was not so certain about Damon.

Tomorrow she would return to school; soon she would have completed her education. Where would she go? Surely not back to Savannah. There was nothing, and no one, there for her now.

Bright moonlight filled the room, giving it the appearance of daylight. Royal's head was so filled with thoughts that she knew she would have trouble falling asleep. When she bent forward to blow out the paraffin lamp, there was a knock on the door.

"Come in," she called out, thinking it would be Hannah. She was surprised when Lady Alissa poked her head around the door.

"I hoped you wouldn't be asleep. Do you mind if I come in? Since you will be leaving tomorrow, I feared we would not get a chance to talk."

Royal drew up her legs and encircled them with her arms. "Has the dance ended?"

"Yes, everyone has either gone to bed or left for their own homes."

"You were radiant tonight, Alissa. I don't have to ask if you are happy."

Lady Alissa whirled around and dropped down on the bed. "I am deliriously happy, Royal! I never knew anyone could be as wonderful as Holden."

Royal smiled. "I told your mother that you and Lord Holden were made for each other."

Her friend unhooked the pearl necklace at her throat and toyed with the catch, as if she had something on her mind. At last she spoke. "Preston told me he is going to ask you to marry him." She peeped at Royal through her lashes. "How do you feel about that?"

Royal laid her head against her knees, wishing the ache in her heart would go away. "I'll tell him 'no.' "

Lady Alissa looked deeply into her friend's eyes as if she wanted to read her thoughts. "You know there is nothing I would like better than to have you as my sister, but it can never be. You would be crucified by society and never be accepted into Preston's world. I could not bear to think of anyone shunning you."

"I know everything you say is true. You needn't worry, Alissa. I will tell Preston tomorrow that I don't return his feelings."

"Will that be the truth, Royal?"

"I only know I would never be the object of any dissension within your family. Because, in the end, Preston would be hurt, and I care too much for him to have that happen."

"You have always had a wisdom that went beyond your years."

"I don't feel wise at the moment, Alissa. I feel rather battered and bruised."

"I know you are hurt, but there is no help for it." Alissa was quiet for a moment, and when she spoke her voice trembled. "Did Preston tell you he will be going away?"

"No, he didn't, but perhaps that will be the solution for him."

Lady Alissa turned her head so Royal would not see the tears glistening in her eyes. "I cannot believe he is leaving."

"Where is he going?" Royal asked hurriedly.

"On some mission for the prime minister. He was rather vague about the details. I don't think Mother is pleased about it at all."

Suddenly a horrible thought tore at Royal's heart, and she grasped Alissa's hand. "Surely Preston is not going to the Colonies to fight in that awful conflict? Tell me that isn't so!"

"He *is* sailing for the Colonies," Lady Alissa admitted, "but not to fight. As Nathan's heir, Preston can't buy a commission, of course. He will be on some sort of diplomatic mission." Although Lady Alissa was disturbed about Preston leaving, she managed to speak encouragingly. "Mother says women are not supposed to think about wars and conflicts. We shall just have to think of Preston as being away on an extended holiday." Her smile was not convincing. "That's what I'm going to think."

Royal couldn't speak. The ache inside her was too new—not to be able to see Preston would be painful indeed.

"Oh, I almost forgot," Lady Alissa proclaimed. "A letter came for you this evening. I told the maid to bring it to you. Did you get it?"

Royal slid off the bed and moved to the dressing table. She immediately recognized John Bartholomew's handwriting on the envelope. "It's from my guardian's secretary," she said, reluctant to open it.

"I'll leave you alone," Lady Alissa said, hugging Royal. "I hope you will believe that I care about you, Royal. Preston can take care of himself, but I will not have you hurt."

Royal watched Lady Alissa slip out the door, closing it behind her. Then, with trepidation, she opened the letter and began to read:

> Dear Mistress Bradford,
> Since your education is coming to an end, and acting on Mr. Routhland's instructions, I have notified Mr. Webber to arrange passage for your return voyage home. Mr. Routhland has asked me to convey his pledge that you need have no fear because of

the war. Every precaution will be taken to assure you safe passage. When the plans have been finalized, you will be notified.

Respectfully yours,
John Bartholomew

Royal stared at the letter with unseeing eyes. The day she had once longed for had come at last, only now she did not want to return to Savannah. She wondered if Damon Routhland's power was such that he could reach across a warring sea and order her home.

No, she thought, flinging the letter aside, she would *not* return to Savannah. She was not the same girl who had left Georgia four years ago. She felt no kinship with the rebels. Her life was here, and she never wanted to go back!

She dropped down on the bed, thinking she would certainly tell Mr. Bartholomew "no."

"You can't make me return, Damon," she cried, turning her face into her pillow.

Her mind was whirling, and she pressed her fingers against her temples to stop the aching throb. Perhaps she could ask Mrs. Fortescue to employ her as a teacher at Fulham. That was certainly a respectable profession.

Hot tears gathered in her eyes. She thought of Damon Routhland. She could still see the softness of his eyes as he had assured her that he would take care of her, but so had Preston. Yet somehow she needed the comfort thoughts of Damon invoked.

Suddenly she remembered something she had pushed to the back of her mind. Now it was as if she could hear the sound of Damon Routhland's voice as he had talked to her at their parting.

"*Will you remember me?*" she had asked childishly.

"*Forever and a day, Royal,*" he had pledged. "*For you are etched in my mind.*"

"*Is that a promise?*" she had continued to question.

"*That's a promise,*" he had assured her.

What am I to do? she cried. Where do I belong?

Dearest Papa,

At this confusing time in my life, I wish I had the benefit of your wisdom. I don't know where the future will take me, I only know I must turn Preston away this morning. And, oh, it hurts so badly, Papa.

Chapter 15

Even though a brisk wind was blowing, it was a warm day. Occasionally, high thin clouds would move across the sky to block out the sun.

Royal urged her mount up a grassy slope and reined in so Preston could catch up with her.

When he rode up beside Royal, he noticed her hair had come loose from her jaunty little hat and was blowing across her face. He reached forward and tucked a golden strand behind her ear while staring at her, his eyes soft with longing. Royal's cheeks were flushed, and there was a light of challenge in her eyes.

"I outdistanced you by a good five lengths," she said, using her expert horsemanship to control the spirited Enchantress, who pranced beneath her.

He reached out and covered her hand with his. "I never mind

losing to such a charming opponent." His gaze moved to the distant view of his home, and he was silent for a moment.

Royal could sense in him a restlessness, and she dreaded the confrontation that was to come. "Is something amiss?" she inquired, knowing well why he appeared so troubled.

"If you look carefully," he said, nodding toward his ancestral home, "you can see where the old moat once surrounded the castle."

"Yes, I see it," she answered, aware that he was making polite conversation because he could not yet say what was in his heart. "I observed last spring that the grass is greener where the moat once was, and the ground is a bit sunken. When was the moat filled in?"

He shrugged. "I'm not certain. Alissa could tell you more about it than I. All I know is that the castle was built in 1461 during the War of the Roses, and it has always been in my family."

She saw him draw in a deep breath and look toward the heavens. "Why don't you tell me what is really on your mind, Preston?" she suggested.

He didn't answer her at once, and when he did he turned to her. "I hardly slept last night for wondering what this day would bring. I knew you would either give me my heart's desire or leave me in the depths of despair. Don't send me away without hope."

"Oh, Preston, don't do this to us. You know to love me is forbidden."

He was suddenly aware of the burden he was putting on her—she was so young she could not know how the thought of never possessing her tormented him. He had to curb his passion so he wouldn't frighten her. "Forgive me for taking unfair advantage of your youth."

"Preston," she said, unable to deal with his distress, "Alissa has told me you are going away. Perhaps by the time you return, you will have forgotten all about me."

"That's not likely," he said, turning to watch a hawk circle above them. "But perhaps we should talk of other matters. Are you aware that I am going to the Colonies? It isn't likely that I shall be in any danger since my mission is a diplomatic one and not military."

Her breathing closed off, and she felt a heaviness in her heart. "You will be missed."

"By you?"

"Yes, me and your family."

His turned his face up to the sky and felt the cooling breeze touch his cheek. "Which is to be for me, Royal . . . happiness or despair?"

"I can't marry you, Preston. I could no more fit into your world than you could function in mine. Surely you see this."

She glanced across the green valley to the imposing brick structure with its wide turrets and vaulted windows. Somehow she had to convince Preston that she was not destined to live in that castle. She turned back to find him watching her with expectation, and it broke her heart.

"If two people love enough, they can overcome any obstacle."

She felt herself weakening until she remembered her conversations with his mother and sister. "I do care a great deal for you, Preston. And I shall say a prayer for your safety every night."

"It is not your prayers I want, Royal. I want you to be my wife!"

She turned away, wishing she could say yes. Oh, how she wanted him to take her in his arms—how she wanted to confess the tender feelings she had for him. Surely it was love that tugged at her heart.

"No, Preston, I will not marry you . . . not without your mother's permission."

His eyes clouded with suspicion. "So that's what this is all about. My mother has been talking to you. She told you to refuse me, didn't she?"

She dared not look into his eyes for fear he would see the truth. "She only told me what we both already know. You will one day be a duke, Preston. The only family I have is an actress—not that I'm ashamed of Aunt Arabella, but how would it look if we were married, and we sat her at the dinner table along with your friends?"

His lips twitched. "Your aunt is a very good actress. I imagine she would add merriment to any occasion."

"Be serious," she admonished him. "You know I am not suited to your way of life."

"Will you send me away without hope in my heart?"

"Preston, don't say anything more that you might regret," she implored. "We both know there can be nothing between us but friendship."

He reached for her hand and pushed her glove aside to place his lips at her wrist. "It's more than friendship I feel for you. Perhaps it was a mistake for me to speak of marriage at this time."

She touched his cheek with her free hand. "You are the gentlest man I have ever known, and I am honored to be loved by you. I'll always treasure this moment, even when I'm very old." A lone tear fell from her lashes and trailed down her cheek. "I will remember the dashingly handsome Englishman who touched my life."

As she spoke, she watched anguish move over Preston's face. "My dearest love, my heart will always be empty without you to fill it."

She shook her head, masking her confusion as she watched him leap from his horse and hold his arms up to her. She was grasped in his strong arms and placed on the ground. Preston pulled her to him, and she laid her face against his rough coat. Silently they stood there, each lost in anguish.

For the moment she felt cherished, but she was only borrowing love that belonged to someone else. She raised her head and looked into his soft eyes. "Perhaps in another world and another time it would have been possible for us to love one another. But not here, and not at this time."

He tilted his head, looking heartbreakingly handsome in his blue coat against the backdrop of blue sky. "I think," he said, pulling her closer, "that you are wise beyond your years. But you do not know me if you think I will give you up so easily." He tilted her chin up and covered her lips with his in a kiss that was filled with yearning.

Royal was stirred by a sweetness that filled her body, and an emotion she had never felt before stirred deep inside her. Yes, she thought, it was so right that Preston should be the first man to kiss her.

When he raised his head his eyes were intense, his breathing uneven. He turned away from her and ran a nervous hand through his hair. "If it were not for this war, I would whisk you away and marry you with or without your consent. You cannot possibly know the depths of feelings you arouse in a man, can you?"

Her eyes were wide and innocent as she shook her head.

"No, of course you can't." His eyes flamed. "I will one day show you what I mean."

She leaned her head against his shoulder. "When must you leave?"

"Soon. I don't know the exact date."

"Will I see you again before you depart?" she asked with a heavy heart.

He turned her to face him, bending to kiss her gently. When she did not protest, he deepened the kiss. At last he released her and groaned, trying not to think of how she had responded. "If possible, I will come to you before I leave." He embraced her so tightly she could scarcely breathe. "If I cannot come to you, I will write."

Royal raised her head, feeling as if her whole body were filled with love for this man who, but for an accident of birth, might have become her husband.

He lowered his head and kissed her with a new desperation. "I love you," he whispered in a passionate voice. "I will keep a vision within my heart of the way you look at this moment. I will take the memory of the blueness of your eyes with me always. And know that when I return I will claim you as my own."

Royal closed her eyes, wanting to hold on to this moment. She thought how strange life was with its little twists of fate. "Take the greatest care of yourself," she said, looking at him with sadness. She buried her face against his shoulder. "Promise me that you won't allow anything to happen to you, Preston."

He laughed. "That is one promise I intend to keep. I have every reason to return. Come," he said, leading her to her horse and lifting her onto the saddle. "You have to journey to London today."

As Royal helped Hannah pack her trunks, Lady Alissa came to her room. "Preston is very quiet, Royal. I take it that you discouraged his suit."

Royal looked at her friend with anger. "Yes, I did all the things you and your family expected of me. It was bitterly cruel, Alissa! I hurt Preston today."

"I know," she said in understanding. "But it was the only way."

"He has not given up," Royal warned. "He still believes we can be together."

"I know that, too. But your answer must always be the same."

"Alissa, I have done all you and your mother asked, but please, let's not talk about it anymore."

Lady Alissa moved out the door, overcome with sadness. There was a gulf between her and Royal. She had known secretly this day would come because of Preston's feelings for her friend. She would miss the best friend she had ever known.

Royal's head swayed back and forth with the rolling motion of the coach. The day's events played through her memory like a sad, sweet song.

Preston's mother had been stiff, almost cold, when she had bid her good-bye today. Royal knew she would not be invited back to Chiswick Castle, nor would she go if asked.

She felt as if the threads of her life were once more coming unraveled. Although she had avoided thinking about Savannah, she was now forced to remember.

The day would soon come when she must consider returning home—she had no choice. She needed to be gone by the time Preston returned to England. If he asked her to marry him again, she might weaken in spite of his family's objections.

It was dusk when the carriage pulled up to Fulham School. Royal was tired and went straight to her room without greeting any of her friends.

She dismissed Hannah and undressed herself in the dark before crawling wearily into bed. She was too numb and hurt to think, yet she remained awake until just before dawn. When she finally fell asleep, she was possessed by a dream that she had not had in a very long time.

In the dream she was a lost little girl, running and searching in the shadows for someone to comfort her. Then out of the gloomy darkness came a comforting hand that brought her warmth and peace of mind.

In her shadowy world, Royal stared into golden eyes that were pulling at her—haunting her—reminding her that she did not belong in England. Her home was in Savannah!

With sheer strength of will, Royal dragged herself out of the dream world to find her pillow wet with tears.

Dearest Papa,

Saying good-bye to my friends at Fulham proved to be very emotional. I was surprised when Mrs. Fortescue called me into her office and with tears in her eyes proclaimed me to be her most exceptional student. It feels strange to no longer be in school. How frightening it is to know that I am considered to be a woman—I do not feel like a woman, Papa.

Chapter 16

It was Royal's last day at school. Most of the girls had already left Fulham for their homes. That afternoon Mr. Webber, the solicitor, and his wife would be arriving to take Royal to stay with them until arrangements were made for her safe passage to Georgia.

St. James's Park was all but deserted as Royal maneuvered Enchantress down the snow-packed trail for her last ride in London. Like slivers of glass, the bitter cold winds swept through the hedges and stung Royal's face. She pulled the hood of her cape about her head as heavy snowflakes drifted earthward.

She raised her gaze to the slate gray skies, then across the wide avenue where the houses nestled among a world of winter white. She would miss this city where she had spent so many of her growing years. It would be painful to leave.

"It's back to the stables with you, Enchantress," she said, leaning forward and patting the horse's long neck. "The bitter weather has taken the joy out of riding. We seem to be the only fools to venture forth today."

With the slightest nudge from the heel of Royal's boot, Enchantress moved in the direction of the school. Royal hoped that today's post would bring word from Preston, who had already sailed for the Colonies.

When she reached the warmth of her room, she glanced at the trunks that were packed and waiting to be taken downstairs. For so long this room had been her home. She had laughed and cried in this room—she had grown to womanhood behind these walls.

She saw two letters lying on the bed. One was from her aunt Arabella and the other from John Bartholomew. She picked up her aunt's first, since she had not heard from her in over a year.

Royal smiled when she read that her aunt Arabella had married an Italian count and now resided in his villa high in the hills above Rome. Royal was certain her aunt would make a most respectable countess. Perhaps this would be the greatest role she would ever play—but, no doubt, Aunt Arabella would play it to perfection.

She was reluctant to open the letter from Mr. Bartholomew, but it would do no good to ignore it because she would not be able to put it out of her mind anyway. Finally, with a resigned sigh, she broke the seal.

> Dear Mistress Bradford,
> It falls to me to inform you that it would not be wise for you to return at this time. As you know, Savannah is still in the hands of the British. Colonel Routhland has instructed me to make arrangements for you to stay in London until such time as he feels it safe for you to make the homeward voyage. Do not be distressed. Mr. Webber and his wife will see to your needs.

Royal stared in disbelief at the letter. Until now the war had only been the monster that had taken the lives of so many young men. Now she was forced to think of invading armies walking the streets of Savannah.

She reread the part about Damon. So he was a colonel. She had not considered him being a soldier, but of course he would have joined the Continental army. He was not a man who would remain passive, and he would never have joined the Loyalists.

In confusion she realized that she wanted to go home.

She was not aware that the door had opened until she heard someone crying. She was bewildered when she saw Lady Alissa. What was she doing here?

Royal reached out to her. "I thought you were at Chiswick. What has happened? Why are you crying?"

"It's Preston. Something terrible has happened to him. Mother has asked that you come to her at once—she's in the sitting room downstairs. You're the only one who can help us now."

Fear gnawed at Royal's insides, and she felt her head swimming. "Not Preston!" she whispered. "He isn't . . . tell me he's not . . ."

"No, Preston is not dead—at least, we don't think so. But he is a prisoner, and Mother wants him home."

"No, not a prisoner! When did this happen?"

Lady Alissa took Royal's hand and pulled her forward. "A message came from the prime minister only yesterday. Mother will tell you all she knows. Come, she is most distressed and wants to see you at once."

"Take a sip of this," the duke of Chiswick urged his mother, who lay back on a lounge looking pale and shaken, while her daughter-in-law declared they were making much too much of this incident about Preston. Mrs. Fortescue hovered in the background, ready to help if called upon to do so.

The dowager pushed the glass away and glared at her son. "I don't want strong spirits, I want your brother."

Royal went to Preston's mother and knelt down beside her. "Please don't distress yourself. It could have been worse, Your Grace. At least he is alive."

The dowager held a handkerchief to her eyes. "Yes, we can be thankful for that. This has been a shock for us all, my dear. Everything possible has been done to find him, but no one has been successful."

"I am certain Lord Preston will be treated well by his captors, Your Grace."

The dowager's eyes were hopeful. "I want to believe that." She glanced up at her eldest son.

Nathan dusted an imaginary speck from his sleeve. "This was bound to happen, Mother. But Preston insisted on having his own way, as always."

"Yes," his wife agreed. "You always indulged and spoiled him, giving in to whatever he wanted."

The dowager seemed not to hear them. "While Alissa is the heart of this family, Preston is its soul. I want all my children under my roof."

"He will come to no harm. You must believe that, Your Grace," Royal said, wanting to ease the dear woman's distress while she herself feared for Preston.

The dowager put a trembling hand to Royal's cheek. "We have treated you badly, Royal. But I hope you will not hold it against us."

For the first time, Royal began to wonder why the Seaton family had sought her out. "Of course not, Your Grace."

"You have it within your power to help Preston," the duke spoke up. "I wonder if I dare ask it of you?"

"I don't understand how I can help, Your Grace," Royal said in confusion. "But I will do anything I can. You must know that."

The dowager duchess grasped Royal's hand. "The prime minister has assured us that your guardian, Mr. Routhland, is a powerful and influential man in the Colonies. If you ask it of him, surely he will use that influence to free my son. You *must* go to him and beseech him to do this!"

"I don't know that my guardian would be able to help you. I just received a letter from his secretary, and he informs me that my guardian is a colonel in the Continental army."

Lady Alissa's face whitened. "Surely he would help gain my brother's release if you asked it of him!"

Royal shook her head. "I don't know. If there was a chance, you know I would do it. Have you any information on where he is being held?"

"No," the duke said. "Sir Henry Clinton informed the prime minister by dispatch that my brother was taken with three others just outside Savannah, Georgia. That's another reason we think your guardian could help."

The dowager gripped Royal's hand even tighter. "The other men captured with my son were later found dead."

Royal swallowed her fear. "Have no fear, Your Grace. If he was taken around Georgia, perhaps my guardian can help."

"Yes, and since he is familiar with the area, he must know where my son is being held." The old woman's eyes pleaded with Royal. "You must go to him and beg him to intervene for Preston. Surely he will listen to you."

Royal stood up slowly, feeling the weight of their trust. "I don't know what my guardian can do. Mr. Bartholomew told me in his letter that Savannah is under British jurisdiction."

"You must try, Royal," Lady Alissa urged, adding her plea to her mother's. "You *must* try!"

Royal glanced at the duke. "It would seem that Savannah is the place where I must start my search. How will I get to the Colonies, Your Grace?"

"As you pointed out, Savannah is in our hands now. I will find a way to transport you there."

Lady Alissa looked at Royal with tearful eyes. "Please help my brother, Royal. He needs you."

Royal squared her shoulders. "I will do what I can."

She felt opposing loyalties battling inside her. She knew two powerful men—could she use one to save the other?

"How soon can I leave?" she asked.

"Time is of the utmost importance," the dowager said, her eyes bright and hopeful. "I cannot stand to think of my son in prison and being ill treated."

"I will make arrangements immediately for your departure," the duke said.

"If you ask me, too much fuss is being made over this," the duchess told her husband. "I'm sure your brother will come to no harm. Perhaps this experience will help curb his impetuous ways."

The dowager turned to her eldest son. "If you don't control your wife's tongue, I'll insist that she leave."

The duke gave his wife a warning glance, and she lapsed into a sulky silence.

The dowager turned her attention on Royal. "It is not proper that a young woman such as yourself should travel alone."

"There's a war going on, Mother, and we can't be worried about what's proper," the duke said.

He took Royal aside and informed her in a lowered voice so his mother couldn't hear, "Preston, as heir presumptive to the dukedom, could be used as a political tool against the king. I want him back for my mother's sake, but also I do not want him to be used to bring pressure against his country."

"I understand, Your Grace," Royal stated. "But don't put too much reliance on my ability to free your brother."

The duke looked at her with new respect. "You are a brave young lady. It must be frightening for you to return to Savannah with war raging. No matter what happens, you will always have our gratitude."

Lady Alissa hugged Royal. "Know that you are not alone. We will be with you in spirit."

Royal smiled. "I will remember that and take comfort from it."

The wind dipping low over the Atlantic Ocean was bitter cold. Royal stood at the railing of the HMS *Dover*, staring into the night. There were no lights blinking from the distant shore, but still she knew they were nearing Savannah Harbor. She could feel it deep within her.

A strange excitement took hold of her. This was the land of

her birth. Her mother and father had been buried here, which made her a part of this land, no matter how she had denied it in the past.

The canvas sails whipped in the wind, and she glanced upward as a voice called out, "Land ho, Captain. Savannah Harbor off the starboard bow."

An hour later the ship glided into the Savannah River. A steady breeze brought with it a heady fragrance that was familiar to Royal, and it awakened old memories both pleasant and unpleasant.

Yes, she thought with a pounding heart, she had not realized until this moment how much she had missed Savannah. Staring into the darkness, she wondered where she would find Damon Routhland. And when she found him, would he be willing to help her free Preston?

Captain Ferris appeared beside Royal. He did not understand why such a beautiful woman would be traveling alone and why everything about her was so secretive, but she must be on a mission of great import, for his orders had been to see her safely to her destination.

"I was informed by the duke of Chiswick, ma'am, to escort you to the headquarters of the commander of our forces in Savannah, Colonel Archibald Campbell. I have a letter to present to Colonel Campbell, asking that he give you every assistance."

"Thank you, Captain." She smiled up at him. "And thank you for the courtesy you and your crew have extended to me. I am most grateful."

He bowed respectfully. "It was my pleasure, ma'am. Now, if your trunks are packed, I'll have my men bring them on deck so we can get you ashore before daylight."

The crew members were scampering around to bring the *Dover* into port. After a while the captain again appeared at Royal's side. "If you are ready, ma'am, I'll take you ashore. No one will witness our arrival."

So I'm to sneak home, she thought, like a thief in the night. This was not how she had imagined her homecoming.

Royal turned her gaze toward the shore. Although it was dark, the imprint of Savannah had been stamped on her mind. She could imagine the shops and warehouses situated high atop Yamacraw Bluff. The streets were paved with ballast stones that had been left behind by long-forgotten sailing ships.

Savannah was a city of charm and beauty, where church steeples spiraled to the sky and quiet streets were filled with moss-laden oak. A paradise where winter hardly ever intruded, and when it did, it was with a gentle hand.

Royal closed her eyes and thought of the graveyard where her mother and father were buried.

"I have come home, Papa," she whispered.

Dearest Papa,

I tremble with fear at the uncertainty in my life. Last night I was brought before the British commander, Colonel Campbell, and he appeared most eager to aid me in any way. I know I cannot find Preston without the help of Damon Routhland. My first dilemma will be locating Damon. If that is accomplished, I will still have to convince him to help me free Preston.

Chapter 17

Royal had been given a room at the British headquarters, where she spent her first night in Savannah. It was now early morning, and she had politely refused the military escort Colonel Campbell had offered her. But she had accepted his offer of a horse-drawn buggy and a nonmilitary driver.

If she was to find Damon, she would have to begin her search at Swanhouse Plantation, and she could hardly go there under the protection of British soldiers. Her only hope was that John Bartholomew would know where to find her guardian.

The horses were clipping along at a good pace beneath the canopy of blue skies. As Royal looked for familiar faces, she saw mostly Redcoat soldiers, and for some reason she resented their presence in Savannah.

She was heartsick at the destruction the war had wreaked on

the city—houses had been burned and storefront windows broken. She wondered how her own home had fared, but she had no time to find out. Her first task was to locate Damon.

Suddenly Royal felt strangely elated as she glanced out at the familiar sights. Though tattered and bruised from the ravages of war, Savannah had survived—Royal had the feeling it always would.

When the buggy crossed Bull Street, Royal strained her eyes to see her house, but it was hidden by the trees. She wondered about Tobias and Alba, and she was anxious to see them—but not yet. Every day Preston was held prisoner was agony for his family and for her.

When the buggy turned down Oglethorpe Avenue, she instructed the driver to stop at the cemetery. She could not pass without visiting her father's grave. Time whirled backward as she pushed open the iron gate and moved down the path to his gravesite. She stopped beneath the oak tree and clasped her hands together in prayer.

How long ago it seemed that she had last visited the cemetery, a lost child in the rain, saying good-bye to her father. Now she was here as a woman, but still lost and searching all the same. The last time she had stood here, newly turned earth blanketed her father's grave; now it was covered with grass.

Royal saw that her parents' graves had been well tended. This, she realized in a burst of gratitude, would be attributed to Alba and Tobias's devotion.

She touched her fingers to her lips, placed them to her father's headstone, repeated the same gesture at her mother's headstone, then turned to leave. It was time to look after the living—Preston needed her.

As the buggy came in sight of Swanhouse Plantation, the stately Georgian mansion loomed against the sky. Royal let out a pent-up breath. She had been afraid that Swanhouse would be ravaged by war. Apparently it had survived.

The three-story structure had been built of red brick and was wondrous to behold. Along a watery avenue, a crystal pool caught the reflection of the house in its shimmering depths. There were four huge fountains in the shape of swans, and though the fountains were now silent, live swans floated upon the mirror-bright surface.

When the buggy pulled to a stop before the massive steps, Royal stared in awe at the house. She had only heard about Swanhouse from her father, but his description had not done it justice. Over the massive double doors was a large wood carving of two swans with their long necks intertwined. Beneath the carving were the words:

MAY ALL WHO PASS THESE PORTALS FIND SHELTER

"Wait for me here," Royal told the driver. "I don't expect to be long."

She moved up the steps and approached the front door. When she raised her gloved hand to knock, the door swung open and an elderly butler greeted her with an astonished look on his face. "Yes, ma'am, how can I help you?"

"Can I assume your master is not at home?"

The black eyes looked back at her suspiciously. "Master Damon ain't been home these many months."

Royal could see that the butler was distrustful of her and was about to close the door. She stopped him. "Take me to John Bartholomew," she said in a clear voice.

The butler looked hesitant. "I don't know if Mr. Bartholomew will see you. Who should I tell him is calling, ma'am?"

She stepped into the entry hall. "Royal Bradford."

Seeing that she was determined, the butler relented. "If you'll follow me, ma'am," he said, leading the way past the entry hall and down a long corridor, where her footsteps sank into luxurious Turkish carpet.

"Please wait in here," the man instructed, stopping before a door and pushing it open. "I'll inform Mr. Bartholomew you're here."

When the butler departed, closing the door behind him, Royal moved about the room, inspecting it carefully. She could almost feel Damon's presence. It was obviously the library, judging from the floor-to-ceiling bookshelves and the deep-set bow windows that caught the morning sunlight.

The walls were covered with mellow red silk that matched the heavy curtains made of Utrecht velvet. Family portraits painted by European masters hung on the wall, and a desk was situated near the fireplace. It was an elegant room, and one that bespoke great wealth.

Two black-and-white spaniels lay before the immense fireplace and all but ignored Royal. Again, she could feel the presence of their master here, leading her to believe that Damon must have spent a great deal of time in this room.

Suddenly the door opened, and a sprite little man appeared. He walked toward Royal with jerky motions, all the while looking her over with care.

Royal studied the secretary, who had been her only link with Savannah for the past four years. He looked very much as she had pictured him, perhaps a little grayer and somewhat older. "I hoped you would know me, Mr. Bartholomew. I believe I should have known you if we had met on the street."

She smiled at John Bartholomew, thinking his personality fit his style of letter writing—stiff, authoritative, and loyal. When still he failed to respond, she laughed impishly. "Oh, Mr. Bartholomew, don't you know me? Even though we have never met in person, we have carried on a lively correspondence for quite some time."

His eyes snapped open wider, and he studied her more intently. Her hair was arranged in curls and powdered. Her green brocade gown bespoke an elegant European styling. "Can you really be Miss Bradford? But you are . . . should be . . . a child."

She turned around for his inspection. "I can assure you it is I—all the way from England—and all grown up."

For just a moment his professional mask slipped, and she saw warmth in his quick smile. "I cannot believe you are here, Miss Bradford." Then he frowned as he remembered Damon Routhland's instructions regarding his ward. "Did you not get my correspondence telling you it was unsafe to return to Savannah at this time? Mr. Routhland will not be pleased that you have disobeyed him."

"I did get your letter, Mr. Bartholomew, but I had to come. A friend of mine is in trouble, and I hope my guardian can help him."

John shook his head. "Mr. Routhland isn't here."

She gave him her most winsome smile. "But you *can* tell me how to get in touch with him, Mr. Bartholomew."

He looked skeptical. "I might be persuaded to help you, if you can prove to me that you are truly Mistress Bradford. You sound very British to me."

She laughed in amusement. "How would you expect me to sound? I was, after all, educated in an English school." Her gaze became serious. "What must I do to prove my identity?"

He was thoughtful for a moment. "What is the name of the horse that was shipped to Miss Bradford from Swanhouse?"

"Enchantress," she stated, then added, "My father's name was Douglas, my aunt is Arabella. Alba and Tobias are my servants. Does that convince you?"

"Many people might be privy to that information."

"I am glad you are protective of my guardian. But it is truly I, Mr. Bartholomew." Then Royal gave him a special smile. "What if I tell you that I was always grateful you never forgot my birthday, and even though my gifts bore my guardian's name, I was aware that you had selected them."

She moved forward with a quickness that took him by surprise and pressed her cheek to his. "I thank you for never neglecting me."

John blushed, but he could not hide the pleasure in his eyes. "Yes, you are surely Miss Bradford. No one else would be as precocious as you."

"Will you tell me how I can reach Mr. Routhland? It is imperative that I contact him as quickly as possible."

He looked at her grimly. "I know where he was a month ago, but no one can be sure of anything these days."

"Please tell me," she implored.

Charles Town, South Carolina

A heady breeze stirred a damp mist from the marshes of the lowlands, encasing the night in an eerie fog. The weather, however, did not discourage the guests, who with supervised regularity arrived at Major Leaman's mansion on Meeting Street. Each carriage deposited its passengers at the front door, then pulled away to make room for the next.

Colonel Damon Routhland, in full dress uniform, leaned against the stairs, watching the dancing couples whirl by. He was aware that Major Leaman's daughter was trying to catch his eye, but he pretended not to notice. He had been in no mood to attend this party and had done so only because he felt compelled by good manners to make an appearance. He decided he would leave as soon as he could without seeming rude.

Damon did not know what made him turn, but when he swung around to face the door, his eyes collided with a woman who held not only his attention, but everyone else's as well.

If the woman was aware that everyone was staring at her, she did not show it. With the gracefulness of a swan, she descended the steps that brought her into the ballroom.

She was as lovely as an angel, delicate and ethereal in a fragile white gown with gold braiding along the hem. Her hair was powdered and dressed in the latest style. Her beautiful face was unsmiling, and it appeared that she was carved out of delicate porcelain.

Damon watched her as she glided gracefully across the room. It soon became apparent to him and everyone else that she was walking right toward him. He wondered why she had chosen him, because he did not know her, he was certain of that. He would never have forgotten her.

Royal clutched her hands to her side to still their trembling. Could Damon sense her distress? she wondered. Could he tell by looking at her that she was frightened? She felt a strange kind of sweetness stirring deep within her body at seeing him again.

She had come to the ball uninvited, but no one at the door had challenged her right to be there. She extended one foot in front of the other, forcing herself to approach Damon, when in truth she wanted to run away.

When she stopped before him, she stared into those now familiar golden eyes, not daring to look away for fear she would lose her courage. She had not remembered him being so tall or his shoulders so broad. He was dressed in a blue uniform with gold epaulets on the shoulders and looked dashing indeed.

Had he always been this handsome? His dark hair was unpowdered and tied back in a queue. He was tanned and exuded leashed strength that reminded her of a caged tiger.

She waited for some sign that he was glad to see her, but she could not be certain. Perhaps he was angry that she had disobeyed him by leaving England.

Damon lowered his lashes over those glorious eyes and smiled. Clicking his booted heels together, he bowed to her. His voice was deep as he spoke. "Let me live in fool's paradise, lovely angel. Allow me to believe that you came here tonight to see only me."

She was hurt and confused. Damon had promised never to forget her, and yet he did not recognize her—how could that be? Perplexed, she decided she was not going to be so quick to reveal her identity. She would flirt with him, toy with him, torment him, before admitting who she was.

"I am here to see only you, Colonel Routhland," she said in a throaty voice.

He arched a dark brow. "If that is so, Miss . . ."

She placed a gloved finger to his lips. "Please, no names tonight. Would you like to dance with me?"

He had not missed her British accent, and her gown could only have come from London. "You have me at a disadvantage. You know who I am, yet I don't know you."

For the first time in her life, Royal felt flirtatious. Anonymity somehow made her bold. Mrs. Fortescue would probably faint dead away if she could witness her prize pupil's performance tonight. But Charles Town was a long way from London and Fulham School.

"Do you not like a mystery, Colonel?"

He took her hand and led her into the stream of dancing couples. "Not . . . usually," he whispered, staring at her full lips. "But you are a mystery I will enjoy . . . solving."

"Do you think you can?" she taunted.

Again he arched an eyebrow. "I'll give it my best effort."

As he led her forward in a reel, she smiled. "I will issue you a challenge, Colonel. If you can guess who I am before sunrise, I will reward you."

"What is my reward?" he asked guardedly.

Excitement throbbed throughout her body. "That will be determined if, and when, you win."

He stared at her. "You are daring, and I like that in a woman." He bowed to the woman opposite him and then turned back to Royal. "Do I get any hints?"

"Of course." She was thoughtful for a moment. "The first hint is—let me see, you *do* know me, Colonel. We have met on at least two occasions."

The music had stopped, and he guided her away from the crowd. "How can it be that we have met before, mystery lady? I would never forget someone like you."

"Nevertheless, you know me . . . quite well."

He had never been so intrigued by a woman before. She was beguiling, beautiful, mysterious. He found himself wanting to learn everything about her. "I don't know what game you are playing, but I will willingly play with you all the same."

She noticed for the first time that they were attracting everyone's attention, and she felt embarrassed. "Would it be possible for us to leave?" she asked hurriedly before she lost her courage.

Damon was immediately suspicious. What trap was being laid for him? This woman was obviously of good breeding and superior education. Someone with her beauty would not have to seek male companionship; she most probably had to discourage admirers. He decided to humor her—for the time being.

"Where would you like to go?" he asked, wondering how far she was willing to play her game.

"I am unfamiliar with Charles Town since I have never been here before. Perhaps you know of a place where we could be alone, Colonel?"

Excitement coursed through his body. He was losing his ability to reason. No woman had ever affected him as she did. His gaze drifted down to her smooth shoulders and her long creamy neck. "We could go to my quarters. It's a small cottage near the waterfront, and we will not be disturbed there." He expected her to refuse his outrageous suggestion.

"Could we leave now?"

Without another word, he took her elbow and escorted her across the floor. When the butler held out her cape, Damon placed it around her shoulders. As they stood side by side on the steps, he was aware only of her. He had not noticed that the fog now shrouded the landscape, impeding the view, making it impossible to see any distance.

When his carriage drew up, Damon helped the lovely vision inside and seated himself across from her so he could study her more clearly in the swaying lantern light.

"Why are you doing this?" he asked in a harsh whisper.

Royal made a pretense of working her fingers into her white kid gloves. "I have issued you a challenge, and you have accepted."

"Yes, but you have failed to tell me what you will gain if I lose."

She raised her eyes to his. "It's very simple. I will ask a favor of you, and you will grant it."

"Ah, I see. It becomes clear."

"Then you know who I am?"

"Madam, I have never seen you before tonight. I believe I know your game, however. You will swear that I met you at some ball or party, and I will be unable to deny it for fear of offending you."

She looked at him innocently. "Why do you think I would do that?"

"Because," he said dryly, "women are always doing that to me."

Royal's smile was provocative. "No, Colonel, when I finally admit to you who I am, you will realize I am not pretending when I say we have met before."

"Let me see," he said, still doubtful of her motives. "Oh, yes, I have also had this one tried on me before. You have a brother"—he looked at her inquiringly—"or perhaps a lover, who would like to be promoted to a higher rank. You foolishly believe if you . . . beguile me, I will recommend him."

"Colonel," she said softly, "would you have me believe that women only approach you to gain rank for their brothers, or their lovers?"

Damon frowned. She was an intriguing woman with a clever mind. It was not too late to stop this game, and he knew he should. She could mean trouble for him, but that would not deter him. He had to know who she was and what she wanted of him. He would play this game to the end.

"Tell me what favor you want from me should you win."

"You will learn that *when* I win."

The clopping of the horses' hooves was muted by the fog. Riding with Damon in the closed carriage, Royal could almost believe no one else existed but the two of them. The lantern swayed back and forth, sometimes casting Damon's face in shadows.

Suddenly, in a move that took Royal by surprise, he reached out and pulled her across his lap. "I can tell if I ever kissed you," he said rakishly. "I never forget a kiss—if it is memorable." His gaze touched her lips. "If I had kissed you, it would have been memorable."

Before Royal could protest, his mouth covered hers. She pushed against him, twisting and turning, trying to escape his grasp. This was not part of her plan. What was he doing?

Damon's hands were rough as he caught the back of her head and stilled her movement. When she became aware of the heat of his mouth, all the fight went out of her. His lips were demanding a response from her—his tongue circled her lips, and she thought she would faint from want of air. Her head was reeling, and her heart pounded—she did not want him to stop.

Just when she thought she would swoon, he released her, and she fell back against the seat, her heart racing.

"I have never kissed you before," he said with assurance. "Nor, I'll wager, has any man. You are not as worldly as you would have me believe."

"I have been kissed," she said, her voice coming out in a breathless whisper, her chest heaving with indignation.

He laughed in amusement. "Yes, perhaps you have. Perhaps your innocence is all part of your game."

She stared at him, wondering how he could react so calmly to a kiss that had the blood racing through her body. When Preston had kissed her, she had not responded like this.

Feeling somehow disloyal to Preston, and remembering the reason for her mission, Royal turned her head away from Damon's inquiring eyes. "You still have not guessed my identity, Colonel Routhland."

"You said you would give me until sunup, and that is a good six hours yet."

"Yes, until sunup," she agreed. "Then I shall ask my favor of you. Do you give me your word that you will honor my request?"

He quirked an eyebrow at her. "If it is within my power to grant your wish, I shall certainly do so."

"Oh, it will be, Colonel. You can be assured of that."

Dearest Papa,

Why am I having these feelings for Damon? When I think of him, I tremble, my heart beats faster, and I feel weak all over. What can be happening to me?

Chapter 18

The carriage came to a halt, and Damon helped Royal alight, then led her to the door of a small cottage.

Once they were inside, Damon's aide came forward to take his cape. Since he was accustomed to having his colonel entertain attractive women in his quarters, Corporal Thomas was well trained. He did not look at the colonel's companion or acknowledge her presence.

Damon handed Thomas his greatcoat. "I won't be needing you tonight, Corporal. You may go."

With a formal nod, the aide withdrew.

When Royal and Damon were alone, he turned to find her hovering near the door. He could sense a nervousness in her. Although she tried to hide it, he did not miss the light of uncertainty in her eyes. Aware that he was now in control of the situation, he went to her and took her cape.

"You will find it more agreeable near the fire," he suggested, "for there is a nip in the air tonight."

Royal moved woodenly to the crackling fire, holding out her trembling hands to the flame. Apprehensively she looked about the orderly room. The furnishings consisted of two chairs, a desk piled high with documents, and a bed in the corner—she looked away from the bed quickly.

Damon came forward to tower over her. "Are you comfortable?" he asked.

Royal thought she might be more comfortable if she could put some distance between them; his nearness was too disturbing to her peace of mind. She decided to open the conversation with pointless chatter. Perhaps that would allow her time to gather her courage.

"Seeing the amount of correspondence on your desk, I would venture to guess that you miss Mr. Bartholomew's efficiency," she remarked, voicing the first thing that came to mind.

He stared at her in astonishment. "How can you know so much about me? Who are you?" His eyes narrowed. "More important, why are you here?"

Royal dropped down on a chair because her legs were ready to buckle. "I will not satisfy your curiosity," she murmured. "You'll have to find those answers for yourself."

He leaned against the mantel, casting a long shadow across her face. Royal was reminded of another time, another place, when he had stood thus. She had been a lost child then, with no one to turn to but him. Her whole world had tilted, and this man had righted it for her. Would he do the same for her now? she wondered.

Damon's eyes took on a rakish glow. "Just how much will I discover about you tonight? How far are you willing to go with this game?"

It was as if he could read her innermost thoughts as he stared at her with impassioned golden eyes.

"I . . . as far as necessary."

He swooped down and clasped her shoulders, pulling her to her feet. "Take care that you do not arouse in me that which you may be unwilling to satisfy."

She tried to look away from him. "You mistake my reason for coming here. I want merely to—"

"The time for playing games is over." His fingers bit into her flesh. "It is not hard for me to guess that you are fresh off a ship from England. I don't know what you want from me, but if you have been given to believe that I will betray my country's secrets to a beautiful woman, you have been badly misled."

She met his gaze with a haughty glare of her own. "If you think I am here to ask that you betray the Colonies, you are wrong."

His eyes narrowed. "I was right, however, that you have come from England. Only an Englishwoman would be so arrogant as to refer to my country as the 'Colonies' rather than America."

"I will not deny that I have come from England. I will even tell you that I landed only this last week. But, Colonel, I will remind you of our bargain. It is not yet daylight, and you have still to discover my identity."

A wicked smile touched his lips. "Let me think." His long fingers drifted down her slender neck, and he toyed with the pearl necklace nestled in the hollow of her throat. "I am trying to recall all the English ladies I have been . . . shall we say"—he groped for the right word—"acquainted with. You are not one of them."

Insulted, she pushed his hand away. "We both know we have not been . . . on intimate terms."

Undaunted, he traced the outline of her lips. "No," he answered in a soft, penetrating whisper. "Not . . . yet. But when a woman seeks a man out, what else is he to think?"

She glanced at the clock on the mantel. How would she be able to withstand him the three hours remaining until sunrise? "You are wrong in what you are thinking, Colonel. I am not . . . have never . . ."

He took her arm and pulled her against him. "We both know why you're here. If you come to a man's room alone, you are bound to give him notions, and you should be willing to take the consequences. But you know that, don't you? You knew that when you agreed to come here."

She thought of Preston. "I . . . am willing to do what I must, Colonel Routhland. But shouldn't you be trying to guess who I am?" she said, trying to distract him.

Damon shook his head to clear it. He was not certain if she was experienced or an innocent. If she was experienced, she was a hell of a good actress, pretending innocence. "So, the game continues."

He moved over to his desk, picked up a glass, and filled it from a decanter of wine. "Perhaps a drink to fortify us for what is to come?"

She hesitantly accepted the glass and watched him take a sip from his own before taking a sip herself. Her first taste of strong spirits burned a trail down her throat and brought stinging tears to her eyes. Damon laughed in amusement when she coughed to catch her breath.

"That settles one of my questions. You are not a heavy drinker. Perhaps you are just out of the schoolroom, though I hope that is not the case. I have never been accused of seducing schoolgirls."

His assessment had come too close to the truth. With defiance in her eyes, she deliberately raised the glass and downed a large gulp. This time the warmth spread through her body, and she began to feel giddy. Full of false bravado, she said, "Let the contest continue, Colonel. You may ask your questions, and I will answer them honestly."

He took her glass and placed it on the desk, then returned to her. "Shall we be seated?"

She dropped down in the chair he had indicated, and he sat opposite. "Let me see, mystery lady. We have already established that you have but recently come from England."

"That is correct."

"Is it fair for me to assume that you have been in my country before?"

"You can assume that." She tilted her face up to him. "In the past, I was here for a long period of time."

His eyes swept her face, and somewhere buried in his subconscious was a vague memory of sad blue eyes like hers. "I could not have been well acquainted with you." He shook his head. "I am not so addle-brained that I would ever forget you."

She thought of Damon's relationship with her aunt Arabella. "Let us say you were more acquainted with a female relative of mine than you were with me."

"Good Lord," he cried in mock horror. "Don't tell me I was intimate with your sister, and please don't tell me it was your mother—or even both."

She smiled. "Surely you give yourself too much credit, Colonel."

He leaned forward. "Are you a spy for the British? Remember you promised to answer with honesty."

"I am not a spy."

"Did someone send you with the intention of gaining information from me?"

"I am here because you have helped me in the past—I am hoping you will do so again."

He looked perplexed as he said, "I want to know everything about you. What color is your hair beneath that powder? Can anyone's eyes really be as blue as yours? What are your thoughts—whom do you favor in this war? Do I excite you as you excite me?"

Royal had never had a man say these things to her before, and she was trembling inside to the vibrations of his deep voice. She could remember when her fondest girlhood dream had been to grow up to be beautiful so Damon would notice her. Now her wish had come true, if she judged his reaction correctly.

Pretending a sophistication she did not feel, Royal gazed at him through a veil of thick lashes. "You once knew the color of my hair. It has not changed."

With a sudden motion, Damon stood up, unbuttoned his coat, and moved away from her. "It looks to be a long night. Do you mind if I make myself comfortable?"

"No, not at all."

He draped his coat over the back of a chair. Royal's eyes followed his lithe movements, noticing his lean, muscled body. His long legs fit snugly inside the uniform trousers. The ruffle at the wrist of his stark white shirt fell across strong, sun-browned hands. Unable to look into his eyes, she stared instead at the high shine of his knee-length boots.

He was making her forget her reason for being there. She must not lose sight of her objective.

Damon stood over her, willing her to look at him. When she did, he smiled. "I have decided that you have all the advantages. It's only fair if I make the contest more equal. Is that agreeable with you?"

She nodded. "As you wish, Colonel."

He pulled her to her feet and rested his hand on her shoulder. "We have never kissed before?"

The liquor had loosened her tongue and encouraged her to speak daringly. "With the exception of the kiss in your carriage—no."

"Of course, I was not counting that kiss."

He removed her gloves one by one, his eyes looking into hers all the while. He then dipped his head and pulled her to him. "Perhaps . . . another kiss to revive my memory."

She did not pull away when his mouth settled at the corner of hers, and he whispered: "A taste of heaven, mystery lady. You do sorely tempt me."

She felt the room spinning and held on to his shirtfront to keep her balance.

His lips hovered inches from hers, and his breath fanned her face. "If it was your intention to make me a mindless slave, you may have succeeded in that. Never have I desired a woman as I desire you at this moment."

She closed her eyes, loving the feel of his hard body pressed against hers. "Perhaps this was my intention all along," she admitted in a throaty voice.

Then she pulled away from him. "Can we strike a bargain, Colonel?"

His voice came out in a harsh whisper. "At this moment, you can ask what you want of me, and I shall grant it."

"Will you promise to help me?"

He pressed her face between his two hands and made her look at him. "No more games. It is time for truth. What do you want of me?"

Daringly she parted her lips, and innocent as she was, she could not help but know that she was tempting this man almost beyond endurance. "We will talk of that later, Colonel."

With a smothered moan, he lifted her in his arms and carried her to his bed. Royal's mind was whirling, but still she did not realize the danger. She laughed lightly. "Am I to be tucked in like a child, Colonel?"

Damon set her on her feet. "You are no child," he told her, his glance moving down her bodice to her narrow waist. "No, certainly no child."

She was not concerned when he began unlacing the back of her gown, because she had no fear of him. What harm would it do to entice him further? she thought. She would stop him before he went too far.

Somewhere inside, a voice cautioned her that she was not acting rationally, but she ignored the warning.

With practiced hands, Damon had her gown unlaced and pushed off her shoulders before she realized it. She shook her head and backed away when his hands went to her stays. "You go too fast," she said, wishing she had not drunk the spirits because her judgment was clouding. In reality, she did not want him to stop. She wanted him to touch her, to show her what it meant to be a woman, but it was wrong.

She was lifted in strong arms and placed on the bed. Nothing but her thin chemise stood between her naked flesh and his burning glance. She tried to remember Preston, but golden eyes were holding her prisoner. "I had not expected—"

He dropped down beside her, his eyes sweeping her face, her shoulders, the swell of her breasts above the thin fabric. "What did you expect?" he asked gruffly. "If you want me to stop, there is still time."

But already his magic hand was drifting down her neck to play with the blue ribbon that would unfasten her chemise. When she made no attempt to stop him, he pulled the ribbon and the material fell aside, revealing her satiny breasts.

Royal whimpered with unleashed longing as his hand moved to stroke her swollen breasts. She ached from his gentle touch, yet she knew she should stop him. Instead her arms moved as if she had no control over them to slide around his shoulders, and her fingers twined through his hair. She had the feeling she was drifting, floating, living in a fanciful dream world.

Now his golden eyes were burning into hers. Passion blazed inside Damon like fire to dry wood. There was no turning back now. Bending forward, he buried his face against her silken breasts, drinking in the intoxicating scent of her perfume. "What are you doing to me?" he asked in a last moment of sanity.

"I want to be with you," she replied with honesty. "I feel as if nothing can touch me when you hold me like this."

He raised his head and stared down at her. He could swear there were tears swimming in her blue eyes, but surely he was mistaken. "Be aware that I will not stop with a few kisses." His words hung like a warning. "I have wanted this from the moment I saw you this evening. Say you want it, too."

Royal found herself experiencing emotions she had never felt before. She touched his face and parted her lips. "I will take the essence of you inside me, so when you are gone, I will still have the feel of you with me."

A low groan issued from his lips, and he pulled her tightly against him. "Damn you, I may get burned by you, but I will have you all the same."

His mouth teased the lobe of her ear, tested her lips in a long, drugging kiss, and, when she was mindless, moved down her neck to settle on the tip of one swollen breast.

She arched closer to him, wondering why she felt his hot flesh against hers. When had he removed her chemise? When had he discarded his own clothing? It didn't matter—nothing did, but the feelings that ran like hot lava in her veins.

Everywhere he touched brought new and exciting sensations to Royal. These unexplored desires were ruling her consciousness. She knew there was more to come, and she ached for it.

"Love me, Damon," she cried. "Love me."

"Yes," he murmured, burning to possess this woman, needing her to soothe the raw ache deep inside. "I will have all of you."

At that moment there was a heavy rap on the door, and Damon raised his head and muttered an oath. He waited and listened, but the knock came again.

"Colonel," came a loud voice from the other side of the door, "the troop is moving out in one hour."

Damon took a deep, steadying breath and looked at Royal regretfully. "It seems you are saved, mystery lady." He moved off the bed, pulled on his trousers, and slipped into his shirt.

Royal watched him move to the door and step outside to converse with his aide. She blinked her eyes, feeling somehow cheated. At the same time she was shocked by what had happened. She hurriedly pulled on her clothing, making a vow never again to drink strong spirits. Not bothering to tie her laces, she reached for her cape and fastened it about her neck.

When Damon returned she avoided his eyes in the pretense of slipping on her gloves. "Tonight was a mistake, Colonel. I am glad we were saved at the last moment."

He smiled wryly. "Do not expect me to share your sentiments. I think there will be many nights that I will lie awake and wonder about you." He shrugged. "Regretfully, I am in something of a hurry. I have made my carriage available to you. The driver will take you where you wish to go."

"Colonel, t-thank you."

He took her hand and pulled her against him. "The sun is not yet up, but will you not tell me your name?"

She hestitated. "We are destined to meet again, Colonel Routhland. Perhaps then you will learn all."

He was reluctant to let her go, fearing she would disappear forever. "When will I see you again?"

"Soon. I still need my favor, Colonel."

"You don't know where to find me."

"I will always find you," she said, turning to leave. "Good-bye, Colonel."

Damon reached out to stop her, but already she was gone. He did not know who she was, but she had touched him in some secret place in his heart tonight, and he knew he would never again be the same. He was sure if he closed his eyes, he would still be able to feel her silken skin.

She had said she would see him again, and he was counting on that.

Royal moved silently up the stairs of the Seaport Inn, hoping no one would see her returning at such a late hour. She would gather her belongings and wait until sunup, when she would instruct her driver to take her back to Savannah.

She sat at the window, watching the first golden streaks of sunlight play flirtatiously across the shimmering water. Unconsciously, as was her habit, she reached for her journal and began to write:

> My Dearest Damon,
> Tonight I realized that I have strong feelings for you. . . .

Royal stared at the words she had written. The truth struck her like an arrow in the heart, and tears splashed down her cheeks and fell onto the page.

"Oh, Papa," she cried, "I now realize that through all these years, although I have addressed my journal to you, the words must have been meant for Damon Routhland all along."

Had she loved Damon even as a child? Yes, she had loved him even then. But he was unattainable to her—Damon, whose heart many women had tried to capture and failed.

She could never belong to him. He would hate her after he learned who she was and that her reason for seeking him out was to enlist his aid in freeing an enemy.

She could not think about that now. Preston's family trusted her to help him. And help him she would, at any cost to herself.

She thought of how boldly she had approached Damon and how wantonly she had set out to torture him. What could have possessed her to be so unmaidenly? She sobbed in agony, wondering how she would ever be able to face Damon again. She prayed he would never discover her true identity. What must he think of her behavior tonight? She had told herself that she had sought Damon out for Preston's sake. The truth was that she wanted to be with him—to have him hold her—to have him desire her.

She closed the journal and placed it at the bottom of her trunk. It belonged to her past. She was no longer a child who needed to write out her pain. She was a woman embarking on an uncertain future.

As Damon rode out of Charles Town to join his troop, his mind wandered back to the strange and stirring events of the night. Never had he met a more exciting woman—he had been totally under her spell.

She had wanted something from him, and he might have promised her anything if they had not been interrupted. He had to see her again—there was too much left unfinished between them.

Wonderful memories of her childhood came rushing in on Royal as she stood on the steps of her home. Here, the war had not intruded. The grass was clipped, the box hedges had been trimmed, and the green shutters had been recently painted. Apparently Alba and Tobias had not neglected the house and grounds.

She paused to breathe in the aroma of the fragrant flower garden and gazed up at her father's mulberry tree. Yes, everything was as it should be. Apparently only she had changed.

She could have opened the door and gone inside, but she did not wish to startle Alba and Tobias, so she rapped on the door and waited for an answer. When there was no response, she rapped again. Soon she was rewarded when the door swung open and Tobias stood there, looking at her curiously.

"Yes, ma'am, what can—" He stared at her long and hard, then a wide grin creased his face. "Miss Royal, is it you? Glory be, it *is* you!"

She extended her hand to him. "I'm grateful that you recognize me, Tobias. I would not have wanted to come home as a stranger."

He stepped back to allow her entrance. "I'd know you anywhere, Miss Royal. We didn't know you were coming, or we would have had the house made ready for you." His smile widened. "We have been waiting for this day."

Looking around the entry, Royal could see into the front sitting room, where the dust covers were still draped over the furniture. "Where's Alba?" she asked.

Tobias beamed down at her. "She's out in the kitchen, most likely preparing lunch. I'll just go call her. She's gonna be so delighted."

"Who have we here?" Alba herself asked, moving into the entryway. "I didn't know we had a visitor." She looked at Royal searchingly.

"Don't you recognize her, Alba?" Tobias asked, enjoying his wife's confusion.

Alba came closer and squinted at Royal. "My eyes aren't what they used to be."

"It's me, Royal."

Suddenly there was joy in Alba's expression. "Miss Royal . . . it can't be you!"

"I've come home, Alba."

"What a glorious day this is!" the housekeeper cried. "We've been waiting for you."

Royal clasped the woman's hand and looked around her. She was surrounded by dear and familiar things. "It's good to be home," she said.

Alba was reminded of her duties, and she moved to the stairs. But Tobias saw a new spring to her step and heard a happy lilt to her voice as she directed him to the door.

"Don't stand there, Tobias. Get Miss Royal's belongings. Now that the young mistress is home, we have work to do." She beamed at Royal. "You have the look of your beautiful mother about you. You must be famished after your voyage," she chattered. "Are you thirsty? Come upstairs, and I'll help get you settled. The rest of the house is closed, but I always kept your room in readiness—aired it every week, and put beeswax on the furniture twice a year."

Royal untied her bonnet and allowed Alba to babble on, thinking how good it was to be home. As she followed the housekeeper upstairs, she could not help remembering that the last time she had come down these stairs she had been a child. Now she ascended them as a woman.

It was late in the evening when the messenger came from the British commander, Colonel Campbell.

> I regret to inform you that His Grace, the fifteenth Duke of Chiswick, has died in a hunting accident. It is my belief that you should act in all haste to find Lord Preston, as he is now the Duke of Chiswick. I fear that if his captors are privy to this information, they may use it to their advantage. Again, I stand ready to help you in any way I can. My man is still at your disposal should you need a driver.
>
> I remain your servant,
> Colonel Archibald Campbell

Sadness lay heavy on Royal's heart as she moved to the open fireplace. It would not be wise for the letter to fall into the wrong hands, so she dropped it into the flames and watched it burn.

She had not known Preston's brother, Nathan, very well, but she grieved for Alissa and her mother's pain. Colonel Campbell was right; she had to proceed with all haste. More than ever, Preston's life might depend upon her actions.

Outside Charles Town, South Carolina

The encampment was coming to life in the early morning light. Guards had been posted every fifty paces, and they were alert to any movement that might announce the enemy.

Inside a tent, several men were bent over a map, studying the fine details.

"We may as well swallow our pride and admit that Georgia is under the British heel," one of the officers observed bitterly.

Damon nodded. "You are voicing what we all know to be true, Major Leaman. We can do no more than strike at the enemy and then withdraw to lick our wounds."

"If only Congress would send us a commander," Major Leaman complained. "General Washington can be of no assistance to us because he can't abandon the northern campaign and allow our sister states to fall to the British forces."

Damon drew a circle on the map. "It is becoming apparent to us all that England has brought her war to the South. We can do little without sea power. It is only to be hoped that the enemy has overestimated the loyalty they think they will find in the southern states."

The men exchanged glances and nodded in agreement. "It's hard to know who to trust these days," one of the officers admitted.

"Then it's best," Damon said, "to trust no one. These are hard times when one cannot always tell the loyalties of his closest neighbor. We have all seen this, so guard your tongues. Seek out your regiments and have them ready to move on a moment's notice."

The men murmured in accord and withdrew.

Damon moved to his cot and lay down, watching the wind make waves overhead in the heavy tent. Last night his troops had clashed with hostile forces, and they had been outgunned and outnumbered. As a result, they had sustained heavy losses. He was weary and heartsick, but he had to pull his troops together and be ready for another assault within the week.

He had not heard Major Leaman enter and looked up only when his friend cleared his throat.

A light of mischief danced in Leaman's eyes. "A rider delivered a message for you." He held the note to his nose and sniffed. "Smells like it's from a . . . lady."

Damon sat up and motioned him forward. He held his breath as he took the note, hoping it was from her—his mystery lady. "You may go, Major," he said, reminding his friend that he outranked him.

The major laughed, and Damon waited impatiently for him to withdraw. Only when the tent flap closed behind the man did Damon break the seal. The unsigned letter simply said:

> I will be calling on you at your quarters in Charles Town tonight at eight. Please do not disappoint me.

It was from her—he was sure of it.

He did not stop to question how she knew where to locate him—all that mattered was that she had. He had cursed his stupidity in allowing her to get away from him without ensuring that he could find her again. He had been to the inn where his driver had delivered her, but she had already gone, and no one knew where.

Damon had been unable to get her out of his mind—the sweet smell of her, the way she felt in his arms, the way her blue eyes had glowed as he stroked her satiny skin. Nothing mattered but that he see her tonight.

A heavy rain pelted against the window, and Damon paced the floor of his cottage, fearing she would not come because of the storm. Again he checked the clock and saw it was almost eight. Suppose she was only playing with him and had no intention of coming?

Damn her, he thought. She was making him behave like a

schoolboy with his first love, and she hardly out of the schoolroom herself.

He moved to the window and pulled the curtain aside. The downpour had intensified, and now the wind peppered it against the window. No, he thought in agony, she would not come tonight.

In the pouring rain, Royal ran to the door of the cottage and beat against it, hoping Damon would be there. She had convinced herself that he would never want to see her again—not after her disgraceful behavior at their last meeting.

When the door opened, Damon took her arm and pulled her inside. "Come where it's warm," he ordered, leading her to the fireplace.

She turned to face him, wondering if he could hear her pounding heart. He seemed so aloof—his eyes were cold and unfeeling. Was he angry with her?

She was covered by her cloak and hood, and all Damon could see of her was the face that had haunted his dreams and tormented his waking moments. When she reached up to lower her hood, he caught her hand.

"Wait, is your hair powdered?"

She looked at him with a quizzical expression on her face. "No, of course not. I didn't think it would be wise since it's raining."

"Then allow me to guess your hair color. It is a mystery that has caused me no end of speculation in the past few days."

"All right."

He stepped closer and studied her face. "Your hair could be black, but I do not think so with your coloring."

"My hair is not black."

"I thought not. You could be a redhead, but again you do not have the coloring."

She shook her head.

Every move she made was naturally provocative and enticing.

It was all he could do to keep from taking her in his arms and smothering her sensuous lips with kisses. "It seems to me that we are left with two choices, so I must reason this out. I have always been partial to blondes, but I will discount that in your case, for I cannot see you as a blonde."

She was amused. "Then what color hair do you see for me?"

"Brown. Yes, you are definitely a brunette. On the lighter side of brown, I would say."

She reached up to her hood, but again he stayed her hand. "This is my fantasy. Let me be the one to unveil your hair."

Slowly he pushed the hood aside, and her hair spilled down her back, catching the reflection of the fire. He could only stare at her. "Golden," he said in an awed voice. "I should have guessed you would be perfect in every way."

She gave him a shy smile. "I have never before been accused of being perfect, though I am pleased my hair finds favor with you." She pretended to pout. "But do I have many rivals with blond hair?"

He gently touched her golden curls, then let his fingers tangle in the silkiness. "I cannot imagine you having a rival anywhere in this world, or any other."

"You flatter me."

His eyelids fell to half mast. "Do I?"

"I am not accustomed to having men speak so boldly."

"Are you not? Your actions say otherwise, fair lady. You have led me to believe love is a game to you, a game you play very well."

"Actions are often deceiving, Colonel. But surely you do not need me to tell you that."

"After the other night, I am inclined to agree with you. At times you seem innocent, and at other times you appear well versed in how to please a man. I wonder which face is the true one?"

A pretty blush touched her cheeks, and Royal averted her eyes. "I beg you to forget my behavior on that night. I was unaccustomed to strong spirits, and I acted most unwisely. I can only ask you to forgive me."

He propped a booted foot on the iron gate of the fireplace.

"There is nothing to forgive. I was rather charmed by you that night."

"Colonel . . . Damon, I want to drop all pretense and tell you the truth."

"So, I am to know who you are at last?"

"Yes, but you might be angry and ask me to leave when you know the truth."

His brows came together in a frown. "Am I about to learn that you are married?"

She looked into his eyes. "No, I am not married. You see, I need something that only you can give me."

His laughter was soft. "Perhaps you overestimate my prowess with women."

"Damon, I want no more pretense between us. Can you not hear me out?"

He touched her hair and trailed his hand across her cheek as excitement throbbed through his body. "Can we not talk later?" His lips touched her brow, then dipped down to test her trembling mouth. "I have thought of little else but you for days. You came unbidden to me in the daylight and disturbed my sleep at night." He smiled in anticipation. "For this you must pay the price."

Her heart was so filled with love for him that she could hardly speak. "If I allow this to continue, you will only hate me for it later," she warned.

His eyes softened. "Hate is the farthest emotion from my mind when I am near you like this. Don't you know that I have been in torment since I met you?" he asked gruffly. "Don't you know what you have done to me?"

It seemed so natural to lay her head against his shoulder. It was as if she belonged in his arms. A flood of tenderness swept through her, leaving her breathless. What harm would it do to draw on his strength for a moment longer, to feel as if nothing in this unsettled world could touch her?

His arms tightened about her and she sighed contentedly. Soon she would tell him who she was, but not just now.

Gently his hand moved up her arm and he lifted her chin so

he could observe her expression. "I'm mystified and intrigued by you." He laced his finger through the ribbon at the neck of her gown, and with a quick tug it came undone. When she did not move to stop him, he slowly pushed the gown aside so it exposed one creamy shoulder. She watched spellbound while he lowered his dark head to press his lips against the hollow there. "I cannot forget how you felt in my arms the other night," he whispered against her skin. "Do you remember also?"

At first she could not find her voice—she was too aware of his hard, lean body and the hunger in his gaze. Her voice came out in a throaty whisper. "I want you to always remember me."

A smile played on his lips. "It's up to you to decide how much I'll have to remember." He bent to kiss her eyelids. "I believe we can beget beautiful memories together."

His nearness was intoxicating. His words swept through her mind with a wildness that summoned her total surrender. In a last futile effort to save herself she blurted out, "I came here only to talk to you. I did not intend to—"

"Shh," he whispered, once more drawing her against his body. He closed his eyes, wishing he could absorb her into his skin. There was no doubt that she had bewitched him, but what did it matter? Everything had ceased to exist for him but the passionately beautiful woman he held in his arms. His longing heightened—he had to have her, all of her. When he felt her tremble with an answering longing, his arms tightened about her. She was so fragile and delicate that he wanted to precede slowly so he wouldn't frighten her with the untamed passion that raged through his body.

"You look at me with the eyes of a stranger," she said regretfully.

"Yet, not strangers," he said, not understanding her meaning. His mouth trailed down her cheek to her lips. "I have been in torment to taste your kiss again."

Royal gave herself over to the burning lips that drained any resistance she might have had. She felt light-headed, her heart pounding with hot blood that surged through her veins, and her body responded to his urgent desire.

Suddenly a moment of sanity returned. Royal moved out of his embrace and retreated quickly toward the door, all the while pulling her gown back in place. "I did not come here for this," she said with a quiver in her voice that belied her words.

"By your actions last night I find that hard to fathom. I know what you were feeling because I felt it, too. You cannot deny that if we had not been interrupted I would have been your conquest."

"Damon, you don't understand."

He moved to stand over her, and a thread of amusement laced his words. "Then perhaps you will explain it to me."

With shaking fingers she fumbled with the ribbon at her neck, trying to refasten it while he watched her.

At last he grasped her hand, raised it to his lips, and placed a burning kiss on the palm. "I have wearied of this game. Your words may deny that you want me, but your actions say otherwise." He pulled her stiff body against his and heard her sudden intake of breath. "Can you deny that you want me to touch you? That indeed you came here this evening hoping it would happen?"

She raised her eyes to him, unable to deny the truth. Oh, yes, she wanted him to touch her, to hold her, to have him tell her that she was beautiful and desirable.

He cupped her face and pressed a kiss on the tip of her upturned nose. "I am not afraid to admit I desire you and that all I can think about is the blue of your eyes and the softness of your body."

Royal knew she had allowed the situation to go beyond her control. What had started out as harmless teasing had become a dangerous circumstance. She had to gain control over her emotions. "Please, don't touch me anymore. I must talk to you."

"You are the most maddening woman I have ever met." He raised his hands as if to surrender. "You do insist on conversation at the most inopportune moments."

She moved to the fire, turning her back to him. "I have a confession to make, one that I fear will make you most unhappy with me."

With an impatient intake of breath, Damon studied the shadow of her profile reflected on the brick fireplace. "I'm always uncomfortable when a woman wants to bare her soul to me. I feel duty bound to point out that I am ill suited to the role of father confessor."

Slowly she turned to look into his eyes. "I do not need a father confessor. I need a champion."

"You are mistaken if you have cast me as your champion, since you are obviously English." He gestured for her to come closer. "It is a far different role I envisioned for myself in regard to you."

Reluctantly she moved forward until she stood beside him. "I need your help most desperately."

"Let me see if I understand this aright—you wish to strike a bargain with me? You want something from me and are willing to do whatever it takes to obtain it?"

She avoided his gaze. "I'll do whatever it takes to enlist your help," she admitted.

He grabbed her wrists, holding them in a firm grip. "Damn you! I make no bargain with you for what I could have with so little effort on my part. Do you think I don't know when a woman is ripe for the taking?" His eyes flashed with the intensity of a golden flame.

Before she could voice a protest, Damon's lips ground against hers with bruising force, muffling any objections she would have uttered. She tried to breathe, to push him away, but he held her fast. She thought her lungs would burst from want of air as his all-consuming kiss trapped the breath in her body. She twisted her head and tried to wrench free, but he held her in an unrelenting grip.

When Royal thought she could stand it no longer, he gentled his kiss. A mind-destroying flame moved through her body as his hands slid up her rib cage to cup her breasts while he rained kisses on her upturned face. All the fight drained out of her, and she gave herself willingly to the sensuous feelings he invoked.

"This," he whispered in her ear, "is what was meant to happen between us."

"No. It's wrong."

"No, not wrong," he murmured against her parted lips. "This was destined to happen." He raised his head and studied her with golden intensity. "At our first meeting I knew we would be together like this. So did you."

A sob broke from deep inside her, and she leaned her head against his shoulder. "You are mistaken, Damon. At our very first meeting, you never thought of me in this way."

"You are playing games again."

"No, no more games. I should never have allowed it to go this far."

He made no reply as his gaze moved slowly over her features. No memory stirred in his mind. He was certain they had never met before. Why did she keep insisting that he should know her? he wondered in irritation.

"Damon," she cried from the depths of her soul, "don't you know me?" She pulled away from him. "Search your mind. You must remember!"

He held her at arm's length. "No, damn it! I don't know you! Do you think I would ever forget you if we had met before?"

She shook her head sadly. "You once promised you would not forget me, but apparently you have. In the past four years I lived each day hoping for a letter from you, but you never wrote me—not once."

Damon felt as if he had been hit by a thunderbolt as memories stirred to life within his head. He swallowed hard and shook his head in disbelief, while he examined each lovely detail of her face with new awareness.

"My God!" he said, taking a hasty step backward. "Royal Bradford!"

Damon's eyes burned with unleashed rage. "How dare you do this! Do you know me so little that you think I would ravish a child?"

He turned away from her and moved to stand at the window, staring out sightlessly. "When I think about what I did the other night"—he shook his head—"when I think about what could have happened between us—"

He was having difficulty accepting that the woman who had so obsessed him was the same sorrowful child who had been placed under his protection. He closed his eyes and with extraordinary strength tried to forget her sweetly curved body. He must forget how he had almost lost his head. Thank God they had been interrupted, or he might have—

After a moment of gathering his thoughts, he turned back to

Royal. "What is the meaning of your actions, young lady?" he demanded furiously, every inch the outraged guardian.

Royal took a tentative step toward him. "First of all, you have already noticed that I am no longer a child. I grew up while you weren't paying attention, Damon. I've been grown up for a long time, but you didn't care."

"You are a child to me, Royal."

"You didn't feel that way the other night," she reminded him. "Or even a moment ago."

"I am trying to put that out of my mind." His voice came out in a groan of despair. "I can't imagine what possessed you to behave in such an outrageous manner. Did they teach you nothing at that fancy London school?"

"You sent me there and forgot about me." Four years of bitterness laced her words. "You never gave a thought to whether I was lonely, or that I might be homesick. You never answered my letters."

He looked at her with impatient irony. "That's absurd! As I recall, I made certain you had everything you wanted. I denied you nothing. How could you say I had forgotten you?"

"Yes, you denied me nothing, but it was my father's money that allowed me to live so well. It was no sacrifice to you and not of your doing. Mr. Bartholomew was more my guardian than you were."

He lowered his eyes. "As you say, it was no sacrifice to me."

Royal had not wanted to quarrel with Damon. She realized with a feeling of desperation that he was drawing away from her. She wanted him to look at her the way he had the other night, but he never would again. She was certain that because of her foolish actions she now disgusted him.

He was still seeking answers. "Why did you come to me playing games, Royal? What possessed you to behave in such a wanton manner?" His eyes hardened. "I can only hope this is not your usual practice with men."

She tossed her head defiantly and glared at him. "Of course I never acted with any other man the way I did with you," she said scornfully. "Surely you can't have such a low opinion of me?"

"I have always had a high opinion of you. It would seem it was you who held yourself in contempt. Otherwise how could you have behaved so brazenly?"

Every word he spoke was like a dagger in her heart. "It was not my intention to deceive you at first, but when you didn't know me, I merely followed your lead. I admit that what I did was unconventional, but I was desperate, Damon."

"You said there was something you wanted of me. This would be a good time to tell me what it is."

Anxiety clouded her eyes. "After I had enlisted your aid, it was my intention to return to England and never see you again. But tonight I knew I had to tell you the truth. No matter what you think of me, Damon, a lie does not come easily to my lips. Especially to someone I hold in such high regard."

"Did it occur to you simply to ask for my help? Have I ever denied you anything?"

Now her face reddened with shame. "I know that is what I should have done. I'll ask you now. Will you use your influence to gain the release of a man—an Englishman—who has been taken prisoner?"

His eyes burned into hers. "So, it was as I guessed. It was for a lover that you sought me out."

She put out her hand in a beseeching manner and then let it drop to her side. "I had to come to you, Damon. There was no one else who could help me."

Anger splintered inside him that she would use him to help another man. "What is this man to you?" he demanded harshly.

"He . . . I care a great deal for him. He asked me to marry him."

For a long moment silence hung heavy in the room while Royal and Damon stared at one another. She was the first to lower her eyes.

"Will you help me, Damon?" She took a step toward him. "I am desperate."

A strange depression settled on his shoulders, and he went to the window and watched the rain trail down the glass. "I sent you away an American, and you come back to me with the voice and actions of my enemies." He turned back to her and found her standing just behind him. "What possessed you to think I would help you free an Englishman? Do you ask me to turn away from everything I believe?"

Royal reached out to touch him, but he moved away. "I suppose I never thought what it would mean to you. And for that, I'm sorry."

"Yet you still ask it of me?"

"Damon, no one but you can help me. I hoped you would do this out of . . . because you have always given me what I . . . you have always taken care of me."

"I see. You have cast me as your father. How fortunate for me."

"No, you have never been like a father to me. But it has always been a comfort to me to know that you stood between me and harm. I could feel your presence, even in England. You were all I had left."

"You had your aunt Arabella," he reminded her, understanding for the first time how lonely she must have been.

"Yes, but she had her life in France. She's married now and lives in Rome."

He read the hurt in her eyes. "I don't know what you think I can do to help. Even *I* would be hard-pressed to obtain the release of an enemy."

She touched his sleeve imploringly. She hated herself for asking him to turn against his principles to help Preston, but she had no alternative. "But you can do it, Damon—I know you can!"

He shook her hand off. "Your faith may be misplaced, Royal. And understand this, I will not go against my country for anyone, not even you."

"Perhaps you could arrange a prisoner exchange," she pleaded. "Lord Preston is not without importance to England. His family wants him back."

"Lord Preston?"

"Preston Seaton, if you will." She dared not tell even Damon that Preston was now the duke of Chiswick.

"What was he doing here?"

"He didn't take me into his confidence, but he was on a diplomatic mission."

"Do you have any of the particulars as to how and where he was captured?"

"I am told by Colonel Campbell, the British commander in Savannah, that Preston was captured near Savannah in early October."

"So you know Campbell, the man who has devastated Savannah." There was accusation in his voice. "Does it not anger you that enemy soldiers walk the streets of Savannah? Are your loyalties so easily won and lost?"

She was hurt by his words, but she could see why he would think her frivolous in her fidelity. "I am loyal to my friends, Damon. If pressed, I would be loyal to you." There was bewilderment in her expression. "If you, or anyone, can tell me whom to believe in, I'll fall in line behind you. I lived in London, where I heard only the British views on what they call the 'rebellion.' I come here, and I am asked to be loyal to the country of my birth, and you refer to the war as a 'revolution.' Who am I to believe? Which is right, rebellion or revolution?"

Unwillingly his eyes moved down her throbbing throat, and he watched the way her breasts rose and fell with her passionate speech. Her eyes were bright, her head held at a proud angle. He was beginning to see her confusion, and he was partly to blame for it. He had left her to her English friends, so how could she be expected to blindly follow the convictions of many of her countrymen?

She had come to him because she thought he would help her, and he had not the heart to turn away from her. Too many people had abandoned her in her short life. Even her aunt Arabella, who had professed to care about the girl's welfare, had apparently neglected her, as he had suspected she would.

"I'll see what I can find out for you," he told her at last. "But don't expect anything to come of my inquiries. If this man is a prisoner, I will have very little influence over his jailers."

Hope flamed in her eyes. "All I ask is that you find him for me."

Damon wanted to take her by the shoulders and shake her until she begged for mercy. He wanted to erase from her mind the memory of this Englishman for whom she had dared so much. He hated himself for asking, but he had to know. "Have you been intimate with this Preston Seaton?"

Her head snapped up, and she turned on him with a vengeance. "How could you suggest such an outrage? Preston would never touch me in that way. Don't mistake my behavior with you as a chink in my armor—I would never have allowed any other man the liberties I allowed you!"

He frowned, trying to understand her meaning. "Am I to feel honored because you chose *me* to torment?"

In a quick motion she came forward, making her golden hair swirl out about her. "Be outraged with me, Damon, even punish me, condemn my actions if you want to, but help me!"

He resisted the urge to reach out and touch her hair, to caress it between his fingers, to raise it to his lips. "I will see what I can do," he said, standing stiffly beside her.

"You will not regret this, Damon."

"I already regret it." He rubbed his forehead, and she noticed the tired lines beneath his eyes. She realized for the first time how much he was suffering because of this war. "If you will just locate Preston for me, I will ask nothing more of you. You have my promise that I never intend to be a burden to you again."

"You forget, Royal, that until you are married, you are very much my burden."

"I release you from that responsibility."

"You don't have that right, and I am bound by my commitment to your dead father. The question is, what do I do with you now? I cannot send you to Swanhouse."

"I will return to my own home in Savannah and await word from you."

"Am I to take it that the enemy knows that you have enlisted my help?"

"Of course not!" she said with indignation. "I would never tell them your name, any more than I would betray them to you."

She thought she saw pain in his eyes, but surely she was mistaken.

"You are in the enviable position, Royal, of sitting on a fence. You need lean neither this way nor that, but smile on both sides and admonish us when we do not conform to the image of what you think we should be. I wonder if you will always be safe on your fence, or if, one day, you will be called upon to make a choice?"

"Sitting on the fence, as you put it, does not come without its pain. It is agony to see the right and wrong on both sides. As for choosing sides, I will soon leave Savannah forever, but I will leave without ever having sacrificed my principles."

"Principles are not a luxury we can all afford. War is reality, Royal. Men are spilling their blood for something they believe in. We Americans have paid a high cost."

"Even if I am only a woman, I can still understand being willing to die for something I believe in."

"What you believe in is this Englishman you want me to find for you," he said scornfully.

"Yes, I do believe in Preston."

At that moment she was more child than woman, and Damon could see that she was deeply affected by what was happening to her. "I assume you have a pass to get through the British lines," he said, watching her closely.

She studied the floor. "Yes," she admitted, "signed by Colonel Campbell."

His expression did not change. "How are you able to get through our lines?"

She looked embarrassed. "I have a forged pass that Colonel Campbell gave me."

He drew in a heavy breath. "I see. It's dangerous work you do. Beware, Royal, that life does not ask more of you than you can give," he said, moving to the door. "I must leave you now. I'll get word to you if I locate your Preston Seaton."

Her hand went out to him, but he had already reached the door. Without another word to her, he pulled his tricorn over his forehead and disappeared into the rain.

Royal stood for a long moment at the window. "I have already been asked to give more than I can, Damon," she said to the empty room. "By asking you to help an Englishman, I have hurt you, and in so doing, hurt myself."

Would Damon ever forgive her for what she had done to him? Would he ever look at her with respect?

Royal stood before Oliver Greenburg with a disbelieving frown on her face. "You were my father's lawyer, and you say there is no money left in his estate, yet you cannot, or will not, tell me where the money has gone?"

"I am not at liberty to tell you that, Mistress Bradford."

She shook her head. "I've never given the slightest thought to finances. It didn't occur to me that the money would run out."

Oliver Greenburg realized that Damon Routhland had not told Mistress Bradford that her father had left her penniless. If that was what her guardian wanted her to think, he would keep his own counsel.

"If you have questions concerning your estate, Mistress Bradford, you should ask your guardian. I am certain he will tell you the right of it."

Royal left the lawyer's office in shock. If there was no money left, why hadn't Damon informed her?

When she arrived home she went to her room and counted out her money. She had less than twelve pounds. That would hardly pay the butcher.

What was she to do?

Damon had used every means at his disposal to find Lord Preston Seaton. But so far he had not met with success. If the Englishman was a prisoner, he had either been transported north or was using an assumed name. In either instance it was not likely that Damon would locate him.

He had one last possibility to explore; he would have to slip past enemy lines and face a man who had neither scruples nor patriotism. He would go to the camp of a renegade group of cutthroats operating in Georgia and the Carolinas. Although they claimed to support the cause of liberty, often as not they preyed upon their own countrymen as well as the British.

The renegades were led by Vincent Murdock, a notorious bandit. He and his men would strike and disappear into the swamps, and thus far no one had been able to flush them out. Murdock was noted for his brutality. If Seaton had fallen into those murdering hands, God help him!

Damon slid a knife down the side of his knee-length moccasin. Since he would be traveling through British-held territory, he had abandoned his uniform in favor of more suitable buckskin trousers and shirt. He knew if he were captured out of uniform, the English would shoot him as a spy, but that was a chance he must take.

Before he sought out Murdock, he must make certain that Royal was safely in her house under the watchful eyes of Alba and Tobias. There were many English soldiers on the streets of Savannah, so he would have to go to her under the cover of night.

Royal watched the housekeeper polish the copper teakettle. "How did Damon handle the household bills, Alba?" she asked at last.

"We were told to make whatever purchases we needed from Masterson's Store and that the bills would be sent to John Bartholomew."

"It would seem that there is no more money, and that account has been closed."

"The shopkeeper is a Loyalist. I've long expected him to turn away from anyone who doesn't support the king. I suspect he learned that Tobias and I didn't share his love of King George."

"That's not all, Alba. I went to see Mr. Greenburg today because I needed money, and he told me there was none. I don't understand what happened to all the money."

Alba pretended to concentrate on the kettle and rubbed it vigorously. "I'm sure I don't know about such things, Miss Royal. But perhaps the attorney was the wrong person to ask. You should ask Mr. Bartholomew when next you see him, or Mr. Routhland himself."

Royal drew in a deep breath. "I wonder why Damon didn't tell me there is no money left in the estate?"

"Surely you aren't suggesting that Mr. Routhland has done anything wrong in managing your affairs?" Alba questioned, wanting to defend the man she had come to respect.

"No, I would never think that. It must be because of the war."

Alba turned back to her task, thinking Royal should go down on her knees and thank the good Lord that Damon Routhland had seen fit to take her as his ward. It was only because of Mr. Routhland's generosity that they had managed to maintain this house.

Although Mr. Routhland had sworn her and Tobias to secrecy, she wanted desperately to tell Royal that he had even paid them the legacy that Mr. Bradford had left them in his will. Mr. Routhland was an honorable man, and Alba had come to look on him as a true gentleman.

Alba bit back her vexation, knowing she must honor Mr. Routhland's wish for secrecy. Royal would never learn the truth from her lips.

Royal had been at the cemetery, placing flowers on her parents' graves, and had not realized night was falling until she glanced at the blood red sunset. The cobblestone streets were deserted as she hurried home.

Not wanting to enter the house just yet, she made her way to the flower garden at the back of the house. Sadness lay like a weight on her shoulders. Now that there was no money, she was concerned about keeping her house. She had already asked so much of Damon, she dared not ask more.

Tears of despair fell down her cheeks, and she quickly brushed them away. Thinking she was alone, Royal was startled when a deep voice spoke to her from the shadows, quoting a love sonnet: "Alas, sweet maiden, a tear from your eyes would fill an ocean in my heart."

She knew it was Damon even before she turned around. When she saw he was dressed in buckskin, she could only stare. "I . . . thought I . . . was alone," she stammered.

He moved to her side and was looking at her with a soft expression. "Shall I leave, then, Royal?"

She glanced around, fearing someone would see him. "Are you crazed to come here like this? How did you get through the British lines?"

He smiled at her with irony. "I have a pass forged with your Colonel Campbell's signature."

Royal looked at him hopefully. "Why have you come? Do you have word of Preston?"

Damon's lips tightened. "No, I was merely doing my duty by making certain that my ward had come to no harm. With you, I can never be sure." There was a slight smile on his lips that took the sting out of his words.

He wore his long dark hair loose, and Royal resisted the urge to push aside the lock that fell across his forehead. "I am much safer here than you are," she pointed out. "You must go at once."

Damon glanced up at the darkening sky. "How are you faring?"

"My health is good." She moved away from him, somehow disturbed by the warm glow in his eyes. "I paid a visit to Mr. Greenburg today."

Damon seemed to stiffen. "Oh?"

She moved down the path, aware that he followed her. "He has told me that I have no money left." She turned to face Damon. "Can you explain that?"

"What would you have me explain?"

"I was wondering about the investments my father made—how could the money be gone?"

He stepped closer to her and tilted her chin up so she was forced to meet his eyes. "Do I hear an accusation in your voice?"

"No, of course not, but you once told me that I need never worry about money." She blinked her eyes. "If the war has wiped out the inheritance, I need to know."

"Do you think I mismanaged your money, Royal?"

"I would never believe that of you. If anyone is to blame, it's me. I regret that I squandered large sums on clothing, never thinking about the consequences. Now I worry about Alba and Tobias's future, and I'm afraid I won't be able to maintain the house."

Damon was silent for a long moment. "Have no worry, Royal, you are still in possession of a sizable fortune. Had you not come back to Savannah, you would have been able to draw on money in England."

She felt embarrassed to talk about finances with him. Already he had done so much for her. "I didn't want to trouble you, and that's why I went to see Mr. Greenburg. He was certain there was nothing left."

"The attorney would not be in a position to know about your finances, since I handle them myself," Damon bit out. "Only John Bartholomew can help you. Somehow I will send word that he is to see to your needs. I apologize for not doing so before now, but you see, I can't go home. You may not know Swanhouse is being watched by your friends, the British. They would consider it a great feat to take me prisoner."

She placed her hand on his arm. "And yet you put yourself in danger to see me?"

He hesitated for a moment. "There is little danger unless you are expecting Colonel Campbell for dinner."

"Please be careful, Damon, and don't make light of the peril." There was an earnest light in her eyes. "I'm sorry I had to speak to you about money. I suppose I am not accustomed to making decisions on my own, because for so long you have made them for me."

"As you have said, it was John who always took care of your needs. Did you not feel worry free in England?"

"Yes, there was never a time when I worried about my future, and I know I have you to thank for that."

She turned away and watched as the now purple sky darkened even more. "I have been doing a lot of thinking since last we spoke. It is most difficult to be lost between two worlds and to belong to neither of them." She spun around and faced him. "Do you know what it feels like to be me?"

"I am beginning to see how deeply this is affecting you. Perhaps I should never have sent you to England."

"You did what you thought was right. I have known that for some time. You have long been a man I admire."

Suddenly his eyes ran down her face to her neck, and she knew he was remembering what had happened between the two of them at his cottage.

"You give me too much credit, Royal, for I am just a man like any other. When I am tempted by a beautiful woman, I often succumb, as would any man under like circumstances."

She managed a shy smile. "Is this in the way of an apology?"

"It is. I ask that you forgive my behavior on our first meeting."

"It was my fault."

"Yes, it was, but nonetheless I ask that you put it out of your mind." He gripped her shoulders. "And never behave with any man as you did with me—is that understood?"

"I understand," she whispered, wishing she could lay her head against his broad shoulder and have him hold her.

Damon released her and stepped back into the shadows. "I do not know when I shall see you again. Tell no one that I was here."

"I will never betray you," she whispered. But already the shadows were deepening, and he had disappeared among them. She stood for a long time, staring into the night, feeling as if she had hurt Damon in some way.

Damon had ridden all night to reach the swamps where he suspected Vincent Murdock made his encampment. Just through the trees, he saw smoke rise from several campfires, and he knew he had come to the right place.

Dismounting, he removed his rifle from his saddle holster and moved cautiously toward the marshes, aware that the renegades would have posted lookouts and more than likely had been alerted to his presence.

This land was as familiar to him as his own, because as a boy he had hunted every inch of these swamps. He knew where to find fresh water, as well as the quicksand beds and other places to avoid, like those that were stagnant with poison gasses.

A twig snapped behind him, and he spun around just as a man dropped out of a moss-laden cypress tree. Damon aimed his rifle at him. "Take me to Murdock at once."

The man, who was unkempt and dressed in filthy buckskin, only shrugged. "I don't know no one by that name. I'm just a poor farmer, took to the swamps to put meat on my family's table."

Damon shouldered his rifle. "My name is Colonel Damon Routhland, and I have come to discuss an important matter with Murdock."

The man stared into cold golden eyes and quickly relented. He held out his hand for Damon's rifle. "If you aim to be taken to our encampment, you'll have to give me your gun."

Damon handed him the rifle. "Lead the way."

The man scratched his scraggly beard and looked Damon over suspiciously. "Well, if'n you're who you say you are, why ain't you in uniform?"

"For the obvious reason. Loyalist troops are swarming all over this valley. I could hardly leave my calling card."

"I reckon you be right. And I reckon there'll be someone in camp who will know if you are who you say you are." The man jabbed the rifle into Damon's back, motioning for him to walk ahead.

Damon's moccasins sank into the mire as he moved forward. A lone birdcall echoed from deep within the swamp, but all else was strangely silent and eerie. They soon stepped onto a well-worn path, and just ahead Damon could see a clearing. Suddenly they were surrounded by men clad in buckskin, all looking at Damon with malignant eyes and pointing muskets at him.

Damon glanced around the camp with distaste. There were scantily clad, dirty children, playing near reed huts. Several women with matted hair and ragged gowns eyed him boldly. Ferocious dogs chained to trees lunged forward, baring their teeth at anyone who came near.

The man poked the rifle into Damon's ribs again and pushed him in the direction of a lean-to that had been constructed from unseasoned logs.

Damon turned to the man with anger blazing in his eyes. "Do that again, and by God, I'll break it over your head!"

The man merely nodded to a tall, heavyset man dressed in beaded buckskin and knee-high moccasins who had just come out of the lean-to to meet them. A pretty woman with long black hair stood at his shoulder, and a baby clung to her.

Damon looked into the man's serpentlike black eyes. Although Damon had never met him, he knew he faced Vincent Murdock himself.

For a moment the two men stood eye to eye, challenging each other. At last Murdock laughed. "Well, if it ain't the lord of Swan-house Plantation. To what do I owe the pleasure of your company?"

"I am glad you know who I am, because that saves a lot of time. I know you as a man with no loyalties."

The man merely smiled. "I have loyalties, although they are to myself first." He pointed a finger at Damon. "Everyone knows about you." He looked around at his men and said in a taunting voice, "I guess we could say we have here the most influential man in all Georgia, unless you want to count the British, who seem to be in control at the moment. Why do you suppose Colonel Damon Routhland would seek out the likes of us?"

Damon was aware of Murdock's enmity toward him, but he ignored it. "I am searching for someone, and I thought you might be able to help me."

"Now, why should I? I got no respect from your fancy army when I wanted to join, so why should I want to help you now?"

"Perhaps I'm wasting your time and mine. If you'll just have your man return my rifle, I'll be leaving."

Murdock's curiosity had been tapped, and Damon knew it. The man was not about to let him leave without discovering why he had come.

"No use your going off 'til you have eaten and drunk with us, Colonel. We are a neighborly group, aren't we, men?"

There was a lot of head shaking and murmuring from the grinning men.

Damon did not like this man. "I didn't come here to exchange pleasantries or to drink with you. I came in search of a man."

Murdock's eyes narrowed with distrust. "Who would that man be?"

"I seek one Preston Seaton—an Englishman."

Murdock's face became blank. "But, Colonel Routhland, if the man is an Englishman, isn't he your enemy? What would you want with him?"

"That's my affair. Have you seen him?" Damon pressed in a hard voice.

Murdock laughed jovially. "But of course I have seen him. He's my prisoner. You forgot to mention that he is a colonel in the British army. At least that's what the insignia on his red uniform implies."

Damon's eyes burned with the anger of betrayal. Royal had told him that Preston Seaton was on a diplomatic mission. Had she deliberately lied?

Suddenly he took notice that the men were forming a tight circle around him. "Is the Englishman here in your camp?" he demanded.

"But of course, Colonel Routhland. Where else would I take him?"

"I want to see him at once. Take me to him."

Murdock's eyes narrowed. "You might be able to order your men around, Colonel, but I'm in command here." He made a wide sweep with his hand. "I'm lord of this domain."

"Yes," Damon agreed bitingly, glancing around the swamp. "That would make you lord of lizards, owls, and snakes—an enviable command."

"Tread softly, Colonel," Murdock warned. "You are here only because I allow it."

"Take me to Preston Seaton," Damon insisted. "Now!"

A grudging light of respect came into Murdock's eyes. "I'll say one thing for you, Routhland, you got guts."

Murdock had heard that Damon Routhland was a man of commanding force, as fearless as he was legendary—and he had heard right. Vincent Murdock looked around at his battle-hardened men. Routhland might be a legend, but Murdock knew if he gave the word to his men that the colonel was not to leave these swamps alive, even a legend could die.

The two men stared at each other in understanding. "The Englishman?" Damon reminded him.

"Come with me," Murdock relented, "and I'll take you to see him, though he isn't much to look at with his fancy red uniform all torn and bloodstained."

Damon's senses were alert as he moved through the camp beside the renegade leader. He had counted twenty-three men, but of course, there could be more. How in the hell was he going to free Royal's Englishman if Murdock decided to hold on to him? For that matter, how was he going to leave?

Chapter 22

Although he knew it was futile, Preston pulled against the rusty chains that bound him to the moss-laden cypress tree. His wrists were raw, and he was tormented by insects that stung him day and night. This was a bug-infested hell, not fit for humans, he thought bitterly.

He had lost track of the length of time he had been a prisoner, but he had been there long enough to grow a beard. He glanced at his filthy red uniform and dreamed of bathing—of cool, clean water.

Preston tested his sore muscles. He had long ago lost hope of ever being rescued. If this man Murdock who held him prisoner was the measure of the American army, God help any Englishman who fell into their hands!

Murdock and his men had the manners of pigs, and they spoke

unintelligible English. Much of the time Preston could not understand them at all. And the food they fed him was unfit for human consumption. He ate it, though, because that was all there was. He thought it strange what a man would do to stay alive. He had always believed himself to be a civilized man, but he slept and ate like an animal.

He closed his eyes and tried to think of his family at Chiswick Castle. He envisioned green, rolling hills—he thought of Royal, with her honey-gold hair and beautiful blue eyes. How far away England seemed to him. He doubted he would ever leave these swamps alive.

He had been beaten several times because he'd refused to give the rabble the information they wanted. He had been too proud to admit to them that he had not been in the Colonies long enough to be privy to valuable information or secret plans. He had been sent merely to report conditions to the prime minister. And he would not tell them that he was not even in the army. He had merely been given an honorary rank by General Cornwallis, and it was of no great significance.

His only world was now a small island about twelve paces across, and it was surrounded by foul-smelling water. Yes, he had become an animal; his main thoughts were of staying alive.

He squinted his eyes toward his captors' camp when he heard muffled voices and the sound of footsteps coming in his direction. The only access to his little mound of dirt was the log that linked his island with the camp of the rebels. Now the log was dropped into place, and he saw Murdock and another man walking toward him.

His eyes burned with hatred as he looked at Murdock, the instrument of his torture. Apparently the man took sadistic pleasure in inflicting pain, and it didn't matter to him that his victim was helplessly chained. Lord Preston prayed for the chance to have that man in his power one day.

He looked past Murdock to a tall man he had never seen before. He surmised that the stranger must be one of the rebels because he was dressed in buckskin.

"Well, here's your man, Colonel Routhland. Not much to look at, is he?"

The Englishman was chained like an animal, and his red jacket was muddy and tattered. In spite of this, the man stared at Damon with insolence.

"You bastard!" Damon said, turning to Murdock. "How dare you keep a prisoner in such deplorable conditions! Release him at once."

Murdock's eyes snapped. "Not likely. This here's *my* prisoner. I will release him when and *if* I decide."

Preston blinked at the newcomer. Was it possible the man had come to help him?

Damon knelt down beside Preston and, taking a handful of hair, turned his face to the light. He frowned when he saw the bruises and lacerations on the prisoner's cheeks and his blackened eye that was swollen shut.

"This man has a fever and needs medical attention. If you don't release him at once, and something happens to him, I'll not stop until I see you punished."

Again Preston blinked. Was he ill? He hadn't known he had a fever.

"Now ain't that ambitious," Murdock stated in a taunting voice. "And who's going to help you do that? As far as this Englishman goes, he's just one of those lily-soft British officers who can't function out of a nice-smelling drawing room. If he's sick, it's because he's weak."

"I suggest you release him into my custody without delay. It will go hard with you if you don't. You know I have the means to run you into the ground, and make no mistake about it, I'll do it."

Murdock's laughter had an evil ring. "Now if I was you, Colonel Damon Routhland, I wouldn't go making any threats, being as how you are here alone."

"It is you who should be afraid, Murdock," Damon said, undaunted by the man's words.

"You see this key, Colonel Routhland?" Murdock jingled a key that was attached to a leather thong that hung around his neck.

"That's the key to the Englishman's chains, and no one but me can unchain him."

He poked a finger into Lord Preston's chest. "He was such a pretty boy when he fell into our hands, all dressed up in his bright red uniform." His eyes gleamed as he mocked the Englishman. "He's not so pretty now."

Preston strained against his chains to reach his tormentor.

"See how riled he gets, Colonel Routhland? I've taken a liking to him, though. It would grieve me fiercely if I lost him."

Damon dipped his handkerchief in a nearby pail of water and washed the caked mud from the poor wretch's face. He looked into questioning blue eyes, trying to see what there was in this man for Royal to love.

"We are not all animals," Damon told the Englishman. He took a dipper of water and held it to Preston's cracked lips. He leaned in closer and whispered, "Take heart. If possible, I'll be back tonight. Stay alert and watch for me."

Damon stood up, deciding to take another approach. "Will you take money for the release of your prisoner?"

Murdock grinned. "Now, I'd expect a man like you to think you could buy anything you want. But your money won't help you here, Colonel Routhland. My prisoner isn't for sale."

"Is that your last word?"

"Yep. I bent some in allowing you to see my prisoner at all. But my patience is spent, and I want you out of my camp right away—unless you want to join your friend here."

"You'll regret this day, Murdock," Damon informed him. "If the American army doesn't get you, the British are sure to blast you out of these swamps."

"Not likely." Murdock swaggered and danced across the log before turning to look at Damon. "No one is going to outsmart Vincent Murdock."

Damon's eyes grew cold, and the intensity of his golden glare made Murdock halt in his tracks. "If you don't remember this day, Murdock, I'll be back to remind you of it."

Damon crossed the log, forcing Murdock to scramble out of his way. "Expect my return," he warned, moving in the direction of his horse.

When Damon came to the guard who had taken his rifle, he jerked it from the man's hand and shoved him aside. No one made a move to stop him as he left the camp, mounted his horse, and rode away.

Preston rattled his chains, wondering who the man was who had just given him hope. He could not understand why an American colonel would want to help him. There had been something about the man that made Preston trust him. He had said he would be back tonight, and Preston believed he would.

The swamp was at it noisiest just after sundown. The continuous croaking of the frogs harmonized with the distant hooting of a tree owl.

Damon slipped into the swampy water and made his way silently toward Murdock's camp. Holding his rifle over his head, he moved closer to the ring of light from the campfires and watched silently.

There seemed to be a festive mood among Murdock's followers because the men were drinking and he could hear their loud voices raised in song. The women moved among the men, rubbing against them and making suggestive remarks. Damon waited, knowing he could do nothing until the camp slept. He watched the changing of the lookouts and took notice of their positions.

It was to Damon's advantage that Murdock would not expect him to return by way of the quagmire. Damon had spent two of the most uncomfortable hours he had ever known waist deep in swamp water. Mosquitoes were buzzing and pestering him, and at one point a water moccasin slithered right past his hand.

Around midnight the camp grew quiet, and Damon moved forward cautiously. Slowly he inched out of the swamp, ducking behind trees, his gaze on the lean-to where he knew he would find his prey.

At last he stood over Murdock, who had one of the women in

his bed. They both appeared to be sound asleep. Quietly he bent down and felt around Murdock's neck until he found the leather thong. Cautiously he cut the thong and grasped the key in his hand.

Letting out a pent-up breath, Damon moved away from the lean-to. Avoiding the guards and keeping in the shadows, he made his way to the mound where he would find Lord Preston Seaton.

Preston stared into the darkness, keeping his vigil. His spirits, kept up by the man's promise to return, were being dashed. The American colonel was not coming. Drawing in a despairing breath, he wondered how much longer he could live under these brutal conditions. There was no hope, no reason to live.

Suddenly he stiffened. Had he heard something? He strained his eyes, looking for anything that moved in the darkness. When a hand touched his, he jerked away, startled, causing his chains to rattle. The man was no more than a vague shadow, and he had come so silently he had taken Preston by surprise.

Preston felt the man kneel beside him and heard him insert a key into the lock that bound his chains together.

He was free.

Damon placed his fingers to his lips, indicating that the Englishman should be silent.

Preston struggled to stand. Feeling as if his legs would not bear his weight, he collapsed on the ground. This was his only chance at freedom, and his body would not obey his command.

At that moment a wicked laugh came from across the mound. Preston looked up and saw Murdock standing in their path, his legs spread in an arrogant stance, his rifle aimed at Preston's heart.

"I should have told you I'd shoot the prisoner before I'd let you have him, Colonel Routhland. Having heard of your daring, I figured you'd try something like this."

Damon tensed as Murdock cocked the hammer of his rifle.

"Your Englishman is about to die, Colonel Routhland," Murdock promised.

Preston was so weak he could not even move to save his life. He watched in amazement as the American colonel moved in front of him, placing his body between him and Murdock.

The gun exploded, and the American slumped forward for just a moment as the bullet tore through his body. But even as he was hit, Damon raised his knife, took aim, and lobbed it toward Murdock. Murdock moaned in agony, then crumpled to his knees and fell forward on his face.

Damon struggled to stay on his feet. Preston attempted to come to the American's aid but did not have the strength. He saw the irony of the situation; here was his only chance to escape, his rescuer had been wounded, and he was too weak to stand, much less walk. Why had the American taken the bullet for him? They were enemies, were they not?

Damon staggered forward. "Can you walk?" he asked.

With renewed effort, Preston tried to rise, but he fell back, feeling embarrassed. "I'm sorry, I cannot."

Damon reached out and boosted Lord Preston onto his shoulder. "Then I'll have to be your legs until we get out of this hellhole."

Preston could do no more than allow the American to carry him like a helpless rag doll. "Who are you, and why are you doing this for me?" he asked in a whisper.

Damon staggered and fell to his knees, got up again, and plunged into the swamp. His voice came out in a painful gasp: "Be quiet. You ask too many questions, Englishman."

With the added burden of Lord Preston, Damon felt his strength waning. He could not maintain this pace for long. He remembered a small island he had used as a young man and headed in that direction.

He staggered when he tripped over tangled roots but kept his balance. He had to make it out of the water before he collapsed. Just when he thought he could not take another step, he climbed onto a low island and crumpled to his knees. With his last bit of strength, he laid the Englishman on the ground before he fell forward, too weak and exhausted to move.

In the distance he could hear the baying of hound dogs, and he realized that Murdock's men were already in pursuit. Since he had kept to the water, there would be little chance of the hounds picking up his scent. They were safe for a time.

Damon felt wave after wave of nausea sweep over him just before he lost consciousness.

Preston awoke and blinked his eyes. Why was he lying on the damp ground, no longer chained? In total bewilderment he glanced at the veil of stifling humidity. When he could not see the familiar landscape of Murdock's camp, his confusion deepened. Slowly he remembered the daring rescue and looked about for the man who had freed him.

He wondered if he had been delivered from his tormenters only to become a prisoner of this harsh swamp. In the pale moonlight, he noticed that the ground had few high places. The sweltering heat was unbearable, and the water was alive with slithering reptiles. Like an ocean of grass, the low, sharp-edged reeds rippled and waved in the breeze. If he had to walk out on his own, which way would he go? He would surely become lost and be recaptured by the rebels.

His eyes fell on the American colonel, who was lying on his back with one hand dangling in the water. Suddenly Preston remembered that the man had been shot. Perhaps he was dead.

Preston stood up slowly, his legs trembling from weakness. Dropping to his knees, he crawled to the man and placed the palm of his hand against the colonel's chest, where he detected a faint heartbeat. A quick examination of the wound revealed a bullet had torn through his upper thigh and would have to be removed.

Preston realized he had to stop the steady flow of blood, or the man would bleed to death.

He did not yet know why this stranger had risked his life for him, but he would do all he could to save the man. A leather satchel lay beside the American, and he tore it open, hoping it contained something to use as a bandage. He found only a few hard biscuits, dried meat, and a canteen of fresh water.

Preston removed his tattered red jacket and looked down at his shirt. It was filthy, but he had to use it for a tourniquet and then a bandage. Pulling out the tail of the shirt, he ripped off the cleanest strip he could find.

The American groaned in pain as Preston wrapped the wound and applied pressure to the tourniquet. He nodded in satisfaction; the bleeding had stopped. But he was apprehensive, knowing that the bullet would have to be removed—and he would be the one to do it.

The cry of a loon echoed down the vast waterway, reminding Preston of the desolation of his new prison.

Suddenly Damon stirred, opened his eyes, and whispered weakly, "Water . . ."

Preston scampered forward and lifted the canteen to the man's lips, waiting for him to take a drink. "Colonel Routhland, I am going to have to remove that bullet at once. Do you feel up to it?"

Damon rolled to his side and pulled himself up so he could lean against the trunk of a wide cypress tree. "Do what you must," he gritted between clenched teeth, "but do it quickly, because it hurts like hell."

Preston licked his dry lips. "I believe I should confess that I've never done this before."

Damon made a hopeless gesture toward the heavens. "It seems my fate has been intertwined with two inexperienced but well-meaning amateurs—first her, and now you."

Preston paid little heed to the American's comment. "Have you a sharp knife?" he asked.

Damon closed his eyes as a spasm of pain racked his body. "If you will recall, I left my hunting knife sticking in a man who was determined to shoot you."

"Yes. And this bullet was meant for me. I'm grateful to you for what you did."

Damon cursed under his breath as Preston poked at his wound. "If you do that again, Englishman, I'll shoot you myself," he groaned.

"What should I do?" Preston asked. "How can I help you?"

"If you look in my boot, you'll find another knife, though it may be a bit dull. Then you will want to build a fire so you can cauterize the wound once the bullet's been removed."

"Is it safe to light a fire?" Preston inquired. "Suppose Murdock's men see the smoke?"

"No one will be able to detect a fire in this fog," Damon said impatiently.

"I fear the bullet is deep," Preston told him with a sick feeling in his stomach.

"Are you going to help me or talk me to death, Englishman?"

Preston's hands shook as he piled up dry twigs and lit a fire. His gaze then went to the American. "I'm ready."

"Then get on with it."

Preston grasped the knife handle and took a deep breath. He shuddered as the knife touched raw flesh.

Damon clenched his teeth and beads of sweat popped out on his forehead as the blade cut deeper. He glanced upward and tried to concentrate on the ghostlike moss that hung from the tree overhead. But pain seared his thoughts, and everything swirled around, until suddenly he was engulfed in peaceful blackness.

Damon awoke and groaned. He felt as if his whole leg were on fire. He struggled forward, trying to rise, but a hand held him down and a clipped English voice spoke to him. "You should rest, Colonel Routhland. You will need to stay off that leg as long as possible."

Damon licked his lips. "How long have I been unconscious?"

"Since last night."

"And it's night again," Damon observed. "The bullet?"

"I removed it. Hope you didn't want to save it. I tossed it away."

Through his pain, Damon saw the fog had cleared, and he swore in annoyance. "Put out that fire, you fool," he said in a weak whisper. "Light can be seen for great distances here in the swamps."

"But you told me to light a fire—"

"I said it could not be seen in the fog. There's no longer any fog to hide the smoke." He sighed wearily. "Aren't you British given any training before you're sent here?"

Preston quickly extinguished the fire, and he glanced at Damon. "Why did you save my life at a risk to your own?"

Damon met the man's questioning gaze. "Because Royal Bradford asked me to help you," he answered simply.

"Royal? How did you come to know her?"

"I happen to be that tiresome young lady's guardian. It seems she came all the way from England to find you, and she had no misgivings about recruiting me to help."

"Ah, so you're Damon Routhland. Of course I should have known, Royal has often spoken of you in glowing terms."

"I might return the compliment, Englishman. According to her, you are a model of all the virtues."

Preston's eyes glowed. "How like Royal to go rushing headlong into danger without weighing the consequences. I once had to rescue her from . . ." His voice trailed off. "I have never known anyone like her."

"Royal is safely in Savannah," Damon reminded him dryly. "It's you and I who find ourselves in danger."

"Yes," Preston agreed, "but we are both still alive."

"If we don't get shot by Murdock's men, or if I don't get captured by the British, or you by Americans, or if we don't get snakebit, die of fever, thirst, hunger, or get lost forever in these swamps, we are still alive."

"I am a great believer in fate, Damon—may I call you Damon? You may call me Preston."

"Of course, seeing as we are probably going to die together, I can see no reason why not."

"Are you always such a fatalist?"

Again, Damon felt a weakness wash over him. "Not until lately," he said with a slight smile. "But listen to me, and listen carefully. We both know that I can't walk out of these swamps, but if you will do exactly as I tell you, Preston, you may get out alive."

"I'm listening."

"At first light, follow the rising sun, keeping it over your right shoulder. Then in the afternoon, keep the sun at your back. If you do this, by nightfall you should come to a clearing, and just beyond that is a road. The road is patrolled regularly by your Redcoats. You don't need to worry about finding them—they'll find you."

"I am not going to leave you," Preston said stubbornly.

"Yes, you are. You don't have any choice. You aren't strong enough to carry me, and I sure as hell can't walk out."

A determined light sparkled in Preston's eyes. "We'll go together, or we won't go at all."

Damon leaned back and closed his eyes. "You're a stubborn bastard, Preston Seaton. You'll probably get us both killed."

"Oh, no." Preston laughed. "I have too much to live for. Royal will be waiting for me."

Damon thought of Royal and wished it were he she would be waiting for. "She doesn't even know I located you—how could she be waiting for you?" he said sourly.

"We'll tell her together."

Preston staggered through the murky water, feeling as if his muscles were strained to the limit. Damon was leaning heavily on him, and they were making slow progress since Damon was becoming delirious from the fever that ravaged his body.

"Leave me," Damon said weakly. "I am too weary to go on. Why do you torment me?"

"I will not leave you." Preston stopped long enough to uncap the canteen and give Damon a drink. "If I leave you here, you will surely die."

"Let me die, then. Each step is agony. I didn't ask for your help, Englishman."

"You aren't going to die—I won't let you. Royal would never forgive me. We will both get out of here alive."

"Royal," Damon murmured, out of his mind with the high fever. "Beautiful, sad little Royal. I promised her I would not forget . . . I promised."

Preston glanced up at the crescent moon and judged it to be near dawn. Just ahead he saw the clearing Damon had described. With renewed strength he picked Damon up and half carried, half dragged him out of the swamp.

At last they were on firm ground. Exhausted, his muscles screaming in protest, Preston laid Damon on the cool grass and fell down beside him.

"We made it, Damon," he murmured. "Didn't I tell you we would?"

Damon didn't hear. He was lost in a world of darkness where pain was his only companion.

It had been raining incessantly. Preston's lot was miserable as he trudged along in the mud with the weight of Damon Routhland to slow him down.

He heard a noise, so he pulled Damon behind a wide-leaf bush just as a British patrol rode by not ten paces ahead of him. As much as he would have liked to hail them, he had to consider Damon. Since Damon was out of uniform, he would be considered a spy by the British—and that would mean a hanging.

When the troop had passed out of sight, Preston breathed a sigh of relief. With the rain falling on his face, and feeling wretchedly lost, he sat beside Damon wondering what to do next. He knew he had influence and could probably save Damon's life by recounting his daring rescue to a patrol, but he was not willing to take that gamble. If Damon was arrested, Royal would never forgive him.

He hadn't been waiting long when he heard the sound of a wagon rattling down the road. When it was near enough, he stepped in front of it, forcing the driver to draw rein.

"I have a wounded man who needs help," he said to the driver perched on the wagon seat.

The newcomer looked doubtfully at the tattered red uniform. "I ain't a king's man," he admitted, "but I am a Christian, and I'll always be willing to help anyone with troubles."

"The one who needs your help is not a Loyalist. Are you acquainted with Damon Routhland?"

The man stared at Preston long and hard, then quickly nodded. "Well, sure I know Damon. He's one of the finest gentlemen you'll ever meet. But I can't guess how you'd know him."

"Does that matter? He needs your help. He's been wounded. Would you be willing to take him to his home, or perhaps to a doctor you can trust?"

The man looked at Preston suspiciously. The Englishman appeared to be sincere, but one could never tell about them. He secured his team of horses and climbed out of the wagon. "I'll just see Damon for myself."

"I hid him behind those bushes," Preston directed.

"Name's Ezekiel Elman, what's your'n?"

"Names aren't important, Mr. Elman. Come and help me with Mr. Routhland." Lord Preston led Ezekiel to Damon, who was still unconscious.

The old man's face creased in a worried frown, and he dropped down to study Damon. "Yep, that'll be Damon, sure enough. Where's he wounded?"

"In the thigh. You can see the bandage there."

"He appears to be hurt real bad. Wouldn't be good to take him to Swanhouse Plantation, though. I've heard tell your soldiers are always watching for him there—your army would give a whole hell of a lot to get their hands on him." He scratched his head. "Don't know a doctor I'd trust with this man—he's well known to me."

"He needs attention as soon as possible, Mr. Elman. If you can't take him to his home, Perhaps you will take him into Savannah to Miss Royal Bradford's house? She'll see that he is cared for."

"I know the Bradford house. But I didn't know Mistress Royal had come back. We best hide Damon under the hay, so I can sneak him past the patrols."

After Damon was aboard the wagon, Ezekiel turned to Preston. "Why's it that you're willing to help one of us?"

Preston shuddered when he remembered how close he had come to death. "Damon Routhland saved my life. I'm merely repaying him."

Ezekiel nodded, as if that were enough reason. "Will you be needing a ride into Savannah yourself?"

"Yes, I would appreciate that."

"Hop on, then. Savannah is just a few miles around that next bend."

Ezekiel urged his team into a trot. They had gone only a short distance when another patrol approached from behind them. "We might be in for trouble," the old man observed. "I sure wouldn't want them to find Damon."

"Say nothing about your passenger," Preston whispered hurriedly. "Let me do all the talking."

When the patrol drew even with them, a British sergeant waved for Ezekiel to halt. When he saw the tattered uniform of a British colonel, the well-trained sergeant saluted. "Begging your pardon, sir, but you look like you could use our assistance."

Preston gave Ezekiel a warning glance. "Indeed I can, Sergeant. Take me to your commander at once."

"Yes, sir. You can have my mount, sir, and I'll ride double with Corporal Redburn."

Preston mounted the horse, then nodded to Ezekiel. "Thank you for your help, Mr. Elman." He leaned forward and lowered his voice. "Tell Miss Bradford the bullet has been removed."

The old man watched the English patrol ride away. Then, worried about Damon, he whipped his horses forward.

It had stopped raining, so in order to avoid the mud, Royal moved gingerly through the kitchen garden, stepping across a neat row of vegetables. She was restless, and time lay heavy on her hands.

She sat down beneath a mulberry tree, trying to free her mind of troubled thoughts. For so long she had considered her fellow countrymen as rebellious and disloyal. Now, some of the incidents she had witnessed made her blood boil, and her loyalty to the land of her birth flamed to life.

Only yesterday she and Tobias had gone to the market. When they had made their purchases and were ready to leave, three British soldiers had blocked their way. One of them unsheathed his saber and placed the point at poor Tobias's throat.

"Be you Loyalist or rebel?" the man had asked before he grinned at his two companions. When he received only silence from Tobias, the man turned his sword on Royal. "How about you, pretty mistress, be you the king's woman, or do you support the rebels?"

Royal had become so enraged that she pushed the saber aside and turned on the soldiers. "Have you no one other than defenseless citizens to intimidate? Must you vent your strength on my servant and me? Surely you soldiers can find more worthy opponents on whom to practice your tomfoolery."

At least the soldiers had had the good grace to look ashamed, and they had sauntered away without a backward glance.

It had not been their harassment she had minded so much. It was the fact that they had arrogantly displayed an air of superiority over her and Tobias. British soldiers had no right to be here in Savannah. This was not their country—it was hers!

Tobias had told her of other incidents where citizens had been harassed on the streets by the occupying forces. Royal was torn between two loyalties, and it was becoming an agonizing burden for her. She remembered Damon telling her she would one day have to come off her fence and choose sides, but she could not—not yet, anyway.

Royal bent down to pull a weed from the garden while her thoughts tumbled over one another. She owed her loyalty to Preston; after all, if he was found, he would need her. She tried not to think of him locked in a cell in some dark prison or perhaps worse. The uncertainty of not knowing where he was tormented her.

She heard someone come out the back door and pushed her troubled thoughts aside. When she saw Alba hurrying toward her and noticed the worried frown on her face, Royal felt a prickle of fear. Something was wrong!

"You'd better come at once, Miss Royal. A man just brought Colonel Routhland in, and he's in a bad way. He says the colonel was shot. I put him in the front bedroom."

With her heart pounding in fear, Royal raced into the house and up the stairs. When she reached the bedroom she found Tobias bent over a motionless form on the bed. Woodenly she moved forward and saw it was indeed Damon, though it took her a moment to recognize him.

His face was almost as white as the pillow he lay against. His hair was matted with mud, and it was apparent he had not shaved in days.

"Where was he wounded, Tobias?"

"In the leg, Miss Royal. The bandages are filthy and soaked with blood, and that's not good."

"How bad is it?" she asked in a trembling voice.

"I can't tell yet. I have removed his wet clothing, but I haven't examined the wound," Tobias told her, pulling the covers across Damon's chest. "It's strange that he was dressed in buckskins."

She could hardly breathe from the pain of seeing Damon so badly hurt. Softly she laid her hand against his forehead, finding it hot to the touch. "Tobias, you must go for Dr. Habersham at once. The wound is most likely infected."

Tobias was thoughtful for a moment, then shook his head. "Old Doc Habersham, who treated your papa, is the king's man, Miss

Royal. We can't trust him not to turn Mr. Routhland over to the British. All the others with medical training have gone off to join the army."

"Then what shall we do? If Damon doesn't get attention, he may . . . die."

"Any help he's to get must come from us, Miss Royal. Otherwise Mr. Routhland might end up in an English prison. He's in no condition to survive imprisonment."

Royal stroked Damon's dark hair. "What could have happened to him, Tobias?"

"Mr. Elman, who brought Mr. Routhland here, said he was shot. And here's the part I don't understand. The man said that some Englishman told him to bring Mr. Routhland to you."

"How can that be?"

"I can't guess, Miss Royal."

Royal watched as Damon took a ragged breath. "Hurry and fetch Alba," she instructed. "She'll know what to do."

Tobias moved hurriedly to the door. "Don't fret none, Miss Royal. Men like Mr. Routhland are hard to kill. He'll come through this right enough."

When Royal was alone with Damon, she bent forward to touch her cheek to his. "Dearest, what has someone done to you?" Tears blinded her, and she wiped them away. "I will not let you die!" she vowed. "Do you hear me—I will not let you leave me!"

She heard Alba at the door, and she stepped back as the housekeeper poured steaming water into a wash basin. "You'd best go out, Miss Royal. I have to wash him and clean his wound." She took in a deep breath. "Tobias was told that the bullet had been removed, so we don't have to worry about that."

Royal shook her head stubbornly. "I will not leave him. I . . . will help you."

Alba looked doubtful. "Here," she said at last, "you can hold the lamp for me and stay just until I clean the wound. An unmarried girl has no business being in a gentleman's sickroom."

Royal's hand trembled as she watched Alba pull the coverlet

up to Damon's thigh. She gasped when the housekeeper removed the bandage, for the skin around the wound was swollen and red.

"Oh, Alba, what happened to him? What kind of a monster did this?"

The housekeeper bent over Damon to inspect the wound. "I don't know, Miss Royal, but we'll do all we can for him."

Alba dipped a clean cloth in the hot water and began to cleanse the wound. She looked at her husband with inquiring eyes. "We have nothing to apply to the wound. What shall we do?"

Tobias looked pensive for a moment. "I brought along a bottle of Mr. Bradford's rum. It'll have to do."

When at last all was done to make the patient comfortable, Royal agreed to leave the room so Alba could bathe him. Unwilling to be far from Damon, however, she lingered in the hallway outside the bedroom. An hour passed before Alba joined her there.

"How is my guardian?" Royal asked with apprehension.

"I fear he's the same. I'm not a doctor, but I don't believe it looks good. You saw the wound. It's badly infected."

When Alba saw the stricken look on Royal's face, she softened her abrupt manner. "But there now, you're not to worry. I watched you endure your father's illness with bravery. You must do the same now."

Royal choked back her tears. "I cannot stand to watch someone else I love die," she cried, not realizing she had admitted her love for Damon.

"We will do all we can to make him comfortable."

Tobias came out of Damon's bedroom and stood beside his wife. "Do you understand the danger of having Mr. Routhland under your roof, Miss Royal? If the enemy finds him here, I can't guess what they'll to you." He stared at her. "Are you willing to take that risk?"

"I'm not concerned with the danger to me, Tobias. I'm only concerned about Damon."

Tobias grinned with satisfaction. "That's how I knew you'd feel."

"I want to see him now," Royal said, moving to the door.

"Before you go in," Alba intervened, "I want to tell you that Mr. Routhland will need constant care. Tobias and I are prepared to take turns staying with him." She looked at Royal with doubt. "Of course, you are an unmarried young lady, and you must consider what people would say if they found out that you were in Mr. Routhland's bedroom."

Royal met Alba's inquiring gaze. "Do you think I care about what people think?" she asked. "My main concern is not my reputation, but how to keep the British from finding out my guardian is here and to nurse him back to health."

Respect was reflected in Tobias's eyes. He nodded and moved down the hall. He turned at the stairwell. "We'll have to take care not to arouse suspicion. In these days, one never knows who to trust. It'll be safer for Mr. Routhland if we tell no one he's here."

"Has Savannah become a town where neighbors turn on neighbors?"

"I've heard of such things happening. But between the three of us, it'll remain our secret," Alba said.

Royal turned a troubled gaze to the bedroom door. If it were possible, she would pull Damon back from the jaws of death—she just had to!

With strong determination, she entered the bedroom where he lay. She realized Alba stood just behind her. "You can go now, Alba, I'll stay with him."

The housekeeper looked uncertain. "I still don't think it's seemly for you to be alone with Mr. Routhland."

"Oh, Alba, we can't worry about that. I care little about proprieties. Besides, he is little threat to my reputation in his condition. He will need all three of us to nurse him back to health."

Alba agreed with a nod of her head. "That seems sensible, though unconventional."

Royal looked down at Damon with an aching heart, unaware that Alba had left the room. She noticed that either Alba or Tobias had shaved Damon, and she touched his smooth cheek. He was still feverish, so she wet a cloth and applied it to his brow.

"Oh, Damon, who has done this to you?" She took his hand in hers. "You lie so still . . . your skin is so pale."

Sitting down beside the bed, she began her long vigil. Tenderly touching his dark hair, she suppressed a sob. "I will never leave you, Damon."

In Damon's world of darkness there was only throbbing, swirling pain. He felt as if his body were on fire, and he longed for a drink of cool water. In his tortured mind, his thoughts turned to the bubbling, spring-fed streams that cut through the heart of Swanhouse Plantation.

Somewhere in his world of anguish, a voice reached him, and a soft hand soothed his brow. A wet cloth touched his dry lips, making him wish he had strength to draw the moisture from it.

Damon recognized the voice that whispered encouragement to him—it was beautiful Royal, and she somehow brought him comfort.

It was the last dark hour before dawn, and the stillness of the swamp was interrupted by the pounding hooves of many horses. The British brigade that had entered the swampy world was led by the new Duke of Chiswick, whose eyes blazed with angry intensity. He was determined that Vincent Murdock would pay dearly for his acts of insurrection against the British Crown and against humanity.

When the column entered the camp, dogs barked and pulled violently at their chains. The inhabitants, taken by surprise, scattered into the darkness but were quickly rounded up by the soldiers.

The duke rode his mount straight for the lean-to, where he hoped to find Murdock himself. When he dismounted he encountered a poor, pathetic woman who might have been pretty if not for the filthy rags she wore and her matted black hair. She tossed her head and grinned up at the duke.

"You're too late, Englishman," the woman jeered. "Murdock has escaped." Laughter spilled from her lips. "You didn't think you would catch him, did ya?" The woman spat at him. "He's much too smart for you."

The duke moved forward and grabbed the woman. "Where is he?" he demanded between gritted teeth. "Tell me now, woman, or I will cut out your tongue!"

She merely grinned. "One can't know where my Murdock goes. But I got a message for you from him."

He flung her away, feeling sick inside that the man had slipped out of his grasp. "I care nothing about what he has to say," he told her, turning away.

"You'll care 'bout this," she called out. "He says to give you this warning. If you hold anything dear, my Murdock'll find out what it is, and he'll destroy it. Guard well what you treasure."

The duke turned back to look at the woman. "I hold nothing so dear as the sight of him standing before a firing squad."

He led his mount to the center of the camp, where the fugitives had been rounded up by his men. Looking around him in disgust, he issued an order. "Burn everything, and chain the prisoners. Although we did not capture their leader, we have struck a blow to his heart. He will have very few followers to aid him in his evil schemes."

"What about the women and children, Your Grace?" one of the soldiers questioned.

"Leave them," he ordered, mounting his horse. "Let the women carry the news to Murdock." The duke raised his voice in hopes that Murdock would hear. "Tell him that he has staged his last raid against British forces."

His voice echoed down the byways, where Murdock hid behind the trunk of a cypress tree. Watching with hatred in his eyes, he swore a vow of vengeance. "I'll get you for this, Englishman. I'll strike where it will cause you the most pain." His face twisted with rage.

But the hatred Murdock harbored for the Englishman was a puny thing and could not equal the malignant loathing he felt for Damon Routhland.

Murdock reached up to his arm, which rested in a leather sling. Damon Routhland's knife had made its mark the night he'd helped the Englishman escape. Murdock had lost the feeling in his right arm, and it was now completely useless.

"Before I am finished with you, Englishman," he muttered, "and with the mighty Damon Routhland, if he still lives, you will both curse the day you were born, and your mothers for giving you birth!"

Damon's brilliant amber glance met Royal's sparkling blue eyes. She placed her hand on his arm. "You had us all very worried."

He closed his eyes. "So tired," he murmured. "Leave me alone—need sleep."

Royal watched as he slipped into a world of darkness once more, but this time it was a natural sleep that would allow him to heal in mind and body. She raised her head, watching the morning sun dart flirtatiously through the window and then fall across the foot of Damon's bed. She had been on her knees most of the night, hoping if she kept a constant prayer on her lips, God would be merciful and spare Damon's life.

She stood up and stretched her cramped muscles, thinking Alba would soon arrive to relieve her. Bending forward, she clasped

Damon's hands. She recalled the night those hands had gently stroked her trembling flesh. How could a man of such power lie so still and lifeless?

Already the day was hot, and Royal pushed a damp lock of hair from her forehead, picked up a wet cloth, and wiped Damon's face and neck, hoping to cool his fever. When she had done all she could to make him more comfortable, she moved to the window and glanced down at the street.

Rain had fallen during the night, and the cobblestone roadway glistened in the sunlight. Everything outside that window appeared ordinary—even the occasional British soldier who rode by did not seem out of place. How could life go on as if nothing had happened, when Damon was fighting for every breath he took?

She turned back to the bed, dipped the cloth in cool water, and reapplied it to his head. Damon was no better, and she was faced with an agonizing choice. Should she send for Dr. Habersham even though it might mean prison? Surely imprisonment was better than death. She fanned Damon with an ivory-handled fan, wishing she knew what was best to do.

When Alba came bustling into the room, she noticed the circles under Royal's eyes and took the fan from her. "How is he?" she inquired, commencing to fan Damon herself.

"I haven't seen any improvement. What shall we do?"

"Whatever you decide to do will wait until you've rested. You look dead on your feet, Miss Royal. You'd best let me sit with Mr. Routhland while you rest. I laid out your breakfast in the dining room."

Royal nodded. "It's too hot to eat, but I will bathe and put on a fresh gown. If there is any change in Damon's condition, notify me at once."

Not wanting to be away from her patient for long, Royal bathed quickly. She then dressed in a cool, pink cotton gown and pulled her hair back with a matching ribbon.

Entering Damon's sickroom, Royal found Alba still fanning the patient. She met the housekeeper's disapproving frown.

"You couldn't have eaten and bathed in such a short span of time, Miss Royal."

"I can't eat while Damon is unconscious. I just can't," Royal confessed. "You may go now, Alba. I'll sit with him for a while."

Alba cast Royal a sidelong glance and looked as though she might refuse. But finally she handed the fan to her young mistress before moving to the door. "You'll be sick next, Miss Royal. Just mark my words—you will!"

Although Royal had closed the curtains against the afternoon sunlight, the heat was still oppressive. Her clothing was plastered to her with perspiration, and the air she circulated with the ivory fan did little good. Earlier she had instructed Tobias to bathe Damon in cool water, but his temperature was still high, and he had not regained consciousness.

Royal heard Alba's excited voice in the hallway, and she glanced toward the door, wondering what had caused the commotion.

"You can't go in that room! I don't care if you *are* a high-ranking British officer. There's a sick man in there, and I won't allow you to pass!"

The voices were muffled by the closed door, and Royal could not hear the exchange between Alba and whoever stood outside. Nor did she know that the housekeeper blocked the entrance to the room like an avenging angel.

"But I'm a friend, and I have brought a doctor to help your patient."

"We don't need any help from you English," Alba insisted. "Leave this house at once!"

Royal moved closer to Damon, fearing for his safety. Her heart was pounding as she watched the doorknob turn. Her hand closed around the fan as if it were a weapon she could use to defend her patient. She remembered her father's pistol was locked away in his desk and wished she had it with her.

She would not allow anyone to harm Damon. She was prepared to defend him if she must. The door swung wide, and a man wearing the red jacket of a British officer stood on the threshold.

Royal's eyes moved to his face in quick assessment. He had gray hair and soft blue eyes. Her eyes went to his jacket, where she saw he wore the insignia of a doctor.

Her heart was beating with fear as she watched him smile. His expression was kind as he glanced at her. Royal placed her body between the intruder and Damon, in case he intended to harm Damon.

"Who are you?" she asked in a trembling voice, picking up the water pitcher and aiming it at the man. "What do you want here?"

Seeing her look of defiance, the doctor moved aside and nodded to another man in uniform who stood just behind him. "Miss Bradford," he said, bowing to her with a twinkle in his eyes. "Perhaps His Grace can explain to you that we have come to help."

As the doctor's companion stepped into the room, Royal gasped and dropped the pitcher, unmindful that it broke as it clattered to the floor. "Preston! Can it be . . . you? Is it possible?"

The duke held out his arms to her. "It is I, Royal," he assured her while his eyes drank in her loveliness. He nodded at the broken pitcher that lay in pieces on the floor. "Is this any way to greet a man who wants to marry you?"

Tears gathered in her eyes as she raced across the room to be clasped in Preston's arms. "I feared I would never see you again. Oh, Preston, you are alive!" she sobbed as he held her tightly against him.

"Yes, sweetness, I am alive. I would have come sooner, but duty dictated that I be elsewhere."

"But I don't understand." She looked him over carefully. He was thinner, but he still had the same boyish smile, the same softness in his blue eyes. "You're supposed to be a prisoner. How did you escape?"

"It wasn't easy, but I had help." Preston nodded to Damon. "Had it not been for your guardian, most probably I would be dead by now. It's certain I would still be a prisoner."

"I don't understand."

"Your guardian rescued me from the swamp. As a result, he was wounded." He stepped closer to the bed. "Royal, this is Major Cummingwood, a doctor of fine standing. He has agreed to help Damon."

Royal was bewildered, unsure if she should allow an English doctor to examine Damon. The duke, seeing her hesitation, said with assurance, "It's all right, Royal. Dr. Cummingwood is only here at my request—you can trust him."

She turned grateful eyes on Preston, deciding to place Damon in the English doctor's hands. "He's very ill. We have done all we could, but his wound is infected, and he has a fever."

The duke grasped Royal's arm. "We will not be needed here. Let us leave the doctor to examine Damon."

It seemed there was nothing Royal could do but agree. She allowed him to lead her out to the hallway, where, under Alba's watchful eyes, she went into his arms, still unable to believe he was safe.

"I am baffled as to how you came to know my guardian. And you said he saved your life. . . . What are you talking about?"

He still clung to Royal's hand. "I had been captured by a man called Murdock and kept in chains somewhere in the swamps. Damon Routhland found me and freed me. The bullet in his thigh was meant for me."

A tear trailed down Royal's cheek. "It's my fault. I asked Damon to help me find you. How could I have known that he would put himself in danger? I thought he had only to locate you, and then we could bargain for your freedom."

The duke looked over Royal's head to Alba, who was keeping a wary eye on him. "Can you prepare tea for your mistress?" he asked the housekeeper. "I believe she would benefit by it."

Alba drew herself up, and her eyes snapped. "We don't serve tea in this house. We Americans think tea is unpatriotic."

The duke laughed. "Forgive my mistake in thinking you were English. Your manner of speech deceived me."

"Humph. Just because I was born in England don't mean I agree with every pearl that comes out of the king's mouth." Alba's gaze locked challengingly with Royal's. "A person may sometimes get confused as to what's right and wrong. Me and my man are not, and never have been, Loyalists!"

Royal gave Preston a sympathetic glance, thinking it was time to introduce him. "Alba, I would like to present you to His Grace, the Duke of Chiswick. He's a friend of mine."

Alba nodded politely, her manner not so brisk, although she was unimpressed with the man's title. "I should hope so. If you don't have any objections to coffee, Your Grace, I'll just make a nice pot."

He said with pretended seriousness, "Coffee would be most welcome, Alba."

Royal realized that only someone who knew Preston as well as she did would have recognized the teasing light in his blue eyes.

When the housekeeper had withdrawn, the duke could no longer contain his laughter. "I don't think I have had such a dressing-down since my nanny took me to task for turning over the butter churn."

"Alba means well," Royal explained apologetically. "It's just that she's very protective of me and has become a fervent supporter of the patriots. You won't hold that against her, will you?"

The duke had noticed she called the rebels "patriots," but before he could reply, Dr. Cummingwood joined them. "Whoever treated the wound did well. I applied new dressings. Beyond that, there's not much else I can do."

"Will he recover, Doctor?" Royal asked hopefully.

"I believe he will. But he is very weak from loss of blood. You must realize he will need constant care," the doctor instructed. "Which it seems he has."

"But he is still unconscious," Royal pointed out.

"Has he awakened at all?"

"Only briefly."

"I would expect him to stir before another day passes." His glance became guarded as he looked at the duke. "If he does not regain consciousness by tomorrow, Your Grace, I shall then be anxious about his recovery."

Royal looked into the doctor's honest eyes. "I thank you for your concern."

"His Grace has told me all about your guardian. I want to assure you his secret is safe with me. I'll try to drop by tomorrow and have a look at him. Meanwhile, keep him as cool as possible."

"Thank you again, Dr. Cummingwood," Royal said gratefully. "You are most kind. I know it wasn't easy for you to come here."

"Not at all, Miss Bradford. When His Grace asked me to help, I was only too glad to comply."

"Come, Doctor," the duke said. "I'll see you to the door."

When the two men left, Royal returned to the bedroom and stood over Damon. She was tormented by the fact that he had been injured rescuing Preston for her. She felt an ache so deep that her body trembled. If Damon died, it would be her fault. She had not wanted him to save Preston at the cost of his own life.

The duke appeared at her side, and they both looked down at Damon. "He is gravely ill," Royal said. "If only I could see an improvement."

The duke turned her to face him. "It is serious, but the Damon Routhland I met is of a strong and determined character. It will take more than a mere bullet to stop him."

Royal was surprised by his words. "Why, Preston, you admire him!"

"Indeed I do. As I told you, the bullet that tore into his flesh was meant for me." He took her hand and led her to the window. "I understand I also have you to thank for my life, Royal."

She looked into clear blue eyes and saw reflections of what he had suffered. His face was gaunt, and she could see the faint traces of bruises on his cheek.

"Don't thank me, Preston. I did very little."

"Don't make light of what you did, dearest. You came all the way from England to enlist Damon's help. My mother asked you to come, didn't she?"

"I would have come anyway. Have you sent word to your family that you're safe? Your mother and Alissa were so worried."

"Yes, the dispatch went out as soon as I got back to headquarters."

They were unaware that Damon was fighting his way out of a shadowy world where there were no feelings and no light. Pain ripped through his body, and a blinding light made him squeeze his eyes together tightly. With no recollection of what had happened to him, he heard the murmur of voices. For a time he listened to the conversation without comprehending the words. Finally, turning his head, he opened his eyes and saw Royal in the arms of the Englishman.

She laid her head against Preston's shoulder. "I was grieved to hear about your brother's death."

He clung to her. "It wasn't easy to hear that Nathan had died. As you know, I grieve for my brother, and I never wanted to stand in his place. But with you beside me, I can do what is expected of me."

"You will make a most admirable duke, Preston." She shook her head in disbelief. "It is still difficult for me to think of you as the Duke of Chiswick." She pulled back and stared at him with wonder. "You are no longer just Preston." Her face paled. "You are . . . Your . . . Your Grace!"

He smiled and kissed her on her upturned nose. "Yes, and you will soon become the Duchess of Chiswick."

She was bewildered for a moment. Preston had been through so much, and she saw hope in his eyes—hope she was reluctant to dash until he had recovered from his brother's death. "In a world that is changing, I am too confused to know how I feel about anything. I would not make a good duchess, you should know that."

His laughter was soft. "Will you turn away from my love just because I am prepared to lay an old and respected title at your feet?"

She pressed her head against his shoulder. "I wish . . . I wish . . ."

"What do you wish, dearest?"

"I wish the two of you would leave a man in peace," Damon said in a ragged voice. "Where in the hell am I?" he asked, trying to rise and falling back weakly on the pillow.

Royal moved quickly to stand beside him and reached to take his hand, but he merely scowled at her.

"You are at my house, Damon. I have been so concerned about you, but you are going to be all right," she assured him with relief etched on her face.

The duke laughed as he moved beside her and looked down at Damon. "If your ill humor is any indication, I'd say you are well on your way to recovery."

Damon looked from Royal to Preston, wondering why he resented the fact that they were together. "Why don't the two of you take your flowering reunion elsewhere," he said sourly, wondering which hurt the most—the pain from his wound or the ache in his heart.

The duke took Royal's hand and led her toward the door, where she turned back and glanced at Damon with a look of concern. "Will he be all right?"

The duke nodded. "Men like Damon Routhland don't succumb to a mere bullet, and he would never let a man like Vincent Murdock get the better of him."

"Who is this Mr. Murdock?" Royal inquired.

The duke guided her out of the room. "No one you would want to meet. Offer me lunch, and I'll tell you all about him. I warn you, though, it isn't a pretty story."

"I want to hear everything, Preston."

"I only have two hours before I have to leave for General Clinton's headquarters."

"Must you leave?"

"Regretfully. And I don't know how long it will be before we meet again." He drew her into his arms. "Will you miss me, my love?"

She looked up at him with earnest eyes. "You know I will." The two men she cared about most in the world were under her roof. There was much confusion in her life at the moment, but Preston was the steadying force that would hold her world together. She caught the warmth of his expression.

"It was only thoughts of you that brought me through these last few weeks, Royal."

"I'm grateful you are safe, Preston. I don't know what I would have done if anything had happened to you."

"Does that mean you will seriously consider my marriage proposal?"

"No, I cannot do that. Especially not now."

"You will change your mind," he said softly. "I'll not give up until you do."

As they lunched together, Royal listened, horrified, as Preston told her about Vincent Murdock. "He is a truly evil man. I hope never to meet him."

"Nor shall you," Preston assured her. "If we don't run him into the ground, I feel certain the rebel army will."

Damon awoke to an annoying, grating sound. Half in irritation, half in a dream state, he turned his head in the direction of the noise to find a branch of a mulberry tree scraping against the window.

For a moment he frowned with puzzlement, wondering at his unfamiliar surroundings. Then it all came back to him. He was in Royal's house. Apparently Preston had brought him here. Evidently he owed his life to the Englishman, and that did not sit well with him.

With rash impatience he tried to sit up, but weakness overcame him. His wound felt as if someone had just stuck a hot poker to it, and he fell back, groaning in pain.

When the door was whisked open and the housekeeper came

bustling in carrying a tray, he only acknowledged her presence with a slight wave.

"Don't think you have to entertain me, Mr. Routhland. I know you aren't feeling up to socializing. I just thought you might like some nice warm broth and fresh cheese to help you get your strength back."

Damon said firmly, his glance showing his displeasure, "It'll take more than your broth and cheese to help me mend. My leg hurts."

"Men are always such bad patients, Mr. Routhland. If you'd seen the gap you have in your thigh, you'd know why it hurts." Alba set the tray down and handed him a napkin. "Would you like me to spoon-feed you?"

His lips curved into a smile. "You can be a hard woman, Alba." With considerable effort, he managed to come to a sitting position while he looked at the thin broth with distaste. "Here, let me have it. I'm perfectly capable of feeding myself."

She stood by with a pleased expression on her face. "See that you eat it all. The doctor says you can have something substantial by tomorrow."

"The English doctor," he said with contempt. "What does he know?"

"He knew enough to help you when you needed it," Alba reminded him. She turned toward the door. "I'll just leave you for now and come back later to collect the tray."

After she departed, Damon shoved the tray aside, then thought better of it. He picked up the cheese grudgingly and bit into it. He was hungry, and Alba didn't appear to be one to trifle with, he mused, taking a spoonful of broth.

After he had eaten his fill and had a cool drink of apple cider, he had to admit he felt stronger. Still, he seemed to tire so easily. He would just close his eyes for a moment, he thought, drifting off to sleep.

Damon watched Alba admit Dr. Cummingwood into his bedroom. As the man approached his bed, he set his bag down and smiled at the patient.

"No need to ask how you are. I can see by your color that you've improved in health since last we met. I admit you had me worried for a time."

Damon used the bedpost for leverage and pulled himself to a sitting position. "It still seems ironic to me that you have been sent to see to my health, Doctor. We're on opposite sides, you know."

The doctor placed the lamp so the light fell on Damon's leg. "As a man of medicine, I am bound by an ethical code, Colonel Routhland, which is why I helped you. And, to a smaller extent, because the Duke of Chiswick asked it of me." He smiled. "His Grace seems to value your health more than you do."

"Surely the irony of this situation is not lost on you, Doctor. Here you are patching me up so I'll be well enough to return to my unit and engage your countrymen in battle."

"We are all members of the human race, Colonel. The sooner you soldiers realize that, the easier my job will be."

Damon stared at the man with respect. "Perhaps you are right," he said at last. "Perhaps you should be making this speech to Preston Seaton."

The doctor looked puzzled for a moment. "His Grace is not a soldier and never has been. Actually, his mission here is a diplomatic one."

Damon closed his eyes, feeling relieved. So Royal had been telling the truth about Preston not being in the military.

"I just hope the next time you go into battle you'll think about what His Grace has done for you, Colonel Routhland."

"As a soldier yourself, you know when a man goes into battle, he cannot allow himself to think of anything but victory."

"I know. It has always been so . . . it will always be so."

"No matter how this war goes, Dr. Cummingwood, it has been my pleasure to know a man like you. No matter that your sympathies lie with the British."

Dr. Cummingwood removed the bandage and nodded in satisfaction at his handiwork. "Your wound is healing nicely. I believe you can put some weight on that leg starting tomorrow morning. Not too much, mind you. Just try to walk to the door and back." He turned to the housekeeper. "See that he doesn't overdo."

Alba nodded. "I'll do that, Doctor."

He wrapped a clean bandage on the wound. When he was finished he extended his hand to Damon. "I won't be seeing you again. My unit is moving out in the morning."

Damon shook his hand. "You have my gratitude for all you have done. I hope for your sake no one finds out you have aided the enemy."

"No one will condemn me for helping you, Colonel. The officers in my unit know the whole story about how you saved the duke's life. They have looked the other way when I made my calls on you."

Dr. Cummingwood picked up his bag and moved to the door. "It's been a pleasure knowing you, Colonel. Try not to get yourself shot in the future."

Royal was passing Damon's bedroom when she heard a loud thud and the shattering of glass, followed by an angry male voice. Without pausing to knock, she rushed into the room and quickly discovered the catastrophe. Damon was sprawled on the floor, and the three-legged table that had held his medicine was on top of him. Medicine bottles and a broken washbasin were scattered on the floor.

Damon looked up at Royal with a sour expression. "Well, are you going to stand there all day or help me?"

She averted her eyes because he was naked from the waist up and inched her way toward the door. "I'll just get Tobias to help you."

"Confound it, Royal, come here! I don't relish the notion of lingering here on my back while you fetch Tobias."

She ventured closer. "What happened?"

"I wearied of lying abed like an invalid, that's what happened!" His eyes were blazing. "I have no patience with this."

"Yes, I can see that." She clasped his arm with both her hands and steadied herself by bracing her back against the wall. With a quick intake of breath that alerted her that he was in pain, Damon stood upright. "Lean on me," she suggested, putting her arm around his waist. "We'll get you back to bed where you belong."

"It seems I have no choice," he said, limping toward the bed and favoring his injured leg. "I cannot recall ever being ill a day in my life," he snapped.

When they reached the bed, he eased his weight down and fell back against the pillow. Royal noticed his hand trembled and beads of perspiration had popped out on his upper lip. He was obviously in pain and still very weak.

She placed her hand on his forehead. "You must rest. Promise me you won't get up unless someone is with you."

He looked at the ceiling as if he were trying to ignore the pain. "Why haven't you been to see me this last week? I could have died for all you cared."

She shook her head. "It wasn't out of neglect, Damon. It was proper enough for me to nurse you while you were unconscious, but quite another thing for me to be alone with you after you . . ." Her voice trailed off because of the sardonic glance he gave her.

Damon's eyes were a golden fury. "It's too late for you to play the innocent with me, Royal. I assume you have been spending all your time with the Englishman."

She bent to pick up the scattered bottles and to right the table, her long hair hiding her face and the indignation she was feeling. "Preston has gone to New York to join General Clinton. I have not seen him since the last time he visited you."

"Lord, don't mention General Clinton's name in my presence," he said. "I'm in a hotbed of enemies with no way to rejoin my unit."

Royal came to stand beside him. "I'm not your enemy, Damon, nor is Preston. He brought the doctor to tend your wounds. Had he not done so, you might not be here today."

"How naive you are," Damon said scornfully, "if you think he did it for me." He rubbed his throbbing leg and faced her angrily. "I can't stay here. Has there been any word from John?"

"No, but I hadn't expected there would be. Tobias told me that Swanhouse is being watched. I'm sure he'll come as soon as he knows you're here."

Damon glanced at her, thinking how lovely she was with an uncertain smile on her face. God, she looked innocent in her white gown and her hair falling around her face like a golden halo.

"Leave me in peace," he said, turning his face to the wall.

When he straightened out his leg, he groaned. "Thank you for your assistance," he said grudgingly. "I am loath to take advantage of your hospitality, but it seems I have no choice in the matter. If it appears that I am ungrateful, it's just that I have a lot on my mind."

"I know that," she said in understanding. "It can't be easy for you, Damon. Please know that you are welcome to stay as long as there is a need. I'm only concerned with your health." She smiled at him shyly. "I have been wanting to thank you for rescuing Preston."

"I don't want your thanks. I did no more than what you asked of me."

"I never wanted you to endanger yourself."

Royal moved out of the room, leaving Damon to stare at the door she closed behind her.

Ezekiel Elman ambled up the steps and rapped heavily on the door. He had been concerned about Damon and had made a special trip to Savannah to see how he was faring. He assessed the Bradford house with approval. It was a good, strong house that would last many generations.

When the door was opened, he quickly removed his cap and slicked down his unruly hair before smiling at the lovely young woman who looked at him with a puzzled expression.

"Yes?" Royal asked. "What can I do for you, sir?"

He grinned. "You don't recall me, Miss Royal, but I'm Ezekiel Elman. I was a friend of your pa's."

Her face was transformed with a radiant smile. "Of course I remember you, Mr. Elman. What would we have done for fresh milk and butter if you hadn't made your weekly calls?" She stepped aside to allow him to enter the house. "I also have you to thank for bringing Colonel Routhland to me."

Ezekiel stood before her awkwardly. "That's the reason I've come, Miss Royal. My wife and me was worried 'bout Damon, and so I rode into town to see how he's faring."

Royal tried to ignore the mud that Mr. Elman had tracked all over Alba's rug. She hoped Alba wouldn't notice until after the man had gone.

"Why don't you follow me upstairs and see for yourself? I know he will want to thank you for smuggling him past the British troops."

Ezekiel looked pleased. "'Twern't nothing. I owe Damon a heap more than I could ever pay him. When me and the wife was 'bout to lose our place, he loaned us the money to put in new crops and buy more milk cows. Heck fire, I'd do 'bout anything for him!"

Royal smiled at the comical little man. His once red hair was mostly gray now. He was tall and thin and had a scraggly beard that hid most of his face. Still, she thought, he had the kindest, softest brown eyes she had ever seen, and when he smiled his eyes softened even more. "I am finding out that many people owe a debt of gratitude to my guardian, Mr. Elman."

"Did he ever tell you that I taught him to hunt in the swamps?" Ezekiel asked hopefully as he trailed behind Royal.

She paused and looked back at him. "No, I wasn't aware of that. But you see, I have been out of the country for some time, and there is much about my guardian I didn't know."

"Me and the wife was wondering if'n you'd come back when the war started, and we was glad to hear you finally had. We Georgians have to stick together. Me, I'm too old to fight." He suddenly looked crestfallen. "I learned that when I tried to join the regulars, and they turned me down. Said seventy was too old to fight!" His eyes blazed with indignation. "Why, Miss Royal, I can shoot farther and straighter than any man I know!"

"You must remember, Mr. Elman, that this country needs its farmers, too."

He nodded eagerly. "That's kinda what I think. We ain't never had any young'ns of our own, so we just think of all the young soldiers as ours and plant more corn to fill their bellies."

Royal smiled as he talked ceaselessly. When she motioned for him to precede her up the stairs, he was still talking. "I have known Damon since he was a boy. When his pa died, he kinda turned to me. You wouldn't think a man of his standing would waste time with the likes of me, would you?"

"Yes, I would, Mr. Elman. Damon is a man who would treasure all his friends."

Royal moved down the hallway and paused before Damon's door. "I'll just knock and see if he's awake." She did so and heard a muffled voice call out.

Opening the door, she stood aside to allow Ezekiel to enter. "Don't stay too long," she cautioned. "He's still weak and needs lots of rest."

Evening shadows were falling before Ezekiel emerged from Damon's room. He passed Royal in the hallway and grinned. "Be seeing you, Miss Royal. Damon's asked me to come by as often as I'm able. He seems in right good health, though he's crusty as an old bear. I 'spect it's from laying abed so long."

"Yes, I suppose," she agreed, trying to hide a smile. "You are welcome to come as often as you like, Mr. Elman."

"I'll do that, Miss Royal—I surely will."

He stopped short. "He asked me to let them know at Swanhouse about his troubles and to get word to his unit. I'll have to ride hard to notify his unit since it's more than three days from here."

Royal was thoughtful for a moment. "If you will inform his unit, I will notify Mr. Bartholomew."

"You must have a care, Miss Royal. It wouldn't do to let the king's men find out what you were about."

"I'll take every precaution, Mr. Elman."

The man beamed at her as he moved to the door. "I'll be seeing you, Miss Royal," he promised, "just as soon as I can come without drawing attention to myself."

Chapter 26

Royal balanced a dinner tray with one hand while she opened the door with the other. Seeing Damon propped up against the pillows, she smiled at him. "Alba has prepared you a feast. Deep-fried fish, green beans with potatoes, and corn muffins. For dessert she made gingerbread. Have you any notion how difficult it is to get ginger, or any spices, with British warships blockading all the ports?"

He crossed his arms over his chest and gave her a noncommittal glance. "Little I care." His eyes burned into her. "Why haven't you been in to see me today?" he demanded. "All I have to do all day is sit here and look at these four walls."

She placed the tray on the table near his bed, knowing how difficult it was for a man like him to be inactive. "As a matter of fact, I have been at Swanhouse Plantation. I rode out early this morning to inform Mr. Bartholomew that you were here. He sends his compliments and asked me to tell you that he will come to see you as soon as he can do so without raising undue suspicion."

Damon sighed heavily and lay back against the pillow. "I don't know what's going on with this damn war. I'm caught here in Savannah, surrounded by enemy troops, and even the doctor who tended my wounds owes his allegiance to King George." His eyes targeted her parted lips. "And, if it comes to that, I'm not all that certain about your allegiance."

She poured cream into his coffee and placed the tray across his lap, unruffled by his sarcasm. "As soon as I decide, I'll let you know." She shook out a snowy white napkin and handed it to him. "You really should eat. Alba took particular pains so everything would be to your liking."

He picked up a fork and stabbed at the fish. Breaking off a flaky piece, he raised it to his mouth and took a bite. "Alba is to be complimented. I have been wondering if I could steal her away from you. Swanhouse could use a woman with her authority."

Royal warmed to his light banter. "Alba would never leave me."

He cocked his head. "Don't be too certain. She told me just the other day that she grew up on a farm outside Yorkshire and sometimes longs for country living. I could offer her the rule of Swanhouse and that would satisfy her need for country living."

Royal propped her arms on the table and watched him devour the fish. "Don't you have a cook at Swanhouse?"

"Not one who can rival Alba."

She waved her hand in the air. "Alba is most temperamental. I doubt you have the fortitude to endure her imposing presence." She peeped at him with humor dancing in the depths of her blue eyes. "While I, on the other hand, have grown accustomed to dictatorial . . . people."

He paused with the coffee cup halfway to his lips. "If you mean me, I can be as gentle as a lamb when the circumstances warrant it."

She gave him a doubtful glance. "Not from what I've seen."

His eyes sparkled as he looked at her. "I can be gentle," he repeated, his tone reminding her of a time when he had gently taken her into his arms.

For a moment they stared at each other, until Royal stood up and moved to the window. "I believe it's time we talked, Damon." She turned around and found him watching her. "You know about what."

"Yes, you want to talk to me about Preston Seaton."

She was amazed by his perception. "Since you know Preston, it will make it all the easier."

"I owe him my life."

"Preston once saved me from a rather . . . awkward situation. So you see, we both owe him a debt of gratitude."

Damon's lips thinned. "Don't put too much stock in my gratitude."

His eyes ran the length of her hungrily. God, how lovely she was in her soft yellow gown. With the sun playing on her golden head, she looked like the image that every man carried within him of the perfect woman—or, at least, his image of the perfect woman.

Damon was surprised by his own assessment, and his voice came out in a gruff whisper. "I have come to suspect that you intend to marry Preston. What you may have forgotten is that your father endowed me with the right to approve or disapprove of your marriage."

"I hadn't forgotten that."

"Yet you plan to marry him without my consent," he accused in a dry voice.

She looked confused. "Although Preston has asked me to marry him, I haven't agreed. I'm very confused about many things, and his family does not approve of . . . me."

"I cannot think anyone would object to having you in his family."

"Then you are saying you would not object to my marrying Preston?"

"Would it not matter to you that he is an Englishman?"

"Not if I loved him."

"Obviously," he said, his voice deep with insinuation, "it appears you have chosen England over your own country." There was hidden meaning behind his words that went unnoticed by her. His eyes hardened. "Will you tell him about the night you came into my arms?"

She had forgotten how intently those amber eyes could burn into a person. She dropped her eyes and studied the tip of her kidskin slipper. "I . . . no, I will not tell him that."

"I wonder if there is much of your aunt in your character?"

Her head snapped up, and she met his gaze. "How dare you imply that I . . . that . . ."

Both she and Damon knew about her aunt's weakness for men, and though Royal loved her aunt Arabella, she did not want to be compared with her.

Damon lifted the tray and held it out to her. "Take this," he ordered. "I have suddenly lost my appetite."

Royal wanted to strike out at him, to hurt him as he was hurting her. She came forward and took the tray from him, set it on the table, and turned upon him furiously.

"I will marry Preston, with or without your consent."

"Will you?"

She nodded.

"Come here, Royal, and I will explain why that would be a mistake."

She took a step in his direction and then stopped. "I'm making no mistake."

"Perhaps you aspire high, and you are only anxious to become a duchess?"

She shook her head. "That's the only part I don't like. I would much rather Preston were an ordinary man."

He held out his hand to her. "Come here."

Reluctantly she placed her hand in his.

"So you intend to marry Preston out of wild, unbridled love," he said, bringing her closer to him.

"I l-love him," she admitted, her gaze locking with his.

With a sharp tug he pulled her across his chest, and her golden hair fanned across his face. She was unable to move as his hand toyed with a curl that had fallen across her lips. "What are you doing?" she asked in a throaty voice.

"Can't you guess?"

"I . . . no."

She was frozen in his hard embrace and could feel the rise and fall of his chest against her cheek. "Have a care of your wound," she whispered, wondering if he felt the same excitement that coursed through her veins.

He slowly raised her chin so she was forced to look at him. "I will show you, Royal, why you should not marry Preston Seaton." His gaze dipped to her lips. "Just a reminder of how fickle you are in your affections."

She tried to twist away from him, but his grip was too binding.

He raised her so her face was even with his. "I keep reminding myself that I'm your guardian, but it does no good—you're in my head and I can't get you out. Even when you are across the room from me, I can smell your perfume."

He pulled her now pliable body so she lay beside him. He looked into eyes that were sparkling with desire, yet there was also bewilderment reflected there. His finger traced down her neck to toy with the lace around her throat. When he saw her pulse beating there, he brushed his mouth against hers.

"Damon, I don't think we should—"

"Don't you?"

She looked into his eyes and saw desire, but she wanted to see those eyes soften with love. "You are killing my soul," she whispered.

"Really? What I want to do is make you feel more alive than you have ever felt in your life. I can't seem to forget holding you in my arms. Do you ever think of that night, Royal? Do you?"

"Yes," she admitted, pressing her body against his, feeling his arms close about her and crushing her to his chest.

His hands slid into her hair, and he brought her face even with his. "Tell me that you want me. . . ."

"Don't make me say it, Damon!" she cried.

His lips settled on hers in a drugging kiss. She could feel the heat of his hand as he gently caressed her breasts.

"Can your Englishman make you feel like this?" he asked, allowing his hand to move lower, circling her stomach.

"No," she admitted, moving closer, her lips parting. All at once she realized what was happening, and she pulled away from him. "No, Damon, this is wrong."

His eyes hardened. "See what I mean, Royal," he said, pushing her away. "Poor unsuspecting Preston does not deserve a wife who lusts after other men."

Before she could protest, his mouth ground against hers. She pounded against his back, but he caught her hands and clasped them in a tight grip.

Damon was unaware that his anger was caused by jealousy. He did not analyze his need to punish Royal, to make her feel some of his torment.

When she went soft in his arms, he deepened the kiss, and she clung to him, pressing her body tighter against his—his harsh words forgotten.

With a suddenness that took her by surprise, he tore his lips away and stared down at her. "By the saints! Poor Preston is to be pitied after all. Should I give my permission and make him miserable for the rest of his life?" He shoved her away. "No, I do not think so. After all, he deserves better than that."

Royal slid off the bed and wiped her lips with the back of her hand. "I'm not like that," she insisted through trembling lips. "Why are you doing this to me? I was happy with Preston before you . . . before I . . ." She backed away, turned, and fled through the door.

"Damn it!" he uttered with a degree of savagery. Why had he felt the need to punish her? She did not deserve the harsh treatment he had put her through. He knew she was innocent, he could tell.

Torment clouded his eyes. He did not like himself for what he had done to her today—what he had done to himself.

When Royal reached her room, she sat down at her dressing table and stared at her reflection in the mirror, watching a tear trail down her cheek.

"What shall I do?" she asked herself. "Why, why does Damon torture me so? I . . . wanted him to kiss me. I enjoyed it. Is it so wrong when you love a man?

"Merciful heavens," she cried, burying her head in her hands. "Can Damon be right? Am I like Aunt Arabella?"

To Royal, time passed with the tedious slowness of the ticking of a clock. Since her humiliating encounter with Damon, she had not visited his room. Even when he had sent word by Alba that he wanted to see her, she had refused his request.

She was often restless because she had too much time on her hands. Thus far she had received no word from Preston, so she waited and watched, knowing something monumental was about to occur.

For the past three weeks there had been heavy troop movement in and out of Savannah. It was whispered in the market that their destination was Charles Town. In April British frigates had attacked Fort Moultrie, and word was that it had fallen, though this had not as yet been substantiated.

Royal was just descending the stairs when she heard voices at the front door. She recognized the man standing there as Damon's aide, Corporal Thomas. He looked strangely out of place dressed in the guise of a British seaman.

Thomas looked anxiously at Tobias, who had admitted him into the house, and said, "It is imperative that I see Colonel Routhland at once!"

"Come with me, Corporal," Royal told him from the stairway. "I know he will want to see you."

If Corporal Thomas recognized Royal as the girl in Damon's quarters that night in Charles Town, he was too polite to show it.

She led him up the stairs and rapped on Damon's door, and after he gave permission, she pushed it open and stood aside so the corporal could enter.

Damon pulled himself to a sitting position when he saw Corporal Thomas. He knew by his aide's face that something had happened. "What has occurred, Corporal?"

"Colonel," he blurted out, "all hell's broken loose, sir! Charles Town is under the gun!"

"Bloody hell!" Damon swung his legs off the bed, ignoring the pain that shot through his body. "When did this happen?"

"This last week Fort Moultrie fell. Since the fort was the only defendable position before Charles Town, the city may already have fallen." Corporal Thomas's eyes showed the distress he was feeling. "I was told by General Lincoln to inform you to come with all haste if you are able."

"Tell me what you know," Damon commanded.

"Well, sir, those loyal to the cause say that General Washington proved to be too much for the English, so they took their war to the South to avoid his genius in the North. I heard those loyal to the king are claiming that to win the South is to win the war. Whatever the cause, we've come together at Charles Town, and it's too soon to tell which side is winning."

"Tell me more later. Right now I want you to find Miss Bradford and ask her to come to me. I will also want the two servants present."

Royal stood beside Alba while they watched Corporal Thomas packing Damon's valise. "What has happened, Damon?" she asked.

"Charles Town is under siege," he said, watching the reaction on each face. Tobias and Alba were shocked, and Royal's face whitened.

Royal grasped Alba's hand. "Surely not!"

"I fear so," Damon said grimly.

Corporal Thomas snapped Damon's valise shut. Reaching into his inside pocket, he extended a dispatch to Damon. "I almost forgot, sir. These are important documents that—"

"You know better than that, Corporal. Give them to me later."

Corporal Thomas appeared to be flustered as he looked from Royal to Tobias. "I apologize, sir. I just thought—"

"Never mind that," Damon said impatiently. "How did you get here?"

Corporal Thomas smiled. "It was easy, sir. I know the laundress who lives at the edge of town. She's kind of sweet on me," he said in all modesty. "She does laundry for the British and was easily persuaded to supply me with this garb."

Damon's lips twitched. "Do you think your . . . friend could be persuaded to supply me with clothing?"

"It would be no trouble at all, Colonel. I'll just slip on out and return as soon as possible." He nodded at Royal. "Ma'am, I hope you will forgive the abrupt way I invaded your house."

"I understand, Corporal," she said politely.

Corporal Thomas departed to do his colonel's bidding, while Royal and the two servants waited to see why Damon had summoned them.

"Surely you aren't thinking of going to Charles Town!" Royal blurted out. "You're not well enough to leave this room."

Damon glowered at Royal. "Never mind that. My only concern is that the three of you stay close to home. I don't know what will happen, and I don't want to have to worry about you." He turned his attention to the two servants. "Tobias, I'm depending on you to see that Miss Royal follows my instructions."

Alba and Tobias exchanged glances, both knowing that Miss Royal would do whatever came into her head.

"Alba," Damon continued, "I would appreciate it if you would pack some food. Tobias, I fear I will have to take one of your horses—please saddle it for me."

Both servants nodded and quickly left the room.

"Go ahead, kill yourself!" Royal cried once they were alone. "What do I care?"

Damon's gaze was probing, as if he were searching for something in her eyes. "Would you send a soldier into battle with only sharp barbs from your sweet lips?"

Her mouth went dry. "Surely you know how I feel about you."

"No," he said dully, "I do not." Now his eyes were mocking. "Suppose you tell me."

"Little I care what you do," she said, moving out the door. When she was in the hallway, she leaned her head against the wall, her shoulders shaking with silent sobs.

"I do care, Damon Routhland," she whispered. "I wish to God I didn't . . . but I do!"

After reading the dispatch, Damon eased himself off the bed and stood up, holding on to the bedpost. Pain moved like molten lava through his leg, making him close his eyes and grit his teeth.

"May I help you, sir?" Corporal Thomas asked with concern.

"Can't think about the pain," Damon said, taking a tentative step, then stopping to catch his breath. "Damn!" he ground out between a moan. "I must ignore the pain." He paused, then took another step and still another.

He made it to the fireplace and reached for the bottle of wine Tobias had procured for him. Opening the bottle, he drank deeply, caught his breath, and drank deeply again, hoping to dull the pain.

By the time he was dressed in the trappings of a British seaman, the pain had lessened. With a final look around the room that had been his prison for the last few weeks, he walked out the door and down the stairs while Corporal Thomas followed.

Royal waited for Damon at the bottom of the stairs, her eyes pleading as she looked into his face. "Don't do this, Damon. Give yourself a few more days to heal. Suppose the wound were to open again?"

He looked past her to where Colonel Thomas stood waiting for him. "I have a duty to my country." He gazed down at her. "Can you understand that?"

"Yes, but—"

"I want to thank you for your . . . hospitality. Don't think I am ungrateful."

As he moved past her, Royal saw how he limped, and it tore at her heart. "What good can come of doing your duty if it kills you?" she asked, but he did not even bother to answer her.

Damon shook hands with Tobias and smiled at Alba, who presented him with a canvas bag filled with food. With no further word to Royal, he moved out the door and, with considerable pain, managed to mount his horse.

His gaze rested on Royal, who stood on the top step, her eye swimming with tears. Perhaps he had been hard on her, and he didn't know why. "Don't worry about me, Royal."

Nudging his mount, he cantered away beside Corporal Thomas.

"All men are fools," Royal said, turning to Alba.

"Maybe, but if they are, what does that make the women who love them?"

Charles Town, South Carolina

The shallow trenches where defending soldiers stood knee deep in water gave little protection from the continuous cannon fire of the enemy's batteries.

The soldiers' faces were haggard, their eyes glazed with fatigue. The enemy was dug in no more than a few yards away, and as night fell both sides sniped at shadows.

Since Damon had the advantage of knowing Charles Town well, he had no difficulty slipping past enemy lines.

The sunlight had just caught the top of the trees when Damon slipped into General Lincoln's tent. The general was bent over a document, the scratching of his feather pen the only sound that could be heard. He looked up when Damon entered, and with a grim set to his lips, he motioned Damon forward.

"I wasn't certain you would be well enough to join us. Now I wish you hadn't, Damon. All is lost."

Damon eased himself down on a camp stool and stretched his aching leg out in front of him. "That has become obvious to me, sir. Without help from General Washington, you cannot possibly hold out. The British have us cut off from land and sea."

"Yet you managed to slip through."

Damon studied his friend grimly. "I am familiar with the area."

"Can you slip out again?"

"Yes, sir, but I would prefer to stay and fight."

"There are plenty of men who are willing to fight, but few I trust to carry this message to Washington at Morristown in New Jersey. Warn him that General Clinton will be returning to New York as soon as"—he paused as if he could not go on—"as soon as I surrender. His plans are to leave General Cornwallis in charge. Make him understand the urgency of bringing his war to the South."

Damon rubbed his aching leg unconsciously. "I passed several houses and shops that were on fire."

"Yes," General Lincoln said wearily, "and the civilians are begging me to surrender." He made a hopeless gesture. "With all escape routes closed off, what choice have I?"

"None, sir," Damon admitted brokenly. "Perhaps one man, maybe two, could slip through the enemy lines, but certainly not our whole damn army."

General Lincoln rolled up the dispatch and handed it to Damon. "Make haste, Colonel Routhland. Take my horse since it's fresh and don't stop until you are clear of Charles Town."

Damon was weary from riding for two days and nights. His leg ached and throbbed, and he could not recall the last time he had eaten. Still, he stood without wavering before his commander. What General Lincoln faced in the next few days would be difficult indeed. It could not be easy for a commanding officer to ask his men to admit defeat.

"You can depend on me, sir. I'll see that General Washington receives your message."

General Lincoln noted the circles under Damon's eyes and the paleness of his face. "Are you sure you're well enough for this, Damon? I know you've been laid up for several weeks."

"I'll make it, General."

At that moment the earth trembled from cannon fire, and Lincoln grabbed the lantern to keep it from falling. "You'll find the horses tethered fifty paces behind our lines. Just tell the corporal there that I said to give you mine."

The two men shook hands, and Damon looked grave. "God be with you in what you must do, General."

Lincoln nodded. "And with you, Colonel."

Savannah, Georgia

Ezekiel Elman came ambling up the steps and watched while Royal and Alba trimmed the branches of a lilac bush that spilled over the porch railing. The little man had come up so quietly that neither woman had heard him. He removed his cap and smoothed down his thinning gray hair.

"Morning, Miss Bradford," he said, smiling at Royal. "If it weren't for what happened at Charles Town, it would be a right nice day."

"Mr. Elman, how nice to see you," Royal said. "I was wondering how you were faring. I heard there was fighting near your farm."

"Nary a bullet hit my wife or myself, but they was awhizzing around and killed one of my stock. A right good milk cow she was, too."

"I am grateful that neither your wife nor yourself was hurt, Mr. Elman."

Alba gathered up an armload of branches and moved toward the side of the house. "I'll just take care of these," she said, eyeing the man's muddy boots warily. "If you are planning on going inside, make certain you wipe your feet first."

Both Royal and Ezekiel watched the housekeeper disappear, then Royal looked at him apologetically. "Would you like to come in and have something to drink? I believe Alba made some lemonade."

"No, ma'am, I just came to tell you the sad news, thinking you might not have heard about it yet."

Royal held her breath. "Damon . . . has anything happened to him?"

"Not that I know of, Miss Royal. But I got word this morning that Charles Town fell to the Redcoats. It's a sad day for us. This is the worst defeat we've had 'til now."

A sudden rage came over Royal. It came so strong and so unexpectedly that it left her breathless. "They can't do this to us! This is our land, not theirs." She thought of beautiful, graceful Charles Town and clenched and unclenched her fists. "Who's to stop them? Will they drive us to dust before they are finished?"

Ezekiel nodded grimly. "Never you fret—we'll stop 'em. With scrappers like George Washington and Nathanael Greene, we'll drive 'em back across that sea. General Clinton won't feel so proud when we win the final battle."

Royal's heart plummeted. Preston was supposed to be with Lord Clinton. "Was Sir Henry at Charles Town?" she asked.

"Yep. He was there bigger'n life."

When would this agony ever end? Royal tried not to think about Preston and Damon being on opposing sides in that battle. No, she could not bear to think about that.

"Them Redcoat generals must be havin' themselves a fine celebration over this'n! They brought us in the South to our knees!"

Royal fought against her anger, remembering that Damon had once told her the day would come when she would have to choose sides in this war. Apparently she had chosen today.

She moved down the steps to sit on a marble bench. "Sit beside me, Mr. Elman, and tell me what you know about the battle."

The old man adored the young beauty. He thought she was prettier than any female he had ever seen. And she was nice to him and listened to him when he talked, which was rare in young women these days. He would do anything for her—anything!

Sitting on the edge of the seat beside her, he began to tell Royal what he knew. "The way I heard it, the battle raged for forty-five long days until we was beaten and General Lincoln had to surrender."

"Do you know if Mr. Routhland was at the battle?"

"No, ma'am. I didn't hear if he was."

She drew in a deep breath. "Do you know anything else?"

"Well sir, the way I heard it from a man that was there, our officers were allowed to keep their swords until someone started shoutin', 'Long live Congress!' That got the British all het up, and they took the swords. Some men they paroled, and others they took as prisoners."

"Was anyone we know taken prisoner, Mr. Elman?"

"I hadn't heard any names." He chewed on his lower lip reflectively. "Cornwallis made our men endure a painful thing. We wasn't allowed to march out with our colors and was forced to move out to the Turk's March. I 'spect that was meant to ridicule." His eyes took on a steely glint. "But we're proud . . . and we'll remember—we'll remember every insult!"

"I'm just a woman, Mr. Elman, and I don't claim to know what makes war. Why will a man fight over this bit of land or that bit of land? Why can't we all live together in harmony?"

He leaned back and studied her for a long moment. "My own wife feels much as you do, Miss Royal, and I'm not sure a woman will ever understand what drives a man."

"What drives a man like Damon Routhland, Mr. Elman?"

"Without the Damon Routhlands of this world, we wouldn't have no rights and no freedom. He's the kinda man that other men follow—the kinda man we admire and look up to."

"I suppose. Still, I will always detest war."

"Love it or detest it, but always stand by Mr. Routhland while he does what he must. He will need you beside him to soothe him when it goes wrong."

Royal looked stunned. "Not I, Mr. Elman. Damon Routhland is my guardian." She clenched her hands together. "He may need a woman to stand beside him, but it won't be me. He thinks of me as a nuisance and nothing more."

Ezekiel smiled to himself, wondering why young people made everything so complicated. He had lived many years and could see much that a younger man might miss. "He'll need you all right, Miss Royal." The old man stood up and moved down the path. "Just be ready for him, 'cause he's gonna need no one but you—if you can believe anything, believe that."

Royal stared after the departing Ezekiel until he climbed aboard his wagon and moved away. Mr. Elman was wrong, she thought. Damon Routhland would never need any woman, and he certainly did not want her!

A heady wind twisted the branches of the mulberry tree, making it scrape against Royal's bedroom window. Although it was after midnight and Alba and Tobias had been in bed for hours, she lay restlessly upon her bed, listening to the creaking and settling of the house.

Here, alone in her room, Royal allowed herself to reflect on her life. Tears soaked her pillow as her tortured thoughts gave her no peace. Damon could have been forced to surrender at Charles Town, or worse still, he might have been killed.

Burying her head in her pillow, she cried out her agony. If only she knew where he was and if he was safe. But suppose . . . he was—

"No," she said, unwilling to think of the heartbreaking possibilities.

Swinging her legs off the bed, she got up and walked to the window. The night was dark, and she could see only vague outlines. When was this war going to end? She tried to think of her life back in England but couldn't empty her mind of how her own people were suffering. When had she begun to change? Or had the feelings been there all the time?

In the distance she heard the rumble of thunder—or had it been cannon fire? She closed the window and made her way back to bed. If only she could sleep. She did not want to think about the war tonight.

After a while her eyes drifted shut, and she slept a troubled sleep.

Somewhere in the back of the house the wind twisted the branches of the mulberry tree, scraping it against the window again. Royal awoke with a start. Her eyes ran the length of the room where all but the darkened corners were illuminated by flickers of lightening. Her body was rigid as she listened to the sound of the rain pelting against the floor. She sat up in bed, her heart caught in her throat. She had closed the window, she knew she had.

Getting out of bed, she moved across the floor to discover the rug was wet. She closed the window, then turned back to allow her eyes to search the room.

"Is someone here?" she asked, feeling foolish for her fears. Perhaps she had only thought she'd closed the window. "Alba's going to be unhappy about the rug getting wet," she said, glancing around for something to sop up the water.

A jagged streak of lightning illuminated the room, and Royal drew in her breath as she stared at the shadow near her bed. Had it been a trick of her overactive imagination, or was someone hiding in the darkness?

"Don't make a sound, Miss Bradford," came a raspy voice she had never heard before. "You won't get hurt if you just do as I say."

Now the dark outline of a man was clearly visible, and he stood between her and her only exit. Royal retreated a few steps, wishing she had not closed the window. "W-who are you?" she asked in a voice that trembled with fear.

"No one you have cause to know," came the sharp reply.

"What are you doing in my bedroom? Get out of here at once!"

Chilling laughter resounded. "Why, Miss Bradford, is that any way to talk to a man who took great pains to find you? In fact, I have come to take you away with me."

Royal was never so brave as when she was cornered. "Surely

you must be crazed. I will never go anywhere with you! If I scream, my servants will come at once!"

The shadow moved toward her, causing her to take several steps backward. "They cannot help you, Royal Bradford. No one can help you now!"

Alba became concerned when Royal didn't come down for breakfast. She turned to Tobias, who had just entered from the back door with a puzzled look on his face.

"Mind that you wipe your feet, Tobias. I won't have you tracking up my clean floor."

He dropped his armload of wood in the woodbin and removed his cap. "I found muddy tracks all around the house. What's strange is that they seem to disappear into the tree beneath Miss Royal's window."

Alba, who had been dipping spoon bread into a hot skillet, paused at her task. "What do you make of that?"

"I don't know. Where's Miss Royal? I haven't see her all morning."

Alba pushed the hot pan off the stove and turned toward the

door, beginning to worry. "Neither have I. I'd feel better if I see her for myself."

The housekeeper rushed up the stairs and, without bothering to knock, pushed open Royal's door. Her eyes went to the bed, but Royal was not there.

Glancing about the room, she clucked her tongue at the water stains on the rug. But she stopped short when she saw the muddy footprints. They were too large to be Miss Royal's. No, they would have to be a man's footprints, she thought in panic.

"Miss Royal, where are you, girl? Answer me!" She waited for a reply, but there was none, so she rushed to the top of the stairs and called down to her husband. "Tobias, come at once! Something is certainly amiss—hurry!"

By the time Tobias joined her, there was fear in the housekeeper's eyes. "What do you think happened?" she asked, pointing out the tracks.

Tobias frowned as he took in the situation. "I'll tell you what I make of it. Two men came in through that window, but they left by the door."

Alba shook her head. "Where is my Royal?"

Tobias's eyes took on a murderous light. "Apparently they took her with them." He hurried into the hallway and called over his shoulder, "They went out this way, bold as you please, and right out the front door."

Alba sank down on the bed, trying to think clearly past the panic that was welling up inside her. Who would do such a thing to that sweet child? She glanced at the pillow, where the imprint of Royal's head was still visible.

"What's this?" she said, picking up a note that had been placed there.

She ran into the hallway, calling after Tobias. "Listen to this," she said in a trembling voice.

> Damon Routhland,
> By now you will know that your ward is missing, and that I took her. Try to imagine all the horrors she will endure to pay for what

you did to me. Try to sleep at night when she cries out for your help. Try to find her if you dare.

Vincent Murdock

"My God!" Alba cried. "Who is this madman? Why has he taken Miss Royal?"

Tobias looked at his wife in disbelief. "Don't you know who he is? Murdock's the man that shot Mr. Routhland when he rescued the duke."

"What will we do?" Alba asked, beginning to pace the hallway. "Who can we turn to for help?"

Tobias was thoughtful for a moment. "We don't know where Mr. Routhland is, and for that matter, we don't know how to find the duke. We are surrounded by the enemy and don't know who to trust. I don't know, Alba." He shook his head sorrowfully. "I don't know."

Alba stopped her pacing and grabbed Tobias's arm. "Go to Ezekiel Elman. He might be addle-brained, but he'll know what to do. I suspect he would do anything to help Miss Royal. That old fool simply worships her."

"Yes," Tobias agreed, glad at last that he could do something positive. "I'll leave at once."

Royal awoke with a feeling of dread, reached up to her aching head, and found a knot. She had been knocked unconscious by one of the men who had spirited her away, and she was disoriented. Where was she? For a long moment she tried to focus her eyes and remember.

After a while she realized she was lying on a narrow cot with her arms tied in front of her. When she tried to sit up, she discovered her legs were bound as well.

She groaned in pain while she took in her surroundings. The room was small and crudely built. It was made of logs that had not been filled in, and she could see daylight through the wide gaps. There was a dirt floor, and wide palm leaves covered the roof. She doubted they would do much to keep out rain.

There was no window, and the door had no latch, leaving Royal to believe it was locked from the outside. The sounds she heard convinced her that she was in the swamps.

At that moment she was more bewildered than frightened. Who were the men who had taken her from her home, and what did they want with her?

Royal did not have long to wait for answers, for the door was thrust open, and a woman sauntered into the room. The woman's eyes were as black as her hair, which was frizzy and unkempt, and she was barefoot. Her face might have been considered pretty had it not been for the unsightly pout that turned her mouth down and the hardness in her eyes.

"So, the princess is awake," she said. "Bless us all. Can we serve you in any way, Miss High-and-Mighty?"

Royal resented the fact that she was being held in this filthy place against her will, and she refused to let this creature see how frightened she was. She tossed her head, returning the woman's taunts with a look of insolence. "Who is responsible for this?"

"La-te-da, but ain't we grand?"

"Who are you?"

"Name's Marie Grimmet." Her gaze fell on Royal's nightgown, and she leaned closer to examine it more thoroughly. Her dirty hands ran down the sleeve to touch the embroidered roses on the cuff. "This is mighty fine for a sleeping garment. I ain't ever had anything half so fine."

Royal jerked away from the woman. "Let me go, and you can have the gown."

Crackling laughter emitted from the woman's lips. "I can have it anyway, fool. You won't be needing it much longer."

In spite of her resolve to appear unafraid, Royal trembled. "What . . . d-do you mean?"

Marie stabbed a bony finger into Royal's chest. "Don't ya know?" she said slyly. "You're the prisoner of Vincent Murdock. And those what fall into his hands don't never escape!"

Royal tried to overcome the panic that riveted through her body by a show of bravado. "Yes, I recall the name now. But you are mistaken. I know a man who escaped from your Mr. Murdock."

Again the woman laughed. "That Englishman ain't important, you foolish woman," she said scornfully. "My Murdock snatched you to get back at the mighty Damon Routhland. Don't you know that because of him Murdock lost the use of his arm? Damon Routhland will suffer mightily for what he did." The woman gave Royal a smug look. "He ain't the only one who'll suffer. You being such a pretty, dainty little thing, bet you can't take much before you beg for an end to your life. Yep, my man has plans for you."

Royal lowered her head to hide the fear in her eyes. "Damon will kill your Murdock for this. If you value Murdock's life, you'd better help me escape."

The woman suddenly grabbed a handful of golden hair and jerked Royal around to face her. "I've bowed to fancy ladies like you all my life, but I ain't no more. Not since Murdock took me as his woman. Now, fancy lady, you'll bow to me."

"Never!"

"Oh, you will, never fear. My Murdock can be very cruel when the mood strikes him." The woman released her hold on Royal's hair and pushed her filthy white blouse off her shoulders. "See this scar here? Murdock did this in a fit of jealousy. I got whip marks all over my back." Her eyes took on a look of pride. "If my man would do this to someone he loves, just ponder what he'll do to you!"

Royal felt sick inside. "I have done nothing to Mr. Murdock."

"No, but your man has."

"Damon Routhland is not my man—he's my guardian."

"That's not the way I heard it. It seems both him and the Englishman favor you." Her gaze moved over Royal's face. "I 'spect some men do favor your puny kind of looks. But my Murdock likes a woman with meat on her bones."

Royal turned her face away from the hateful Marie Grimmet. Her head ached where she had been struck the night before, and her throat was parched and dry, but she would rather die than ask the woman for a drink of water.

"Leave me alone," she declared haughtily, and turned toward the wall. "I will no longer talk to you."

"I'll leave ya alone, but Murdock won't. He's gone for the day, but he'll be back tomorrow. You might as well get ready for him."

Royal heard the woman leave and latch the door behind her. Curling up on the cot, she began to tremble. Fear ate at her insides like bitter acid.

"Oh, Damon," she cried out, "not even you can help me now!"

The moon was shrouded behind a cloud as Damon plied his oars against the current, sending the small craft noiselessly down the Canoochee River, his destination—Swanhouse Plantation. Damon had not been home in over two years, and he wondered what changes the war had brought to his house and lands.

He hugged the darkened shadows of the riverbank and skillfully eased the boat beneath the pier that jutted out into the river. He climbed out of the boat and made his way up the slopes, taking care to keep within the shadows.

The message from John had said "urgent." He knew his secretary would never have sent for him if it were not a life-or-death situation. Damon had been granted a leave of absence so he could come home.

Slowly the clouds moved away, leaving a bright moon riding high in the sky. Damon held his breath. It appeared that neither time nor war had touched Swanhouse itself. The stately house rose majestically out of the darkness and was now bathed in soft light. Reflections of moonbeams mirrored in her windows, making it appear as if she were sending out a welcoming beacon to her lord and master.

For a long moment he stood motionless, breathing in the pine-scented air. He wondered what his father would have thought of this war. Would he have resented the English marching across

Georgia—scarring the land, killing and plundering—or would he have joined with the country of his birth? Damon believed his father would have supported America.

Damon heard unmistakably English voices coming from the cove just ahead, so he realized the British were still watching Swanhouse, hoping to catch him unaware.

Quietly he circled the enemy camp, his steps noiseless on the pine-needle-carpeted path. With measured caution he reached the back of the house and moved to the door, hoping he would find it unlocked. His firm tug was rewarded. The door opened, and he slipped into the cool darkness of the house.

How strange it was, he thought, to sneak into his own house like a thief in the night. After he had seen John, he would sneak out again and be gone before daylight came.

Damon did not need the benefit of light to guide him through his own home. His foot was on the bottom stair when he heard muffled voices coming from the library. Cautiously he moved to the closed door and listened. He recognized John's voice, though the secretary spoke in an agitated manner rather than with his usual calm.

"What shall we do, gentlemen? If only Mr. Routhland were here, he would know how to proceed."

Damon pushed the door open, and three pairs of startled eyes turned in his direction. He was surprised to find Tobias and Ezekiel with John. He acknowledged their presence with a nod. "Gentlemen, did I hear my name mentioned?"

"Mr. Routhland!" Tobias cried, moving forward to wring Damon's hand. "Thank God you're here! The most horrible thing has happened."

Damon searched the servant's eyes as a hand of dread wrenched his heart. "Has it to do with Miss Bradford?"

John moved forward. "It's most unfortunate, sir—most unfortunate."

"I reckon it couldn't be worse," Ezekiel said, adding his opinion to the conversation. "Nope, it couldn't be worse."

"For God's sake, what's happened to Royal?" Damon demanded. "Where is she?"

John struck a more professional attitude. He fumbled around on the desk until he found the note Tobias had given him earlier. "Vincent Murdock left this for you, sir. I think it will explain everything." John's look was sympathetic.

Damon could not bring himself to read the note. With a feeling of doom, he asked, "What does it say?"

John's eyes clearly showed his distress. "Miss Royal has been taken by Vincent Murdock, sir."

Damon was riveted with emotions—rage that Murdock still lived, disbelief that the man would take something that belonged to him, fear that he might harm her. As a man who was accustomed to making quick decisions, he turned to Ezekiel.

"You and I are the obvious ones to go after her," he said. "Will you come with me?"

"I done made up a pack of everything we'll need."

Damon looked at the old man with gratitude. "I should have known you would anticipate my thoughts."

"I want to get her back as much as you," Ezekiel said, looking grim. "She's a mighty fine little lady, and she don't deserve to be in that madman's hands."

Damon shuddered mentally, thinking of Royal at the mercy of Murdock. "We have to find her, and quickly."

"I figured you'd want to start at his camp, though if'n he was smart, he'd surely be gone by now."

"What can we do to help?" John asked.

"John, I want you to get word to my unit that an urgent matter has come up that requires my immediate attention. Tell them I'll return when I can. There is no need to tell anyone the nature of the crisis." Damon turned to Tobias. "You need to return to Savannah in case Murdock contacts you again. We'll get word to you and Alba as soon as possible."

"What if the duke should come inquiring about Miss Royal?" Tobias wanted to know.

"Under no circumstances are you to tell him what has occurred.

The last thing we need is the whole British army looking over our shoulders. Ezekiel," he said, turning to the man, "we should leave one at a time so we won't draw attention to ourselves. You go first. Take two horses and wait for me by the pond where I swam as a boy. I'll meet you there as soon as possible."

Ezekiel hurried toward the back door. "Have a care, Damon—the Redcoats would still like to get their hands on you."

Damon met Tobias's troubled gaze. "Tell Alba to have faith," he said. "Be assured that I shall do everything possible to find Royal."

"We know you will, Mr. Routhland. And if anyone can bring her safely home, it's you."

It was dark inside the hut with only pale moonlight shining through the cracks beneath the door. With considerable effort, Royal managed to drag herself to a sitting position.

Fear was her constant companion. She had been in this filthy pesthole for what seemed forever. So far she had not seen the dreaded Murdock, but she knew it was only a matter of time until he came.

Royal felt something crawl across her leg, and she shivered in disgust. She tried to move off the cot, knowing it was infested with all kinds of vermin, but the ropes about her wrists were too tight, so she fell back.

In the distance an owl hooted, announcing his nocturnal presence. Royal curled up in a tight little knot, feeling alone and miserable. She closed her eyes and tried to think of something pleasant so she could forget, if only for a moment, the horror of her situation.

She must have slept, for when next she opened her eyes, sunlight was streaming into the room. She dreaded the prospect of another day.

Suddenly the door was thrust open with such force that it banged against the wall. Royal shrank away from the man who stood in the doorway, his huge bulk casting a shadow over her face.

Her gaze moved up the length of him. He was dressed in dirty buckskins, and his hair was matted and tangled. His right arm dangled at his side. His legs were long, his body beefy, his eyes small and black, and the look he cast her sent shivers of terror up her spine.

"So," he said, moving to stand over her, "Royal Bradford, you're the woman who has captured both the Englishman's and Damon Routhland's hearts." His eyes swept her from head to toe. "If they saw you now, they might not think so much of you . . . hmm?"

"You are mistaken, Mr. Murdock, if you think either man has an interest in me."

He touched her golden head, and she cringed but did not pull away. "You can't fool me. I know both men want you. Let me see what they find so desirable in you," he said, grabbing a handful of hair and jerking her head back so her face was turned up to him. "I've been watching you for a long time, but I never got close enough to see you so clearly." His eyes widened when they fell on her lovely face. "Yes, you are indeed a rare beauty."

"Why are you doing this?"

"I don't care so much if the Englishman grieves over your disappearance, but I want Routhland to be in agony."

Although Royal knew Damon would not stop until he found out what had happened to her, she had to make this odious man think he would not care. "You are mistaken, Mr. Murdock. Mr. Routhland will not be overly concerned by my disappearance."

Murdock released his hold on her and sat down beside her. She resisted the urge to scamper to the far side of the cot.

The man laughed while his eyes narrowed in speculation. "I know more about your affairs than you think I do. But I'm curious—what did you do, Miss Bradford, play the one man against the other? Did you dally with one while tormenting the other with your sweetness?"

"I . . . don't know what you are talking about."

He studied her intently. "Maybe you don't. I can't judge a woman of your refined nature since I never knew one before."

Murdock reached out and ran his finger down her cheek. He found himself fascinated by his captive. It was true that he had never before been this close to a woman of her class. "You are the beautiful bait I will use to lure Damon Routhland to me."

"He won't come."

Evil laughter filled the room. "Oh, he'll come right enough. Any man would go through hell to get a woman like you back."

She licked her dry lips, and his eyes followed the movement. "What you need is a man who knows how to treat a woman," he said suggestively.

She glared at him. "I saw evidence of how you treat women. Marie showed me her scars."

He stood up. "It would be different with you. I could be very nice to you. We could be good together."

She threw back her head and met his eyes squarely. "That's something you will never find out. I'd kill myself before I'd let you touch me!"

Ordinarily Murdock would have struck any woman who dared talk to him in such a way, but this one only intrigued him more. He rubbed his hand over the stubble on his face, his eyes thoughtful. "This is no way for a lady such as yourself to live. I'll send Marie to clean the place up and bring you some clothing. We'll talk more this evening."

Murdock left the room, heading for the washtub at the back of the encampment—he would bathe and shave. The notion of possessing a woman who belonged to Damon Routhland was becoming an obsession with him. Her skin was so white, her eyes so clear. He had never seen a woman with hair like spun gold.

Royal felt more afraid than ever. If he had struck her, she could have dealt with it; but his actions had been most disturbing, and she shivered at what might be her fate at his hands.

As Murdock was sharpening his razor, Marie came up to him and rubbed her body against his. "I kept an eye on the woman just like you told me to."

"See that she has water to bathe and take her a gown—and don't go giving her one of your filthy rags. She's a lady."

Marie's eyes filled with suspicion. "What are you thinking, Murdock?"

He applied the razor to his face. "You are beginning to annoy me, Marie. Just do as you're told." He shoved her away with a strength that sent her tumbling to the ground.

She rose slowly to her feet, her whole insides on fire with jealousy. "She won't have nothing to do with you. She's used to fancy men like that Englishman."

He glared at her. "Little you know about her kind. Real ladies like men of strength and character."

"Like Damon Routhland," she taunted. "He had strength enough to cripple you."

Before the luckless woman knew what was happening, Murdock was upon her, pressing the razor against her throat. "Take care that your wagging tongue does not dig your grave," he said between clenched teeth.

Marie blamed herself for his anger. She should have remembered that any reference to Damon Routhland would send him into an uncontrollable rage. She was paralyzed with fear as she felt the cold blade against her throat.

"I'll do whatever you want me to, Murdock," she said in a choked voice. "But don't hurt me again."

She stared into black eyes that bulged with rage, knowing she was only moments away from death. She felt the blade tremble, and then he closed his eyes and shook his head to clear his thoughts.

Marie drew in a deep breath, knowing he could easily have cut her throat. She stood up on trembling legs and backed away from him, still uncertain if his rage was under control.

"I have decided to be generous and let you live," he said lightly as if nothing had happened. "But guard your tongue and do what you are told from now on."

"I will, Murdock," she assured him. "You won't have no trouble from me."

Damon and Ezekiel moved cautiously down the path toward Vincent Murdock's campsite. As they had suspected, it was deserted, and the charred huts gave evidence of a fire.

Ezekiel bent down and examined the ashes. "Looks like it's been burnt several weeks ago."

"Yes," Damon agreed. "My guess is that Preston Seaton had a hand in this. The fool—he's only forced Murdock to go deeper into the swamp."

Damon's eyes were filled with anguish as he fixed them on the far horizon. This painful emotion he was experiencing was so new to him that he did not know how to deal with it. "He's out there somewhere, but where, Ezekiel?"

"Can't rightly say, but I have a passing acquaintance with a man who might know."

Damon turned hopeful eyes on him. "Who is this man?"

"Lester Grimmet. His sister is Murdock's woman. He don't like Murdock any too well, and he might be persuaded to tell us where to find him."

"I feel so helpless. Every moment Royal is in that man's hands is . . . torment to me." The words were torn from his throat. "I can't allow myself to think what she might be . . ." His eyes clouded with anguish. "I'll kill him if he's touched her!"

The old man's eyes blazed with determination. "We'll get her back, Damon. Don't you worry 'bout that. I don't think he plans to harm her—this is his way of luring you to him. I heard tell he has a powerful hatred for you. We best go cautiously so we don't fall into any trap he's set for you."

Marie faced Royal with scorn on her face. "Murdock says you're to wear this," she said, tossing her gown at Royal.

"I can't very well dress if my hands are bound," Royal informed the woman. "Do you intend to keep me tied?"

Marie came forward and with a jerking motion untied the ropes at Royal's feet and hands. "I curse the day you came here. You've caused trouble between me and my man, and I hate you for it."

Royal turned her back on the woman and slipped out of her nightgown, glad at last to have something suitable to wear. The linen gown was rough against her skin, but it was clean, and it would give her more protection against Murdock's prying eyes.

Marie scooped up Royal's discarded nightgown and ran her fingers over the delicate material. "I'm taking this in exchange for my gown." She watched Royal closely as a dog would guard a bone against another dog. She half expected the fancy woman to object.

"Take it, and you are welcome to it." She pushed her tangled hair out of her face. "I find this more suitable to my needs."

With her hands on her hips, Marie walked around Royal. It did not please her that her own gown looked better on this woman than it ever had on her. Her eyes darkened with envy. "I 'spect you're used to men breathin' heavy when you come 'round. You may think Murdock's smitten with you, but it ain't true. He took you 'cause he wants Damon Routhland dead."

"Damon will not be lured into a trap. He's much too intelligent for that."

Marie stopped her circling. "Humph, little you know 'bout men. A woman can make'm rush headlong into danger when their loins rule their heads. I bet Damon Routhland's panting after you like a stallion wanting to get to a mare."

Royal felt sickened by the woman's vulgar inferences. "You couldn't possibly know what goes on inside the mind of a gentleman like Damon Routhland. You are only accustomed to a savage like Murdock."

Royal saw a satisfied smile slowly crease Marie's face as she stared at someone standing just behind Royal. Even before Royal turned around, she knew she would face Murdock.

"So, fancy piece, you think I'm a savage, do you? We'll see about that."

Royal noticed that he had shaved, and his hair was still wet, so he must have bathed. His black eyes bored into her while he snapped his fingers at Marie. "Get out!"

"I won't," Marie said.

He turned on her, grabbed her arm, and shoved her to the door. "Get yourself off, and don't come back. I'm sick of the sight of you!"

Marie lingered in the doorway, ready to take flight if he came too close. "This fancy piece don't want you. You'll come crawlin' back to Marie when this one's wiped her dainty feet on ya."

"Get out!" he roared.

Royal watched the woman flee, wishing she could go with her. She turned her eyes up to the man who towered over her and met his stare without flinching.

"Don't touch me," she addressed him with as much hauteur as she could manage. She hoped he could not guess that her manner was forced and far from what she was feeling.

Respect shone in his beady little eyes. "I should be angry with you for calling me a savage, but I have decided to be lenient. You are an exceptional woman. You will tell me all about yourself."

He motioned to the cot, but she shook her head. "I just want to talk to you, nothing more."

"I have nothing to say to you. I don't enjoy being dragged out of my own house and brought here as a prisoner."

"Oh, you're not a prisoner. You're free to roam about at will. Of course, I think I should warn you that my men are partial to pretty women, and I can't say they won't fall on you. And then the waters hereabouts are infested with alligators. I've seen an alligator gobble up a full-grown man in less time than it would take me to smoke a pipe."

She trembled, knowing he was right. Whether or not he tied her up, she was a prisoner of these swamps.

"Take me back home. I can't mean anything to you."

His eyes blazed. "When I brought you here, it was for revenge—now I keep you because you please me."

She stared at him in disbelief. "You can't just keep me here against my will."

"I can, and I will." He dropped down on the bed and patted it, indicating she should sit beside him. "I only want to talk to you. You have my word that nothing else will happen between us unless you want it to . . . at least, not yet."

"Why should I trust a man like you? You are dishonorable and . . . and . . . a pig!"

His eyes narrowed, but he managed to smile. "Guard your tongue, Royal Bradford. I can only be tested so far."

She realized that this man was close to madness and must be handled carefully. With great trepidation, she sat beside him, deciding the best way to stave off any advances he might make was to keep him talking.

"Tell me about yourself," she said, remembering Mrs. Fortescue had once told her class that men liked to talk about themselves. "Were you born in the swamps?"

He smiled as if he were remembering something pleasant. "Actually, no. I was born in Philadelphia. It might surprise you to learn that my pa was a schoolmaster."

"No," she told him, relaxing just a little. "I can tell by your manner of speech that you had a formal education. Tell me about your boyhood."

Murdock's voice droned on and on as he recounted a time in his life that he had pushed out of his mind. Whenever he paused, Royal would encourage him to continue by asking a question.

"You know," he said, standing up and moving to the open door to stare outside, "I've told you things today that I never told another soul." He frowned. "I had forgotten that I once lived in a world far different from this one."

He swung around and stared at Royal. "But I have not forgotten that Damon Routhland gave me this!" He tapped his useless arm. "And I have not forgotten my vow to see him dead!"

A covey of ruffled grouse came squawking down the path as if someone had disturbed their nesting place. Damon and Ezekiel flattened themselves behind a tree, watching the path for whatever, or whoever, had frightened the birds. A twig snapped, and then the shadow of a man danced across the trail.

"Lester told the right of it," Ezekiel whispered. "That's one of Murdock's men. The camp must be just ahead. 'Course, we can't be sure that Lester didn't send word to Murdock to expect us."

The man went whistling by and disappeared around a bend. Damon and Ezekiel moved forward cautiously, staying to the bushes and avoiding the path whenever possible. It was slow progress since they had to cut their way through the tangled undergrowth.

At last they spotted puffs of smoke and knew the camp was just ahead. They dropped down on their knees and looked across the watery swamp.

"It won't be easy to get to," Damon observed, pointing to a large alligator that floated lazily on the surface of the water with only the top of his head and his eyes showing.

There was caution in the old man's expression. "You know Murdock'll be awaitin' for ya."

"Without a doubt." Damon turned to look at his companion. "That's why you aren't going in with me. I need you to stay here and watch."

A stubborn light gleamed in Ezekiel's eyes. "I ain't likely gonna let you go in there without me."

"You don't have any choice, my friend. I want you to wait here, and if I haven't come out by morning, then you will know I have failed, and it will be up to you to rescue Royal."

Ezekiel nodded reluctantly. "I can see the sense of that, but I don't like it none. You won't have anyone to watch your back if I'm not there."

"I am thinking of Royal. We are her only hope. The way I figure it, if we split up, she will have twice as good a chance of getting away."

"I reckon," Ezekiel admitted grudgingly.

For the rest of the afternoon they watched the comings and goings at Murdock's camp. They studied the lay of the land, looking for any vulnerable spot, but there was none—Murdock had chosen well. His encampment was an island surrounded by quicksand and alligators, and it was accessible only by raft or boat.

"I can't see any way to get to it without rafting across," Ezekiel stated, voicing Damon's conclusion.

"So it seems," Damon said grimly. "There must be a raft tied around here somewhere. We'll locate it, then I'll wait for dark before I cross."

Ezekiel looked at the waning sun. "There'll be a bright moon tonight," he said pessimistically.

Damon checked his rifle and tested the blade of his knife before pushing it into his boot. "I could wish it otherwise."

"You keep watch while I locate the raft," Ezekiel said, moving into the shadows. "Mayhap you can locate Miss Royal."

Damon nodded, his eyes already on a hut latched from the outside that would be the obvious place for them to keep Royal. But perhaps that was what Murdock wanted him to think. His gaze moved to a small hut set apart from the others. That, he decided, was where Royal would be.

He settled down to watch, forcing his impatience to the back of his mind. He wanted to go charging across the swamp and take Royal away from this hellhole, but he had to consider her safety, so he had to wait and bide his time.

Ezekiel located the raft and was in the process of returning to Damon when the man they had seen earlier came upon him.

"Who be you?" the man barked out, aiming his musket at Ezekiel's chest.

"Name's Ezekiel Elman," he answered, looking around for his weapon. He spied his rifle where he had propped it against a tree and knew he could never reach it in time.

"Well, Ezekiel Elman, you just lived your last day on this earth. Ain't no one comes near Vincent Murdock's camp and lives to tell 'bout it."

"I reckon that's fair," Ezekiel agreed, diving for the ground and rolling behind a clump of bushes. He could hear the man lumbering toward him, so he looked around for something to defend himself with. Seeing a stone, he picked it up.

When the man came in sight, Ezekiel lobbed it at him and was surprised when it caught the man in the forehead and he dropped like a tree that had been felled.

Ezekiel crawled forward and scooped up the man's musket from where it had fallen. Aiming it at the prone figure, he waited, amazed when the man did not move. Cautiously he crept forward and reached out his hand to the man's throat. There was no pulse beat.

"Thunderation!" the old man exclaimed in disbelief, "he's dead! Like David, I done slew Goliath!"

Dark had settled over the swamp world that Royal had come to abhor. Everything was always damp. The smell of mildew was ever present, and the air was heavy and oppressive. She longed for a cleansing breath—she wished for a day when she did not have to fear for her life.

For over a week Murdock had come each day to her hut and stayed for hours, his dark eyes raking her body, his callused hand often brushing against her. So far she had been able to keep him occupied by encouraging him to talk about himself, but the time would come when talk would not keep him away.

She moved to an eye level crack in the wall to watch the moon, like a giant ball of fire, rise over the swamp. Royal's whole being was filled with melancholy and a strange yearning. Her thoughts were of Damon.

Murdock seemed confident that Damon would come to rescue her, but she hoped not since a trap awaited him. She couldn't stand to think of him coming to harm because of her.

Suddenly gunfire erupted at the far side of the island. She turned her head to look in that direction and saw a raft floating toward the island with a man on board. She cried out as bullets tore through the figure on the raft, because she feared it was Damon.

The door burst open, and Marie stood there, her hands on her hips, a malicious grin on her face.

"Your Damon Routhland's come for ya. Ain't it a pity he's dead."

Royal shook her head, unwilling to accept what the woman was telling her. "It . . . cannot be true."

"It is true. If you'd seen what I seen, you'd know it. Ain't no way he's alive."

"No," Royal moaned.

"Bold as you please," Marie taunted, "he sailed to meet death. When he got near enough, Murdock and his men peppered his body with shot."

Royal clutched her hands together, her heart shattered. "No, it cannot be."

"I'll say this for your man," Marie admitted grudgingly. "He's brave, though foolish. I don't think Murdock would do the same for me."

"I must go to him," Royal cried, her eyes wild with grief. "I will not let anyone touch him but me."

Marie stepped in front of her. "Murdock tole me to keep you here, and I aim ta do just that."

Royal's grief was now tempered with anger. She reached out and grabbed a handful of black hair and pulled Marie forward. "You can't stop me!" She flung Marie aside and rushed for the door.

Just when she thought she was safely outside, Marie caught up with her, grabbed her around the waist, and flung her to the ground. Royal did not feel the pain of her impact, she was too frantic. She jumped to her feet and tackled Marie, making them both roll down a slope, where they landed in the mud.

Both women struggled for supremacy, and finally Royal swung her fists and caught Marie a stunning blow across the temple. The woman crumpled and lay still. But before Royal could gain her feet, she was caught from behind by strong arms, and she swung out again, catching her assailant hard on the jaw.

"Dammit, Royal, it's me!" Damon called out in pain, dangling her in the air while she struggled to get free.

She whirled around, unable to believe her eyes. "Damon! Oh, Damon, they told me you were dead!"

He tested his jaw. "I was doing all right until I encountered you. You strike a good blow."

"How did you—"

"No time to explain," he said, pulling her into the shadows. "Our first concern is how in the hell to get out of here."

There was the sound of shouts and running feet, and Damon

knew Murdock and his men were heading in their direction. "If you know how to pray, Royal, now would be a good time."

He scooped her up in his arms and moved toward the water. "Here's where we make a decision. Do we swim with alligators or take on Murdock and his vermin?"

"Mayhap a boat ride would suit ya better."

They both recognized Ezekiel's voice. The old man applied his oars and bumped against the water's edge. "You best hurry, Damon, Murdock's fannin' your rear."

With a loud whoop, Damon jumped from the bank with Royal still in his arms, soared through the air, and landed in the boat. For a moment the small craft teetered and swayed, and it appeared they would all three be dumped in the water, but Ezekiel's expert paddling soon brought the craft under control.

"Let's get the hell out of here," Damon said, depositing Royal none too gently on the floor of the boat and taking up oars to help Ezekiel paddle.

Shots rang out, and Damon pushed Royal's head down.

"I'll get you for this, Damon Routhland!" Murdock swore, raising his one good arm in the air and shaking his fist. "There's no place on earth where you can hide her. I'll get her back—I swear I will!"

Royal raised her head and found Murdock standing knee deep in the water, shaking his fist at the heavens. She shivered at his grim warning.

Damon and Ezekiel were applying strong strokes, and Murdock and his men soon disappeared from sight.

"Will they follow?" Royal asked, still frightened.

Ezekiel laughed merrily. "They'd like to, Miss Royal, but they can't till they repair their boats. You see, I had me this lucky stone." He drew it from his inside pocket, tossed it in the air, and then put it away. "I just busted the bottom of all their boats, 'ceptin' this one."

Damon's laughter joined the old man's. "When will I ever learn not to underestimate you, Ezekiel? Heaven help the British if we let you loose on them."

Royal was emotionally spent. She lay in the boat, too weary to lift her head. "I never thought I would get out alive, Damon."

He secured his oars and lifted Royal into his arms. "Don't think about that now. You're safe."

She rested her head against his shoulder, feeling as if nothing could harm her now. "They told me you were dead."

"They thought I was."

"But I don't understand. I saw the body on the raft and the bullets—"

"That wasn't me, it was one of Murdock's sentries, and he was already dead. I had this notion that if Murdock and his men were pulled to the other end of the island, that would leave me free to come to you."

She smiled up at him. "That was brilliant."

"What about me?" Ezekiel asked eagerly.

"You were brilliant, too." She reached forward and kissed the old man on the cheek, and he beamed with pleasure.

"What about me?" Damon asked lightly.

"How can I thank the two of you?" she said, leaning forward and brushing her lips against his.

He smiled down at her. "That's payment enough, wouldn't you say, Ezekiel?"

"Yep, sure 'nuf."

Ezekiel turned back to his oars and concentrated on the tricky twists and turns of the byways.

Damon shifted Royal's weight so she was lying across his lap. "Sleep, little one," he said softly. "I'll take care of you now."

She nestled her head against his broad chest, comforted by the steady beat of his heart. She loved him so desperately it hurt.

"Was I in time? Are you . . . did Murdock—" Damon could not voice his deepest fear.

"No," she told him. "I was not harmed in any way."

He let out a sigh of relief. "Thank God." Then: "You could do with a bath," he said lightly. "You're covered with mud, you know."

"Perhaps, but I have the satisfaction of knowing that Marie fared no better."

"A most unmaidenly display, I must say." He tried to act stern, but his lips twitched into a smile. "Is that the kind of behavior they endorsed at that school?"

She looked up at him. "I know it was unladylike, but Marie said you were dead, and she wouldn't let me go to you."

"So you took her on."

"I hope she feels every bruise. I don't like her in the least." She yawned and smiled apologetically. "She deserves a man like Murdock."

It took only a moment for Royal to drift off to sleep. Lying in Damon's arms and lulled by the gentle rocking of the boat, she slept deeply.

Ezekiel glanced at Damon's face where a bruise was visible on his cheek. "I thought you said ya didn't tangle with Murdock's men."

"I didn't."

"Then how did you get that bruise?"

He glanced down at Royal's sleeping form. "I tangled with a little wildcat."

Ezekiel chuckled. "I see. She whupped you and Marie both. Feisty little lady, ain't she?"

"Remarkable."

"We lost our horses," the old man reminded him.

"We could have lost our lives," Damon said. "If it hadn't been for you, we'd be in Murdock's hands by now."

"The little lady didn't suffer at his hands, did she?"

"No. I don't believe so—at least she says not—but emotionally, she must have lived through hell."

"She's got spunk, I've seen this for myself."

"Yes, but she's never had to deal with a man like Murdock. And I pray God she never will again."

"She'll get over this."

Damon watched Ezekiel move through the narrow channels with the expertise of one born to the swamps. After an hour Ezekiel guided the boat onto the Canoochee River, which carried them swiftly along in its current.

Damon glanced down at Royal. Her face was muddy, her hair tangled, her gown torn and dirty. He could only guess what horrors she had suffered. His arms tightened about her protectively. This incident with Murdock had made him realize how important she was to him. He had done a lot of thinking and had come to a conclusion. He could not return to his unit until she was safe.

She sighed in her sleep when he touched her cheek. Preston Seaton was a good man, and a duke at that. She would be safe with him. But how could he give her up?

"Ezekiel, does Reverend Camdon still live outside Savannah?"

"He did as of a week ago."

"I want you to bring him to the hunting lodge when we arrive."

The old man nodded. "I wondered when you would come to that."

"I have no choice, Ezekiel."

The old man laughed merrily. "I see what you can't, Damon. But then, I always did have a keener eye than you."

"Damn it! I have to give her the protection of my name and move her to Swanhouse. Otherwise how can I know she will be safe?"

"I reckon you best ask her 'bout that. She may just not care to let you sacrifice yourself for her." Ezekiel snickered. "Mighty noble of ya, I'd say."

Damon scowled. "You think I'm doing this for another reason?"

"You'll know that better'n me. But I never knew a man to make a sacrifice 'less'n he was gettin' somethin' out of it for himself," the old man said, chuckling.

Could Ezekiel be right? Was he fooling himself by acting noble in offering protection to Royal when all along it was what he wanted? Was this his last effort to keep her from marrying the Englishman, who would surely take her to England where he would never see her again?

Why did he feel this cold emptiness inside? Damon wondered. Why did he ache with a feeling of great loss?

Royal was awakened when the boat bumped against something solid. It was near sunrise, and she opened her eyes when Damon stood with her in his arms.

"Where are we?" she asked sleepily.

"At my hunting lodge," Damon informed her.

She lay back against his shoulder, still too weary to move.

He carried her up the steps and into the lodge. Moving through the outer room, he placed her on the bed in the sparsely furnished bedroom. He pulled the covers over her and watched her as she slept.

Ezekiel lit a candle and waited for Damon. Tiptoeing out of the room, Damon closed the door and joined Ezekiel, who had a fire going in the hearth and coffee brewing.

"You still want me to get the reverend?"

"I haven't changed my mind. If I let her go back to Savannah, Murdock might get to her again. But as my wife, she will go to Swanhouse, where she'll be well protected."

"Why didn't you take her straightaway to Swanhouse?"

"You know I can't do that unless we're married. I thought it might be wise for her to stay here until she regains her strength. You can gather supplies and inform Alba and Tobias that she's safe."

"I'll fetch the reverend by tomorrow night."

Damon nodded. "That will give me time to talk to her."

"I know'd how you feel about her—it's clear as a day in April. And I reckon that for a long time she's felt the same 'bout you."

"Are you forgetting the Englishman?"

"You could always hand her over to him." Ezekiel smiled as if he knew a secret. "Or don't you want to let her go?"

"Let her go? Hell, she's not mine to keep."

Damon walked to the window and stared out at the gathering dawn. "I can't recall a time in my life when I was so unsure of myself, Ezekiel. Georgia is under the heel of the British, and General Washington stays in the North while we flounder. I don't know what the hell is going to happen from day to day."

"That's not what's really bothering you tonight," Ezekiel observed. "It's the little lady what's got you in a spin." He poured a cup of coffee and carried it over to Damon. "I've seen women come in your life, and I've seen 'em go, but I ain't never seen one get to you like this one has."

"I know," Damon admitted reluctantly.

"She's the kind you marry—the kind you make a ma to your offspring."

"I know that, too."

"Why don't you send for the Englishman?"

"You have a long night ahead of you, Ezekiel," Damon reminded him in an irritated voice.

"You're a fool, Damon Routhland."

"Among other things."

Damon watched the wind ruffle the branches of the pine trees outside the lodge. "I have to go back to Murdock's camp after Royal is safely at Swanhouse."

"I kinda figured you would."

"If I don't, he'll try to take her again."

"That'd be my thought. Say when you're ready to go, and I'll go with ya."

Ezekiel picked up his pack and headed for the door. "As for Miss Royal, seems to me you might want to ask her about her feelings." He paused with the door open. "I'll be back soon as I can."

"I'll expect the minister by tomorrow," Damon insisted.

Ezekiel gave a mocking salute and was gone with a parting shot. "Yes, sir, Colonel."

Damon stood at the window, watching the sun streak the eastern sky with its brilliance. He was weary, so he moved to the leather chair and sat down, placing his coffee cup on the floor beside him. Leaning his head back, he fell asleep immediately.

Royal awoke and looked about her, expecting to see the crude walls of the hut. But these walls were of polished logs—and instead of the dingy cot she had lain upon in Murdock's camp, she was tucked beneath a soft down comforter.

Blinking her eyes, she remembered that she was in Damon's hunting lodge. She eased herself out of bed and groaned from the bruises on her body. Marie had got in her blows, she thought with irony.

Pushing the door open, she moved cautiously into the outer room. Her gaze ran the length of the log walls, taking in every detail. This was definitely a man's room, with unpolished wooden floors, a bearskin rug, leather chairs, and a table made out of logs. Along the walls were several stuffed animal heads. Over the mantel hung a musket.

Her eyes fell on the chair near the window, and she saw Damon asleep there. She moved forward tentatively, not wanting to disturb him. When she stood over him, she had the strongest urge to reach out and touch him. With his guard down, he looked so vulnerable. His dark hair fell across his forehead, his long lashes made shadows against his cheek. His firm mouth was parted just a bit, and she remembered vividly how those lips had once awakened a fire within her body.

Troubled by her thoughts, she glanced down at her mud-caked hands. As quietly as she could, she moved out the front door.

A warm sun beat down on her. It was glorious to be free of Murdock!

She walked along the river until she could no longer see the cabin. She waded into the river until she was waist deep in the cold water. Like tiny needles, the swift current made her tingle as it washed the mud from her gown and body. She then dunked her head and scrubbed her long golden tresses, wishing for some of her rose-scented soap.

"Royal, what in the hell do you think you're doing?"

Damon stood on shore, hands on hips, glaring at her. "Come out of that water at once!"

A mischievous light danced in her eyes. "Why don't you come in and get me?"

There was irritation in his voice. "Royal, the river is swift, and if you aren't a good swimmer, you can be carried downstream. I'm in no mood to dive in and pull you to shore."

She smiled to herself as she dove under the water, kicking her feet so she would not surface. Alissa had taught her to swim at Chiswick one summer, and over the years she had become quite proficient.

Damon waited tensely for Royal to surface, and when she didn't he plunged into the river, boots and all. Frantically he dove under the water, searching for her. At last he came up for air and found her nearby, laughing at him.

He was amused by her, and his irritation melted away. "You little baggage, I thought you were drowning."

She swam over to him and clasped his arm playfully. "You're wet," she taunted.

His dark brows came together, the smile faded, and his jawline hardened. "And you are a naughty little girl who needs to be taught a lesson."

Her laughter chimed out, and she dove under the water, trying to evade him, but he reached out and caught her gown and dragged her to him.

"So," he said, his irritation returning, "I see you still like to play games. What does one do with a naughty little girl?"

She tossed her head back and looked up at him. "Anything you wish, sir. You are my lord and master." Her mouth clamped shut as the words were spoken. Yes, she thought, he *was* her lord and master.

The amber in his eyes deepened to a bright gold while he inspected her closely. "I know what I'd like to do." His hand drifted up to her hair, and he pulled her closer. "I'd like to torment you the way you have tormented me. I want to invade your dreams the way you have invaded mine."

The sunbeams dancing on the surface of the water were reflected in the depths of her blue eyes. "I . . . feel . . . I want . . ." She shook her head in confusion, unable to voice the deep love she felt for him. It was too overpowering, too unsettling.

His fingers bit into her flesh. "Do you love Preston Seaton?" He had to know.

"Yes, but—"

Damon had been watching her, and when he spoke, his words puzzled her.

"Are you cold marble or warm flesh, Royal?"

She took his hand and placed it against her cheek, knowing her action was provocative. "As you can feel, I am flesh like any other woman," she said softly.

"Damn you," he ground out, lifting her in his arms and carrying her ashore. "Have you no notion about how to behave with a man?"

He placed her on her feet and glared at her. "Are you so innocent that you don't know what you're doing?"

There was a ring of longing in her voice, and her eyes were wistful and seeking. "I don't know how to act with you, Damon. You are the authority in my life. When I asked you to find Preston for me, you did, at risk to your own life. You came to me like an avenging angel when I was taken by Murdock. How should I act with you?"

He steered her toward the lodge. "If this is your way of saying you are grateful to me, a simple 'thank you' would be sufficient."

He pulled her along so swiftly that she had to run to keep up with him. She glanced at him and found a scowl on his face. She had displeased him again. Would she always make him angry?

Once inside the lodge, he pointed to the bedroom. "Get those wet clothes off. You'll find a robe to put on until they dry."

"I'm hungry," she told him, pausing to lean against the door frame.

"After you have changed, you can eat while we talk. There is something I want to discuss with you." There was an expression in his eyes that she couldn't interpret.

"We could talk now," she suggested, curious as to what he wanted to discuss with her.

"Sometimes you're a woman, and sometimes you remind me of a little girl," he said in exasperation. "Will you get that wet gown off?"

Royal was seated before the fireplace with a plate of fried trout in her lap. "This is wonderful," she said, licking her fingers. "I wish I could eat like this every day."

Damon was seated with his back propped against the wall, one long leg drawn up in front of him. "It is nice, isn't it? When I was a boy, my father and I would come here to hunt and fish. At night we would sit here as you and I are doing now and eat our catch."

She stood up and moved to the table. "You don't get much chance to do that anymore, do you, Damon?" she asked, picking up a dirty dish and plunging it into sudsy water.

He handed her his plate, while he picked up a drying towel. "No, but it is always kept in readiness. Ezekiel sees to that. This is the one place where I can escape when the world comes crashing in on me."

She turned to look at him. "Does the world crash in on you often?"

He smiled down on her. Royal was shapeless in his robe, which was too long for her and had to be belted at the waist. She had rolled the sleeves up to the elbows, making her look like a little girl playing dress-up. "Since you landed on our shores, my world has tottered a few times."

"I have caused you a lot of grief, haven't I?"

He took his finger and dabbed at a speck of soap on the tip of her nose. "Just a bit."

His hands moved into her hair, and he turned her face up to him. "When a woman looks like you, I suppose she can't help how men react to her."

There was puzzlement in her eyes. "Do you truly think I am pretty?"

He rubbed her golden hair through his thumb and forefinger. "You are devastatingly beautiful," he admitted huskily. With a jolting shock, he realized that he had pulled her into his arms, and he pushed her away and stepped back a pace, striking a pose of indifference he was far from feeling.

"Don't worry about the dishes," he said harshly. "Just go to bed."

Royal watched him move to the window, and she went to him, troubled by his sudden coldness. "Have I done something to displease you, Damon?"

"No, it's nothing you've done."

He pushed open the window, needing fresh air, and a sudden gust of wind blew out the candle. The only light came from the dying embers in the fireplace and the moon riding high over the treetops. He was fighting the urge to take her in his arms and hold her until his body stopped trembling. He gripped the edge of the window and turned his back to her.

"Go to bed, Royal."

She placed her hand on his shoulder. "But, Damon—"

"I said go to bed!"

"You said you wanted to talk to me."

"That can wait until morning. Get some rest."

"Could I ask you something first?"

He turned to her impatiently. "What is it?"

There was a look of bafflement on her face. "You have told me that I don't know what I do to a man, and you're right. I am often puzzled about the attraction between a man and a woman."

"I don't think we should be having this conversation."

"You are my guardian," she reasoned. "Whom would I go to for advice if not to you?"

"Good Lord, Royal, has no woman in your life ever talked to you about this?"

"No, should they have?"

"Perhaps if your mother had lived," he reasoned. "I can't help you. You should ask Alba. Yes," he said in a rush of relief, "that's what you should do."

She shook her head. "You know Alba well enough to know that would not be possible. She's adamant about what is proper and what isn't."

"She would not approve of this conversation, and I don't either." His voice was filled with kindness. "Perhaps you really should go to bed now."

She was not willing to let him off so easily. "Can't I be with you just a while longer?"

He watched the way the moon played across her hair. "I don't think so."

She took a step that brought her even with him. "I like to be with you, Damon. While I was at school, I always pretended I belonged to you. You are the closest thing I have to a family, you know."

He was touched by a strange sadness. Apparently she had suffered a great deal from loneliness. He gathered her into his arms, wanting to insure that she never knew another day of hurt. She was hard to resist, and he wondered if she knew what was happening between them.

Royal sighed. "Perhaps I am tired. May I just kiss you good night?" She stretched up and pressed her mouth against his.

When their lips met, it was as if the night were charged with electricity, and try as he might, Damon found himself pulling her against him. . . .

Royal reveled in being in Damon's arms. She belonged to him as surely as any person could belong to another. She raised her head and looked at him. Raw, intense feelings were reflected in his eyes.

"Royal," he murmured, "why do you do this to me? You are tearing my insides out."

She trembled, waiting for the touch of his mouth against hers. Softly his breath touched her cheek, and she closed her eyes, wanting so badly to be a part of him—to become one with him, to feel every breath he took, to feel every pain he experienced—to be happy when he felt joy.

"I tell myself this is wrong," he whispered just a fraction away from her lips, "but I cannot stop myself."

Her young, inexperienced body throbbed with a yearning that was like a physical pain. "Oh, Damon, I want to be with you."

His lips brushed against hers, and he felt her draw in a breath. His hand moved to the belt at her waist. "Yes," he said, untying the sash. Opening the robe, he slipped his hands around her tiny waist. "I remember the feel of you so well," he said in a voice deep with passion.

Damon pulled her closer to him, unable to stop the longing that had taken possession of him. "You belong to me," he whispered, his lips pressing against her silken lashes, drifting down her cheek, and, at last, fusing with her mouth.

Royal's head was spinning, and she was drifting in a world where the only sound was the beating of her heart and the only feelings were the wonderful hands that caressed her.

"I have always belonged to you, Damon," she told him, her eyes shimmering. "I want to be one with you tonight."

Damon's trembling hand touched silken flesh, and he closed his eyes, trying to keep from ravishing her on the spot. He was half-mad with desire, and yet he fought to keep that desire under control. Royal was innocent, and he was man with a great deal of experience. He must be strong because she was not aware of the consequences of her actions.

He pulled back and shook his head to clear it. "You are consuming me." His voice came out in a groan. "Now, will you go to bed?"

She took his hand and raised it to her lips, kissing the fingers one by one. "I know that you will soon be gone, and I will be alone again. Do not leave me until you have given me something to hold on to," she pleaded.

With a heavy groan, he pulled her forward. "I have always been in control where women were concerned, but not with you. From the very beginning, you have had me in hell."

"Oh, Damon, I don't mean to—I only want—"

His mouth dipped to cover hers, and he felt as if the whole world consisted only of the taste and feel of her. He had no will of his own as his hands cupped her waist. The kiss deepened, and his hands slid upward, stopping just where her young breasts swelled.

She rolled her head from side to side as his lips drifted down her neck. Slowly and sensuously his hands inched up her breasts to circle, tantalize, and torture. "Sweet, sweet," he murmured against her lips.

Her eyes were feverish with newly aroused desire.

"Tell me again you have never done this with a man before," he insisted, needing to know he was the first to be with her.

"I have never wanted this with another man," she answered in a breathless voice.

Royal slowly unfastened his shirt, and her hands inched up his chest to brush against the dark hair there. "I have no knowledge of lovemaking, Damon. I want to learn from you."

Her hands boldly stroked up his neck to lace through his hair. She moved forward and pressed her soft, velvety lips to his.

Slowly Damon slipped the robe off her shoulders while the silvery moonlight cast flirtatious shadows across her beautiful body.

Lifting Royal in his arms, he gently placed her on the bearskin rug and then stood over her while he tossed his shirt aside. His other clothing soon followed. While he was undressing, Damon stared down at her, holding her spellbound.

Royal watched, fascinated as he stood before her with the flickering firelight dancing across his body. His legs were long and muscled, his waist narrow, his shoulders wide. She allowed her eyes to follow the dark hair that covered his chest, then narrowed across his stomach. Her eyes widened when she saw the evidence of his desire, swollen and throbbing.

Damon dropped down beside her and circled her neck with his hand, bringing her lips to within a breath of his own. "Don't you know you should never look at a man like that?" His voice was raw with longing.

He lowered his head, and his mouth brushed her arched neck. He knew just where to touch . . . to arouse . . . to excite. His hand moved across her taut stomach, circling, enticing.

Royal's eyes were glazed with pleasure and pain. "Ohhh," she breathed when his hand moved lower, his finger sliding in the warm, velvet softness of her. He came up against a barrier that told him she had never been with a man, and in a moment of sanity, he moved his hand and sat back.

"Damon, don't leave me!" she cried, clutching him by the arm and pulling him to her.

He should have known she was ripe for a man's touch. He closed his eyes, furious with himself that he had brought her to this state.

Royal pressed her body against his, and an aching tide washed over her. How right it was to be in Damon's arms, she thought.

He whispered harshly against her lips, "If I don't stop now, it will be too late."

Her fingers twined into his dark hair, and her lips parted to receive the hot kiss that would not be denied. He could no longer control his hands as they roamed over her body, touching, feeling, molding.

Royal felt his lips drawing every emotion out of her. His hands took a sensuous path, up her spine, across her shoulders, and down to tenderly circle her breasts. She gave a sharp intake of breath when his lips touched the rosy tips ever so softly. Looking into his golden eyes, she had the feeling that they were swirling tides of passion.

A tremor shook her body when Damon ran his hands over her hips and brought her beneath him. An aching started in her heart and traveled throughout her body when he smiled at her tenderly.

"If you don't want this," he murmured, "say so now, and I will walk away." He waited for her answer, knowing what it would be.

"I don't want you to stop," she confessed, groping for his hand and placing it on her swollen breast.

Damon groaned. He already knew she would bring him a deeper satisfaction than he had ever felt before, and his body ached to take what belonged to him.

He pushed her head back against the rug and positioned himself between her legs. His mouth burned into hers as he slowly lowered his body, first brushing against her soft flesh and then pressing his body against hers.

Royal could not catch her breath as his body fused to hers. She gasped and finally drew air into her lungs. His life-giving shaft probed between her legs, and she stared at him with bewilderment in her eyes.

"I don't know how to—"

"Shh," he whispered, tracing her face with a lean finger and loving her with every fiber of his being. "I will teach you all you need to know."

"I don't want to displease you."

"Tonight, I will take all you have to give, but I will also give to you. Do you believe this?"

"Yes."

She laid her face against his, thinking how right this felt. She loved him—and had for a long time. Perhaps even from that day long ago when he'd promised a young girl he would not forget her. If she gave herself to him now, would she be able to hold on to him? No, perhaps not, but she would have this little bit of him to keep forever.

His hands moved over her hips, circling, enticing, pulling her closer to the heat of his body. He closed his eyes, allowing pure ecstasy to wash over his body as her satiny warmth closed in around him. He was more alive tonight than he had ever been in his life.

His dark hair mingled with her golden curtain of hair. Their minds merged, and their bodies trembled and quaked.

With tenderness in his expression, Damon eased himself slowly into her body, knowing with regret that at any moment he would cause her pain. "You pilfer all of a man's mind, seductress," he groaned. "Will you leave me with nothing?"

Royal ran her hand down his back, wondering how he could ask such a question. Did he not know that she had just given him her life, her will, and her whole heart?

"I will give you all I have to give, Damon. If that isn't enough, I have no more to give."

He moved deeper within her and felt her stiffen. "It will but sting," he cautioned.

Her lips parted, and he was caught under her spell, needing all of her, wanting to keep her with him from this day forward. Pride of possession flamed in his eyes.

Gently he slipped to the barrier within her, then, with a forceful thrust, broke through. She gasped and her eyes widened with surprise as she tore her lips from his.

"It was necessary," he said, holding her to him, trying to absorb the ache that tore at her virginal body. "There will be no more pain, I promise. I will make your body sing."

He was right, she thought as she clutched him tightly. He set a rhythmic motion that sent the blood throbbing through her veins. Pleasure and passion reflected in her eyes with his gentle movements. Each time he thrust forward, she caught her breath with pleasure, and each time he eased back, she clung to him.

Her velvet smoothness caressed his pulsating desire, taking him higher and higher to an elevation of pleasure.

Soon Royal's body caught his rhythm, and she moved with him, enhancing her pleasure and bringing a shuddering gasp from him. She nipped at his ear with her teeth, ran her hands up and down his hips, and pushed against him, giving and taking pleasure.

"What are you doing to me?" he murmured in a passion-laced voice.

"Making you remember me," she whispered. "When you go away, I don't want you to forget me."

Forget her, he thought, how could he forget her when she was in every thought he had, every breath he took?

The pleasure became so intense that it felt as if his loins would burst, and relief came moments later when he drove deeper into her and erupted with life-giving fluid.

Royal's body quaked and trembled as Damon clasped her ever tighter against him. She reached deeply for a breath and clung to him as if he were her very life.

Swirling joy sang through her like a love song. She opened her eyes and saw tenderness in his golden gaze. For a long moment they lay in each other's arms, reliving the closeness they had captured.

Royal watched the moon playing tag through the tall pine trees and turned to Damon. Her blue eyes held a new awareness. "I have never felt so alive."

"Nor I," he admitted. His finger trailed down her flat stomach, and he felt her melt against him. To his delight, he found he wanted her again as she turned to him and pressed herself against him.

Eagerly she responded to his every move. She filled his needs and made him feel immortal.

When at last she lay exhausted in his arms, he began to question his actions. He was not as noble as he would have hoped. He must have known all along that this would happen. Since the night she had tantalized him as the mystery lady, he had been unable to get her out of his mind.

Angry with himself, he gazed coldly at the object of his obsession.

"I belong to you now," she said, touching his mouth with her lips.

"Yes," he agreed, knowing what he must do. "Royal, I have asked Ezekiel to bring the parson tomorrow."

Her eyes were sparkling. "Do you want . . . to marry . . . me?" she asked, almost afraid to hope.

He pulled her to a sitting position and stared at her. "Do you realize the consequences of what just happened between us?"

"I am not so innocent that I don't know that." She smiled. "I never knew that such wonderful—"

"For God's sake, Royal, I have to think!"

Her hand teased the hair just over his ear. "I want you to think of me."

He caught her hand and held it in a firm grip. "We will be married tomorrow night."

Tears were swimming in her eyes as she laid her head against his shoulder. "Yes, I should be your wife after tonight," she agreed.

"I need to ask you again, Royal. How do you feel about Preston?"

She was quiet for a moment. "I have known two fine men in my life. You are one—Preston is the other."

"You know you can't marry Preston now, don't you?"

She tossed her head back and met his inquiring gaze. "I want to stay with you forever."

He held her to him, wondering if what she was feeling was the lingering effects of their lovemaking. He was experienced enough that he knew how to please a woman, but that was not necessarily love.

He stood up and scooped her into his arms and carried her outside. Royal looked at him as if he were crazed. "Surely we should not go out without our clothing?"

He walked toward the river. "No one will see us." He waded into the swift current and held her while the river rushed over them.

Royal squealed in delight as he dumped her in the water. Laughingly she reached for him, and he pulled her to him.

Damon's lips clung to hers hungrily, and she found herself lying on the cool grass with him hovering above her. She pulled him forward and offered him her lips, an offer he did not refuse.

Ezekiel, being a romantic, had gathered up all the candles he could find and set them around so the lodge was aglow for the wedding ceremony.

Royal stood beside Damon, her eyes shining, while Reverend Camdon recited the beautiful words that made her Damon's wife. She was puzzled when she sensed a tenseness about Damon. He repeated the marriage vows in a stiff, clipped voice. She wanted him to look at her, but for some reason he avoided her eyes.

All too soon the ceremony was over, and Royal was dazed when Reverend Camdon shook her hand.

"I wish you happiness, Mrs. Routhland."

"Thank you," she murmured as Damon coolly accepted the minister's good wishes.

Ezekiel wrung Damon's hand. "She's the best thing that's ever happened to ya. I hope you see that afore it's too late."

"You had better get started if you are going to get the reverend home," Damon reminded him.

"I'm going, but I'll leave ya with this thought—the best of a man is a good wife, and the worst of him is if he prizes her too lightly."

Damon picked up the old man's hat and shoved it at him. "The reverend is waiting. You be back by tomorrow."

Ezekiel moved to stand before Royal, and a smile curved her lips. "You're gonna know great happiness, Miss Royal. If'n I was you, I'd make this a marriage," he whispered. "And don't wait too long."

She smiled at him and kissed his cheek. "I will, Ezekiel." He looked pleased that she had called him by his first name, and he decided to do the same.

" 'Night, Royal." He moved to the door. "Let's go, Reverend, it'll be midnight now afore we get you home."

When Damon and Royal were alone, she went into his outstretched arms. "Well, that's done," she said, smiling. "You can't get away from me now." Her eyes took on a serious light. "I truly belong to someone now, Damon."

He hugged her tightly. "You belong to me."

Suddenly his gaze was sorrowful as he looked at her tattered gown. "I'm sorry this was such a shabby affair for you."

"That's not important to me."

He felt light-hearted. "You are an exceptional woman, did you know that?"

She tossed her head and pretended seriousness. "What else would you expect from Mrs. Damon Routhland of Swanhouse Plantation?"

He was aware that she grew soft in his arms. How little it took for her to pull him into the prison of her silken web, he thought. Like a man with no will of his own, he covered her lips with his.

Royal awoke and reached out to discover Damon was not with her. Smelling the strong aroma of coffee, she slipped out of bed and pulled on the wrinkled gown.

She was Damon's wife! Her hand moved to her stomach, and she remembered with awe how he had held her in his arms and taken her from the world of a girl into the world of a woman.

Damon poked his shirt into his trousers and dismissed the cup of coffee Ezekiel held out to him. "For a new bridegroom, you're up awful early this mornin', ain't ya, Damon?"

"I have to rejoin my unit as soon as possible."

The old man stroked his chin thoughtfully. "I'd 'a been hard-pressed to leave a wife like Royal if I's you."

"I'm able to leave her because she'll be safe at Swanhouse. You know I have no choice in the matter. I will give you a letter to take to John instructing him to watch out for Murdock."

"I'll kinda keep my eye on her."

"I am depending on that. I'll just take your mount, Ezekiel, and you can take Royal to Swanhouse for me. She is asleep, so I'm not going to wake her."

"She won't like it none when she wakes up and finds you gone."

"You will explain to her that I had to leave."

"I'd rather you did."

Royal chose that moment to open the bedroom door. Neither man knew that she could hear their exchange.

Damon looked at his friend, his mind troubled. "I don't know where to place a wife in my life, Ezekiel. Royal would have been better off with the Englishman."

"You might have thought of that before last night."

"What choice had I? If I hadn't married her, I would not have been able to take her to Swanhouse where Murdock can't get his hands on her."

Royal felt her heart shatter, and she softly closed the bedroom door and leaned against it. Her eyes were wild with grief at what she had heard. Damon had not wanted to marry her. He had felt it was his duty.

Blinded by tears, she sat on the edge of the bed, knowing she could not face him just yet. Although he had not said he loved her, she had supposed he felt the same way she did.

She heard the outer door open, and a short time later a horse rode away. Royal knew without being told that Damon had left without telling her good-bye, and, oh, it did hurt so deeply!

Wiping her tears away, she opened the door to the outer room. With her chin held high and a proud tilt to her head, she moved out of the bedroom. Her eyes fell on Ezekiel, who was bending over the open hearth, poking at the embers.

"Mornin', Royal." He grinned. "Most likely you'd like coffee. I'll get it for you."

"Damon's gone, isn't he, Ezekiel?"

The old man's eyes were sympathetic. "Said ta tell you he's gone back to his unit. Said I was to take you to Swanhouse."

"I would rather go to Savannah. Will you take me home?"

He studied her closely. "Now, I can't rightly do that, seeing as how Damon told me to take you to Swanhouse. If'n I was you, I'd do what he says. You can't be too careful with Murdock lurkin' about."

"I'll go to Swanhouse for now," she said with a resigned sigh. "But I will only stay until Murdock is no longer a threat."

"That's a good girl."

"I know you admire Damon. Ezekiel, will you help me understand him?" It was almost a plea.

"The way I see it, there ain't much to understand 'bout him. He's honorable, upright, and he's doin' what he thinks is best for you. Sometimes he slips in his judgment, but the best thing he's ever done is marry you."

She smiled at the dear little man. "Thank you for that, but I'm not certain he would agree." She didn't tell him she had overheard Damon when he'd admitted his reason for marrying her.

"You best eat, and then we'll be off. I want to get you settled in afore I take to the swamps."

"Are you going to join Damon?"

"No, I'm gonna keep an eye on Murdock. Me and Damon figure it's best to know where he's at all the time."

"Can you tell me where Damon has gone?"

"Nope. Don't know. He keeps his private business to hisself."

She accepted the cup of coffee Ezekiel offered her and took a sip, then wrinkled her nose.

He grinned down at her. "I'm accused of brewing coffee so strong it'll stand alone."

She took another sip and gulped. "Your accusers are right."

While Ezekiel loaded the boat, Royal moved about the room where she had been so happy. Last night she had become a wife . . . today she was alone again.

The trip down the Canoochee River to Swanhouse Plantation went without incident. Ezekiel helped Royal up the sloping lawn to the plantation house, where she found, to her surprise, that they were expected.

John Bartholomew stood stiffly at the bottom of the steps, his formal mask in place. If he found her rumpled appearance strange, he was too well trained to show it. "Welcome, Mrs. Routhland," he said. His voice sounded devoid of feeling, but the pleasure he felt at having her as mistress of Swanhouse could be measured in the light of his eyes.

"I am proud to welcome you, and I believe I speak for us all when I say we are glad your ordeal is over at last."

She gave him her hand and allowed him to assist her up the last three steps. "Thank you, John." She looked around at the faces of the slaves and servants—they were strangers to her, but she could see the welcome in their smiles.

"John, can I assume my housekeeper and her husband have been informed that I will be residing at Swanhouse?"

"Indeed, yes, madam. Mr. Routhland wrote them in his own hand, and I had the letter delivered this morning."

Ezekiel looked somehow sad as he clutched his cap in his fingers. "I'll be going now, Royal. If'n you want anything, John'll know where to find me."

Ezekiel was a crusty, kind-hearted character, Royal thought, and she was going to miss him. "Visit when you can, Ezekiel."

His eyes lit up with pleasure. "I'll do that, Royal." He stumbled backward, looked apologetic, and lumbered off toward the boat.

"Ezekiel, have a care!" she called after him. "Don't take any unnecessary chances with Murdock."

"I won't," he called out.

He hopped into the boat with the agility of a much younger man, raised his hand to her, and paddled upstream.

She turned to John. "If you will be so kind as to show me to my room, I will require a bath." She was thoughtful for a moment. "I don't suppose there are any gowns that I could wear until mine arrive from Savannah?"

"Your trunks have already arrived, and I had the upstairs maid unpack for you, madam."

"I should have known," she said, comforted by his thoroughness. "You always did think of everything, John."

If he was pleased by her compliment, it did not show in his expression. "If you will follow me, I will show you to your room."

Royal could not know that John had insisted on seeing her settled in because he was the one person at Swanhouse who was familiar to her. She also did not know that there were seven guards who would watch the house day and night so Vincent Murdock could not get to her.

Royal climbed the stairs beside John, feeling like an intruder in Damon's house. It didn't matter—she had already decided she would stay only until Murdock was captured; then she would leave.

John paused before a wide double door. "I have put you in the master suite, madam."

"My needs are not so grand, John. I would much prefer a guest bedroom."

He stared at her for a long moment, understanding her reasons better than she thought. "Very good, madam. I will put you at the end of the hallway."

Christmas had come and gone, and Royal waited for some word from Damon, but none came. An unusual calm hung over Swanhouse—a calm that Royal knew could be interrupted at any moment by the war that raged about them.

There were reports that General Washington's troops were mutinous and had deserted in large numbers. They had not been paid, and they grew weary of fighting a war that seemed to favor the superior British forces. The British controlled the seas, and most of the South was under their rule.

The house in Savannah had been boarded up, and Alba and Tobias had been installed at Swanhouse Plantation. In no time at all the forceful Alba was running the house and everyone in it. John Bartholomew seemed amiable to the arrangement. Royal suspected he was glad to be rid of that responsibility. Tobias had fallen naturally into overseeing the gardens and grounds and was content to spend most of his days outdoors.

Everyone but Royal seemed to know his place—she had yet to learn where she belonged.

It was a particularly cold day when Tobias rushed in from the stables calling for Royal. She came out onto the back veranda and watched him, his eyes dancing with delight, his breath coming out in frosty puffs.

"What it, Tobias?" she asked, smiling at his enthusiasm.

"You will never guess, Miss Royal—the most wonderful thing has happened."

Alba came out the door wiping her hands on her apron, looking at her husband as if he had lost his mind. "Tobias, just tell us what's so wonderful," she insisted.

"Two men just delivered a horse to the stables. They say the animal was sent all the way from England."

Royal put her hand to her throat. "Enchantress," she gasped. "Enchantress is here?"

"Yes, madam." He held out a letter to her. "I was told to deliver this into your hands."

She took the letter and saw Alissa's dear, familiar handwriting. It made her feel ashamed that she had neglected to write her friend. Opening the letter, she read:

My Dearest Friend,
Neither time nor tide stand still, nor do our lives. Holden and I are married, and I am deliriously happy. To add to my happiness is the news that you were successful in procuring Preston's release. My mother and I were astounded to learn of Damon Routhland's heroic rescue of Preston. We will be eternally grateful to him. We are sending Enchantress to you, knowing how much you love her. That's the least we can do for you after all you have done for this family. I miss you, dear friend, and want to see you back in England soon. Perhaps I am giving away secrets, but I know Preston plans to bring you home with him, and it is with my mother's consent.

Royal folded the letter and slipped it into her pocket. So the dowager duchess had decided that she was worthy of her son after all. She smiled sadly, thinking how much that would have meant to her at one time. Now it was too late for her to think of a life with Preston.

She moved down the steps toward the stable, while a puzzled Tobias stared after her. "I thought she'd be happy about the mare. She didn't seem happy to me."

"Hush," Alba said, her shrewd eyes seeing more than her husband's. "I swear you men don't know anything."

Tobias scratched his head, willing to admit his wife was right, at least about him. "I guess it's the war," he concluded. "Having to abandon her home and all."

"Tobias," Alba said impatiently, "haven't you noticed that Miss Royal has put on weight?"

"No, don't say as I have."

Alba poked a stray hair back into her white cap. "She's with child. She's going to have Mr. Routhland's baby."

"W-when?"

"In about four months, I'd judge."

"Why didn't you tell me?"

"Because," Alba replied, her mind troubled as she watched Royal disappear into the stable, "she hasn't told me yet."

She took Tobias by the shoulder and pointed him toward the

house. "You best look in on Mr. Bartholomew. He's got a fever, and the poor man isn't able to get out of bed."

The clock had just struck seven when Alba came to Royal in the solarium. "Will you be wanting your supper in here, Miss Royal?"

"I'm not hungry, Alba."

The housekeeper stared down at Royal with the same determined light she had used when Royal had been an unruly child. "You need to eat. I'll just have Tobias bring the tray in here."

"I say I'm not hungry," she insisted.

"Nevertheless, in your condition, you need to eat."

Silence ensued as Royal stared into Alba's eyes. At last Royal asked, "How long have you known about the baby?"

"Most probably longer than you have."

She reached out and clutched the housekeeper's hand. "You must tell no one." There was desperation in her eyes. "Swear you will keep my secret."

"I already told my suspicions to Tobias," Alba admitted.

"Then swear him to secrecy. Promise me you will."

"Mr. Routhland should only hear about the baby from you. However, I'm certain Mr. Bartholomew could get a message to him on something this important."

Royal was thoughtful for a moment. "I will tell Damon myself when the time is right. Speaking of John," she said, changing the subject, "how is he today?"

"His fever is still high, and his chest hurts. I put a poultice on him and steamed his room. I don't know what else to do. The poor man is beside himself because he keeps complaining that he needs to make an entry in his log. Something about selling several horses."

"I should see him. It's not like John to give up and go to bed. He must be truly ill."

"I reckon you should see him. I'll just go along with you. It may be that you can calm him. But, first, you eat."

Royal drew in a resigned breath, knowing Alba would have her way. "Yes, I will have something light. Perhaps one of your crêpes with blueberry sauce."

"And a glass of milk," Alba cajoled.

"And a glass of milk," Royal agreed.

John Bartholomew attempted to rise up on his elbows when the young mistress entered his quarters. "You shouldn't be here, madam."

Royal saw how pale he was and how his eyes were fever bright. "Nonsense. You are ill, and I want to help you. Perhaps I should send for a doctor."

"No," he protested. "It is just a recurrence of fever. It will pass in a day or two."

"Alba has told me you are concerned about your bookkeeping. Would it ease your mind if I made the daily entries for you?" She smiled at him, knowing how meticulous he was about his work. "If you will recall, I made high marks in mathematics."

He began to tremble, and his forehead broke out in perspiration. Royal could see it was an effort for him to talk. "I know, madam.

Your marks were a great source of pride for me." His eyes took on a hopeful glow. "Perhaps you could just enter the financial reports. It has been my habit to make entries daily. Several transactions have been of great concern to me."

She patted his hand. "You just concentrate on getting well. I promise I will keep your entries up to date. I'll get started first thing in the morning."

He was flooded with gratitude. "Thank you, madam. That is a great relief to me."

Bright and early the next morning, Royal was bent over John's account books. It was easy to follow his method, and she painstakingly added figures to the column of neat numbers.

She soon became so engrossed in John's method of bookkeeping, which included narratives of the transactions, that she found herself thumbing back through the pages, which read like a diary. He had made notations of daily events on the plantation, recorded births, deaths, and marriages.

At one particular entry, she smiled with delight. John wrote of the dilemma that occurred on the marriage of two slaves, Joe and Mary. It seemed the two had been gifted with a sow. The animal got loose and was running through the manor house, despoiling valuable rugs. Royal laughed aloud, trying to imagine the meticulous little man chasing across the polished floors in pursuit of a fugitive pig.

She thumbed back through the log, fascinated by the daily events that occurred at Swanhouse. When she came to a page with her name, she began to read:

> Miss Royal is so far away and friendless. It grieves me to receive her letters begging to come home. Although I have never met her, I feel she is an exceptional young lady. I hope one day to meet her for myself.

She was touched by his concern for her all those years she had been away at school. He was such a stoic little man, she had not known that he had taken such a personal interest in her well-being. Feeling somewhat like an eavesdropper, she turned back the pages, looking for any mention of her name. She found many.

> I talked to Mr. Routhland today about Royal Bradford's financial situation. It was my belief that she was spending far too much on frivolity. But when I pointed this out to Mr. Routhland, he instructed me to let her have whatever she wanted. He wants her never to know that her father left her penniless. Mr. Routhland was adamant that she never know that it is he who pays for her education and expenses. I gained a great insight to his personality only yesterday. When he discovered how lonely his ward was in England, he instructed me to ship to her his finest mare, Enchantress.

Royal stared at the yellowed pages, reading about her life with a new insight. Tears fell, smudging the ink.

"Oh, Damon," she cried, burying her head in her hands. "I never knew. Why . . . why didn't you tell me?"

For over an hour Royal sat at the desk, trying to compose her feelings. All those years she thought that no one cared about her. John Bartholomew had cared . . . Damon had cared.

She remembered the day in her garden when she had questioned Damon about her money. Even then he had not admitted that he had been supporting her since her father's death. She thumbed back still farther through the pages and read her whole story through John's eyes. Another passage caught her interest.

> Today Mr. Routhland had me pay off all Douglas Bradford's debts, and they were considerable. When I questioned why he would pay such an amount to settle another man's debts, he informed me he had looked into a little girl's eyes and seen pain. I am not certain I know what he meant.

Damon had looked into her eyes and seen pain. He had done all in his power to make it go away. He was truly a noble man. At every turn in her life, he had been the strength behind her without her being aware. Even though John Bartholomew had written her the letters, the words had come from Damon.

"Oh, Damon, if you could look into my eyes now and see the pain, would you make everything all right? I am not a little girl anymore, but a woman who loves you desperately and is going to have your baby."

She dried her tears and closed the log. Today she had looked into Damon's soul and found him the most worthy of men. He had helped her out of kindness. But she wanted more from him—she wanted his heart.

Dare she hope that he would one day love her as his wife? She had no notion where he was. He could even be hurt, and she would not know.

Royal's hand went to her rounded abdomen where Damon's child lay. This precious life she carried within her body was the greatest gift of all, given by a man who had looked into her eyes and seen pain.

May 1781

It was on the day that Royal learned General Cornwallis had moved his troops northward into Virginia that she gave birth to Damon's son.

The morning started out normally enough. Royal was helping Alba arrange dried fruit in the dugout when the first pain ripped through her body. She clutched at the side of the dirt wall, trying to catch her breath.

"I knew you shouldn't have come down here, Miss Royal," Alba chastised.

"Just help me to the house, Alba. Then send for the midwife."

As they walked slowly up the steps with Royal leaning heavily on Alba, the housekeeper looked at her with some concern. "You should have a doctor."

"No, I will not have that Loyalist Dr. Habersham deliver Damon's baby."

Royal drew in a deep breath and continued on toward the house. "I don't even want that man at Swanhouse."

"You have certainly changed since you first returned home," Alba said. "There was a time when I thought you were loyal to the British."

Up the steps to the house they went slowly. "It's a curious thing, Alba, but it seemed that the more battles we lost, and the stronger the enemy grew, the more loyal I became."

They were in the house now, and Alba glanced at John Bartholomew, who had come into the hallway. "It's time," Alba told him. "I'll get Miss Royal upstairs. You know what to do."

For the first time since Royal had known John, she saw his calm mask slip.

"Are you all right, madam?" he inquired, reaching out to her. "Perhaps I should carry you upstairs?"

"I'm all right, John, truly I am," Royal assured him.

Royal labored all afternoon and long into the night. She was attended by Alba and the midwife, Josey Evens.

Downstairs, John, Tobias, and Ezekiel waited for some news of what was happening with Royal. The room was silent but for the ticking of the clock and an occasional nervous cough from one of the men.

It was almost dawn when a small cry was at last heard. At first John stood up and walked out of the library, listening at the bottom of the stairs. "Was that a baby's cry?" Then he heard the sound again, only this time louder.

Three men watched the top of the stairs expectantly. After what seemed like hours, Alba appeared, carrying a tiny bundle as if it were the most precious thing in the world. When she reached the bottom step, she pulled the blanket aside to reveal a tiny little face with black hair. "Mr. Routhland has a son," she announced proudly.

"How's Royal?" Ezekiel inquired.

"She's doing just fine," Alba assured him. "She had a long, hard time, but she's sleeping now."

Ezekial, John, and Tobias stood awkwardly at the foot of Royal's bed, admiring the young master of Swanhouse.

Royal held him out so they could have a better view. "Is he not wonderful?" she asked proudly.

"He has the look of his father," Tobias observed.

"No," Ezekiel insisted, peering at the little face. "I see Royal in him."

"Nonsense," John said. "All babies look alike. You can't tell whom they look like until they are older." A rare smile touched his lips. "He is handsome, though."

Royal looked at the people in the room and assessed how dear they were to her. John, always so formal and precise, had a nurturing heart—she had many times been the beneficiary of his caring. Tobias, strong and sturdy as an old oak tree, silently lent his strength. Ezekiel, dear and loving, eager to help, was a friend on whom one could always depend. Then there was Alba, the staying force, loyal and dependable. Royal smiled to herself, thinking how peremptory Alba could be, but only with those she cared about and only when she was sure it was for their own good.

Yes, she thought, looking down at her son, who slept contentedly in her arms, her world was here—it had always been here.

Ezekiel ambled closer, his eyes filled with awe. "I still say he looks like you, Royal," he maintained. "What's his name?"

"I don't intend to name him until his father comes home."

Ezekiel nodded in approval. "Seems right to me."

"Would you like to hold him, Ezekiel?"

Now his eyes danced. "Could I?"

She nodded and handed him the baby. He clutched the infant to him as if he were the most precious person in the world. "Soon as he's old enough, Royal, I'm gonna take him out and teach him to shoot, just like I did his pa."

"I will expect you to."

The baby let out a loud cry, and Royal laughed when Ezekiel quickly handed him back to her.

Alba appeared at the door. Looking disapproving, she shooed the men out so Royal could rest.

Royal curled up with her baby, touching his cheek, his tiny nose, and counting his tiny fingers. "He's perfect, Alba," she said, placing a kiss on the soft lips.

"Of course he is," Alba agreed. "You get to sleep so you can regain your health." She scooped the baby into her arms, carried him to the other room, and placed him in the cradle.

Royal stretched her arms over her head and closed her eyes, falling asleep.

Alba returned to the room and smiled down at her sleeping charge. Then, pulling the coverlet over Royal, she tiptoed out.

August 1781

A sweltering dome of heat hung over Georgia. There was not a breeze stirring, and the sky showed no sign of rain to cool the land.

The master of Swanhouse was still absent, and no one had received word from him.

Sketchy news of the war reached the residents of Swanhouse Plantation, and none of it favored the American forces. The South was still in the clutches of the enemy, and there seemed no end to the war.

Cornwallis swept across Virginia. If he were to retain his hold, the whole South would fall to the British and the war would reach a sad conclusion for the Americans.

Royal was riding across the pastureland, noting that the cattle and sheep seemed to thrive on the abundant grassland. She removed her hat and blotted her forehead with the sleeve of her riding habit. It was too hot to ride, she decided, looking at the sun and gauging it to be midafternoon. She turned Enchantress toward the house, thinking a cool bath would feel wonderful.

When she reached the stable, she found Tobias waiting for her. "The duke is here to see you," he informed her, helping her dismount from the prancing Enchantress.

"Preston!"

"Alba put him on the veranda with a glass of lemonade—said it would be cooler there."

Royal smiled happily. "It will be good to see him again. I want to hear all about his family."

She walked in the direction of the house, and when she rounded the corner she saw Preston waiting for her. She raised her hand to him, and he came bounding down the steps to enfold her in his arms.

"I have been in agony wanting to see you and not knowing where to find you. No one could tell me where you were. At last I decided to ride out to Swanhouse this morning, and here you are. It was wise of you to move out of Savannah."

She smiled up at him and linked her arm through his. "You look good, Preston. The air in America seems to agree with you."

He raised an eyebrow. "It's unhealthy for most Englishmen."

"I had thought you would have returned to England by now."

"I had. But the prime minister wanted me to return. All is not as well as it might be. I am to join Cornwallis in Virginia."

They had reached the shade of the veranda, and Royal leaned against the railing. "I would rather your Cornwallis returned to England."

There was a look of irritation on Preston's face. "So would I. I am weary of generals. Take General Clinton. He is always issuing orders about one fool thing or another," he said sardonically. "I believe he thinks he can win this war by proclamation."

"That will not be so easy here," she stated proudly.

"True. Cornwallis is finding out much to his amazement that the Southerners are a churlish lot. They will neither join his army nor agree to feed them. They won't furnish him with information, and when he sends out dispatch riders, they are attacked, and the perpetrators just disappear."

Royal laughed. "Please be seated, Preston," she told him, motioning to the chairs that faced the river. "Perhaps you should not talk so freely about military matters."

He held a chair for her, and when she was seated he sat beside her and reached for her hand. "Why? We have always spoken freely about the war."

"That was before I gave my allegiance to my own country."

He frowned, his gaze sweeping her face. "When did this happen?"

"I suppose it's been there all the time. But it grew bolder as your generals gobbled up more of our land. I cannot support a government that oppresses its own."

He looked into her eyes and saw the truth. "Even if this is so, it will make no difference between you and me. When the war is over, you will return to England with me, as my wife."

She looked into blue eyes that were aglow with love, and it broke her heart to have to cause him pain. "I cannot do that, Preston."

"I know that you were hurt by my mother. She confessed all to me. But she has changed, Royal. She wants you to become a daughter to her. She has agreed to our marriage."

"You don't understand. I can't marry you because I'm married to Damon."

He stared at her in disbelief.

"It's true, Preston."

"But I always thought that we would . . . that you and I would be married."

She shook her head. "Even if I had not married Damon, I could never have been your wife. I just don't love you the way you deserve to be loved."

He turned away from her, struggling to control his emotions. "Damon is a fine—" His voice broke, and he could say no more.

Her eyes were sad, and teardrops clung to her long lashes. "Dearest Preston, you are one of the finest men I have ever known. And I'll admit that a part of me will always love you. But not with the love of a woman for a man. One day you will meet someone you adore, someone worthy of you." She smiled at him through her tears.

He reached out a trembling hand to her, then pulled it back. "With all my heart and soul I envy Damon Routhland. I would have given up everything to have you love me." He took her dainty hand in his and studied it for a long moment. "Mother and Alissa will be disappointed."

"Tell them I will write, and tell them I will always remember their kindness to me."

Preston felt his eyes stinging, and he wanted to crush Royal in his arms—to never let her go. "Can I hold you just once before I go?" he asked, coming to his feet and carrying her with him.

A sob built up inside Royal, and she went readily into his arms. "Oh, Preston, I want so much for you to be happy."

His arms tightened about her, and he tried to absorb the feel of her, so he would remember it always. "I will not so easily forget you, Royal."

She stepped back and looked into his eyes. "Don't ever forget me. I won't ever forget you."

He released her and stepped back. "I will take some comfort in that."

Preston looked toward the fields and then down to the river. "I'll think of you living here. This is a good land, and whatever happens, I want you to know that no one will bother you here."

"I don't understand what you mean."

"Have you not wondered why Swanhouse Plantation hasn't been touched when her master is a known rebel?"

"I suppose I never thought about it." She looked at him with understanding. "It is because of you, is it not?"

"I thought I owed that much to Damon."

She touched his cheek. "Thank you for that."

He caught her hand and brought it to his lips. "I will always remember how you looked today—I'll remember you forever . . . my love."

He turned away and moved across the veranda without looking

back. The Duke of Chiswick held his head high, his shoulders upright. Only Royal knew that his heart was breaking.

She moved slowly into the house and up the stairs. Dear Preston, with his gentle nature and loving heart. Why could she not have loved him instead of the dark, brooding Damon Routhland?

Royal was not aware of what had awakened her. The baby was in the connecting room; perhaps he was stirring. She slipped out of bed and came up against something solid.

Suddenly she remembered the night Vincent Murdock had come to her room and taken her captive. With all the strength she possessed, she swung out at the intruder, only to have her hand caught and held in a firm grip.

"For God's sake, Royal, it's me."

She went limp with relief and joy. "Damon! I thought you were Murdock."

"You will never have to worry about him again. Ezekiel saw to that—didn't he tell you that Murdock is dead?"

"No, he didn't," she said, remembering that she had told Ezekiel she would not stay in Damon's house once Murdock was no longer a threat. He had deliberately kept the information from her.

Damon seated Royal on the bed, fumbled around until he found a candle, then lit it.

They stared at each other for a long moment. She noticed his face was haggard, and he looked tired. There was so much to say, and yet Royal suddenly felt shy with him. She decided not to speak of anything concerning the two of them.

"We are all rejoicing about the victory at Yorktown, Damon. Were you there?"

He pulled up a chair and straddled it, feasting his eyes on her. "Yes, I was there."

Her blue eyes took on a hurt expression. "I waited for some word from you. Why didn't you write, or at least send a messenger?"

His gaze swept her face. There was a new maturity about her, a glow that had not been there previously. "I wasn't certain you would care to hear from me."

She studied him closely, remembering what she had read in John's logs. Yes, she could see it now—he loved her. But she had to have him say the words.

"How long have you been home?"

"Since eleven. I ate and bathed while John gave me a report on what's been going on at Swanhouse."

She wondered if John had told Damon about his son. "Do you find everything to your liking?"

His eyes ran down her neck to rest on her breasts, just visible through the filmy nightgown she wore. "Not entirely."

She blushed at the way his eyes reminded her of the closeness they had once shared. "Oh? And what was not to your satisfaction?"

Damon stood up and moved across the room. "First, I expected to find you in the master suite. And, second, John told me that the Englishman was here."

A thrill went through Royal's body. He was jealous! "Yes, Preston was here."

Damon stared out into the dark night. "I suppose if he hasn't returned to England, he soon will."

"I suppose. He was with Cornwallis," she informed Damon.

"I see. Perhaps you have already had his account of the battle?"

"Preston's gone."

He turned quickly back to her, seeking something in her face. "I thought—"

The cry of an infant cut Damon short. It appeared to be coming from the other room. He stared at Royal in bewilderment. "What is that?" he asked.

"It's a baby boy who doesn't have a name."

"I see. I suppose a slave's baby was ill, and you, with your kind heart, brought him into the house to nurse back to health?"

She smiled to herself. Damon had no notion that he had a son—John had not told him everything. "Would you like to see the baby?"

"Not really," he said in irritation. He had been away for a year; he wanted to talk to her about something important, and all she could think of was an infant crying in the next room.

He watched her leave and return with the baby in her arms. When she laid the child on the bed, he hardly gave it any notice.

"We have things to settle between us, Royal. I know how you feel about Preston."

She smiled and picked up the child. "Do you?"

"Did you make arrangements to meet him in England?"

"I can't leave you, Damon."

Hope burned in his eyes. "Why not?"

She pulled the blanket aside and held the baby out for his inspection. "This is why."

He looked puzzled as his gaze moved over the dark hair, the white skin—the golden eyes!

"What is this?" he asked, feeling as if someone had just delivered a blow to his midsection.

"This," she said, "is a baby, or to be more accurate, your son."

Damon's golden eyes flamed with pride and then became piercing with anguish. He reached out and touched the soft black hair as feelings he had never experienced riveted through his body. "But how?"

She gave him a sideways look. "I believe we both know how."

Damon, who was always in control, was now completely at a loss. "I never considered—never thought . . . about a child." He shook his head when Royal placed the baby in his arms.

"It's time the two of you became acquainted. And it's time his father gave him a name."

Damon stared down at the child, who had closed his eyes. Raising his son to his cheek, he breathed in the sweet baby smell, his senses overcome. "My son," he said, and Royal was certain his voice had cracked.

Damon watched the candlelight flicker across Royal's beautiful face, trying to fathom her true feelings. "I can see why you didn't feel you could join Preston. I blame myself for this."

She pretended seriousness. "I blame you for it also. Two nights with you, and you impregnate me."

His face fell. "I can't tell you how bad I feel about this."

She still could not resist teasing him, for she was now certain he loved her. "Oh? You don't like your son?"

He handed the child to her. "Give me time to grow accustomed to the idea. I thought I was coming here tonight to give you your freedom." His eyes hardened. "Make no mistake about it, Royal, I will never allow you to take my son to England."

"I can see that you want to keep your son. Would you consider allowing me to leave if the baby remained with you?"

Damon's head snapped up, and he looked at her long and hard. "Could you give up your baby?"

She wanted to reach out to him because she was aware that he was feeling pain. But she had to make him admit he loved her. "Could you give up your wife?" she countered.

For the first time there was hope in his eyes. "I would rather you stay. A boy needs his mother."

"Suppose I no longer want to go to England, Damon? Suppose I want to stay with my son—and you?"

He watched her place the baby down on the bed and come to him.

"Suppose I told you that I love you, Damon—that I have always loved you?"

His golden eyes flamed as if they were on fire. He reached out to her, touching her arm, allowing his fingers to curl around her hand, pulling her toward him gently. "Don't tell me this if it isn't true, Royal. I could not bear it if you gave me hope and then dashed my dreams."

Tears danced in her eyes as she smiled at him. "Oh, my dearest love, how can you claim to know so much about women and yet know so little about your own wife? I have loved you for a very long time."

A deep tremor shook Damon's body as he pulled her tightly against him. His hands ran up and down her back as if he were becoming reacquainted with the feel of her. He closed his eyes and held her tight, wanting never to let her go.

"Royal, sweet Royal, you have always had my heart, first as a child, now as a woman. I have lived in agony these last months, believing that when I returned home, I would have to let you go. I thought you loved Preston . . . you said you did."

"And I do. But the love I feel for him is as a brother, a dear friend, nothing more. My heart is so filled with you, there is little room for anyone else." She glanced up at him. "When did you first love me?"

"I can't even remember not loving you. When you were in England, I would dream about you and wake up feeling sad that you were not here. I believe I was born to love you."

She pressed her cheek to his. "And I you, Damon." She pulled back and gave him a tantalizing smile. "I warn you, you will never be rid of me."

He pulled her into his arms, allowing her sweetness to fill his whole being. "I will never let you go. You belong to me—you always have."

He moved away from her, scooped up his son, and deposited

him in the cradle in the next room. When he returned he picked up his wife and carried her to the bed.

When he lay down beside her, he didn't take her in his arms as she expected. Instead he laced his hands behind his head and stretched out his long legs.

"Before I can become your husband," he told her, trying not to smile, "I would ask you to release me from being your guardian. That has been damned awkward for me on numerous occasions."

Royal smiled and rolled over, propping her head up on her elbow. "I will never release you. I want you tied to me in every legal way that's known to man."

His expression became serious. "I love you, Royal. And I want you in every way a man can want his wife."

He pulled her to him, his lips inches away from hers. "This time, I take you without guilt."

"Yes," she whispered, her hands unbuttoning his shirt. She lowered her head and pressed her lips against his.

Everything else was forgotten as he took command of her body, tying her to him with threads of love.

Royal reached for her journal and began to write:

> Dearest Papa,
> I love, and I am loved. Happiness is my constant companion.
> Good-bye, Papa.

She closed the journal, knowing she had just made her last entry. Life was to look forward. The past could never be again.

Constance O'Banyon is frequently on Waldenbooks Bestselling Romance list. She has written eighteen books and lives in San Antonio, Texas.